ALL THE TIDES OF FATE

ADALYN GRACE

TITANBOOKS

All the Tides of Fate
Print edition ISBN: 9781789095135
E-book edition ISBN: 9781789095142

Published by Titan Books
A division of Titan Publishing Group Ltd.
144 Southwark Street, London, SE1 0UP
www.titanbooks.com

First Titan edition: February 2021
10 9 8 7 6 5 4 3 2 1

This is a work of fiction. All of the characters, organizations, and events portrayed in this novel are either products of the author's imagination or are used fictitiously.

A CIP catalogue record for this title is available from the British Library.

Map art by Dave Stevenson

Printed and bound by CPI Group Ltd, CR0 4YY

To Josh—
For telling me to write this series,
and for believing in me while I did.

To Tomi—
Because there's no one I'd rather be doing this with.

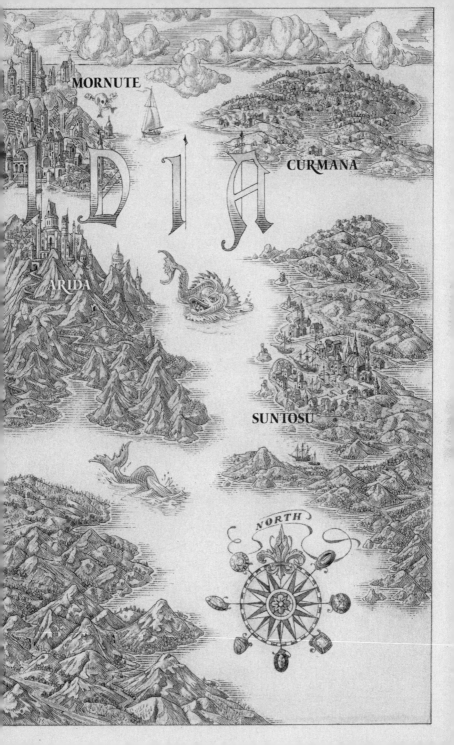

MORNUTE

CURMANA

IDIA

ARIDA

SUNTOSU

NORTH

THE KINGDOM OF VISIDIA

ARIDA
Island of soul magic
Represented by sapphire

VALUKA
Island of elemental magic
Represented by ruby

MORNUTE
Island of enchantment magic
Represented by rose beryl

CURMANA
Island of mind magic
Represented by onyx

KEROST
Island of time magic
Represented by amethyst

SUNTOSU
Island of restoration magic
Represented by emerald

ZUDOH
Island of curse magic
Represented by opal

ONE

This water is fierce.

It snarls as it thrashes against *The Duchess*, who lets herself be jarred by the wrath of winter's tides. She tests her new captain, knocking me against the weatherworn helm as grainy seawater slickens the wood and dampens my fingers.

But I won't slip. Not this time.

"Back the mainsail!" I dig my boots into the deck and grip the helm tight, refusing to let the ship bait me. I am the captain. If *The Duchess* refuses to listen, I've no choice but to make her.

Today there's no promise of neighboring islands in the distance. None of Mornute's mountains are visible through the milky-white haze that blows in from the north. It wets the air, seeping into my pores and plastering dampened curls to my neck.

The ship buckles from another blow of the tides, and I brace myself for what's coming as I see the faint shadow of the fast-approaching buoy I anchored to the sea a full season ago. I shut my eyes and pray under my breath to any god who might listen as we approach, begging them to spare me. Begging them to let this be the day that the boundaries of my curse are pushed further.

But as always, the gods refuse to listen.

The moment *The Duchess* passes the buoy, my knees buckle as white-hot pain rips up my spine and through my skull like a too-familiar blade cleaving through me. I bite the inside of my cheek until I taste blood, doing everything I can to keep my pain contained so that the crew won't grow suspicious. I dig my fingernails into the helm, cool sweat licking at my neck as my vision flickers in and out. Desperate, I give Vataea the signal.

She leans over the stern at once, whispering a chant so fierce that every word that passes her lips is a clap of thunder. The sea regards her curiously at first, then obeys Vataea's siren magic with a snap, twisting the direction of the tides. Some of the crew mumble with irritation as we turn back toward the docks, wondering why I have them do this same silly trip every day—not even half a morning long, and never to any specific destination. But at least out loud, they don't complain. They're not foolish enough to go against their queen.

The moment *The Duchess* is southbound toward Arida, the tension against my skull eases and my ragged breathing steadies. Only when my vision begins to clear do I loosen my grip.

Vataea presses a tentative hand upon my back. "Perhaps it's time we stop this." The mermaid's voice never fails to sound like the sweetest of songs, even if the words threaten to cleave me again. "Maybe it's time to stop fighting your curse, and to make the best of it."

I say nothing. Until someone's had half their soul ripped away and cursed into another living person, I don't care to hear their suggestions. Vataea will never know what it feels like to have part of her being merged with someone else. To be able to feel their presence. Their strongest emotions. Their *everything*.

She doesn't get to be the one who's fatigued from trying to break this curse.

Vataea's hand slips from my back, leaving my skin cold. "I'm sorry for what happened, but being reckless isn't going to cure you any faster."

I want to bristle. I want to turn and yell about all the things she doesn't understand. But instead, the air in my lungs deflates as she turns and makes her way to the bow.

Those are the limits of my curse. A curse that means half my soul—and all my magic—lives within Bastian.

And like today, every attempt to break it only ends in failure.

The docks are filled with royal soldiers and servants who draw back as we approach Arida's docks, where the fog camouflages the visiting ships, turning their sails opaque. Instinctively my chest seizes when I see the figures waiting there for me, knowing it's no longer time to be a captain, but a queen.

"Toss the anchors!" I twist the helm and the ship groans as I force her against the waves, slowing our brisk speed. My crew obeys, and the two anchors catch the bottom of the shallow water, jarring us. Someone slams into the ship's ledge and slips face-first onto the deck, but I can't help them. I twist the helm the opposite way, forcing the ship to oblige. To obey.

She steadies herself, and my grip loosens as my muscles relax.

The moment we hit the shore, my crew spurs into action. Some focus on righting the anchors and dropping the sails while others toss themselves upon the shore to secure the ship. They lower the ramp onto sand red as blood, where Mira, my lady-in-waiting, stands in a thick black cape with a collar of white wolf fur that stretches to her modest chin, tight and suffocating. Her matching gloved hands are folded

3

before her, eyes narrowed with the perpetual worry I've grown accustomed to.

"You're late." Her breath steams the air, creating whorls that shroud the faces of royal staff who straighten as I approach. Two of them hold a plush sapphire pillow with elegant silver-and-gold embroidery, and balanced atop it sits my crown—the head of a giant Valuna eel, its mouth open and waiting to sit upon my head and clamp around my jaw. Waiting to devour me.

The gem-encrusted spine glistens from the dampness of the fog, making my throat thick as I consider how natural this false crown looked on Father. It's a crown made for imposters, and as it's fitted swiftly upon my head, I can't help but think how natural it must look on me now, too.

"I'm never late." I fasten my sapphire coat tight and straighten my crown as the eel's jagged teeth graze my jaw and temples. "I'm the queen."

I'm quick to match the smile Mira flashes at me, though our playfulness is nothing but a farce. This is a game we've played since summer, one that's expected by my kingdom. They smile and I smile back, no questions asked. I'm their queen now, and despite all that's happened, I'm meant to show my people that we're still strong. That while Visidia has suffered loss, we will unite to surpass our hardships and restore the kingdom.

"Tell that to everyone waiting. It's your first advisory meeting as Visidia's queen; you ought to make a better impression." Mira's tired eyes roll; it's something she never would have done before last summer, before she was nearly killed during Kaven's attack on Arida. Now though, she's relaxed, willing to tell anyone what's on her mind—including me.

I'm glad for it. I'm glad for the color in her cheeks and

4

the energy in her step. I'm glad that she's *alive*. Not everyone was so lucky.

"The queen dowager is waiting with the advisers in the throne room," Mira begins, but those words ignite a wicked chill within me. It blossoms in my stomach and wraps claws around my throat.

"Don't call her that." *Dowager*. I practically hiss at the title, not needing an additional reminder that Father is dead, the remnants of his charred body feeding the fish as he rests at the bottom of the sea. "When you're in my presence, call her by her name."

Mira's cheeks flush, and I try not to let the embarrassment from my outburst show. When she opens her mouth, I wave her words away, not wanting the apology that lingers on her tongue. The last thing I need is more people tiptoeing around me—especially when they've no idea what really happened the night Father died. That if I'd been able to stop Kaven before he reached Arida, Father would still be alive. I'd be the princess, and my soul would still be in one piece.

But that's far from the fate the gods cursed me with.

I shove my hands deep into my coat pockets before anyone can see how fiercely they tremble, and raise my chin high for those watching. "Take me to the advisers."

TWO

The throne room falls silent when I enter, the last tendrils of conversation evaporating like smoke as the heels of my boots snap against the marble floor.

Bitter air and the prickle of ghosts brushing against my skin welcome me into a room I've not stepped foot in since I fought Kaven here last summer. It's one that no longer shows signs of the fire that destroyed it, or even a drop of the blood I remember flowing so freely from Father's corpse when he drove a sword through his own stomach to sever his connection to Kaven and give Bastian and me the ability to fight him.

I don't stop to observe the advisers who stand and bow their heads until after I've taken a seat at the head of an oversize black quartz table, rubbing my fingers over the charred bones of my throne—freshly lacquered since the fire so that it's sturdy enough to sit upon.

It's a cruel punishment to hold our council meeting here, but no one says a word, likely thinking the same thing I am— one of us is sitting in the very spot where Father died.

Mother sits after I do. Her curls are slicked back, fashioned into plaits that are so tight they lift her forehead, making her eyebrows high and alert. Once, her beautiful brown skin glowed radiant as the seaside cliffs at sunrise. Now it's sallow and sunken, and she holds her lips like she's just taken a bite of something thoroughly unsatisfying. Perhaps she feels the wrongness of this room as much as I do.

Advisers from each of the islands—with the notable but not unexpected exception of Kerost—take their seats around us. Feathered quills and parchments full of notes lie before them. There's an empty seat on my right meant for my leading adviser, Ferrick, but I wave for a royal guard to take his chair away.

"Ferrick has duties elsewhere today," I tell the advisers before they can ask, jutting my jaw so that I might look as authoritative as possible beneath my crown. "I'll speak on behalf of Arida myself."

Next to me, Mother's voice chides in a whisper only I can hear, "Mind your tone, Amora. You're not here to fight; we all want the same thing."

Her words force my lips into a thin line. Ever since I took the throne, there's been no shortage of those who question my authority. But she's right; confronting Visidia's advisers as though I'm prepared to fight them will do me no good.

Digging deep into myself, I find my will to continue playing the game Mira and I started back on the docks—the same tired game I've been playing with the kingdom since taking the throne. I plaster a smile to my lips.

"Thank you all for coming." I make myself sound lighter this time. Friendlier. "I know things are difficult for all of us right now, so I appreciate everyone's willingness to meet."

"I'm glad we finally have the chance." The voice that speaks is deceptively tender. It belongs to Zale, the newly appointed adviser of Zudoh, an island we're working on reintroducing into the kingdom after my father wrongly banished them eleven years ago. Though her people cruelly suffered, Zale was kind enough to offer my crew and me shelter and protection when we arrived in Zudoh on our quest to find Kaven—even despite Bastian being his brother.

Ever since her island was freed from Kaven's reign, she's developed a lively glow to her warm skin, and her once hollow eyes have filled with a brilliance that rivals the brightest malachite. She's gorgeous in her silky white robes, but there's a fierceness in her that's not to be overlooked. Zale's one of the sharpest and most determined women I've ever met.

Beside her, Lord Bargas sits as proudly as one can be while bundled in a ruby coat so thick that it's practically a blanket. Accompanied by his young successor, they represent Valuka, the kingdom of elemental magic. My heart skips a beat when I see him, as I'm reminded sharply of Bastian and how he'd pretended to be the baron's son on the night we first met to gain entry to my birthday celebration. The baron and his crew had been left out at sea, disarmed, disrobed, and under the heavy influence of Curmanan sleeping powder.

"Hello, Your Majesty." His lips pull into the kind of smile that could melt ice during the coldest winter. He's the oldest adviser, nearly sixty, and seeing him not only reminds me of Bastian, but also of the way Father liked to joke with the baron. The way he would clap Lord Bargas on the shoulder and roar with one of his chest-rattling laughs.

"It's a pleasure to see you again, Lord Bargas." I clear my throat and the emotion swelling within it, tucking it away for a later time when eyes are less prying. "I hear you were sleeping the last time we all met." That earns me a few chuckles, even from the lord and the young woman sitting next to him.

"I assure you, it wasn't by choice." There's a conspiring gleam in his eyes. "That blasted pirate even stole one of my favorite swords. Be sure to get that back for me, would you?"

I match his lively smile. "I'll see what I can do. Who's this you've brought with you?"

He claps a firm hand upon the young woman's shoulder. "This is Azami Bargas, the daughter of my eldest brother, and my new successor. Azami will be fully taking over by spring."

"It's a pleasure to meet you, Azami."

She bows her head quick and low. "Likewise, Your Majesty."

I'm surprised to find there are other faces here I don't recognize. While most watch me with intrigue, Mornute's new adviser steeples their fingers on the marble table, then taps anxious patterns upon it. With each tap of their fingers, tiny constellations dance around their lacquered black nails. When they catch me looking, they jolt to attention.

"Leo Gavel, Your Majesty!" Leo's face is pleasantly youthful, with full peachy cheeks sprinkled with freckles enchanted to look like stars. Physically, Leo is small and plump, with striking features that give me a tinge of jealousy for all those able to practice enchantment magic. They've piercing yellow eyes and matching buzzed hair, and wear a lavender pantsuit with winged liner in a similar shade around their eyes. "We haven't been able to meet since Mornute's previous adviser was killed during the attack, but I assure you that I'm well trained. I look forward to working together."

"As do I." But my words are forced as my thoughts linger on the night of the attack, wondering how many people I let die. Because I couldn't kill Kaven the first time he and I fought on Zudoh, how much blood am I responsible for spilling?

There's yet another new face—the adviser representing Curmana, the island of mind magic, judging from his loose onyx pants and shimmering cape.

"I'm Elias Freebourne, and I'll be filling in for my sister, who went into labor the morning we were loading the ship to journey here. I look forward to serving you, Your Majesty." There's a glint in his striking green eyes that warms my skin. I turn quickly away.

"This meeting is to discuss the unification of Visidia," I tell them. "I'd like to focus on our restoration efforts with Zudoh and Kerost. While relations with the former are going as well as we can expect, we need to figure out a way to restore Kerost's trust in us before they secede from the kingdom." We let them suffer from the storms for far too long. We ignored them as a time trader profited off their pain and stole years of their lives. If we want to make it up to them, we're going to have our work cut out for us.

Mornute's adviser stirs. "I'm more than happy to discuss restoration efforts, Your Majesty. But my primary purpose for coming here is to discuss the well-being of Mornute, and how it's being impacted by Visidia's recent . . . changes."

At once I know Leo is referring to my abolishment of the law preventing Visidians from practicing more than one magic. A law that was crafted upon the kingdom's biggest lie, and that I put an end to the moment I took the throne.

For centuries the Montaras kept Visidians weak, ensuring they only practiced one magic—and never even had the ability to learn soul magic—so that no one could single-handedly overpower our family. They crafted a legend of a beast that would cause Visidia's ruin should they break the law. A legend that tricked my people into believing that the Montaras alone could use dangerous soul magic to protect them. The story became so ingrained in our kingdom's foundation that few people ever strayed.

Even now, my people don't know what the Montaras—my family—did. They believe I vanquished the beast and freed magic. If they knew the truth, I wouldn't be on the throne. I'd never have the chance to make things right.

So long as I wear this crown, I have only one goal: repent for the mistakes of my ancestors by breaking the Montara curse and freeing soul magic from our bloodline. I'll make this kingdom whole by giving my people everything they were always meant to have, and finally tell them the truth.

And then, I'll accept whatever punishment they see fit.

"I, too, would like to discuss how these changes are affecting our individual islands," says the Suntosan adviser, Lord Garrison. He's a stout man with a thick red beard that conceals half his face from view. It's meticulously styled every time I've seen him, and soft, too. Like he coats it in oil every night. "Some of us have traveled great lengths to be here. It's only right that we get to address our concerns."

Mother's reminder rings in my head—*you're not here to fight them.* But gods, between his proud chin and assessing eyes, I can't help myself. "I know our geography, Lord Garrison," I say tersely, satisfied at the way his eyes narrow in surprise. "I'm very aware of how far you've traveled. I'm certainly happy to listen to everyone's—"

"In the past," he says, rolling over my words as though I haven't spoken, "King Audric would open these meetings with each of us presenting our own thoughts and needs for the islands we represent, rather than opening himself—"

At the mention of Father, something in me snaps. Mother's hand finds my knee beneath the table, squeezing it in warning. But her presence isn't enough to prevent the malice that cracks my smile.

Lord Garrison was always loyal to Father, but like the rest of the advisers, he was politely cold to me. Up until this past fall, I was hardly allowed any interaction with the advisers. Father held too many secrets; until I earned the title of heir to the throne, I was never allowed details of these meetings. It was purposeless and frustrating, especially now as I sit at the head of a room, meant to lead a group of advisers who hardly know me and whose trust they believe I've not yet earned.

But they're mistaken. I earned my place on this throne the moment I stabbed Kaven. I earned this seat with his blood and mine. I earned it with my magic, and the sacrifice of every life I took to get here.

Trust be damned. I've earned this crown with my soul.

"Thank you for letting me know how my father ran things. We all know he was a perfect ruler, never making a single mistake." I straighten in my seat, pinning my eyes to Lord Garrison's. "And considering how I was never allowed in those meetings, and that no one ever thought to include me, your information is *very* helpful. But I'd like to remind you, Lord Garrison, that my father is dead." I don't look away as he flinches, nor do I turn to Mother as her hand goes limp on my thigh. Instead, I keep my focus trained on the Suntosan adviser as he shifts with discomfort.

When he opens his mouth to speak, I hold up my hand and continue. "However the late king used to rule doesn't matter, because he's no longer the one who sits on the throne; I am. I'm not sure if you felt it was okay to condescend to me because I'm a woman, because of my age, or simply because I'm new to this position and you felt the need to establish some sort of dominance you do not and will never have. But the next time you open your mouth to speak to me, remember that you're talking to your queen. Do you understand?"

From the corner of my eye, I catch Mornute's adviser slack-jawed in their seat while the others look away in uncomfortable silence. Lord Garrison's face turns scarlet, and I'm glad for his embarrassment. He deserves it.

"I understand, Your Majesty," he practically huffs, as if uncertain whether to be surprised or apologetic.

"Good. Then I suppose we can continue with the discussion I've laid out?" I roll my shoulders back, making it a point to show that I'm relaxed, and not a tensed coil ready to spring again. "I am, of course, interested in discussing the aforementioned 'changes,' as well, as I suggested before your outburst. We can start with Leo." Mornute's adviser turns to me, and I smile once more, trying to ease their shock. Though most of the advisers are reserved, this one is still so new that they wear their expressions clearly on their face, and I like it. It makes me trust them more than most in this room.

Leo jolts to attention and grabs the parchment before them, rifling through it to gather their thoughts. "I want to discuss how the abolishment of this law will negatively impact our island. Our port town, Ikae, is the largest tourist destination in all Visidia, and is our most prominent source of income. We worry that if our magic makes its way to other islands, we'll no longer be able to generate the same tourism

13

we currently do. If anyone can make their town dazzling with enchantments, why will ours continue to be so appealing? I'm worried Mornute will be looking at a massive decrease in income due to this change."

Their worry is a legitimate one, but it's one I've already considered. "You're right that this law will change things," I tell Leo. "But Visidia has been due for a change for some time. And as it evolves, we must focus on evolving with it. While you're right that Mornute is primarily a tourist destination, I believe you're overlooking the monetary value of its alcohol exports." The glimmer of curiosity that sparks in Leo's eyes tells me I'm right; this isn't something they've deeply considered. "Mornute's climate lends itself well to being one of the few areas that can grow the ingredients needed to make great ale and wine in massive quantities. You can focus on expanding production; if the tourism rate in other towns goes up, so will its alcohol consumption, and they'll need to import spirits from somewhere. There will be more of a demand for your products than ever, and perhaps even greater revenue as well.

"My suggestion to you is to get a head start on preparing for more alcohol sales," I continue. "Expand the vineyards on the mountainsides. Plant more barley. And while you're at it, consider developing a style of alcohol that's unique to Ikae. Make enthusiats come directly to the island if they want to experience it."

Leo sits on this for a moment before they grin at their parchment, jotting notes. "It's certainly something to consider. I'll take this idea back to the island and see what we can do with it."

I'm glad someone here is easy to communicate with. So

long as Mornute can keep up with demand, it should never have to worry, and my idea seems to have put Leo at ease. The people of Mornute, especially those in the port city of Ikae, appreciate lavish lifestyles; I'm confident they'll come up with plenty of other innovative ways to maintain that.

I hadn't realized I'd been so stiff and rigid in my chair until Mother's hand drifts away. I relax, knowing it's a sign of her approval. My response seems to appease several of the other advisers as well, all of whom had been sitting at the edge of their seats, anxious to see how I'd do.

After the way I handled Lord Garrison, it takes most of the newer advisers time to work up the nerve to speak. But soon enough I settle into my confidence, appreciating the steady pattern of conversation we fall into. I relax into the conversation, stirring only when there's a muffled shout at the double doors. I'm out of my seat, dagger in hand, when those doors are shoved open, much to the protest of the guards standing watch.

But my fingers weaken on the hilt as I see that the one standing there at the threshold, slipping around Casem's reach, is the last person on this island that I want to see right now.

Bastian.

THREE

Standing at the door is the boy I've been avoiding for nearly a full season.

The boy who holds the missing half of my soul.

Dressed in sleek black pants and an iridescent opal shirt with the top several buttons left open, Bastian stands with a proud arrogance that makes him feel every bit the royal adviser he pretended to be the night we met. Hazel eyes catching mine, he brushes his hands across the dark stubble on his cheeks. The luster in his eyes is unmistakable.

He's frustratingly handsome, and the bastard knows it.

Bastian strolls in without invitation, hesitating for only the briefest second at the sight of the polished, unscathed room. There's a quick hitch in his jaw. Because of our curse, I feel the quick burst of terror in his chest that echoes within my own. Like me, he must be remembering the last night we were in this room, drowning in a river of Father's blood. But he has no choice but to right himself, pulling Ferrick's discarded chair from the corner and dragging it to the table. Wood screeches against marble, but the sound doesn't deter him even as the advisers grimace.

I try to catch Bastian's eye, but he doesn't look at me even when he sits between me and Zale. Only then does he smile, so irritatingly charming that I want to reach out and use my nails to swipe it from his lips.

"Sorry I'm late." He offers a casual wave of his hand. "Please, continue. No need to pause on my account."

I press my hands into my lap so no one can see the nails digging in my palms as I ask him, "*What* are you *doing*?"

Bastian still doesn't look at me as he combs his fingers over coiffed hair and stares wistfully ahead. "I'm here for the meeting."

Every hair along my body bristles. "This meeting is for advisers only, Bastian."

"Oh, so you do remember my name. It's been so long since we've spoken that I was beginning to wonder." His own voice lowers, and the huskiness within it does strange things to my stomach. "And I can do whatever I want, *Princess*. I helped save this kingdom."

Princess. The nickname flares goose bumps across my skin.

"Besides, what are you going to do?" He leans in, whispering the next part only to me. "Kick me off the island?"

"You can't make yourself an adviser," Zale interrupts, eyes smiling despite the tension in her jaw. "But I would like to personally offer you a seat, Bastian. On behalf of Zudoh, we welcome your opinion."

It takes everything in me to relax my hands. Knowing better than to go against Zale, I ignore the smugness that eats Bastian's lips as he untucks a quill from behind his ear, licks the tip, and sets several slips of parchment on the table. He winks when he catches me staring.

Never has there been a time when I wanted to learn Curmanan mind speak more than this moment. If I practiced it,

I'd be sure to tell Bastian exactly where he could shove that quill.

"We've a long way to go to help Zudoh," Zale continues, steering us swiftly back on track. "We're progressing, but it'll take time for our island to recover from the neglect."

"What about the water?" The smugness has left Bastian's lips, and the sincerity that pulses within the words runs deep. Since Kaven's death, the desire to restore Zudoh has nearly consumed him. Feeling his passion as potently as I feel my own, my anger wanes.

"Valukans are helping clear out the water, making it more habitable for sea life after the toll of Kaven's curse," Zale answers. "It'll take time for fish to reappear, but we're already seeing improvement."

"I'm glad to hear it," I say. "Lord Bargas, we should discuss how best to divide the restoration efforts of the Valukans between Kerost and Zudoh . . ."

We speak for hours, back and forth, sharing ideas and coming to terms with changes that need to be made. And though the meeting started off rocky, by the end of it I'm relaxed in my seat, having taken off my crown to better focus. Some of the advisers have fresh perspectives, while others are stubbornly set in their old ways. But there isn't one of us who doesn't want what's best for our people. And despite his grand entrance, I'm surprised to find that everyone is receptive to Bastian. Loath as I am to admit it, his ideas are valuable, and the love he has for his home island is genuine.

But as well as everything has gone so far, the challenge in Lord Garrison's eyes is enough to warn me that it won't all be so easy.

"Leo," he says casually when it's his turn to speak. "I

believe it's time Her Majesty knew about the papers."

Leo's eyes widen. Sharply, they turn to Lord Garrison. "I've already told you, the situation is handled."

But Lord Garrison ignores them, huffing into his beard as he reaches deep into the inner pockets of his emerald coat. Parchment crinkles beneath his calloused fingertips as he slams it onto the table before us. I reach forward and grab it.

One of Ikae's latest trends is parchment that's been enchanted with moving images to show off the latest gossip and fashion. Vataea and my cousin Yuriel have been poring over them for weeks, but I've been too distracted to focus on what any of them have to say.

Apparently, that was a significant mistake on my part.

HER MAJESTY, AMORA MONTARA: QUEEN OF OUR KINGDOM, OR VISIDIA'S BIGGEST THREAT?

Last summer, Queen Amora turned our kingdom on its head with the announcement that Visidians would no longer be forced to honor the centuries-old practice of using only a single magic.

While some have long desired this change, many are skeptical. The announcement came only days after the death of the late King Audric, and after Queen Amora was forced to take the throne despite her previous failure to perform the duties necessary of an animancer. Though our queen claims the beast that has lived within the Montara bloodline for centuries—the reason behind our single-magic law—was vanquished in the

same fight that killed King Audric and Kaven Altair,
it's difficult to overlook the convenient timing.

From the moment our queen took the throne, the
state of Visidia has been tumultuous to say the least.
If the rapidly changing dynamics of magic aren't
enough to worry you, the shifting state of our kingdom
should be. With Zudoh's effort to rejoin the kingdom
happening among threats of Kerost attempting to
secede, one must wonder what Her Majesty is thinking
with all these changes.

Perhaps it's because she's a young woman, or
perhaps it's because no one is around to tame her, but
whatever the reason, one thing is certain—our queen
is destroying Visidia. And if something doesn't change
with her soon, I fear the worst is yet to come.

There's an accompanying picture of me from the day of
my coronation, sitting before my people in the same scorched
throne I sit in, now. Mother is placing the eel crown upon
my head, and the people before me bow. I look stern and
confident, shoulders back and chin held high.

But I remember that moment, and if one were to look
hard enough at the corners of my eyes and the furrow of my
brows beneath the jaws of the eel, they would see fear.

Fear that I wouldn't be able to fix Visidia alone.

Fear that my people would discover the truth of the
Montaras, and kill me before I could even try.

Not wanting to relive the memory, I draw my attention
from the image and instead skim back to a single line, reading
it repeatedly.

Our queen is destroying Visidia.

"Our people don't trust you, Your Majesty." The smugness in Lord Garrison's voice is hardly enough to distract me from the anger that scalds my skin. "Ever since you failed to sufficiently perform soul magic during your performance last summer, they fear you're unable to handle your magic."

Thank the gods my people don't know that I can't even use my magic at all right now. My curse prevents me from accessing my soul magic, given that half of my soul is cursed within Bastian.

I am the High Animancer. The queen. If I cannot perform soul magic sufficiently, there's little that would stop my people from ripping the crown from my head.

Mother's face screws tight as she reads over the parchment; I can practically see her biting her tongue. Even Bastian opens his mouth to protest, but words die uselessly at his lips as he reads it again.

"What do you propose I do to change the kingdom's perception of me?" I clench my hands against the arms of the chair and stare Lord Garrison dead in the eye. "Tell funnier jokes? Throw parties where the kingdom may dance and drink merrily? I didn't just save Visidia from Kaven; I returned magic to this kingdom. And yet I need to be *tamed*?" I strike my fist upon the table. "For the sake of the gods, I am a *queen*!"

When Lord Garrison straightens, resentment poisons my mouth and coats my tongue. I drag my fists away and onto my lap, hiding my scraped knuckles beneath the table.

"You may have the title of a queen," Lord Garrison says coolly, "but in the eyes of too many, you are still little more than a girl who fled her kingdom, who cannot be trusted with the power she wields."

I hate him for not losing his temper. But I hate him even more because, after everything I learned about the Montaras last summer, I know he speaks the truth. "What Visidia needs is stability. We can't only throw hardships at our people and expect them to be comfortable with a mere promise that, one day, things might be better. They need to trust you. They need to feel like they still have not only a queen, but a protector."

I press my lips together and sink back into the chair. "I take it you have a solution in mind?"

It's as though no other adviser's in the room when Lord Garrison looks at me, confident and calculated. "I propose we give Visidia a distraction; something for them to focus on while we working toward changing the foundation of our kingdom. I want to give them a reason to root for you."

The way he says it sends electricity flooding through my veins.

"You're the queen, now." He savors each word. "Your duty is to your kingdom, and part of this duty is that you'll be expected to continue the Montara lineage by providing the throne's next heir as soon as possible. Because of this, you'll need to take a husband."

Perhaps it's because no one is around to tame her.

I feel Bastian's resentment spike, just as bitter as my own. But when he sets his hands on the table as though he's about to stand, I kick his shin and fix him with a look that demands he remain seated. This isn't his battle.

"Technically I don't need a *husband* to produce an heir," I start, but Mother cuts me with a pointed look. I can't help but notice she's taken no stance against his suggestion. "What are your thoughts?" I ask her sharply.

"I just want you to be safe," she answers with every drop of the exhaustion that's rattling my bones. "If a husband can settle our kingdom . . . it might be worth considering."

"So what," Bastian growls, ignoring me when I knock my boot against his shin for the second time. "You want to marry her off? She's your queen, not your pawn."

Lord Garrison sets his hands on the table, keeping himself tall. "Politics is a game, son. Everyone is a pawn."

From the rest of the advisers, an overwhelming silence is their only response.

"I propose we send notice to each of the islands," Lord Garrison continues, though I no longer look at him. I press a hand to my forehead instead, willing away the headache blossoming against my temples. "We'll tell them you're on your way to meet their most eligible bachelors. We'll be loud about it, and ensure everyone's attention is on you. We'll distract the kingdom from how quickly everything around them is changing."

"It's a clever idea." Zale's voice is soft and regretful when she chimes in. "We could use it as an opportunity for you to curry favor, Amora, and have the islands get to know you. The people would feel engaged; like you're one of them, and part of this kingdom. Love also makes you vulnerable. It makes you soft, and that softness is what people need to see from you. This could give Visidia hope."

It takes everything in me not to let her feel the extent of my rage, even as the rest of the advisers nod their agreement.

It's barely been two seasons since I broke off the engagement with Ferrick, and already they're trying to pawn me off on another man. Just the idea of it's enough for me to push from the table, rising on legs that threaten to shake with anger.

"I've spent over eighteen years training to be in the position I'm in." I grit the words through my teeth, having to reel in my emotions with each one. "I've studied the books of our history. The maps. Magic. Weapons. Strategy. Court. Tell me, what man is out there who has done the same? What man could possibly be ready to sit at my side and help lead a kingdom?" I try to steady my wavering voice; it's not one that comes from nerves, but from hate. Not at Lord Garrison or the other advisers, but at the sheer fact that, deep down, I recognize this idea has its merits.

The kingdom needs *something* to distract them, and I told myself I'd do whatever it took to right the wrongs left behind by the Montaras. But *this*?

Across the table, Lord Garrison remains calm as the summer sea. "I admire your tenacity to strengthen the kingdom, but as I've already said, Visidians need to trust their ruler. No one has even *seen* your strength. You may have stopped Kaven, but since you failed during your ceremony last summer, no one has seen your magic. With Arida's prisons at capacity, many have their hesitations about you, Your Majesty. Rumors you can't use your magic at the level of a High Animancer have been circulating; many believe you don't have the control over your soul magic to even execute prisoners, let alone protect Visidia. It's time for damage control. It's time to show the kingdom that you're vulnerable—that you're so open to listening to the concerns of commoners that you'd even consider bringing one of them into the kingdom as your husband."

Mother's face slackens as I freeze. This is the first I've heard whispers about my magic.

"There've been more urgent concerns than executing prisoners." It's Bastian's sharp voice that cuts in, and I'm thankful for the moment it gives me to collect myself. "Her magic is fine."

Though Lord Garrison nods, the corners of his eyes crease with a scrutiny that says he doesn't fully believe the lie. "Of course. That's why a tour like this would be so beneficial, so that Her Majesty might show the kingdom she's not only powerful, but that she's someone they can trust. That she hears their worries and will do what's best for the kingdom."

I taste the start of blood at my bottom lip from how roughly I worry at it. "I'll put an end to any rumors about my magic tonight," I say before I can decide better of it. "I'll address all prisoners who've been sentenced to an execution by my magic, and I invite you to watch, Lord Garrison. And if anyone else here is concerned about my magic, you're welcome to join us."

Both Mother and Bastian try to catch my eye, but I refuse to pay them any mind. Here before the others, I must maintain my most dismissive calm even as my heart races so fiercely that it can't be long before I crack.

I need to get out of here. I need to plan and think, far from whispers or advisers and the swirling mass of Bastian's nerves that eat at me.

The sooner I can squash those rumors about my magic, the better. On top of everything else, the discovery of my missing magic is the last thing I need.

"I'll consider this proposal, Lord Garrison," I announce to the table, hiding my shaking hands. "And I'll see you tonight."

∽ FOUR

Bastian catches up to me before I can escape back to my room, breathless as he seizes hold of my wrist.

I jump from the jolt of his skin on mine. His touch blazes through me like fire, igniting my veins. It makes me want to give myself to him, to let him hold me and just burn.

It's why I've been doing everything in my power to stay away from him.

"You're really going to run out like that?" he demands, his hair windswept from running, hazel eyes fixed on mine. "You have no *magic*, Amora. How do you think you're going to get away with this, especially with others watching?"

"You don't get it, do you?" I whip my hand back from him, as though he's a flame threatening to char my skin. "I *need* others to watch. That's the only way I have a chance at putting a stop to the rumors that something happened to my magic."

His fists are clenched, the muscles in his neck taut. "But do you have a *plan*? You know, that thing where you pause to think about what you're doing before you announce to an entire room that you're going to do it?"

"Of course I do," I argue. "I have a . . . a contingency plan."

He cocks his head to the side. "Oh? What kind of contingency plan?"

I clamp my teeth together, tempering the frustration that's bubbling within me. "One that will work." But also, one I hoped I'd never have to use. One with too many variables, when we have only one chance to get this right. I know full well how risky it is—one misstep, and my entire reign will go down in flames before it's even begun. But I've known this day would come since the moment I took the throne, and this is the only idea that stands a chance.

Bastian sighs. "You don't need to do this by yourself. Just . . . *talk* to me. You and I are better together; let me help you."

For a fleeting moment, I want little more than exactly that. But I trusted Father with everything, and look where that got me. I will not put my faith solely in another person, again.

"You can help me by staying away tonight." I keep my voice terse, trying to ignore the way his grief slices into me. Every fiber of my body buzzes with the wrongness of this emotion that isn't my own. "You're a distraction, Bastian. And I can't have any distractions when I'm down in the prison."

Maybe they're cruel words. But as his face falls, I know they've worked. For now, that's all that matters.

"You've been avoiding me all fall. I'm sure I can manage to stay away from you for one night." He leans away from me and crosses his arms over his chest. The stance looks almost casual, but I'm not fooled. Frustration boils within him, heating my skin. "But what about what they said in the meeting? Are you . . . Is that something you want?"

"Getting married?" I snort. "Of course it isn't. But you can't deny the idea has merit."

"It's a *safe* idea," he challenges, gritting the words between clenched teeth. His anger is a dark and vicious storm of emotions that swells within me.

"There's nothing wrong with trying to be safe." I haven't had the chance to truly consider the idea, but I can't help but want Bastian to feel a little sting from my words. I want him to know that, regardless of this curse linking us, he doesn't own me. He is not my destiny, and though I might want him, I don't *need* him. "Visidia's lost too much. My *mother* has lost too much. What's wrong with having some stability?"

"There's nothing wrong with stability. But it shouldn't mean sacrificing who you are." He steps forward and reaches out as if to touch me. Though every inch of my body burns for that touch, I flinch back, only realizing a moment too late what I've done.

Bastian stills, stricken. His chest doesn't move—for a moment, he doesn't breathe.

"You just got out of one engagement; don't trap yourself again." His words have turned to a whisper, soft and pleading.

"This isn't a sudden suggestion." I keep my voice hard. "There's a reason my family engaged me to Ferrick last summer, and now there are too few options left to be the heir. I have to consider it—I'll do whatever it takes to repair this kingdom, and if that means I must put a ring on my finger to do it, or fake whatever I must fake so that my people can rest easy, then I will."

His jaw snaps shut, and I can practically hear his teeth grinding together. I'm about to dismiss myself, unable to bear the tension any longer, when his posture relaxes.

"Fine." Bastian speaks with such finality that, for a moment, I'm almost offended he hasn't tried harder to stop me. At the very least I expected an outburst, yet his anger comes cool and bitter.

"Fine?"

"That's what I said." His voice is calm, but brisk. "It's

fine. In fact, you *should* do it."

It's as though he's struck me straight in the chest. I turn away, unwilling to let him see the anger festering inside me. "This is all it took you to back off? Stars, maybe I should have begun courting ages ago."

Bastian's laugh is smooth as wine. In his nearness, I can practically taste the familiar sea-salt scent of his skin. "Who said anything about backing off? The plan would be to meet the most eligible bachelors in all Visidia, right? And see if you have a connection with any of them?"

I watch him warily, eyes narrowed. "That's correct."

His breathing settles. Though his eyes are dark, determination has hardened them. The smile he flashes is nearly enough to melt me to the floor, warm and rich and brilliant. "Then if that's what you decide to do, let's not forget that I'm a bachelor, too. And I'm very, very eligible."

As the shock of his words settles in, I find I can barely move my lips, let alone form words. Sweat coats my palms, and I wipe them by pretending to smooth out my dress. My mouth is dry and my cheeks hot and flustered. The last thing I want is for him to notice, though the attempt is useless. This boy can feel my very soul.

"If you'll excuse me." I turn away before my thundering heart can betray me to him and the entire kingdom. "I have to prepare for this evening."

The last thing I see from Bastian is that he bows his head. There's a smirk in his voice as he calls out, "You won't be able to ignore me forever, Princess."

But until I can sort out these emotions roiling within me, I'm sure as stars going to try.

FIVE

My boots sink into blood-red sand as Casem and I lead the advisers to the prison beneath the cast of a silver moon. Only two have showed up—Lord Garrison and Lord Freebourne. For the others, I'm sure the grotesque rumors of my magic have outweighed their curiosity.

Growing up, Father and I journeyed into these prisons once every year for a single purpose—to rid Visidia of its most dangerous criminals, by using our magic to execute them. Back then I'd thought I was protecting Visidia with my magic, as my kingdom still wrongly believes. The soul magic that Father and I practiced was corrupt and grotesque, but until this past summer I didn't know any better. Our magic is the result of a curse on our bloodline to punish my ancestor Cato, who originally tricked everyone into believing they could only practice one magic for their protection.

Once I break *both* the Montara curse and my curse to Bastian, my soul magic should return to the way it was always intended to be used—as something peaceful and protective that allows its users to read souls and the intent of them. And though I'm excited to get to know that version of my magic, I can't help but acknowledge the sliver of fear.

Grotesque as my magic may have been, I'd always

believed I was using it to protect others. And for that reason, I grew to love it.

"Are you feeling okay about this?" It's Casem's whisper that breaks our silence, pulling me from my thoughts. This isn't the time to feel mournful.

"Now is as good a time as any," I tell him. "Let's get this over with."

I guide the others up a steep cliffside and deep into a thicket of rainbow eucalyptus, inwardly pleased by Lord Garrison's huffing and stumbling. Unlike him, I need nothing more than starlight to guide me through this island I know so well. This island that has etched itself inside my soul. In my lungs. In the salt that burns the cracked skin of my palms. I could close my eyes and still lead the others through Arida without missing a step.

Built like a cavern into the cliffside, the prison's exit is guarded by three skilled soldiers—two Valukans with an affinity toward earth and air, and a Curmanan with mind magic, skilled with levitation. As they step aside to let us through, even more guards wait within the prison.

Typically, Father would send them away for our executions. But whether it's because I'm new to doing this on my own or because they're suspicious of why I've avoided the prisons for so long, several guards tail us from a distance, as if expecting me to give the command for them to leave at any moment. But it's good that the guards are here. The more people who witness this, the better.

Sweat beads my temples as we journey through the dank tunnels, taking the musty dirt path that leads to the section of the prison that hosts the worst of the criminals. As we arrive, nerves seize my chest as I peer into the tiny window carved into an iron door.

A willowy, blond-haired woman glares back at me. Her skin is pale and eyes hollow; on her neck is the familiar black tattoo of an X—the mark of someone charged and tried for premeditated murder. Her hands are bound tightly before her, covered with a thick burlap sack. Every inch of her skin is covered with cloth, and on her feet are irremovable metal boots that tell me she's a Valukan with an affinity toward earth. Without being able to connect her body with the earth through touch, her ability to control the element is nonexistent.

There are others behind her—five total, bound by chains to the wall. All of whom are to be executed tonight.

I hold my position outside the cell as the guard opens the door. Curiosity is ablaze within all the guards' eyes. The majority of them stand to the side as I enter, arms folded behind them as they watch with hawklike focus. The advisers stand with them, and Lord Garrison watches expectantly as the woman's gags are torn from her.

"I was beginning to think you'd never show up." She keeps her voice playful even when her eyes flit this way and that, searching for the nearest exit. With as many guards as there are patrolling the prison, it'd be pointless for her to run. But that hasn't stopped prisoners from trying.

I close the remaining space between her and pluck a hair from her scalp. When she flinches away from my touch, I see the mark I'm looking for. On her bound hands, just above the edge of the burlap that's meant to be covering all of her, is a faint lilac tattoo on her inner forearm—two skeletal fish forming crossbones beneath a skull. It's tiny, nearly impossible to see, but it gives me all the courage I need to press on. Clutching the hair in my fist, I say a silent prayer that this will work.

"I need fire," I tell the closest guard.

Soul magic is based upon equivalent exchange; if I want to take a bone from someone, I must offer a bone and something of their person—usually a hair. If I want their tooth, then I offer a tooth in return. And if I want to kill them, I must use their blood.

However, there's no one way to use soul magic; everyone who has ever wielded it has done so in a unique way. My father used water for drowning, my aunt swallows the bones and uses the acid in her stomach to destroy them. I use fire to burn the blood and bones of my victims.

Likely anticipating my request, a Valukan guard obliges by drawing a powerful breath from her gut. When she breathes out again it's with an extended palm. In it, a tiny flame flickers and stretches to life, building each time the Valukan exhales. She sets the flames upon a small pit built into the cell, created for exactly this purpose, and it flares brightly. I open my palm and dangle the hair above it.

"What's your name?"

The prisoner's easy demeanor falters. Her expression becomes tart as she attempts to rise to her feet, but the heavy boots trip her, and there's nowhere for her to go. Only bound prisoners wait behind her, and a handful of Visidia's strongest magic wielders before her.

"Don't try it," I warn as her eyes flick toward the single exit. "I'll ask you one more time—what's your name?" I reach for the satchel on my hip, relishing the way my skin buzzes against the burnished leather, missing having a reason to reach for it. From it, I draw a single tooth and wind the prisoner's hair around it.

For me, teeth are the most humane way I know to get the amount of blood I need to end a person's life. While uncomfortable, it's fairly painless.

I dangle the tooth over the writhing fire, watching as the woman's jaw twitches in response. Her hard demeanor shatters.

"Please don't do this," the woman pleads. "Please, give me another chance."

My own jaw twitches too, though unlike hers, mine's from annoyance. I hate being made the villain, especially in front of a crowd. "I asked for your name."

"Riley," she says. "It's Riley Pierce."

"Riley Pierce, as the Queen of Visidia, it's my job to keep the kingdom safe. Your soul is a blight; it's grown corrupted from your crimes, and the people of Visidia have chosen execution as your punishment. If you have any last words, say them now."

She drops her head, shoulders shaking as I press my palm against them, keeping her on her knees should she try anything.

When she raises her chin again, there's ice in her eyes. "I hope that you burn."

They're words that jolt my mind back two seasons prior, and I think of Father's lifeless corpse burning in a sea of fire, skin charring and melting from his bones. His blood pooling and boiling around him, turning to tar. I sway as the walls of the prison close in and force myself to draw a deep breath through my nose to steady myself.

Not right now. Not right here. The memories can haunt me later, as they do every time I shut my eyes. But right now, I must maintain my composure.

"One day," I tell the prisoner, "I'm sure that I will."

34

Riley's eyes flicker to me, confused, but my only response is to drop the tooth wound with her hair into the flame. Her body spasms as blood pools from her gums, staining her teeth and spilling down her lips. I bend to run my finger over it, coating my skin, then smear the blood over two bones—one from a human spine, and another small shard of a skull.

Taking only the briefest moment, I turn to look back at the advisers' faces. Lord Garrison has gone bone white, while Lord Freebourne's dark brows furrow as though he's unsure whether to be appalled or intrigued.

I drop the bloodied bones into the fire, and as they crackle the woman falls. Her spine twists sharply and her skull caves in. She takes one surprised gasp of air before she shudders to the ground, dead.

Death by my hand is never painless—I don't have the luxury of giving people that—but it can certainly be quick.

With Riley's limp body before me, I turn to the advisers to see that Lord Garrison has turned away. It's clear any doubts he had about my magic are gone; I've given him what he wanted, yet he didn't even have the stomach to watch.

"Casem, you stay. The rest of you, there's no need to torture yourselves." I crouch before Riley's body, setting my hand upon the sheath of my steel dagger. "Unless you want to watch me drain the bodies and harvest their bones, take your leave. I'll handle the rest of the prisoners alone."

Relief floods from Lord Garrison in waves that knot my stomach. Though Lord Freebourne hesitates, seeming half-inclined to stay, both men eventually nod and take their leave without protest. The guards are quick to follow, handing Casem the copper key ring so that I may finish my work in peace. This wasn't even my true magic, and still it disgusts them.

"Lord Garrison?" I call as he's nearly out the door.

Sheet white as he fights against shaking hands, he turns to me, unable to look me in the eye. "Your Majesty?"

"Should I hear even a whisper about my magic, especially from the mouth of a Suntosan, I'll have you to take it up with."

"Yes, Your Majesty." And then he's gone.

Casem stands with his hands folded behind him, gaze firmly on the ground. Only when we can no longer hear the footsteps of the others does he exhale a tightly held breath.

"Blood of the gods, I can't believe you pulled that off."

"It's not over, yet." I untie the binds on Riley's wrists and turn her so that she's no longer lying face-first on the grimy floor, but with the back of her head on my lap. "Go and guard the perimeter."

Casem moves to obey, but something stops him mid-step. Quietly, he whispers, "You don't have to do the rest of this, you know. We can find another way."

"There is no other way." As much as I want to believe those words, they're a lie. This is my duty, just as Lord Garrison said earlier. And if I can't even do this—something I've trained for my entire life, something my people believe to be an act of protection—why do I still wear this crown? "Make sure no one enters."

Though he waits a beat too long, Casem bows his head and excuses himself. Only when he's gone do I take Riley's face in my hands and squeeze her cheeks.

"Nice show," I tell her. "Now get up, we need to move quickly."

She stirs, the blond of her hair slowly melting into a soft

36

pastel pink. The lilac tattoo on her wrist wriggles and melts back into her skin. The woman opens eyes that are no longer hazel, but a startling, magical ruby, and it's Shanty who beams at me.

She's a face-shifter from Ikae who we met on our journey last summer. She helped disguise us long enough to escape off the island, and was the one to tell us where to find Vataea.

Her teeth are stained red, and with the back of her hand she wipes blood from her lips and peels back a tiny, empty pouch of pig's blood from the top of her gums.

"For future reference, this stuff is *revolting*." She spits it on the floor with a grimace. "You owe me big-time."

The yells of the prisoners who wait behind her are muffled by their gags as Shanty's enchantment wears off. The rest of them, unfortunately, are real. And the one Shanty was doubling for waits in the lineup, her own face altered with enchantment magic.

Shanty takes my offered hand and pops onto her feet, brushing dirt from her cream tunic and linen lilac pants.

"They believed it." Relief fills me when I say it aloud, settling the nerves that turned my skin to gooseflesh. The relief nearly makes me laugh. "They fell for it completely. You were amazing."

She bats a baby-pink curl from her shoulder and smiles with lips red as rubies. "Did you ever doubt me?" Her voice is a proud purr.

Though I was hesitant to add to the list of people who know I'm unable to access my magic, hiring Shanty was a necessity. She's been here on Arida since the fall, likely living with a new face every day. It was Ferrick's idea to invite her here, and to keep her secret, just in case we needed her skills.

Few people know she's here on Arida.

It was a good call. As fragile as Visidia is right now, ensuring that my people still believe they're protected by a powerful animancer is necessary. It's as Lord Garrison said — sometimes we must distract our people from the truth long enough to get the job done.

"Have Casem help you get out of here," I tell her. "And make sure you're not seen."

"Like I'd be caught before I collected payment," Shanty muses. "Staying hidden is my specialty, Your Majesty. I'll see you on the other side."

She gives a tiny salute, leaving me to focus instead on the five real prisoners before me. At my side rests two daggers — Rukan, the blade I forged from the poisoned tentacle of the Lusca, a sea beast I bested last summer, and the steel blade I've had since Father gifted it to me in this prison thirteen years ago. That's the one whose hilt I take now, clutching it tightly as I crouch before the first prisoner I'm to execute. The man lifts his eyes to me as I tear off his gags, assessing my crown.

"Do your people know their queen is as much of a liar as the rest of her family?" He spits on my hands, then looks at me as though he expects me to reel back. But this is far from the first time I've been spat on. I wipe it on my pants.

This isn't the way it should be; his blood on my hands is not what I want, and without my magic, I can't even look into his soul to ensure his execution is just. But for the sake of making Visidia believe in me and my protection until I can restore the kingdom and all of its magics, this is what I must do.

Perhaps Lord Garrison was right; maybe I am nothing more than a pawn in this game.

"May the gods judge each of you as you deserve." Without lingering a moment longer, I stab my dagger into the man's heart and twist the blade, pressing one hand against his shoulders to steady his body until the convulsing stops. As life drains from his lungs, I lean his corpse against the wall and peel the dagger away.

I move on to the next prisoner. Though I try to make every kill as quick as possible, a blade through the body is far from painless, and I can't control a body's desire to live. Some go quickly, while others are slow and painful. One man takes so long and suffers so greatly that I take to slitting his throat so that he might pass on swiftly.

The whimpers of the remaining prisoners turn to tears as they wait, which then turn to sobs and screams muffled by the fabric that gags them.

Their blood stains my hands in such a violent shade that, no matter how hard I may scrub, I know it'll never come off. For each heart that my blade pierces, a piece of my already withering soul chips away. But I don't stop until the last prisoner has fallen and my boots bathe in a pool of their mixed blood. And even then, I'm not done; leaving five stabbed bodies is too suspicious when my magic doesn't rely on a blade to kill. If I had more fire and a bigger room, I'd burn the bodies. But my only option to conceal the wounds is by cutting through them, draining them, and collecting the valuable bones one by one.

For some, I take many bones. For others, I harvest only a few important ones each—one from the clavicle and spine. Just enough to make it appear as though I had good reason to stab into the chests of each of them.

It's a process I'm used to, but one that's different this time around, now that I know the truth about soul magic. Now that I know it never needed to be like this.

Nausea has me cold despite the seething fire, and it takes everything in me not to lose my stomach. It takes hours until I'm gathering the bloodied bones to be washed, keeping the bodies of the prisoners exposed for the guards to feed to the fish.

I've just finished when footsteps echo through the tunnel. Though Shanty's gone and I've done everything I can to stage my lie, a surge of panic rushes through me and I jolt to my feet, expecting Casem or one of the other guards. But it's Ferrick who runs into the prison, his face as red as his hair as he pants for breath.

My chest squeezes with relief at the sight of him, even when his nose scrunches and his breaths stop short at the sight of the blood I may as well have bathed in, and a small mountain of corpses behind me. He squeezes his eyes shut and immediately turns away. My cheeks flush hot.

"You shouldn't be here." Shame sinks into my bones as I wipe my bloodied hands on the dirt. It's been a full season since we were last together, back before I gave him his first official job as my lead adviser. I hate that, in our first moment together again, he has to see me like this.

"We found him," Ferrick pants, ignoring my words. His shoulders shudder with each heavy breath.

I drop the bones into my satchel and cross the floor to him so quickly that my brain can hardly keep up with my movements. "Where's he now?"

"He's being held on the ship. We've got him."

I could kiss Ferrick for those words. I nearly throw my

arms around him until he flinches back, and I remember the blood.

"I'll have him brought here—"

"No." I sheathe my blade, determination straightening my spine. "Take me to him."

SIX

The docks are a ghost of what they were yesterday.

The skies have lightened during my hours in the prison, and dawn fights to break free from beneath a heavy clot of storm clouds. While the sea kept a peaceful rhythm hours ago, now the tides thrash violently against the docks, misting my face with sea salt. They're the type of waves that are a threat to the average sailor, but a call of adventure for the rest of us. The kind of waves that were made to be conquered.

The fresh sea mist is a perfume I coat myself in as each wave beckons. I fill my lungs with it, as if to feed the pit of my soul. Though it was only yesterday that my hands last gripped a helm, desire thickens my throat. Sailing around the bay, failing to expand the perimeters of my curse to Bastian, is a far cry from the sailing I long for.

Staring ahead at the docked ships, my body aches for the days back on *Keel Haul*. For the mornings where I woke with the sun, and the nights I spent counting the stars with a mermaid, a pirate, and a stowaway at my side.

All my life I wanted nothing more than to one day rule Visidia. But now that it's mine, all I can think about is the day when I'm finally able to pass on the responsibility and have my body returned to the sea where it belongs.

Ferrick climbs up the docks, waving me toward the small cargo ship he arrived on. Having kept the crew as tight as possible, only a few trusted soldiers wait for us, their faces somber and tired. They know nothing of the man I sent them after, or the revolting crimes he's escaped punishment from for far too long. While all soldiers are swift to bow, several look purposely away from the blood that stains my skin and clothing, while others stare.

"You all did wonderfully." I grab the rope ladder dangling from the ship and haul myself onto it with practiced ease. "Go clean up and return to your families. You've earned a break."

Some hesitate, surprised I'm dismissing them so swiftly. But they obey their orders, and I wait with Ferrick in the silence until they're too far down the shore to hear me ask, "Where did you find him?"

"Off the coast of Suntosu. I got a tip from someone who knew him back in Kerost. They said he's been traveling, searching for someone."

I clasp a hand on Ferrick's shoulder and squeeze it, just once, and it's a gesture that earns his attention. He turns, slow to look me over. Even though I'm covered in blood, he winds his arms around my shoulders and pulls me in close. I don't fight him, letting myself melt into his body, thankful for his safe return.

Back when I was forced to be his betrothed, I hadn't always been the kindest to Ferrick. But after our journey last summer, I can't imagine life without him. I hug him fiercely, letting him be the first to ease away.

"I didn't mean for it to take so long." He combs his fingers through loose red curls that are in desperate need of

43

trimming. "How have things been, here? How are you?"

My skin cools, not wanting to consider the weight behind the question. "I'm glad you're home, but let's save the catching up for later. I need to see him."

The skin between Ferrick's brows wrinkles, but he nods all the same. "We've got him tied down below. I can come with you—"

I shake my head. "Stay here and guard the door. I don't want Vataea finding out about him until it comes from me."

"She's doing well, then?" he asks, innocent but hopeful enough that the light in his eyes warms my heart.

"She's adapted to palace life as well as we expected. And she'll be thrilled when she finds out who you've brought her."

Cheeks flushed with satisfaction, Ferrick nods and steps aside so I can access the stairs leading below deck. I take them quickly, and with a ship this small, it doesn't take long to find who I'm looking for.

He's fastened to a post, bound tightly at the waist and hands. Though I know it's him, his face isn't one I recognize upon first glance. He's aged significantly since we last met, his skin wrinkled and sun damaged. His once smooth, clean-shaven face is now covered with a thick gray beard that stretches down the length of his stout neck. But as different as he looks, I recognize his jaded green eyes, the burnt skin of his throat, and his missing left finger—wounds left over from our fight last summer.

Blarthe.

A man directly responsible for illegally time trading on over a hundred counts. One responsible for poaching a mermaid, the most endangered, protected species in our kingdom. He destroyed the lives of dozens and took

44

advantage of their suffering in a time of need, and subjected Vataea to years of atrocity.

This is a man who deserves every bit of what he got, and more. He's one whose execution I would not hesitate to sentence. He deserves to burn before all of Kerost for the damage he's caused.

"Hello, Princess." Blarthe flashes teeth that are no longer pearly white, but blackened with rot and decay. Several are missing from where I burned them away.

"You'll address me as queen, now." I crouch before the time trader, taking in how poorly he's aged. "Is this what you really look like? Gods, no wonder you took to time trading. Someone should have put you out to sea ages ago."

He spits at my feet, but I don't flinch. With all the blood that stains them now, I'd planned to have these boots burned. But Blarthe needs to remember who's in charge.

In one fluid motion I have Rukan out of its sheath and against his throat. His focus narrows on the strange navy blade as he tries to retract from the tiny iridescent specks that move within it.

"I'm sure you've heard of the Lusca? I took this from it as a parting gift." I press the hooked blade forward enough to scare him, but am careful enough not to break skin. The last thing I want is to poison him when I still need him alive. He's not only a gift for Vataea, after all. His capture is how I'll win back Kerost's trust.

Spite darkens his eyes. "I've heard the rumors about you, you know. They say the new queen refuses to use her magic."

"Look at the blood I wear on my clothes and skin and you'll see those are nothing more than rumors." I tease the tip of Rukan against the knob of his throat, heat boiling within me. But it's not enough to make him shut up.

"You forget I was there when Kaven tried to take Kerost. Unlike so many, I saw what his magic could do. I know he had the ability to curse away magic."

I sheathe Rukan before I'm tempted to poison Blarthe and be done with it. "Say another word and I'll take your tongue."

Blarthe doesn't falter, though there's a tremor in his words that he fights to conceal. "Anyone who knows Kaven's magic will be able to figure it out, girl. Take my tongue if you must, but know this—silence me, and you'll never get your magic back. I can help you."

The laugh that rips through me is practically a bark. "Do you take me for a fool?"

"I take you for someone who knows that not all myths are fake." His eyes flicker to Rukan's hilt, and I clench the blade tighter. "Aren't you curious what I was searching for when your soldiers found me?"

"Not particularly. I brought you here to be tried for your crimes, and because there's a mermaid who I'm sure would love to have a say in your punishment. I've no interest in whatever you were searching for." But that last part's a lie. The edge in his voice has admittedly made my blasted curiosity flare more than I care to admit.

"I was searching for an artifact the legends say was left behind by the gods themselves." Blarthe's focus doesn't waver as he presses on with the desperation of a man fighting for his life. "It's one that has the power to enhance magic more than you could ever believe. It's said that, with it, a person could wield the power of the gods."

46

"No person is meant to have that kind of power." Gods, I can't believe I'm even entertaining him. I lean back, ready to fetch Vataea and end this, but his next words freeze me in place.

"But imagine what *you* could do with it." He tips his head back against the post. "You want your magic back, don't you? There's no use hiding it; Kaven cursed you. You'd be threatening me with more than a blade, if you still had it."

Blarthe's words cause the memories to leech in, obscuring his face and making it Father's. There's smoke around his body. Though I know it's not real, fire devours his pants, and blood trails from the sword now protruding from his stomach and onto the ground below. Reminding me that I couldn't save him. That he's dead because of me.

If I wasn't cursed—if I'd had my magic—I could have saved Father that night. I could have saved so many lives.

"You're lying." It takes effort to find my words, and to keep my hands wound tight around me so he can't see how much they shake. "The list of your crimes could stretch from here to Ikae. What makes you think I'd ever trust a word you say?"

Though sweat beads his forehead, he shrugs as though this is a situation he's in every day. "Because there's more in it for you than for me if we were to strike a deal. Leave me here while you search for it, if that's what it takes. Why would I lie when I'm the only one risking anything?"

I peer back at the door, looking beneath the cracks to ensure Ferrick's shadow isn't waiting outside. Though I see nothing, I crouch once more and drop my voice. "What you're offering sounds like something of a legend." But even saying it, I know from experience that every legend is rooted in the truth. The very dagger I carry with me now is from a beast that I once believed was little more than a story.

A cruel laugh rattles his chest, splitting his dry lips. "If you believed that, you wouldn't still be listening."

I don't want to hope. But every time I shut my eyes, Father's there waiting for me, his face shrouded in smoke and his hand stretched out, begging me to help him. Night after night I'm reminded of the void within me where my magic used to sit. I'm reminded that Visidia isn't whole, and neither am I.

I need to break the curses that've been put on me—both the one on the Montara bloodline that keeps soul magic from my people, and the one that connects me to Bastian in the same way he was once connected to his ship.

Even if it's too good to be true, can I turn away from this opportunity without trying?

"This object is the closest you'll ever get to being a god yourself," Blarthe presses, as though he can sense my hesitation. "With it, you'd have the power to amplify magic to impossible extents. If I use it to amplify time magic, I could reverse what's happened to your body. I could restore your magic."

I let myself drop to the floor, leaning back against the wall because I no longer trust my legs to keep me steady. "Why tell me this? What's in it for you?" I'm as foolish as a fish, taking the bait he's lured me with. And yet I can't turn away.

Though we're beneath the deck, it's as though the storm itself fills his eyes. "I am a man who values his life. Isn't that enough? Promise me my freedom, and I'll lend you my magic."

"I'll find someone else—"

"Another time trader?" he snorts. "Best of luck. We're as rare as they come."

My hands tense with irritation, but he continues as

though I've already agreed. "During my travels I met a young adventurer who claimed to be the child of a man who'd used the power of the gods in the past. I don't remember much of their story; we'd probably had a barrel of wine between the two of us. But if you want to find the location of the artifact, finding them is your best bet."

"And where can I find this adventurer?" When he doesn't respond, I drag my hands down my face, groaning into my palms. "Do you at least know their name?" Without it, trying to find this amplifier will be no better than continuing to search for whatever charm Kaven had used when creating my curse. It'd be like searching the sea for a single shell.

"I'll give you a name, and I'll even show you how to use the artifact once you have it. But first I'm going to need you to do something for me."

I clench my fists, knowing the threat of my daggers won't be enough this time. Even with the skin beneath my fingernails stained black from the blood and innards of the prisoners I killed, Blarthe knows he won't suffer the same fate tonight. Gods know I wouldn't let him touch the artifact. But if I'm to search for it, I'll need him around until I'm certain of how to use it. I'll need him alive.

It takes nearly everything out of me, but I grit my teeth together and growl between them, "Name your price."

"I need a promise," he says. "A guarantee that you'll not only let me go, but that you'll pardon whatever past indiscretions might linger to convict me. Once we're on the other side, I don't want you looking for me."

"*Indiscretions?*" I sink my teeth into the inside of my cheek. The first one that comes to mind is Vataea, then

Kerost, and guilt buries itself within me thinking of them. Pardoning Blarthe and pretending he's not out there taking advantage of others by time trading would not only mean soiling my kingdom, but also betraying my friend. It'd mean letting her abuser go free.

But how do I say no to this?

Visidia could be whole, again. *I* could be whole, again.

No more lies. No more curse.

Though I wish with everything in me that it didn't have to be this way, there's one belief I've spent my entire life practicing: one life is not more important than the entirety of Visidia.

And besides, Blarthe is giving me too much credit. I may be extending his life, but in accepting his offer I am in no way sparing it. I will keep his presence here a secret for now, but the moment I have what I need from him, his life will end.

I'm not just Visidia's queen, after all. I am its protector. Its monster.

Vataea and Kerost can wait, because this goes beyond them. This is how I fix *everything*.

Squaring my shoulders, I look Blarthe dead in the eye. "Give me a name, and you have yourself a deal."

His voice is sweet as sap. "Ornell Rosenblathe."

SEVEN

It takes hours to get the blood off my skin. Even after I've bathed, I can still feel the remains of those I killed only hours ago. Though I've scrubbed myself clean, it's as if the blood's part of me, now. Always and forever there.

I do everything in my power to distract myself as I lounge on the chaise in my sitting room, skimming through leather-bound tomes gathered from the library, while trying not to pick at the skin beneath my nails.

Though much of the library was destroyed in the fires last summer, I managed to find three salvaged books on seafaring legends. I've been poring over them for hours, reading stories of sailors who've watched friends be dragged into the sea by mermaids, only to claim they saw that friend's face again years later, ghostly beneath the surface of the water. Myths of a giant serpent that's said to live in the Valukan volcanos, and stories of water horses that carry people into the depths to steal their bodies for one full year before that body deteriorates and they're forced to find another vessel or crawl back into the sea.

The goose bumps on my skin double with every picture and story, knowing full well that there's truth to at least some of these legends. But as for whatever this item is that's rumored to have been left by the gods, I cannot find a single word on it. There are pages that've been torn away by greedy sailors, or doused in ink and made illegible, likely by those whose prayers have made them paranoid. Perhaps I could find more stories if I looked hard enough, but it's as Blarthe said—while I'm out searching, he'll be withering away in the prisons. He's clinging to the chance to live; there's nothing in this for him, especially if I fail. So perhaps there's at least some truth to his tale, after all.

"Amora?"

My hands still upon the pages at the sound of Mother's voice. I kick the extra tomes behind the chaise before opening the one on my lap to the least offensive page—something fantastical and ridiculous, about a treasure-filled kingdom rumored to exist within the clouds, only touching the ground once every hundred years. "Come in."

The door cracks open, and tears fill Mother's eyes the moment she sees me. Though I know it's from relief, the fact that she even had to worry about the execution stings. She crosses the floor and practically throws her arms around me, pulling me tight to her body. In her nightgown, she's frailer than she appeared when I last saw her in the throne room, her bones sharp and delicate, as though she'll snap if I hug her too tightly.

"Oh, thank the gods. You did it, then?"

I draw back to get a better look at her. Either I was too distracted during the council meeting to notice the heavy shadows weighing her eyes and the sharpness of her cheekbones, or her handmaiden is incredibly skilled at masking them. Mother doesn't look as though she's been eating.

Day by day it's becoming harder to look at her. Because when I do, I think of Father.

Mother's skin would still glow if he were alive. Her cheeks would still be healthy and full.

But I took him away from her.

As much as I scrutinize her, she does the same to me. I've not slept for at least a full day, and my eyes are heavy and bloodshot. I don't need to see my reflection to know there are likely bags beneath them, and that the color is slowly being leeched from my skin.

"Shanty really came through." I try to ease away from her scrutiny, focusing instead on the flicker of movement over her shoulder. Aunt Kalea steps into the room and shuts the door behind her. Her arms are folded as though she's hugging herself, lips pressed together and her head dipped like a scolded pup, uncertain if she's welcome.

The muscles in my neck tighten as she approaches. Since her betrayal last summer, our relationship hasn't been the same. It's not for the lack of effort, or for my lack of desire of wanting things to go back to how they were, but my trust in her has shattered.

Kalea was meant to hold off on selecting her magic until I claimed my title as heir to Visidia's throne and proved myself to the kingdom. But instead, she learned enchantment magic, making herself ineligible to even attempt becoming the future animancer in my place. Because of her, I thought I'd had no other choice but to go on a journey to save the kingdom. Because of her, I lost my magic.

Because of her, Father is dead.

I clench my fist as she hesitantly steps forward, digging my nails into my palm to steady myself. For the sake of our family, I do my best to keep things civil around her. But even now I find myself gripping the pages of the tome too fiercely, creasing them.

What would have happened last summer, if only she'd kept quiet and never revealed her secret to me? If she hadn't put the pressure of the entire kingdom upon my shoulders, would I still be trying to carry the weight of the crown today?

"We wanted to make sure you were okay." Aunt Kalea's voice is low and cautious, and for Mother's sake, it's all I can do to bite down my bitterness as it bubbles to the surface. She doesn't need any more pain where pain can be spared.

"No one suspected a thing," I tell them both, drawing slowly away from Mother and easing her arms back to her sides. "But it's not a farce I'll be able to keep up forever. What we have is a bandage, not a solution."

Mother draws my hand into her own, nodding softly. "We'll find a way to get back your magic, Amora."

"Or maybe you could learn a new one," Aunt Kalea offers. She stiffens as my eyes find hers, likely oozing with every ounce of anger and resentment I feel. "The laws are different, now. You could learn a new magic; show the kingdom you're just as strong and capable with something that isn't so . . . vicious."

The anger can no longer be swallowed down. My tongue is a poisonous, acidic thing. "You'd know all about that, wouldn't you? How dare you say that to me, after everything you've done?"

I refuse to feel bad for the way her face crumples. The only sliver of guilt I feel comes when Mother sinks into the cushions, a shadow of the woman she once was. Tension swells around us, its pressure excruciating.

There's someone here who's missing, and each of us feels the significance of his absence. This pain isn't just mental. It's physical, like claws shredding my chest from the inside out.

"I can't learn any magic with half of my soul missing." I sit straighter, tucking my feet beneath me. "And as well as my lie in the prisons went, the only thing the barracudas bought us is extra time. Shanty's not someone I'd like to be indebted to; we can only use her services for so long. There are too many risks that come with needing to involve so many."

What I need is a way to change Visidia. To find the legendary artifact and change my fate. Break my curses. Restore Visidia once and for all.

But I'm not able to do that here on Arida.

"I've been thinking about yesterday's meeting." I look at my lap, curling my toes and hesitating, as though I hadn't been kept awake thinking up this plan. I have to sell this story. If I pretend to be excited, or give in too easily, Mother will suspect something. "The advisers were right; Visidia is too divided. I need to win our people's trust now more than ever. They need to know that I'm here to protect them, and that practicing multiple magics is the way of our future."

Mother cups my hands in hers. She doesn't want to seem too excited, but it's not difficult to see that this is what she wants. She thinks I'll be safer this way, romancing all of Visidia and finding us a new king—one that our people will look to and adore. One she likely thinks will protect me.

That idea alone is enough to curdle my stomach, but I maintain the facade.

"I know this isn't what you want," Mother says, "but Visidia needs a distraction. We're trying to change too much, too quickly. Our people need stability—a leader they trust and adore. The promise of a stable future, with heirs who will one day rule.

"I wish this wasn't a burden you had to carry," she continues. "It's not easy for women in our position. Your father was seen as a capable and trusted ruler from the moment he was poised to take the throne. But us? If we are too firm with our beliefs, then we have cold hearts. If we don't smile, we are uncaring. There are different standards for you and me, but *especially* for you as the queen of this kingdom. And part of those standards—part of your job—is marriage and children."

I tense on cue, making it a point of looking away from her. Parading me around to bachelors is so far beneath a queen it's sickening. "Father would never have had to do anything like this. He would have laughed at the idea."

"Your father had the privilege of being a man, Amora. No matter how capable you are, things will be harder for you than they were for him." She works at her jaw, like saying the words aloud is grating. But she doesn't need to convince me; a distraction is exactly what it's going to take to get me off Arida, so that I might find the adventurer who will lead us to the legendary artifact—Ornell Rosenblathe, who will hopefully be one of the many bachelors I'm to meet.

"So, you want me to parade around with men, making a show of it all while my kingdom is still suffering?" I make my voice bitter, not letting her think I'm giving in too easily.

"I want you to play the age-old game of court." Mother buys into my nerves, squeezing my hand tighter. "The Montara line is dwindling, and our kingdom needs to feel that it's secure. So give them a queen they will want to *protect*, and a royal family they will bow to. I'm not saying it's fair or that it's right, but it's easier for the public to love and trust a woman who they see as kind and vulnerable. One who has a charming man at their side. Play their game and show them what they want to see. Put on a show and earn their trust all while doing the work to rebuild this kingdom. Make them love you, Amora. Can you do that?"

It's not right. I shouldn't have to smile or change how others perceive me to be viewed as a strong ruler. I earned this crown by far more than blood right; who cares whether I smile as I give commands?

But I need to get off the island to break the curses, and this is the best shot I have at it. All that matters is that I find the artifact.

And for that reason, I exhale a deep breath and bow my head. "I can."

The relief in Mother's sigh squeezes my guilty heart. Her eyes water as she brings our connected hands to her lips, kissing them before setting her forehead against them. Under her breath, she whispers a quiet prayer I can't fully make out.

She leans away and releases my hands. "You're the queen now. The seas are rough this time of year, and we're only just beginning to understand this new state of our kingdom. I need you to promise you'll be more careful than ever. None of *that*." She gestures toward Rukan, still sheathed at my hip.

I force myself to nod even though it's perhaps the biggest lie I've told today. "Of course. And I'll bring the strongest crew Visidia has to offer."

"I'll have my mind speakers watch over you, too," Mother says. "No matter where you are, I'll have eyes on you. Should anything happen, I'll have you brought home or soldiers deployed right away. Bring Ferrick, all right? And that boy, too." I hate the pitying way she says it. It awakens an angry heat within me, and I peel my hands away from her at the mention of Bastian.

"It's not like it's possible to leave without him." The words hold every ounce of bitterness I feel. This time, I don't bother attempting to contain it. "Believe me, I've tried."

She lifts her hand as if to set it on my shoulder, then hesitates and returns it to her side. The movement's enough to snatch my breath, reminding me so sharply of Father. I feel the ghost of his hand on my shoulder. The single squeeze — just one — and my knees nearly buckle. It's everything I can do to pretend like I didn't notice. To pretend that I'm fine. That Father didn't die and leave me with a broken kingdom in his wake.

"I would never wish what happened to you on my worst enemy." Mother folds her hands before her and as far from my shoulders as possible. Distracted as I am by the ghost of Father's touch, her words are distant. If I focus hard enough, it's almost like I can smell him — a familiar scent of sea and sandalwood. I can nearly feel the lingering warmth of the sun on his skin as he returned from a day out on *The Duchess*.

If only he were still here.

The sound of Mother lifting herself off the chaise stirs me, and Father's ghost slips away once more, out of reach. "I'll leave the crew to you, and you leave the planning and the fanfare to me. You'll set sail in two days' time." She bends to kiss the top of my head. "Sweet dreams, Amora." And then she's gone, the door shutting quietly behind her. Only then does Aunt Kalea lift her head to look at me fully. I stare back, smothering my resentment.

"You need to take care of her." I am a snake with venom so lethal that even my words are deadly. "I don't care what you have to do, or what it comes down to. You'll protect her with your life." With Mother gone, I no longer care about civility. My aunt flinches but doesn't protest. She deserves every ounce of my anger and more.

"Keira's strong," she says. "Focus on yourself instead of worrying for her."

I have to bite back the laughter as it roils deep and vicious within me. "Let me worry about fixing my kingdom. That's what you always wanted, after all."

Again, she takes the insults in stride, which causes something within me to sear and fester. I want her to bite back, to fight me. What happened is as much her fault as it is mine, and there's nothing more I want than for her to know it. To scream it at her over and over again, and bury my anger so deeply within her that she feels every last drop of it.

But she doesn't fight me, nor does she bite back. Kalea takes my punches one after another, snuffing the blazing fire right out of me. When I speak again it's no longer with wrath, but with the coldness of facts. "I've no intention of returning until my people are willing to fall on swords for me. In my absence, I'm entrusting my mother with caring for Arida. But I swear upon every last god, Kalea, if anything happens to her while I'm gone, I'll have your head. I will not lose another parent because of you."

And with that, I return to the tomes on my lap and dismiss her without another look.

EIGHT

I find a freshly bathed Ferrick in his room the next morning, droplets of water dripping from his trimmed hair. Back turned to the door I crack open, he's in a fighting stance with his rapier raised before him. One hand is behind his back as he lunges, backs away, breathes in deeply, and shifts his feet into a new position.

I lean against the frame to watch, fascinated by how he doesn't waver. By how the muscles in his bare shoulders and back flex and tighten, stronger now. Without his coat, it's easier to see how much he's filled out since the summer. Though he's still lankier than Bastian, his shoulders and arms have swelled to nearly double the size since he took up weapon training with Casem.

Behind him, shelves of herbs and plants take over an entire wall, with bottles and glass jars stuffed full of moss and other things I can't make sense of.

"What are you doing?"

He practically yelps, jolting so fiercely that the rapier drops from his hand and falls to his toes. I grimace when he curses, stumbling onto his bed. Grabbing a discarded tunic from the open luggage he's got beside it, he hugs it to his chest to cover himself.

"By the *gods*, Amora, don't you know how to knock?" His cheeks flush such a vibrant red that, despite everything, I can't hold back my laugh.

"Queens don't have to knock," I tease. "What were you doing?"

"What does it look like I was doing?" He crumples his shirt in his hands, huffing. "I was training."

"Wet and half naked?"

"I'm not half . . . You know what? You never know what the conditions are going to be like, all right? Gods know you find trouble everywhere; if I'm going to be your adviser, I need to be the best."

"Right. I feel much safer knowing you can fight under these conditions." Stars, I missed Ferrick. "But you might not want to unpack. We're heading out again first thing tomorrow."

His freckled face falls. Looking at him now, clean after half a season out at sea, I see that his cheeks are glaringly sunburnt, and that there are thin wrinkles around his eyes from spending too many days squinting into the sun.

"No way" is all he says at first, turning away. After another moment, he groans. "Please tell me this is a joke."

When I say nothing, he runs his fingers through his hair and tosses the shirt he's been holding back into his travel chest. "This is a cruel punishment, Amora. I have *feet*. Feet are meant to be on *land*." His hand drifts to his stomach, and I don't need to read minds to know he's thinking of his seasickness. "Do I need to procure a ship?"

"It's already done. We'll be taking *The Duchess*, with a crew as small as we can get it. I'd like you as our healer, Vataea to command the waters, and Bastian . . .

because he's a requirement."

Slowly, Ferrick's lips curve upward. "It's our old crew."

I wonder if that warms his heart as much as it does mine. Our crew, back together again. But it's little more than a dream, because our crew is a ghost of what it once was, and it's my fault; I'm the one who can't manage being in the same room as Bastian.

"Our crew and then some," I say eventually. "I'm adding Casem, to use his affinity toward air to help with the sailing, and because Mira's been teaching him mind speak and Mother insists I stay in communication with her and the islands. There's one other person I might add as well, if they're up for it."

"What's our mission?" He takes a seat across from me and offers his hand. I don't hesitate to take it, letting him cup his hands around mine.

"I'm to make the kingdom adore me." I flash my most practiced smile before explaining our strategy to tour the kingdom and meet its eligible bachelors. Something in Ferrick's expression has cracked by the time I finish, though I can't tell whether it's curiosity or disbelief that wars in the creases of his forehead. "You're going to get *married*?"

"Again, you don't need to be married to have a—"

"I know how it works." He cuts me off, skin flushing pink. "I just figured you'd want to break your curse with Bastian and try things with him, first. You know, considering how hard you were fighting against marriage and all that when *we* were engaged." He screws his brows tight and squints at me. "You're being serious, right? Still not a joke?"

"Still not a joke," I echo. "That's what everyone wants for me. But . . . that's not what's really going to happen." I wait until his curiosity piques before quietly adding, "I may have found a way to break my family's curse. While the kingdom thinks I'm courting, we're going to have a different goal."

To this, Ferrick's shoulders ease. "Ah, yes, that sounds much more like you. For a second there I thought some wicked sea spirit must have possessed you."

I laugh, jabbing him in the arm, but Ferrick swats my hand and ignores it. "You know we've looked everywhere for that charm, right? We've done everything but physically tear Zudoh apart looking for whatever Kaven might have used to create your curse, and we haven't been able to find anything. What makes you think you'll find it in Kerost?"

"I don't," I say. "I've no doubt whatever object Kaven used is lost forever. This is something new."

"Something that Blarthe told you about?" Ferrick's too smart for his own good. He exhales hard, my lack of an answer enough of a confirmation. "And what happens to Blarthe once you find this rumored object?"

"Then I'll proceed with him as planned," I say easily. "He has no power; I just need to keep him around until I see whether his lead goes anywhere." And for his help with time magic, though Ferrick doesn't need to know that.

"He wouldn't have told you unless he has something up his sleeve, Amora. He's too self-preserving for that."

It's a thought that's been eating at me, too. But when Ferrick says it, I'm immediately defensive.

"If he tries anything, we'll be ready. For now, he's in the prisons, bound and gagged. We have time."

Leaning back on his hands, Ferrick nods. Though still skeptical, he doesn't fight me or say that he knows better.

Whether he agrees with me or not, Ferrick's stepped into his role as my leading adviser, and is backing my decision.

My appreciation for him is warm enough to burn a hole through my heart. For a fleeting moment, I get the urge to tell him everything—not just about the long night I spent awake, reading up on legends, but about what's been happening every time I shut my eyes—how all that waits for me behind them is death.

I think to tell him how I see a mass of Visidia's fallen, with Father standing between a sea of dead bodies. Of the blood that falls like a river from his stomach, and smoke that shrouds his face and body, but never the hand that's always reaching out for me, begging me to save him. I think to tell him of how breathing is more painful than ever now, and that it sometimes doesn't come at all.

I want to tell Ferrick that I know how ridiculous it sounds, because I'm meant to be the one protecting Visidia. I'm meant to be restoring it. But that sometimes I worry these nightmares will stay with me forever. Bodies woven in red, soaking in seas of blood.

I want to tell him that I am willing to risk anything—*everything*—to make up for my family's past and send these memories to the bottom of the sea where they belong.

Instead, I take the easier route, the safe route. Because the last thing I need right now is anyone's judgment. Especially his.

I give his knee a quick pat as I stand and make my way for the door.

"Tell Bastian to pack too, all right?" I add quietly, not ready to share the news with him myself. "But . . . Just tell him when to meet us on the docks. I need to be the one to tell him the rest."

You won't be able to ignore me forever, Princess.

I shudder at the memory of Bastian's words. He's right—come tomorrow, I won't be able to ignore him any longer. Come tomorrow, we'll be forced on the same ship for gods know how long.

Ferrick runs pale fingers through his damp red hair. "Of course. I want to be clear that I absolutely hate this idea and am totally against every part of it . . . But of course. I won't say anything until you talk to him, but what about Vataea?" There's a hopeful edge in his voice. A gleam in his eyes. "She and I . . . I mean, I know we're taking it slow, but I'd like to see where it could go. You're asking me to keep a huge secret by not telling her about Blarthe."

"And I'm sorry to do it. But you know as well as I do what will happen if Vataea knows we have him. Until I find the artifact, I need Blarthe alive."

"But—"

"Ferrick." I turn to him fully now. "It's an order."

Surprise flashes in his eyes before he rights himself, bowing his head. "All right then, Your Majesty. I won't say a word."

Once Ferrick and Casem have both been alerted, and a request for another crew member made, it's time to see Vataea.

The mermaid lounges on her balcony, long legs and smooth stomach exposed as she tries to summon the sun to tan her skin. She sprawls the fingers of one hand out in front of her, each of them topped with a miniature amabon that's skewered into her nails. She pops one of them into her mouth as I enter, her smile turning toothy when she spots me. Waving me in, she kicks her feet onto the chaise longue she's dragged onto the balcony.

My cousin Yuriel has been making the most of her presence at the palace. The two have been practically inseparable. Even now he lounges beside her, sipping from a deep goblet of sangria as though we're in the middle of summer. Though Vataea was set to leave Arida weeks ago to set out exploring the kingdom, she's grown accustomed to the lavish life of a royal guest in the palace. But after everything she endured with Blarthe, I'm glad she put her travel plans on hold to settle for a while. To stay somewhere she could feel safe and comfortable.

"You know it's freezing, right?" I cross my arms around myself and pull my coat in tight. The sapphire satin curtains around Vataea's open window buckle in the heavy breeze, and yet she remains unbothered, wearing just enough not to expose herself. Yuriel at least wears a glimmering coat that's been enchanted to look as though it's made from lilac fox fur.

"Sangria keeps you warm," he says lazily, not bothering to look up at me. He turns the page of an Ikaean parchment, laughing at one of the moving images. I nearly bristle until he turns it to Vataea and I see that it's not the same parchment Lord Garrison shared with me, but one of a seemingly drunk man whose bubble pants took a turn for the worst at a party. Vataea leans over Yuriel to snatch the parchment. One look, and she dissolves into wicked laughter.

When I clear my throat, she rolls her eyes and sets the parchment and its moving images aside.

"It's much warmer out here than it is at the bottom of the sea." She pops another amabon into her mouth and dips her head back against the chaise. "Would you like wine? As the *honored guest* of the palace, all I have to do is ring a bell and we'll be brought as much as we can drink." Another amabon, and then a toothy grin. "Put away your serious face, Amora. Come, eat and drink with me for one night."

"Another time." I cross the floor to pluck an amabon off her finger and pop it into my mouth. The deliciously fluffy bun practically melts on my tongue, filled with a sweet plum paste. When I groan, Vataea laughs and finishes off the last two. She looks entirely too relaxed, and I try not to let that make me feel guilty. If she knew Blarthe was in Arida's prisons as we speak, this would be an entirely different afternoon.

"How do you feel about another adventure?" I lick the last of the sugar from my lips. "A proper one, this time. Not just to the buoy and back."

Vataea's eyes narrow into slits as she turns to assess me. Within them, I swear I see the glimmer of dark delight. "How proper are we talking?"

"I'm to sail the kingdom. There will be bachelors, a chance to tour the other islands, and most likely far more food and drinks than we could ever want in our lifetimes." When Yuriel perks up, I quickly add, "But we need to keep the crew as small as possible. I'll need your help sailing."

She tosses her legs over the chaise and stretches her arms wide. Some time on land has done her well—her skin is warm with the sun and her belly's full and healthy.

"Who am I to deny an adventure?" Though she speaks wistfully, there's mirth in her eyes as they meet mine. "Where to first?"

Guilt is a piranha, devouring me whole as I force out the truth. "Kerost."

I don't want to ask her to return to the place we rescued her from—one of the several places she was held captive by Blarthe and shown off like a trophy. I understand fully the vengeance Vataea seeks on him, and once he's served his purpose, Vataea can have her turn with him. But for now I'm to follow his lead in Kerost and find Ornell Rosenblathe. "You can stay on the ship, if you'd like. You don't have to come ashore."

She flashes her teeth, sharp and dangerous. "I refuse to let that man keep me from enjoying my life. I will go. I take it the boys are coming with us?"

"Of course they are," I nearly growl, reminded sharply of Bastian and his outburst in the throne room.

The more I think about Bastian, the more I think about my curse. And the more I think about my curse, the more my resentment grows and my mind crawls into itself. The edges of my vision darken, tunneling. Tunneling. Tunneling. Until I see smoke. Fire. Blood. Bastian writhing on the floor. Father dead, a sword between his ribs. I search for his face in the smoke that shrouds it, but all I find are the faces of a thousand dead spirits circling behind him. Watching me.

"Amora?"

I inhale a breath at Vataea's songlike voice. I focus on it, using it as an anchor to drag my focus back. There's a tightness in my chest and a hollowness in my stomach, but I do everything I can to ignore it and focus instead on pushing my shoulders back and standing tall.

"Have your things packed before nightfall." I make my voice firm, silently begging her to leave it at that. Because if she presses, I'll surely waver. "We leave at dawn."

NINE

The fur along Mother's cloak billows behind her as we stand at the edge of the docks. She looks like a spirit, her expression no less haunted than the mist surrounding us or the wood that groans beneath our boots.

Her gaunt face is turned toward the roiling tides, creased with a concern so deep that it settles its way into her hands, which clench and unclench against her cloak in an anxious rhythm.

"We can postpone the tour until summer." The squawking seagulls nearly drown out her voice. "It'll be safer to travel, then."

I follow her gaze, watching as thick sea foam thrashes against the shore, trying to claim scuttling crabs that seek refuge in the rocks. I understand Mother's hesitation, but unlike that crab, I don't fear the sea. The ocean holds my soul firm. Salt and mist settle against my skin like a coat, luring me into its comfort. I lean into the feeling, welcoming it.

"The sooner we get this kingdom under control, the better." I keep my words devoid of the eagerness that stirs within me.

Freedom for Visidia is only an ocean away.

Freedom from my *curses* is only an ocean away.

I won't be waiting until summer to set sail.

Our departure is quieter than I expected. Since everyone who lives on Arida works for the royal family, there are no cheering crowds to send us off. The few who stop by come quietly and don't linger, mostly palace chefs who bring gifts of meats and pastries, while maids stock the ship with gowns and soaps.

"The islands have themselves in a tizzy trying to get everything prepared in time." Mother clasps her hands together in an effort to stop fidgeting with her cloak. "But everything's been arranged, and should you need something—or if *anything* happens, Amora—have Casem contact me."

I wish I didn't have to see the pain in her eyes, or the fear of losing someone else in her life. I wish there was *somewhere* for me to look without seeing Father. "I'm going to fix everything, I promise."

I hug my own cloak tight as soldiers weave around us, loading our supplies onto *The Duchess*. Though the island will warm throughout the day, here in the early morning fog my breath plumes in thick gray clouds. I breathe in the brine so deeply it stings my nose, catching my fingers beating a fast rhythm against my sides.

I shouldn't be this eager. I've been on *The Duchess* nearly every day since I recovered from my fight with Kaven. But as I try to remind myself of that, a flash of full white sails floats in the corner of my vision, and my fingers still.

The approaching ship is one I've not seen since Arida took a bite out of it last summer. Somehow the splendid white bow has been mended with Zudian birch, and the entire ship polished to perfection. The barnacles that once ate their way along the wood have been stripped away, and the glossy white figurehead of a seething sea dragon looms over us, larger and fiercer than ever.

Keel Haul is and will always be the most brilliant ship,

and as my eyes linger on its captain, I have to bite my tongue.

Bastian's not behind the helm where I expect him, but seated atop the figurehead, impeccable in a fitted scarlet coat and khaki breeches. His leather boots are polished, and his chestnut hair is loose and curling against the wind. He's gorgeous, but that's not what makes my heart take pause and my stomach twist fiercely with desire.

It's his smile. The same boisterous, cocky smirk he wore when I first met him. The smile of someone who reeks of charm. Who wants to be noticed and thrives off it.

It's the smile of the pirate I fell for, back for the first time in ages.

"That boy certainly likes to make an entrance." I ignore the hint of amusement that lightens Mother's words. "I suppose that means it's time for me to get back to the palace. But remember what I said—be *safe*. I'm only a sail away." She pulls me into her chest without warning, burying me in the warmth of her furs for a moment too long before peeling away, keeping her face ducked out of view. "I'm sorry for this burden, but you're going to be an amazing queen, Amora. I just know it."

She's halfway down the docks before I can process her words, her footsteps hurried, not looking back. If she does, we both know she'll try to stop me.

I force my attention from Mother's retreating figure and ahead to the sea. *Keel Haul*'s sails billow as the ship approaches, and Vataea stands at the bow, her lips moving in a steady chant. Though I can't hear her, it's clear she's commanding the tides as they roll and bend to her will, easing the ship onto the docks beside Father's ship, *The Duchess*.

"Ahoy, Your Majesty!" Bastian cups his hands over his

mouth to call to me, and I fight the urge to roll my eyes. The last thing he needs to do is yell; we can all hear him. "Tell your soldiers to transfer the cargo onto my ship." He's got one foot dangling off the dragon, while he bends the other at the knee and leans against it, looking perfectly confident. Perfectly at ease. Just . . . perfect, really. It's incredibly annoying.

Though he once told me he wanted nothing more than to take a break from the sea and settle, looking at him now, it's clear that Bastian will never belong to an easy life on the shore. Perhaps he wanted a taste of it, just to see if it satisfied his craving. But I know what that craving's like, and it will never be satisfied. His soul is one that's made to be moving, always on the hunt for the next adventure.

Keel Haul groans as she settles into the sand, and I shove my hands deep within my cloak for fear their trembling will give away how desperate my fingers are to reach out and graze her cool wood. Or how desperate my body is to settle into my place on its deck. To return to my cabin and be lulled to sleep in a hammock, surrounded by nothing more than waves and wood.

No politics. No pain. No fake magic.

As quickly as that wanting swells within me, I snuff it out, digging my nails into my palms to quell the anticipation.

This isn't meant to be an *adventure*.

"We're taking *The Duchess*," I announce stubbornly, lifting my chin to watch his brows crinkle. It's impossible to tell whether it's with amusement or annoyance.

"No, we're taking *Keel Haul*," he challenges, voice light as air and as overly confident as only men can be. "You want to make an impression on your people, don't you? You want everyone to take notice from the moment you arrive, ready to break the hearts of some poor bastards?" Lithe from experience, Bastian shimmies down the neck of the figurehead. He knows exactly where to grab to get himself low enough to safely jump onto the sand.

"*The Duchess* is a great ship," he says, "but she's no *Keel Haul*. This ship has gotten us through one adventure together, and she's fit to get us through another." Up close, I see his face isn't as confident as I thought. Though he maintains his ease and charm, the corners of that smile waver. While his eyes dance with hope, anxiety creases its way onto his skin.

"If you think that being on *Keel Haul* will somehow make everything between us back to normal . . ."

He shakes his head. "Stop being stubborn and give the order. You know you'd rather take my ship. She's quicker. We'll be able to cut down our travel time between the islands." Behind him, Vataea laughs, and I shoot her a glare for letting herself get roped into Bastian's antics.

I open my mouth to argue, afraid of how being on *Keel Haul* with Bastian might make me feel. But before I can, there's a hand on my shoulder. I jump, exhaling a sigh of relief when I see it's only Ferrick.

Ferrick's dressed in his adviser uniform, wearing a deep green frock inlaid with elegant gold stitching that snakes up its collar, forming the shape of leaves and ivy. It's no longer a rapier he carries at his side, but a gorgeous gold broadsword with a pommel that's decorated with a sapphire on one side, and a fierce emerald on the other.

Though the green he picked for his coat doesn't *quite* match his goldenrod pants, he's getting better with his wardrobe. Though they'll never admit it, I suspect he and Bastian have been selecting clothing together, recently.

"I think it's a good idea to take *Keel Haul*." Ferrick's words are quiet, meant just for me. "We're trying to keep the crew small, and she's an easier ship to maneuver. Plus, we're comfortable with her. Bastian's right, you're being stubborn." He ruffles my hair, frizzing it with the friction, but the tension in my chest eases. They're right.

Rather than look back at Bastian, I turn to the soldiers. "Thank you for your work, but plans have changed. Get everything loaded onto *Keel Haul* as quickly as possible."

If they're annoyed, they don't show it. Fortunately we've only just started loading *The Duchess*, and the soldiers are quick to adjust their route and get moving with the cargo. As they do, Ferrick grins at me.

"It's okay to be excited," he says, as if he's able to sense the eagerness I'm desperately trying to conceal. "You love sailing; don't be ashamed of that. You may have to keep a brave face for Visidia, but you're with friends here. All right?"

"All right." I raise my hand to let my palm set atop his, settled upon my shoulder. Though I don't fully believe his words, I appreciate them.

Since Father's death, it's Ferrick who's been my rock. A tiny, trusted light in a haze of gray. Though Bastian's tried to be there, how could I let him comfort me when I can't do the same for him?

Ferrick and I do not have a romantic love, and we never will. But I trust him more than anyone. He is, undoubtedly, my best friend.

"I'm glad you're back," I tell him, and he responds with a smile and a quick kiss to the top of my head.

"I'm glad, too." His tone, however, doesn't match his words. "I just . . . I can't help but feel guilty about this. After everything Vataea's been through, she deserves to know about Blarthe."

"She does." I fix him with a serious look. "But if I tell Vataea now, she'll march right to his cell and slit his throat herself."

"Would she be wrong to?" Ferrick asks, and I half expect him to be joking. Last summer, he'd never have said such a thing. But his eyes are shadowed now, and his lips are pressed into a thin, straight line. I realize that, this time, he's serious.

It's as though every time I blink I see another part of Ferrick that's changed. He was the one who delivered the final blow that killed Kaven, after all. Even if it was to save me, he's taken a life. I know from experience how much that can change a person.

"No," I admit. "At least, I don't think she'd be." As much as Ferrick has changed, so have I. Once, I would have readily agreed that Vataea should slit his throat and be done with it. Gods, she could even bite his throat out with her own teeth and I would have supported her. But since learning the truth about the Montaras—since learning that every single person I killed wasn't for the good of the kingdom like I was raised to believe—I'm not certain anymore.

I will absolutely do whatever it takes to serve my people and lead them into a stronger future. If I must kill or get my hands dirty to do that, I will.

But does that mean it's not *wrong*? What makes me any better than those I kill?

"For now, I need him alive." I push through the strain in my voice, refusing to let the thoughts linger. "If we're

75

keeping our crew as small as possible, we'll need Vataea's magic. We'll need her sharp."

Though it's with a sigh, Ferrick relents. His hand shifts to the small of my back as he pushes forward, urging me toward *Keel Haul* and to the boy who stands on the sand before it, waiting.

Let's not forget that I'm a bachelor, too.

Thinking back to Bastian's words, my skin grows hot. With everything in me I wish I could allow myself to fall into the weight of those words and *feel* them. I wish I could take his face in my hands and press my lips against his. Taste the salt and the sea that I'm sure has never left them.

There's desperation in his bones and a hungry pulse of his soul that tells me Bastian feels the same. But I can't let his sideways smirk or the stars dancing in his eyes sway me, no matter how much my body wants to be swayed.

Bastian's quick to climb the ladder and lower *Keel Haul's* ramp, and I weave through the royal soldiers to climb aboard. But the moment I pass by, he whispers, "Welcome aboard," and just like that, I'm transported back to the night we met.

I still, and his knowing expression is enough to tell me he's perfectly aware of what he's doing to me. Without a word, I force my feet to obey and pass him, making my way to Vataea.

"Are you certain you'll be able to guide the ship?" I ask, lifting placating hands when her stare turns venomous. "I'm not doubting you. I just don't want you wearing yourself out."

"I've been practicing." Haughtily she juts her hip to the side, arms folded. With the added weight she's put on since being on Arida, her curves are generous and difficult to look away from. Behind me a soldier trips and drops a chest full of cargo, forgetting herself at the sight of Vataea. The mermaid's eyes flash briefly to the soldier, look her over once, and then return to me.

"Practice all you want," I say, "but that doesn't mean you'll never wear down. You're not invincible, Vataea."

"Perhaps not." She bats strands of raven-black hair over her shoulder. "But I'm the closest thing to it. Besides, he'll be around to help."

When Vataea points her long dark nails behind me, I turn to find Casem and Mira. He's got his bow slung across his back, one hand free to hold Mira's. I try not to scrutinize her too much as she makes her way down the shore. There's color in her cheeks now, and a healthy glow to her skin. But I can't help thinking of when I saw her crumpled to the floor, dying from the stab wound in her chest. Even with the help of the Suntosans, it's taken her a long while to heal. She favors her left side, and the hitch in her step tells me she's not as recovered as she lets on. None of us are.

At the bottom of the ramp, Casem turns to Mira and pulls her in close. He whispers something I can't hear, but that I know is intimate enough that I should look away. And yet, I can't. Not even as she pushes onto her toes and grabs his face, kissing him with more fierceness than I'd known her capable of. When she eases away, her pearl engagement ring catches the light of the breaking dawn, and I find myself staring at it with a burning heat in my veins.

I'm happy for them. I really, truly am. But I can't help but envy how easy this is for her. She loves Casem, and he loves her. There's nothing confusing or difficult about it.

Only after making sure she's bundled tightly in her coat does Casem plant another firm kiss to her lips and begin to draw back. His footsteps are slow, dragging across the sand.

I wish I didn't have to take him with me. But Mira's been teaching him mind speak, and coupled with his ability to manipulate air, he's too valuable to leave behind.

"That's nearly everyone," I say, mostly to myself, though Vataea's lips press thin with surprise.

"Nearly?" she echoes as a royal soldier approaches. It's one I don't recognize, the same woman who stumbled at the sight of Vataea. She's tall, with broad shoulders and cropped red hair. Freckles kiss her face, and her green eyes are bright and devious as she looks us over. On her wrist is a small bracelet that looks as though it's been made from dainty fish bones and plated in rose gold.

"Forgive my eavesdropping"—her voice is a purr I recognize instantly—"but did I hear correctly? You're waiting on another crew member?"

Vataea's eyes flash as she turns to me, as if to ask, *Is this person serious?*

I try not to laugh as the soldier's grin turns toothy. The red of her hair lightens and lengthens down her spine, turning into baby-pink waves. Her green eyes deepen into the shade of fresh blood, and her curves widen while she shrinks in height. Slowly, her body continues to morph until it's clearly Shanty who stands before us.

"Hey there, Captain," she purrs. "Care to introduce me to your friend?"

I bite back a smirk as Vataea's neck contracts with initial surprise. But she levels her expression and lets curiosity take its place. Her eyes linger slowly up Shanty, taking their time.

"Vataea," she answers for herself, but keeps her arms

folded across her chest, not offering a hand.

"You must be the mermaid." Shanty offers her hand anyway, and smiles deviously when Vataea eventually takes it. "I'm Shanty."

"Shanty's the one who tipped us off about where to find you," I offer. "She uses Ikaean enchantment magic in a way I'd never seen before I met her. Calls herself a face-shifter."

"Not just faces, anymore," Shanty corrects. "I can enchant parts of my body now, too. I'm better with the top half than I am with the lower, but I'm working on it."

The first time I met Shanty was in the hidden Barracuda Lounge on Ikae. She'd seemed dangerous then, among the color-flashing lights and leading a gang that wouldn't hesitate to slit our throats if she asked them to. But here, as the sun is peeking through the fog, I'm surprised by how *normal* she seems.

Shanty's shorter than I remembered, nearly reaching my shoulders. And though the red color she prefers to keep her eyes is unnerving, she's strangely approachable. Clever and ruthless, Shanty is also beautiful, with full pink cheeks and a smile that lies, convincing the world she's not a threat. She's the type of girl people find themselves drawn to, never really knowing why; the type you give your trust to far too easily, even if they're the type who might betray you the moment they're given the chance.

Though I pardoned Shanty and the barracudas for their past crimes thanks to her helping us find Vataea, it was before I knew they were hired mercenaries. While Shanty knows I've got my eye on her, no part of me believes that the barracudas aren't still taking jobs.

"Are we waiting for anyone else?" Vataea asks as the soldiers finish bringing up the last of the cargo, and I scan the deck to see the crew we've assembled:

Ferrick, Casem, Vataea, Shanty, Bastian, and me. A crew of six, which normally would never be enough to maintain a ship of this size. But it's a perfect crew.

A healer.

A mind speaker who can wield air.

A mermaid who can turn the tides with a single song.

A face-shifter.

A pirate with curse magic, as well as the magic I once had.

And . . . me. Who, without any magic or skills other than knowing how and where to stab a person for maximum efficiency, adds exactly nothing to the skill set of the crew.

But that's exactly what I'm here to fix.

As the ramp to *Keel Haul* is drawn up and the soldiers return to the shore to wave to us, wishing me luck, Bastian takes hold of the helm.

"Where to first?" He's barely able to conceal the hopeful edge in his voice. Though I know he wants nothing more than for us to return to Zudoh, first I need to chase Blarthe's lead and see what I can find about the artifact.

"We'll go to Kerost."

Bastian nods and gives the helm a sharp twist. "Vataea, that means we need to head southwest. It's a long trip, so if you'd be so kind . . ."

Vataea's quick to take her place at the bow. She leans over the railing, whispering a chant so quietly that at first it sounds like she's mumbling. But as the tides stir, her chanting grows louder and louder until the waves practically take hold of our ship and throw us forward. The initial jolt sends me stumbling into Ferrick, who catches me as he tries to keep his footing.

"By the gods," he mutters, and I look up to see that his face is turning green. Ferrick practically drops me on the deck and darts for the railing, barely making it in time.

Bastian takes one look at him and rolls his eyes, and despite everything, my stomach warms.

Even with everything that's going on, I let myself sink into this feeling. Because for the first time since summer, I'm finally home.

TEN

It isn't until Arida's no longer in sight and the sea sinks into my skin that I realize this is real. We're doing this.

The fierce wind rips through my curls as I settle into the damp air, pulling my cloak tight as I stare at the buoy. It sways behind us, and my chest swells with a feeling I nearly don't recognize—freedom. No longer am I cooped up on Arida, but here on the open sea, ready for another adventure.

The crew lounges on the deck behind me, Casem and Bastian plotting our course while Shanty leans against the mast, using enchantment magic to repeatedly alter the color of her nails, having difficulty landing on any one shade.

Beside her, Vataea tips her head back against the dim sunlight, eating contentedly from a jar of pickled herring while Ferrick fidgets, working up the nerve to speak to her.

Vataea catches him from the corner of her eye, and her lip twitches with amusement before she hands him the jar in offering.

"Herring?" My stomach curls as a slimy fin disappears between her lips. She makes a satisfied groan before she starts on another one.

"Yes, thank you." Ferrick clears his throat and takes the offering, not hesitating to bite into it. His entire body seizes the moment he does, forced to disguise his choking by coughing into his sleeve. "Delicious." He nearly wheezes when he says it, forcing himself to politely finish the entire thing. "Just a little . . . salty."

I grab a handful of dried meat and smother my laugh, heading to the bow to leave them to their conversation. *Keel Haul*'s a fighter, today. She tramples over the winter waves, jarring the ship enough for me to have to grip the railing to steady myself as I look out at the horizon.

One day we'll go on a journey together, Father once told me as he carried me off the first ship I'd tried to stow away on. *I'll show you the entire kingdom. I'll show you every jewel and every secret it has to offer.*

I shut my eyes, trying to remember what it felt like against his chest. With each day that passes, I find myself chasing Father even more. Chasing the memory of his smile, or the sound of his laugh that always seems to evade me. The longer I try to keep hold of Father's memory, the more my mind skews his image.

Crimson blood soaks through his vest and onto my hands, staining them. He drops me as the blood leaks from his mouth, shadows pooling like smoke from empty eye sockets, masking his face. Behind him, a sea of dead Visidians rise. Each of them stares at me, unblinking, and I recognize a few of their faces from the massacre that happened on Arida last summer. Where their eyes should be are holes filled with blood that runs like rivulets down their cheeks.

I reach out to Father as the blood pools around me, but every time I push forward, the dead pull him out of reach. Their rage clatters my bones, nearly piercing enough to split my head open.

They know what the Montaras have done to them, and the lies Father kept. They know this is our fault.

The last thing I see is Father clutching his stomach with one hand, while the other reaches for me through the dead that seize him tight. I push harder and harder to reach him, screaming when the dead devour him.

It's my fault he's dead.

It's my fault they're all dead.

It's my fault—

"Amora?"

The voice snaps Father's image away, and I open my eyes. My hands are gripping the railing so tightly that they tremble, nails digging into the splintering wood. There's a strangled gasping sound, and I don't realize I'm the one making it until someone has one hand on my back and another on my shoulder.

"Oh, gods. Hey, take a breath, all right? Try to breathe." The voice is feminine, but not enough like a song to be Vataea's. Though I can barely focus, I try my best to do as Shanty says. "Good. Listen to my voice."

And though I expect her to keep telling me to breathe, it's with a jolt of surprise that I realize she's no longer talking, but singing so quietly I have to focus to hear it's a popular sea shanty.

Her voice is nothing like Vataea's. It's like a ship grating across sand, completely off pitch. But the familiar rhythm of the words beats in my head, and I follow it.

By the time the song's done, my vision has steadied, and Shanty eases her grip. She's likely the only reason I'm still standing.

"Thank you," I manage to say between leveled breaths, letting the ocean's brine lull me back into its comfort. Slowly but surely, the pain of the memories ebbs away—still there, and still a constant weight, but no longer too much to contain.

Beside me, Shanty leans her arms against the railing. "There's nothing to thank. I know it doesn't seem like it now, but . . . Stuff like this? It gets better. Maybe not for a while, and maybe never entirely, but it gets better."

I still, almost afraid to ask. "This has happened to you?"

She looks behind her, making sure no one's paying attention before she whispers, "I imagine we have different reasons. But when my reasons feel like they're too big to deal with, I know how suffocating that can feel. It doesn't happen to me as often, anymore. But for me, music helps. Usually if it's a song I know, I can focus on the words instead of the memories. My thoughts can get dark sometimes, so I try to trick them into something happier."

I'm surprised by how comfortable she looks on a ship. I expected her to feel out of place, yet she's perfectly at ease as she leans against the bow. Even now, it's hard for me to get a grasp on who Shanty is. I know she didn't come here out of good faith, but for the payment that comes with helping a queen. And yet, in this moment, it doesn't feel like she has any ulterior motive. She seems like she would have stopped to help anyone who'd been going through what I was.

I'd always thought of Shanty as someone fearsome. Someone who next to nothing could shake. But here she is, the same as me.

"I didn't expect you to come." My words are as loud as my shaking voice can manage—hardly any louder than the wind. "Will the barracudas be fine without you?"

"The barracudas can take care of themselves," she says.

"This is a job, just like any other. They know I'll come back to them, and my pockets will be nice and fat when I do."

I set my arms over the railing and lean my head into them. "Please, don't tell anyone about what happened. They wouldn't understand."

For a moment she says nothing, and if I didn't feel the presence of her body beside me, I would think she'd left. Eventually though, her response comes. "It's not mine to tell. But some of them might understand more than you think, you know."

"You said it got better for you." Behind her, I catch sight of the others sneaking glances at us, but between the distance and the roaring winds, I can't imagine they've heard any of what's happened. "When?"

"When I stopped running from it." There's something fond about the way she says it. "I had the help of my barracudas. They helped me embrace my past, when running from it became too exhausting."

Again, my bones stiffen. Chills run up my spine and I shudder, though I play it off as only the wind.

"What do you say we get some breakfast?" Shanty insists. "Casem's relaying notes from your mother about how to impress the bachelors, and her tips are making for some of the best entertainment in all of Visidia. You really ought to come and hear them."

"I'll be right there," I say. "Give me a minute."

"Of course." She squeezes my shoulder in a way that seizes my heart and reminds me sharply of Father before she excuses herself. In her absence, I let the weight of her words sink in.

I had the help of my barracudas.

And I have my crew, but Shanty's wrong. They're frustrated enough with me and how I've had to handle my curse as it is. They'd never understand.

I stopped running from it.

But that's not an option for me. My hands are stained with the blood of those who were killed on Arida the night of Kaven's attack. They're stained with the blood of my father.

If I stop running, it would mean accepting their deaths, as well as my curse. It would mean accepting that I only have half of my soul, and that soul magic will never belong to me or the rest of Visidia ever again.

Until I find the artifact—until I do everything in my power to repay Visidia for the damage I've caused—there's no stopping. There's no forgiving, no forgetting.

For now, I must keep running.

ELEVEN

With our course set, I head to the cabin Vataea and I are to share and set to work unpacking my chest. It's with a heavy heart that I run my fingers over the fraying ropes of my hammock, remembering my first night lying here upon the sea. The start of a journey that would give me everything I've ever wanted, while taking away everything I loved most.

A quiet stomping of boots down the steps stills me, and I know they belong to Bastian even before he approaches with a second hammock in hand. Ours eyes catch, but he passes by wordlessly. I flinch at the sound of the first strike as he hammers the hammock into *Keel Haul*.

Staring at the tension in his body and the anger in his strikes, I know now's the time to tell him the truth: that I'm here to find an artifact that can break our curse, not to take a husband. But as the words are nearly out of my mouth, Bastian breaks the silence.

"This would have been incredibly painful to do last summer." Wiping sweat from his brow, he strikes another nail into the wood.

It takes me a second to understand he's referencing his previous curse—the one that had his soul connected to *Keel Haul*—and I fold my hands as I take a seat across from him.

"You must be glad not to be connected to a ship anymore."

Gods. Small talk is bad enough on its own, but small talk with Bastian makes me want to chew off my own arm.

The breath he lets out sounds almost like laughter, but far too bitter. "I'd take my last curse to this one any day, Amora."

Tell him, a voice inside me urges. *Tell him the truth.* But hesitation wins out, and I ignore the voice. "Is that why you never unpacked?" Inwardly, I curse myself for asking. I want to go on *ignoring* Bastian, just as I've tried to do since fall. But wanting and doing are something my mind and body wage a constant war between, especially now that we've been forced into such tight quarters. "You hardly had anything for the soldiers to load onto the ship."

He continues his hammering, gaze never straying from his work. "It was in case I had to leave."

I stiffen, biting down my surprise. "You can't *leave*. What about our curse?"

"We're not going to be cursed forever." Another hammer strike. "I was getting ready for when we found a way to break it, and you decided you no longer want me on Arida. It's impossible to get comfortable in a place I might not be welcomed to stay."

My fingers still their anxious tapping. "Why would you think I wouldn't want you there? I thought you *wanted* Arida to be your home."

Finally he drops the hammer to his side, but the look Bastian cuts me is one of exhaustion, so unlike the assured arrogance he displayed on the shore this morning. "How can I feel welcome when you go out of your way to avoid me? When you flinch if I try to touch you?" He finishes Vataea's hammock and takes a seat to test it, dragging his hands down

89

his face. "Zudoh is my home. If you'd take the time to listen to me for five minutes, maybe you'd realize that."

I tense before I realize there's no harshness to his words. They're flat and factual, and that alone halts my building tension.

"This curse affects me, too," he says, "and it'd be nice if you remembered that. Wherever you go, I've no choice but to follow. So when you're stuck on Arida, or parading around the islands with *suitors*, remember that I have to be there too, when all I want is to return to Zudoh and help repair the damage done to my home."

"That's *all* you want?" And gods, I don't know why I ask. Part of me wants to swallow the words the moment they're out, but the other part wants to hear him say it, because I can't stop the feelings. The rage. The want.

The most vicious part of me wants to know he's feeling the same way.

Tell him, Amora. Tell him the truth.

"You know it's not." Bastian stands, and I can barely breathe when he crosses the floor. Every step he takes toward me is one I draw back, until I'm flush against the wall and we stand chest to chest. He pins an arm on one side of my head and leans his face down so that his breath warms my lips. Never once do his hazel eyes stray from mine until his hand fists into my curls and I shut my eyes, dropping my head against the wall as my body practically breaks beneath his touch, wanting nothing more than for him to kiss me. To touch me.

I stiffen, expectant, but nothing comes. I force my eyes open only to watch him frown.

"I want you." Something in his voice fractures with those words. "I just can't tell if you want me, too. With you, I'd be

90

happy on Arida. But every time you see me, it's like you'd prefer me not to exist. And yet here we are, like this, and you're not exactly running away. So tell me what I'm supposed to think." He pushes away, and my chest aches when he's no longer against it. But the moment there's distance between us, it's like the fog retreats from my mind, clearing a path for my thoughts.

"Tell me what you want me to do and I'll do it," he urges. "I would move mountains for you. I would chase down the stars just so you could hold one. But if you don't want that, then tell me now, because I won't pine. I'm doing everything I can, Amora, but you have to tell me what you need."

They're words I've never heard before. Words that stir a fluttering in my chest. A rising pressure in my blood. An overwhelming sensation that this moment is fragile, and that with one wrong move, I'll fracture everything.

"I wish it were that easy." It's not what I want to say; it's what I have to. "I feel things for you that I've never felt for anyone, but part of my soul is *inside your body*, Bastian. How can I trust that any of this is real?"

"Because it was real from the moment we first met." His voice is firm with determination. "I know you felt that same spark I did. It wasn't an issue the first time we kissed, or the second, or when we were in Zudoh and nearly slept together. You and I had feelings for each other long before this curse."

He's right, and while I want to agree, I know in my gut it's not the same. I will not be with someone who will chase down the stars for me if I cannot give them the moon in return. If I cannot be whole, then I cannot be with anyone.

This is my last chance to tell him the truth. But Bastian's a tide that won't stop reeling me in, and I need to be as unyielding as an anchor. I need him to feel a growing distance between us. Because I will not let this boy claim me, and if this is what it takes for him to realize that, so be it.

"I wish I could trust that." I have to pull the words out of me. Each one is serrated, ripping me apart. "But whenever I'm near you, it feels like you own me. I'm not okay living like that."

He draws back, and as he rubs a hand down his mouth and the dark stubble peppering it, I'm struck by how much older he seems. The shadows in his eyes have hardened since losing his brother, and his square jaw has turned to steel. I've always considered Bastian strong, but he's more filled out now, with added muscle upon his bones and strength in his shoulders.

No one who meets Bastian now could call him a *boy*. While I wasn't looking, he turned into a man. And now, there's a spark in that man's eyes.

"I'm no fool, Amora." His voice comes cool as frost, and his nose crinkles as though he's sampled a new wine only to discover he doesn't have the taste for it. "If you thought settling down was what's best for Visidia, you wouldn't have broken off your engagement with Ferrick. He's everything your kingdom could have wanted in a king."

My chest seizes. I know this is my chance to tell Bastian the truth, and yet . . . I can't seem to get the words out. I don't want him to know that there's a chance to break our curse. I don't want him to know what I'm after, because I don't need his opinions. Bastian has too much of a hold on me as it is. If I told him everything, it would mean letting him in. It would mean sharing this journey together.

And I'm not sure I'm ready for that.

"I know you well enough to know that you're hiding

something," he says. "There's more to this than you're telling me. But I'll play your game, and I hope you give it your best shot with those boys. Because you're going to be sorely disappointed when you discover that not one of them is me." With every word, his confidence blossoms. "They'll never be able to make you feel even half the things I make you feel."

His pirate swagger snaps back as he steps forward again. One foot. Another. And then his hand is on my waist. At first it's hesitant, giving me the chance to pull back. But my knees tremble, and I can barely keep standing. The last thing I want is for him to let go.

"And if you find someone who does," he continues, voice a low growl, "then I'll stop trying. We'll chalk half of what you feel for me up to the curse. But the other half? I'm going to call that real. And if there's anyone out there who makes you feel more than that, I won't try to stop you from being with them. I want you to be happy. *But*"—he leans down so that his forehead is pressed against mine, his words brushing hot breath across my lips—"since we're playing, I'm making a new rule. I'm going to prove to you that what you feel for me is real. Whatever those other guys get to do to try to woo you, I'll be right there playing along. I get to do everything they do."

No longer able to tell whether I'm breathing, I ball my hands into fists and press them against the wall so they won't touch him and betray me.

"*Woo* me," I scoff, doing everything in my power not to let him see the influence he has over me. "As if I'm so easily—"

"Amora." The sound of my name stops me short. "I've no family left. My brother destroyed my home, and yet I can't return to Zudoh to help my people because I'm *cursed to you*.

93

Your magic is running through my veins, and because I'm not a Montara, we've no idea how long I'll be able to maintain it, or what it might do to me. You are not the only one affected by this.

"As you can hopefully understand," he continues, "my life has certainly been better. And yet I've asked you for nothing, because I know how much stress you've been under. Stars, I *feel* how much stress you've been under. I've been saving my one ask, and this is it. I don't need special favors. Keep your secrets, I don't care. But if I have to go along with this charade, then I want a fair chance. Please. Give me a fair chance."

There's no argument for that, no matter how hard I try to find one. As much as I want my space from Bastian, he's right that he doesn't deserve the way I've been treating him. It's not his fault we're cursed. None of this is his fault.

It's mine.

Now though, I have a chance to fix my mistakes. I have a chance to fix everything. But if that's going to happen, then this constant bickering with Bastian needs to stop.

"Fine," I relent, having to push the words out of me. "Whatever festivities are being planned for the suitors, you may join."

"Wonderful." Bastian masks the relief in his voice with a smile as he pushes away from me to pick up his discarded hammer. My lips grow cold and numb from his absence as he heads toward the door.

Over his shoulder, Bastian casts me a wink I have half a mind to burn him for. "I'm glad we can finally agree on something. Sleep well, Princess."

〜

TWELVE

With *Keel Haul's* speed, the force of Casem's wind bloating the sails, and Vataea's magic willing the sea to push us onward, we make it to Kerost in just over two days.

The air's sharp and cool when we arrive, and as it scrapes against my cheek I'm reminded of the last time I was here. Last summer there'd been signs something was amiss in the kingdom, but it wasn't until I stepped upon Kerost's pebble stone beach to a choir of hammering that I understood how bad the state of my kingdom had gotten.

Fortunately, things are better, now. No longer do the strikes of hammers permeate the air; instead I hear rueful voices and laughter.

No longer withered and forgotten, the docks are packed full of ships with emerald and ruby banners strung across them. Curmanans with the ability to levitate objects and the elementally gifted Valukans are ashore, using their magic to rebuild the island, as I commanded when I first took the throne. Pride heats my chest as we lower *Keel Haul's* ramp, a strange feeling considering that out of our need to be ready to flee at a moment's notice, we'd only used the ladder on our last adventure.

"Look how much it's changed." Relief grips me as we make

our way down the shore. The pavement is solid and fresh beneath our feet, no longer the cracked and chipping stone I remember. When I last saw Kerost, it was devastatingly poor, and Blarthe had swooped in to prey upon its citizens. While he gave the Kers the supplies they needed to rebuild their island, he traded time off their lives in exchange. But the supplies he gave them were never going to be strong enough to withstand the extreme storms that plague their island every few years.

Now though, they're learning the skills they need to survive.

There's a small group of talented Valukan metalworkers who've made the trek to Kerost as well, using their affinity toward earth to enforce the structures so they're sturdy enough to withstand the storms.

Near the water opposite the docks are several other Valukans who instruct a class of Kers on how to manipulate the water. Their motions are like the most elegant dance, and I find myself straying from the crew so that I might get close enough to hear them.

"People often mistake water as the gentlest of the elements," says a small Valukan girl. Though she's younger than the rest, her movements are by far the most graceful and precise. "But that's not true. Water can be fierce. It can be unruly. If you go in thinking you're going to master it, you'll never learn. Instead, you must think of it as an extension of your body." As she draws her hands above her head, seawater spirals above her in a clean arc. When she swings her hands down, it follows. She grinds a foot into the sand and turns slow circles, letting the water follow her graceful dance. It builds until it looks as though she's standing in the middle of a raging whirlpool. I can barely see her raising her hand between the gaps of the water, but when she drops it, the whirlpool zips back into the sea with a sharp *smack*.

The Kers watching are enthusiastic with their applause, eyes bright with excitement for this new magic they're eager to finally learn. "Now, everyone, come stand by me on the shore," the young girl says. "We're going to start with the basics . . ."

Watching them settle close fills me with a pleasure that's bone deep. *This* is what Kerost has always needed. If only they'd been given the ability to learn multiple magics years ago, so much of their pain and suffering could have been prevented.

At least they're finally learning, now.

Yet, for as much as there *is* in Kerost, it's impossible not to recognize what there *isn't*.

There was no ceremony upon *Keel Haul's* arrival. There are no banners. No royal adviser or Kers waiting to greet me and whisk me away to meet their bachelors.

If I didn't know any better, I'd think the island had no idea I was arriving today. But I was there when Mother made the arrangements; this isn't something she'd overlook.

I recognize one of the Kers training as the boy we first met upon coming to Kerost—Armin. We'd spent hours hammering beside him, after which Ferrick had healed the boy's aching hands. Armin doesn't see us, but the older woman observing him from a sea-slickened rock above the shore does. My heart skips a beat as her bitter green eyes pierce through me. For a moment I stand still, fists clenched, because I remember her last words to me.

The next time you come here, it better be with an entire fleet.

The moment I took the throne, I sent her just that.

The woman holds her chin proud, and it's with a start that I catch sight of the shimmering gold emblem on the shoulder of her amethyst cloak. She's Kerost's adviser; the one who didn't show up for the meeting on Arida. And she's waiting for me.

"Wait here," I tell the others, though Casem's quick to respond.

"You're not to be left alone, Amora. It isn't safe."

I flash him my deepest scowl, but Casem's unfazed.

"She's their *adviser*," I argue.

"And I'm your guard." His arms fold as his eyes flicker away. "Something here isn't right, and it's my duty to protect you." The heat in his voice is enough for me to read between the lines, and with the dawning realization comes a pit in my stomach.

Casem's father, Olin, was my father's most trusted friend and protector, until Olin betrayed him. I've no resentment for Casem, who had no idea his father had teamed up with Kaven until it was too late. As someone who is also indirectly responsible for the deaths of too many, I can only sympathize.

"You're not your father." My voice is soft as his shoulders deflate. "And I am not mine. I'm here for my people to get to know me. They need to feel like I've dropped my guard around them, and that's not going to happen with you as my shadow. I've been sparring with you for years, Casem. Do you think you've taught me well?"

His face retracts with confusion. "Of course I have—"

"Then stop worrying about me. Magic or not, I can take care of myself."

Casem grinds his jaw, but eventually bows his head in defeat and steps back with the others. With his blessing, I stalk through the shore and up a sandy cliffside until I reach Kerost's adviser. In the time it's taken me to climb, she's scooted herself over so that I might have a spot beside her on the large rock. Silently, I take it.

"So you're our queen, now," she says after a moment, still observing the boy I can only assume is her grandson.

"I am." I've no idea why my words feel so grating, or why nerves eat the lining of my stomach raw. "And it looks as though you're the new adviser."

The title causes her lips to twist so fiercely I nearly flinch. "It wasn't my choice, but a decision made by those who remain here on Kerost."

My own lips sour now. Like the Montara family, advisers typically come from the same lineage. But I don't need to ask for it to be clear that whoever *was* the adviser must have died in the most recent storm. Kerost must have improvised by choosing their own ruler.

This woman, at least, is a good fit.

"It would've been nice to see you at the council meeting." I'm careful with my words, understandably on thin ice. "I never even got your name."

"Ephra Tost," she says stonily, still looking ahead.

I'm painfully aware of how *slow* Ephra's movements are. The last time I saw her, she'd been using time magic to speed up her body. Now, each of her movements appears deliberate, slow and pained. Though she's an elder, her hair has grayed and her skin has wrinkled well beyond her years. Looking at her, I can't help but recognize that while Kerost finally has a chance at stability, I was still too late. So much time was taken from too many people, and they'll never get it back. No matter how hard I tried, I've still failed them. But as I'm about to apologize, Lady Tost extends a shaky hand and sets it atop my lap, taking hold of my hand.

"You did well." She keeps her eyes on her grandson, never looking directly at me. "You have done more for my people in two seasons than any High Animancer has done for us in their lifetime." I try to draw my hand back, an argument burning my tongue, but she holds tight. "My son and his wife were killed in a storm. Their house and everything in it was destroyed; only Armin made it. He was buried beneath their bodies, crying, when I found him." She nods to the boy on the shore, who falls back into the sand as the water he was attempting to control smacks him hard in the face.

"But as well as you're doing, I'm afraid Kerost cannot forgive you so easily," Lady Tost continues. "All it would have taken was someone who was willing to give us the tools necessary to take care of ourselves. This is why I couldn't come to Arida. While I appreciate that you were finally the one to give us those tools, we don't want instructions on how we must use them. I know all about your reason for being here, and about the husband you must find. But I invited you here to this island so you could see our progress, not to celebrate you after what we've endured. While you parade around with bachelors, our efforts will be focused on restoring our island. Kerost wants no part in this charade."

Every word stings like venom seeping into my skin. I finally manage to slide my hand away from hers, knots of nerves coiled like snakes in my throat.

I understand where she's coming from—we took too long, and left Kerost with too much pain because of it. If I were in her position, I'd do the same for my island. I'd demand better, just as she is.

But I'm not Ephra. I am Visidia's queen, and already my plans of traveling the islands and finding this legendary artifact are being interrupted. And we haven't even been ashore for an hour.

If I'm to continue this journey, I can't let the rest of Visidia see that I was turned away by Kerost, or let them believe they can get away with the same treatment. And I certainly can't let myself get kicked off the island until I find out more about Ornell, the only person with the information on the artifact I'm to find.

"I don't expect your forgiveness so easily." The tension tightening my muscles has me tripping over my words. "And I understand you not wanting to participate, though I assure you, I've no intention to parade. But if you invited me here to see the progress of this island, surely you can allow my crew and me at least the night here? I'd like to see how Kerost is faring."

Ephra's snort is a rueful sound. "I can't stop the queen from staying however long she wishes; we haven't seceded from Visidia, yet. Do whatever you'd like. But know that Kerost isn't the home I once knew, and I expect you'll find it's a different island entirely. I dare say that Blarthe's influence on our island actually left us with something good."

My brows crease. "What do you mean?"

She pats my thigh before drawing her hand back into her own lap. "Go and pay a visit to Vice." She says it with such finality that one might think she herself was queen. I leave only after thanking her, and head back down the cliffs to rejoin the others.

Vataea's the first one I see waiting for me. Her eyes flit back and forth over the beach, body coiled and ready to spring. Though she's said nothing, I imagine that being back on the island she was forced to live on for so long against her will is a torment.

"Are you all right?" I ask her quietly. "No one will think anything of it if you need to wait on *Keel Haul*."

She only shakes her head and says, "If that bastard's still hiding here, I want to be the first to find him."

Ferrick's throat bobs as he swallows, and I cut him a quick look to remind him not to say anything. I'll tell Vataea the truth about Blarthe soon. Just . . . not until after I find the artifact.

"If you change your mind, you can leave any time. But for now, it sounds like we're headed to Vice."

Kerost is far from the easiest island to navigate to. Tucked at the southwest edge of the kingdom, it lacks sights like the beautiful gardens of Arida, the volcanos and hot springs in Valuka, or the lavish glam of Mornute. It's Visidia's smallest island, and without any natural draw, it's never been a stopping place for travelers. But as we round the hill toward Vice, it becomes increasingly clear that Kerost is far from the island it once was.

"What in the gods' names . . ." Ferrick's surprise mirrors my own as we're forced to group tightly together, not wanting to get lost in the crowd that packs the streets. For the sake of keeping a low profile and experiencing Kerost without drawing attention to myself, I pull my cloak tight—enchanted to be Ker amethyst rather than sapphire, thanks to Shanty—and raise my hood.

"BILLIARDS AND BLACKJACK!" yells a woman clad in a skintight amethyst dress. It's cut so low in the front that my skin heats, never having seen anyone daring enough to wear something like that. The rest of the crew stares too, shameless, and I clear my throat as the woman yells again, "Come test your luck at billiards and blackjack!"

Another woman stands at a newly erected structure across from her, calling out to the crowd with matching enthusiasm, "Ladies, we've got the most beautiful gentlemen in the entire kingdom waiting to serve you." She slings her arm around one of two young women who take pause, and lures her toward the entrance with well-practiced charm. "That's right, come on in. Right this way."

Farther down the street, patrons lift their ale to the skies before splashing mugs together with rowdy laughter. Their skin is flushed and their eyes bloodshot as they yell bets on what sounds like some kind of race.

While many of the patrons roaming the streets of Kerost wear the striking amethyst shade that marks them as a Ker— someone who once would only have specialized in time magic—dozens of other patrons fill the streets, as well. From the lavish styles they wear, it's easy to make out that the majority are from Ikae. It appears today's Ikaean fashion trend is clouds, which all try their best to resemble by wearing shades of pinks, lavenders, soft blues, and cream. Most look like puff pastries, but one cleverly styled patron has dressed like a raging storm. An occasional bolt of lightning strikes through his navy suit every few minutes, turning it a startling shade of yellow. Another Ikaean woman has dressed in all gray tulle; she must practice Valukan magic now as well, for she's created her own personal rain cloud above her head. Though it drips a steady stream of rain upon her, she never gets wet.

There are many Valukans as well, and even some Aridians

weaving in and out of the gray stone buildings. Some stumble, intoxicated, while others yell about how their money was stolen and how all the games are rigged.

On one corner, a young man is taking his chance at conversing with a small group of women. On the opposite corner, a child sells stacks of moving parchments.

"Queen Amora is looking for a husband! Just a single piece of sea glass to read! That's right, folks, step right up for your copy . . ."

All the activity happening on these streets is so disorienting that Casem draws a protective step closer to me.

"Seem like they've turned themselves into a giant gambling den." There's no malice or judgment in Bastian's words. If anything, he sounds impressed. I follow his focus when he points ahead, to the sign that reads VICE. It's been painted since we were last here at Blarthe's old place, now boasting a flashy silver background with bold amethyst letters. Women who venture into the establishment wear short dresses or shimmering suits beneath the coats they leave at the door, while the men don their finest. Everything is flashy in a way I've never before seen; it's overwhelming, loud, and with this much alcohol and money floating around, it's certainly not safe.

"Everyone keep close," Casem demands, hands flexing to the pommel of his sword. "This place is dangerous."

"This place is incredible," I argue.

"It's *remarkable*," Shanty echoes, lifting her hood and dipping her face so that others in the crowd don't notice the enchantment leeching over her skin as she presses two fingertips against her cheeks. She softens her eyes and makes her hair longer and her lips pouty and full, transforming herself into someone with the kind of sweet innocence too many men like to take advantage of. The dress that's taking form beneath her coat, however, is anything but innocent.

"If you need me," she says with a grin so wicked I second-guess that pardon I gave her, "I'll be at the tables, bleeding everyone dry."

"You mean their pockets," Ferrick says, a deep crease forming between his brows. "Right? You'll be bleeding their pockets dry?"

Shanty only smiles. "I suppose that'll depend on how the night goes." With the tiniest wave, she disappears into the crowd, reminding me once more how dangerous a crew I've assembled. Shanty could have a knife to my throat in a single second, and I'd never see her coming.

Though I knew Visidia would change following Father's death, I expected for it to come slowly, for the islands to need more support. Shanty's right, though—what the Kers have done for their home is both necessary and ingenious. But it's also a reminder of how quickly Visidia's changing, and how little control I have at steering it.

Now that they're getting training to protect themselves from the worst of the storms—now that they're *safe*—all they had left to deal with was figuring out a way to drive more revenue.

And they have.

The sun falls behind the stone buildings, beginning a quick descent into dusk. Dazzling lights spark to life, bathing the night in flashing neons that are impossible to turn away from. They're not meant to be a beautiful arrangement of colors like the ones in Ikae, but so flashy and over the top that they're almost gaudy. And yet there's something magnetic about them. Something *exciting*.

This is exactly what Kerost needs. This is their lure, their draw for tourists to visit and spend their money. They took what Blarthe gave them and made it their own, and I don't think I've ever felt prouder of my people.

Like Shanty, I want to take off down the brightly lit streets and explore all this city has to offer. I want to find Ornell. But with the crew shadowing me, doing so freely is impossible.

I need a way to search without the others getting too suspicious. Right now, Ferrick is the only one who can know what my true goal is.

"You love it." Bastian's voice draws my attention, quiet and wistful.

"It's incredible." I don't deny it; the evidence is written all over my face. This is the part of traveling I love more than anything—not only seeing my kingdom and its people, but learning how each island operates. Seeing their customs and getting to know them firsthand. I could read about the fashions of Ikae or the monstrous mountains of Valuka a thousand times, but nothing beats experiencing it.

"Look how far they've come in just two seasons."

A smile curls on Bastian's lips, though it falters when he catches sight of something on the street corner. He tips his chin to the left, and I discreetly turn to eye a merchant who's set up at the edge of a thin alleyway. Three metal mugs sit before him, and he shifts them around on the table he sits cross-legged behind. A crowd forms around him as he lifts one of the mugs to reveal a miniature conch shell.

"Keep your eye on the prize," the merchant tells a girl who sits opposite him. She narrows her eyes with intent focus as he covers the shell with the mug and begins to move the cups. His movements are slow at first, easy to follow. But eventually his time magic sets in, and the mugs spin so fast they blur.

Even as the merchant settles and the mugs still, the girl doesn't look put off. She points to the middle cup, boasting confidence. But a frown finds the merchant's face, and when he lifts the mug, nothing sits beneath it.

"You were so close," says the merchant, feigning sympathy. "Care to try again?"

She does.

"There's no way anyone could win that," Ferrick huffs under his breath as we step forward to get a better view. "You can't see anything!"

"Even if you could, you'd still never win." Bastian's got his arms folded across his chest, squinting at the merchant like he's a puzzle that's just been solved. "Once the mugs stop and she's about to guess, watch his hands."

The girl points to the mug on the far right, and sure enough, in a flash of movement so quick I nearly miss it, the merchant uses Valukan magic to alter the air so that the seashell slips from beneath the middle mug and into the sleeve of his coat. When he unveils the empty mug, he offers a shrug. "I guess it's just not your day."

The girl falls back, bewildered. "But I could have sworn . . . Which one's it under, then?"

I watch the merchant's hands, which use a mix of both Ker time and Valukan air magic to slip the shell from his sleeve and back into the middle mug with lightning speed before revealing it fully.

Still not used to seeing multiple magics used so fluidly, my heart skips at the sight. It might be nothing more than a

107

parlor trick, but it's one this boy's skilled at.

Defeated, the girl groans and runs her fingers through her hair dramatically. "That was going to be my next guess. I thought I had it that time!"

And both times, she had.

"Gotta train your eyes to be nice and sharp like mine," says the merchant. "You could always try again if you feel up to it?"

Though the girl looks ready to sacrifice whatever money she's got left in her pockets to prove she can do this, I've no intention of letting her go broke for a rigged game. Not to mention that I need a way to scope out this town without Bastian and Casem breathing down my neck, and this kid's given me an idea.

"Do you fancy a game, Vataea?" I ask, ignoring Casem's tired groan.

A grin curls wickedly onto her lips and she loops her arm in mine. "I thought you'd never ask."

"Wait a second," Ferrick calls as we start forward. "Did I miss something? What are we doing?"

Bastian shrugs. "I've found it best to just follow along, mate." The buckles of his boots clink quietly as he tails us, and Casem and Ferrick follow a second later. Ignoring the protesting huffs and annoyed comments, Vataea and I push our way through the crowd, not stopping until we're directly before the merchant's table. His eyes flick up to me, skeptical.

"Would you mind if I try?" I ask with the sweetest voice I can muster, though I don't wait to take a seat. The girl who'd previously been playing turns to me as if ready to protest, but I slip off the hood of my cloak and let the shock register. It doesn't take long for the quiet gasps and whispers to spread like wildfire through the streets. Thanks to these parchments, now all of Visidia knows my face.

"Your Majesty!" The girl scrambles to her feet, mumbling a stream of apologies as she half bows and half curtsies before stumbling away. "Of course!"

Vataea takes a seat behind me.

"The queen wants to play *my* game?" The merchant tries to be charming about the way he says it, but beads of sweat form a line above his upper lip. This close, I see he's younger than I thought—perhaps fourteen or so—and it's clear he's processing whether it's worth letting me win. He'd be foolish not to. I'm the queen of Visidia, after all. And a queen should always look her best before her people.

By how much he sweats, he must know this. But as I press a solid gold coin onto the table, starved shadows darken his eyes. Though I've no doubt he makes good money from his scheme, a single gold coin is likely worth a week's work for him.

"Don't take it easy on me," I tell him earnestly.

Determined now, the merchant nods and shows me that the shell is still beneath the far-right mug—and I intend for it to remain there. Because seashells come from the sea, after all. And mermaids rule the sea.

The mugs begin to shift. Slowly at first, then impossibly fast. The moment the merchant's time magic kicks in and he's about to slip the shell back into his sleeve, Vataea begins chanting quietly from behind me to keep the shell in place with her magic. I pretend to keep my eye on the mugs all the while, but as his speed increases, it's impossible. My eyes have never been trained to follow time magic, and even if my life were on the line, I'd die before I was able to confidently guess which mug contains the shell. Vataea, however, is prepared.

The moment the mugs stop moving, the tip of her fingernail grazes my left arm, so gently I almost think it's a trick of my brain, and so casually that no one else would notice it.

I point to the left mug.

"Apologies, Your Majesty," the merchant says as he lifts it. "I'm afraid you've chosen—" The crowd roars, and the merchant's face blanches when he looks down to discover the shell.

Vataea claps her hands together, feigning delight. I keep my eyes on the merchant, who clenches his fists tight on the table. His eyes catch mine, and I let my smile turn coy to confirm his suspicions.

He licks his chapped lips, frustration evident in the jerky movements he takes to reach under the table and grab a pouch full of coin. "Your winnings." He can barely contain the spite in his voice. I reach forward, drawing back only my gold coin.

"I don't need your money." I point to the alley behind us. It's dark and nearly empty, blocked off by his table and free from any flashing lights or curious ears. "But I would like to speak with you for a moment, if you wouldn't mind joining me?"

I raise my hood and venture into the alley, the merchant close on my heels. Though glum about it, Casem obeys my order to stand guard at the edge of it while the rest of the crew waits near the booth, watching with sharp eyes to ensure that no one tries anything funny.

Not that anyone would be foolish enough to try; they still believe I've got my magic. And even without it, I'm not defenseless. I've a steel dagger strapped to one hip, while Rukan sits sheathed to the other side.

"Listen, Your Majesty." The boy's voice prickles with

nerves. "I have some coin if you want it, but I've got a family to take care of. A sick sister, and parents who gave up too much of their time trying to rebuild our home after the storm. If you could spare—"

Reaching forward, I take the boy's hand. It's bony and calloused—a working hand—and I hold it softly between both of my own.

"I'm your queen," I tell him, "not your commander. As I've already said, I don't want your money. You do, however, need to be careful with that trick of yours. If I caught onto it this quickly, there will be others. And they will be far more sober and far cleverer than they appear."

Beneath the dim oil lamps, his cheeks flush a faint red.

"It's a clever trick," I add, hoping he'll relax. "But what if you never had to do it, again?"

He goes deathly still, so much so that I can't tell whether he's breathing. "I can't stop, I need the money—"

"But what if you *didn't* need the money?" I press a gold coin into his palm, examining his shifting expression all the while. Though there's some confusion, nothing can outweigh the hunger that flares in his eyes, or the way his fingers twitch desperately around the coin. "What's your name?"

"Ronan," he answers as I pull my hand away, hesitating to pocket the coin as if uncertain whether I'll change my mind.

"Well, Ronan, what if I told you I had plenty more gold coins just like that one? Let's say thirty of them. You'd never have to risk this scheme of yours again. You could take care of your family."

He uses a sleeve to wipe away the sweat on his forehead. Finally, he closes his fist around the gold coin and pockets it. When he looks at me again, his voice grows thick with determination. "What do I have to do?"

This boy is clever. It may be a parlor trick that earned him my attention, but because of that parlor trick I noticed several things. One, he's a great actor. Two, he's got the kind of face that blends in, making him look like any other merchant in these parts. And three, he's desperate for coin.

"I need to find someone." Though I know we're alone, I lower my voice all the same. "But I have too many people with me to do it without raising suspicion. Do you recognize the name Ornell Rosenblathe?"

He shakes his head. "No, but if he lives in Kerost, he shouldn't be hard to find."

"I'm not sure that he does," I admit. "But if not, then I need you to figure out before sunrise where he went. Can you do that?"

"*Sunrise?*" Peering up at the forming stars, he cringes. But one more look at the coin has him straightening his shoulders. "I can do it."

"Good." I nod to the coin in his pocket, the only motivation he should need. "Figure it out, and you'll never worry about money again."

I don't give him time to change his mind or fish for answers I don't have. There's nothing I can do to help; I can only hope, and fight for a reason to stay here another day if Ronan comes up empty-handed.

The hunger in that boy's eyes, however, assures me that won't be the case.

THIRTEEN

Time in Kerost is nonexistent.

Hours have passed since sundown, and yet enchanted lights continue to paint the streets while the bustle and noise keeps them fully awake. The gambling dens remain open, serving liquor and taking bets with no sign of stopping. Casem pulls my cloak's hood over my head as we slink into one, concealing my face. I roll my eyes; these people care little for politics, and they're far too busy with their games to notice my entrance.

Coins are tossed liberally from one greedy hand to another, and workers call to us from beside tables and bar tops, offering ale and wine while imploring us to join their games. I catch Bastian eyeing a blackjack table with curiosity, scanning each individual face in the crowd.

I try not to pay too much attention, but his curiosity prickles within me, making my skin itch. When I can no longer take it, I ask, "What are you looking for?"

He straightens. "Shanty. She'll be trouble if we give her free rein in a place like this."

The way he says it isn't unkind, but concerned. I'd even dare say it was a bit affectionate. Jealousy stirs within me, and I hate myself for it. Though I knew she and Bastian were somehow connected in the past, I never thought about the extent of it. Not until now, anyway.

"You know she can change her face, right? The whole point of her magic is to make her impossible to recognize." The honeyed velvet of Vataea's voice is enough to draw the attention of several patrons seated at the bar. They turn, eyes widening at her overwhelming beauty. If she notices, she doesn't pay them any mind. Having been on land this long, she's become almost desensitized to the ogling of us humans. Though, sometimes, I'll catch her staring back at those watching her with daggers in her unnervingly golden eyes. She'll slip them a toothy smile, showing off her sharp incisors. Usually, that's enough for them to leave her alone.

"Sometimes there are tells," Bastian argues. "Like a tattoo or hair color she favors, or jewelry she chooses not to disguise. Enough for someone who's purposefully looking to be able to find her."

"Just how well did you used to know Shanty?" Discomfort riles my stomach. I've no reason to be concerned about something so trivial, especially when I don't *want* a relationship with Bastian right now. Still, I can't help the curiosity eating at me.

The bone-white smile Bastian flashes is disarming. He knows full well why I'm asking, but to my surprise, he doesn't taunt me. Instead he says, "I knew her before she formed the barracudas. After I first got booted off Zudoh, I spent a period living on Ikae. Shanty was my closest friend from back then, though it didn't take long until I realized that living on the land wasn't going to be possible for me. I met her when she was still learning her magic, and I know sometimes she can get a bit lazy with the changes she makes when she knows no one is suspecting her. She has certain traits she always falls back on. At least, she did back then."

It's strange, thinking about the life Bastian once had before the two of us met. If not for the trouble with the kingdom and the havoc caused by his brother, it's entirely likely the two of us would never have crossed paths. Visidia's a massive kingdom, after all. Even if I explored every inch of it, I doubt I could ever meet everyone. And yet, I can't imagine a life in which I'd never met Bastian. I don't even want to try.

"Come on." He nods toward a table unlike any I've seen before; it's one with numbers on it, where those playing place bets and roll dice. I've no idea how it works, but considering that more than half of those gathered around it are several drinks in, it can't be hard.

"Are you sure we should even be in here?" Casem demands, eyes darting around the crowd. His whole body is surprisingly tense.

Sympathetically, Ferrick places a hand on my guard's shoulder, shaking his head. "It's no use, Casem. Welcome to a crew that knows no reason."

There's a girl standing at the table with curves that could bring a person to their knees, and soft lilac waves. She's on the arm of an Ikaean man with beautiful silver liner winged out into dagger-sharp points around his eyes. His hair is a matching silver against pale skin, and he stands tall in a sharp lilac suit, holding his body in the same way those proud of their money often do.

He's got dice in his hand, and holds them to the woman's full, frosted-pink lips. With a giggle, she blows on the dice, and he tosses them onto the table. When the crowd cheers, I stretch onto my toes to try to get a better look at what's happened, though none of it makes any sense.

"There's no way that's Shanty," I whisper to the others.

Bastian only shrugs. "She's an excellent actor."

"A little help, here?" Ferrick's voice is a sharp whisper as someone takes him by the arm and sets a pair of dice in his hands.

"Your turn," they say, and slap him on the back. He trips to the front of the table, and the woman who might be Shanty arches a curious lilac brow that has Ferrick turning red from his neck up. Hesitantly, he tosses the dice and rolls a seven.

"Seven out, seven out, seven out!"

The entire crowd roars, and Ferrick's face flushes even brighter. "Again," he says, already digging into his pockets for his coin purse. I'm about to grab his collar and steer him away from this trap he's fallen into so easily when the lilac-haired woman frees herself from the Ikaean man—much to his disappointment—and instead winds herself around Ferrick. I see a flash of a rose gold bracelet on her wrist, dainty and in the shape of several dozen slender fish bones.

"Why don't you let me blow on those for you?" Her voice is a low, seductive purr. At once, the rest of us find ourselves nodding.

"Aye," Bastian says, "that's her."

Ferrick, however, doesn't appear to realize this. He darts a look back at Vataea, as if trying to convey his disinterest in this woman by his sheer looks of panic. Without popping blood vessels, he couldn't possibly get any redder. His body grows rigid when Shanty loops an arm over his, giggling. As she leans in, she bumps his hands too hard and makes Ferrick drop the dice. She catches them just in time, and places them back in his hands with flushed pink cheeks.

"Sorry!" she says to the table. "Looks like the bubbly is catching up with me." Ferrick, still stiff as a board from her touch, awkwardly tosses the dice onto the table. I don't see what numbers he rolls, but whatever it is makes the man running the table bulge his eyes, while the rest of the crowd screams and grabs Ferrick by the shoulders. They cheer for him as though they've all been best friends for ages.

"I don't think I've had enough to drink to handle this place," Vataea sighs, slinking away as she catches sight of the bar. "I'll be back."

"Do you need money?" Bastian's quick to ask, about to dip into his own coin purse when Vataea scoffs.

"Have a bit more faith in me, pirate." She disappears into a crowd that parts for her, and with Ferrick happily distracted, I'm acutely aware of Bastian's presence at my side. It's a comfortable feeling, a warm buzz I want nothing more than to sink into and never emerge from. It takes everything in me to ignore it, keeping my attention ahead as Ferrick throws another pair of dice, greeted immediately by more cheers.

"I would have lost the shoes off my feet to this place when I was younger." Bastian sighs, trying to make conversation. "With that kind of cheering, I have to imagine our drinks are all on Ferrick's tab, tonight."

Not a bad idea. Whatever Shanty's doing, it's working. But it's also drawing attention.

Discreetly, I nudge an elbow into Casem's side, nodding my chin a fraction of an inch at two men who are watching

Ferrick from behind the crowd on the opposite end of the table. They're less like men than they are walking boulders, built thick and strong, with massive coiled muscles. Based on the amethyst color of their clothing, they're Kers.

One of the men catches me looking, and recognition sparks a light in his eyes. He elbows his companion, who turns his attention to me. I realize it's not with interest, like I might expect from people who recognize their queen in public, but with malice.

Quietly, I say, "Something tells me we're not going to be having those drinks."

Bastian discreetly catches who I'm staring at and makes a low sound in the back of his throat. "No one would pick a fight with you in public. Attacking you would be grounds for an execution." The men stand, leaving full mugs of ale behind at the bar so that they can instead stalk their way toward me. "Then again, I've been wrong before."

"Out gambling away the money of your people?" The taller man's voice is rough and grating. "I shouldn't be surprised, though I expected more from Visidia's new queen."

The crowd's cheering dies swiftly, and the gambling den quiets to an uncomfortable buzz. Before me, the man stands tall and smug, practically crooning for attention.

"I think we'll cash out now," Shanty says, gathering the chips and shoving some into her pocket and others down her chest before disappearing into the crowd.

I open my mouth to speak, only to find my mouth too dry to form the words I want. In the past, I wouldn't have had any problem putting these men in their place. Now though, Mother's voice rings through my ears: *Make them love you.*

This man wants a fight. He wants to make a fool out of me, and for me to lose my temper. He wants for me to be the monster too many of my people already believe me to be. Already Casem and Bastian both have their hands on the pommels of their swords, ready to draw them at a moment's notice. The tension of Bastian's body feels like sharp pulses of electricity in my veins, jarring me.

"She wasn't wasting anyone's money," he starts to argue, but I press my hand against his chest, stilling him.

There are too many people watching. Too many people stiffen in their seats, waiting to see how their queen will respond.

"I'm on a tour of the kingdom," I say as I lower my hood, letting the words flow through my lips without any bite. It's a struggle to not reach for my dagger when threatened; I instinctively reach for my magic instead, only for my skin to flood with coolness when it doesn't respond.

"We know all about your tour," says the second man, his voice firm. He's shorter, but thick with muscle. "Kerost wants nothing to do with it."

Again Bastian starts to speak, but Casem elbows him in the ribs before he can say anything.

"The only reason I'm here," I continue, "is to see how I can continue to support Kerost. To do that, I need to see what's happening on the island."

Not defending myself or preparing to slice off their tongues for their slander feels . . . odd. I'm not used to it, and clearly neither are these men. They seem unsettled by the way I maneuver around their argument, not fully shirking the blame, but also not accepting everything they say.

"If you'll excuse me," I say firmly, "I'd like to get back to watching the games. But please know that I understand your frustrations, and I'm working to find a solution. If I didn't care, I'd be on another island right now, as their plans for me involve parties and free food." A few voices in the crowd entertain my joke with a laugh, and patrons return to their games. I know I've won this match.

"Right," says one of the men, scratching the back of his neck as noise livens up the gambling den once more. No longer is everyone paying attention to him or waiting for an outburst. I could have easily been the villain in this situation, but instead I've made him look like the fool. Just like that, the men shuffle away.

Bastian and Ferrick are staring at me in surprise, while Casem exhales in relief. Slowly, Bastian drops his hand from the pommel. "Well, that's certainly a new way we're dealing with things."

The sharpness of Ferrick's laugh surprises me. "Gods, that would have been nice for you to have discovered ages ago. Can you imagine how many fights we might have been able to avoid?"

I roll my eyes, thankful when Vataea emerges from the crowd with four giant pints of ale in her hands. She hands two to Casem and me, then sets one with a few sips already taken out of it into Bastian's waiting hand. He's about to protest when her eyes cut to him expectantly. "You didn't pay for it."

He scowls. "Did you?"

A toothy grin crawls across her lips, which is enough of an answer for us all.

Already the gambling hall is in full swing again, but now people watch me more closely, or pull me into the games.

They don't ask for money or for chips; instead they offer them, only wanting me to join in for a game with them. They ask what I'm drinking and order me more. Casem eyes them like a hawk all the while, walking back and forth from the bar every time someone pours me a new drink to make sure they're not slipping anything into it.

None of us have any idea where Shanty's gone, but seeing how much coin she snuck away with, I've no doubt she's already taken a different face. Meanwhile, Vataea and I are at a blackjack table with Ferrick behind my shoulder and Bastian over hers. He eyes her cards with a neutral expression before he bends to whisper something into her ear.

I find my fingers tensing against the cards, my grip becoming tighter as my mind lingers not on the game before us, but on memories of his breath tickling my skin. Of him whispering into *my* ear.

I drink, forcing myself to look away. Forcing myself to laugh when someone makes a joke, and to relax as best I can with the pressure of so many people watching me, expecting gods know what. All I've ever wanted was for my people to know who I was, and to earn their love.

Why, then, does my skin feel as though it's crawling? Why does every word out of my mouth feel like I'm trying to talk through lips that are nailed shut?

Hours pass with no break in the action. No one seems to tire, and the crowd doesn't disperse until dawn. Morning light cracks through the windows and bathes the room. In the brightness, all the cheering feels too loud. All the makeup and shimmering outfits from the night no longer dazzle, but look excessive and out of place.

It's time to get out of here and find Ronan. I pray he's found the answers I need; I'm not sure I can handle back-to-back nights in Kerost.

I made sure not to drink too much, only taking polite sips of anything bought for me. Enough to make people think we're friendly, but not lose my wits. Even so, my head pounds and my eyes blur, though it's likely more from exhaustion than the alcohol.

Gods, I should have slept hours ago. It's going to be a long day on *Keel Haul*.

As the crowd wanes, we make our way back outside, some of us groggy while others—namely Ferrick and Vataea—still buzz with laughter. Each of their footsteps sway a few inches too far, and their cheeks are flushed from both alcohol and breathless laughter.

"Did you *hear* him?" Vataea laughs, wiping at her watering eyes.

Ferrick barks a laugh in response, the sound so fierce that he's having to hold his stomach to contain himself. "*Oy!*" he says in a low, mocking voice. "Aren't you one of those *mermaids*?"

Vataea practically howls, and Bastian and I exchange an amused look that makes my stomach prickle and has me immediately glancing away. Ferrick and Vataea continue on like that, making absolutely no sense to anyone but each other, arms slung around one another. While Ferrick's hand sits comfortably at Vataea's waist, I watch as she shifts so that his hand drops to her hip. She waits for a reaction, and I catch the briefest, sourest pucker of her lips when Ferrick continues on with his drunken laughter, politely shifting his hand back up. Only when she purposefully takes his hand

and lowers it again to her hip does he jolt with surprise. This time, though, he doesn't move it away.

The two of them walk ahead as I take my time, scanning the streets for a head of shaggy black hair. I catch sight of Ronan in a shaded corner beneath the VICE sign, trying not to doze off. When he spots me, his scowl grows deep and he jumps to his feet. "Did you really have to stay there *all* night?"

As the rest of the crew stops to look at the boy's outburst, I draw a sharp breath and freeze, hoping they won't recognize him. But, sure enough, Bastian squints and steps forward.

"You're the kid with the shells," he says briskly. "That was a clever trick you pulled back there."

Ronan lifts his chin, but I grind my teeth together and give him a sharp look to draw his attention. He stills, eyes widening as he catches on. This isn't a conversation we can have in front of the others.

"Give me a minute with him," I whisper to the crew. "Sooner or later someone's going to catch him, and it's never a pretty sight when money is involved. Go ready the ship, all right? I'll only need a minute."

"We're not leaving you—"

I don't stay to listen to Casem's argument. I pull Ronan ahead by the wrist, ignoring the way the sharpening sunlight spins my head. I lead him to the same alleyway we had our discussion in the previous night, and only when I make sure no one is around do I speak.

"Did you find Ornell?" I try not to let my words sound as urgent as I feel. Too long, and surely some of the crew will come looking.

He nods swiftly. "I met a woman who recognized the

name. She said she was a friend of Ornell's mother, and that the last she'd heard, the family had moved to Curmana." He works at his jaw, trying not to let his nerves show. "I'm sorry, that's all I was able to find out. No one knows anything about him, or if he's still there."

It's not much, but it's a lead. And for now, that's enough. I fish a small coin purse from my coat and press it into his palms. "Keep that safe, all right? No more swindling."

He shoves the coins into his shirt, but the smile on his lips lasts only seconds before his eyes lift, looking over my shoulder. Fear settles into him and he shrinks back, making himself smaller. Every muscle in my body rigid, I look to the ground, where not one shadow hulks over me, but two.

FOURTEEN

Slowly, I trail my hand to Rukan's hilt.

"Run," I urge Ronan. He doesn't need to be told twice. The moment he takes off I spin, narrowly avoiding a knife that spirals for my face. It takes a bite of my hair, and I scowl at the man wielding it. "I'm *trying* to grow that back."

It's the men from the gambling hall earlier. They squint at the sun, one of them with a knife drawn while the other brandishes his sword. I grip my own blade hard, refusing to let my face show the panic that comes from fighting a Ker.

Never fight a Ker. My heart is a monster, raging against my chest as I recall Father's old warning. *They'll have a knife to your throat before you even see it coming.*

Time magic isn't one to be used freely. It's the hardest to control, and takes the greatest toll on its wielder's body. But any Ker would be a fool to enter a fight they mean to win without using it to their advantage.

I reach inwardly for my magic, doing everything I can think of—everything I've done a thousand times before—to try to awaken it. But once again, it refuses to listen.

I know my magic's gone, but still I frantically try to pull it around me and make it heed my call. Because without it, I stand no chance in this fight.

The tallest of the men lashes out with his knife, and I'm relieved that the attack isn't quite so fast this time. I take a nasty cut to my forearm but manage to dodge the worst of it, countering with Rukan. But the second before my weapon can slice into skin, Mother's voice rings in my head and I falter. *Make them love you. No matter where you are, I'll have eyes on you.*

I stop just short of striking.

My hesitation doesn't go unnoticed. While the taller of the two hesitates, the shorter, stockier one growls, "You think because you sent us some soldiers, we should bow our heads and thank you? That somehow that's enough to make everything better?"

I sheathe Rukan and make a grab for my steel dagger— maiming but not killing is the only way I can win this. But I'm unable to grab it before the man stands before me, quick as lightning, and slams me against the wall. My back cracks as it hits the stone, knocking the breath from my lungs.

"Get off our island." Each of his words is its own snarl, and the stench of stale alcohol fouls his breath. I cringe as he leans in close, one hand wrapped tight around my neck, squeezing the breath from my lungs while his sword waits ready. I reach desperately for my weapon even as darkness peppers my vision.

Panic rises, bubbling over as I beg my magic to listen. To protect me. As I beg for my hand to reach just a little farther around this man to grab the steel blade waiting for me, if only I can get to it.

His friend, the tall one, starts to back away, face panicked as the one gripping me by the throat lifts his blade. It presses against my coat and I brace myself for the bite of steel I've grown far too familiar with.

But it's not me who's bit.

I fall to my knees, gasping for desperate breaths. My fingers dig into the cobblestones as I heave and blink the fog from my vision.

"You're going to be fine." I know at once it's Bastian's hands that settle upon my shoulders because my lungs breathe easier and my vision sharpens at his touch. I let myself fall into him, rubbing my tender throat.

My attacker lies face-first on the ground, two long needles poking from the skin of his neck. Shanty stands behind him, tucking the remaining needles into the tiny spaces between the bones of her bracelet, and a tiny vial of thick white liquid down her sleeve.

Ferrick's on my left, and I jolt from the sharp sting of his restoration magic on my throat. It flares once at the sharpest point of pain, then ebbs away to nothing but a dull ache. Still, my voice itself is raw as I ask, "Is he . . . ?"

"Dead? No." Shanty kicks at the man's hand, pressing her boot down upon one of his fingers until he groans. "See? Just unconscious. Might wake up with a killer headache, but nothing he wasn't asking for. Casem took off after the second guy."

Good. I could have killed them with Rukan, but the kingdom cannot love a queen who they see as a monster; I've already learned that the hard way. My people expect a queen to be kind and fair, not someone who will bloody their hands unnecessarily.

If I use Rukan's poison to kill, these men will get what they want; I'll forever be thought of as a ruthless, dangerous ruler. It'll go against everything Mother wishes for me to show Visidia, and she would have had me sailing back to Arida within the day.

"We should have never let you out of our sight," Vataea growls, teeth bared at the unconscious man. "We have to arrest them."

I'm about to stop her when Ferrick beats me to it. "We can't. If others found out Amora was attacked at our first stop, after Kerost already refused to participate in our Visidian tour, how do you think that'd look? This could ruin our journey before we've even gotten started."

Bastian practically preens at that news, but Shanty shakes her head.

"Maybe not." She crouches, lifting my chin with a finger to inspect me. "If there's one thing my magic's taught me, it's that people will always see what you show them." Straightening her spine, she turns to Ferrick. "Go get me as much parchment as you can find. And you"—she turns to Vataea—"do something with this man's body. He won't wake for a few hours; put him in the sun and let him burn somewhere."

There's a gleam in the mermaid's eyes as she tucks her hands under the man's arms and lugs him farther into the alleyway, out of sight. I can only hope she's not dragging him directly to the sea.

Ferrick, meanwhile, leaves only after double-checking me for injuries. "Stay here," he says seriously before he turns, hurrying toward the street.

I have no desire to follow. Instead I lean my head against Bastian's chest as he holds me, relaxing into the feeling of wholeness that comes with his touch. Connected like this, I can't tell whether it's my curiosity that spikes or his when Shanty's eyes glimmer with mischief.

"What are you up to?" he asks, to which she squares her shoulders.

"Trust me, pirate. I'm about to be positively brilliant."

I'm leaning against the main mast back on *Keel Haul* when Shanty hands me her creation.

"No need to say thank you." She beams as I grab the parchment. "You can just slip me a bonus when it's time for payment. Make it that navy blade of yours and we'll call it even." There's a hunger in her eyes when she peers at Rukan.

I cover the blade with my coat and out of her sight as I spread the parchment onto my lap, startling at the moving image that plays back at me in a loop. It's . . . me. But it's not a still, captured by an artist. It's in full color, lifelike and dazzling.

I straighten, realizing this parchment is similar to the one Yuriel and Vataea were looking at back on Arida, and like the one Lord Garrison showed me during the council meeting. This one in particular is of me in the gambling den, raising a glass of bubbly with other patrons as we bet together on the games. Merrily we laugh, seemingly having enough fun that anyone would be jealous to have missed out. Below it, the parchment reads:

HER MAJESTY, QUEEN AMORA MONTARA, TO WED!

It looks as though Visidia may be getting a new king sooner than we thought! Her Majesty's tour of Visidia started just days ago, and already she's getting

friendly with the people of Kerost. Could love soon be
in the air for our queen? Better get ready, bachelors.

There's a list of ads at the bottom of the moving
parchment, featuring Ikaean stylists and wardrobe consul-
tants to help get them ready for my visit. It's worthy of an
eye roll, but considering it leaves out the more unfortunate
events of Kerost, it's also brilliant. What's depicted is short,
sweet, and exactly the kind of show expected from me. I
clutch the parchment tight, only truly feeling my tiredness
as relief settles into me.

"This is brilliant," I tell Shanty, to which she bats her pink
hair over her shoulders.

"*I* am brilliant. You're welcome."

Casem sits behind her, eyes the hazy white of someone
using Curmanan magic. "The news is already spreading,"
he says, voice distant. But as the blues of his eyes return, so
does his excitement. "The mind speakers are eating this up.
Ikaeans are replicating the story and taking it back to their
island to be redistributed, and they want more. They want
documentation from each one of your stops. We can spin this
story however we want."

"Only if we're the ones who stay on top of it," Shanty
warns. "These gossip pieces are so popular, lately; people
will be competing for information. The best gossip makes
for the fattest coin purse, so we'll need to get our stories out
the quickest."

Had the purpose of this trip only been about ensuring
my people favor me, this would've been a brilliant strategy.
Now though, it's a nuisance. It just ensures more eyes on

my movements, and that I'll need to be more careful moving forward.

I hand the parchment back to Shanty, and she marvels once more at her work. "We'll see about that bonus," I tell her, "but thank you. I appreciate it."

"For the queen?" she teases. "Any time."

Standing at the helm with a compass in hand, Bastian casts a sour glance at the parchment. He only scoffed when he saw the headline, and now spends his time glaring at his compass, pretending to be unbothered.

"Our itinerary doesn't have us getting to Zudoh for another three days," he says. "We'll have to contact them and let them know we're arriving early." I don't miss the hopeful edge of his voice, and guilt turns my throat thick. I wish it could be Zudoh next as planned, but my main objective is to find Ornell, and figure out what he knows about the legendary artifact.

"We'll go to Curmana first." I try to sound aloof about it, but Bastian's eyes narrow with suspicion and Ferrick stirs from where he sits across from me, brows furrowing. "Casem, contact them and let them know our plans have changed."

Casem stills. "But we have an itinerary."

"Not to mention Curmana is on the complete opposite side of the kingdom," Bastian grumbles. "Going there now wouldn't make any sense. Both your mother and Zale will chew off our heads if we ignore the plans."

"We're not ignoring," I say. "We're protecting ourselves. If we want to stay ahead of the gossip parchments, we don't need all these reporters knowing our next location. They'd mob us." It's a lie that rolls easily off my tongue. One that has enough merit that, for a moment, no one argues.

Ferrick's response is the first to come, quiet and wistful. "Gods, what did I get myself into."

I ignore him and stand on tired legs to lift my chin toward the others. "My mother would want us to take precautions. If something were to go wrong again, the last thing we need are a thousand new gossip parchments." Not to mention that, with so many reporters sniffing around, finding Ornell will only be that much harder. "Tell her we're visiting Curmana next, and that we're keeping our itinerary flexible. She'll understand." I put every ounce of authority I have in my voice, refusing to explain or elaborate—which would require coming up with a lie I don't have.

Bastian's jaw clenches, but even if he can feel that I'm not telling him the full truth, it's not as though he can read my actual thoughts.

"Set our course." I leave him at the helm and head below deck before he or the others can pry any further.

Down in the cabin, Vataea's already sleeping off her alcohol, twisted in the ropes of the hammock like she's been fished straight from the sea. She doesn't so much as twitch as I clamber into my hammock beside her, exhaustion settling into my bones.

When I shut my eyes this time, I pray that, for once, it'll be sleep that waits for me, not Father's ghost.

FIFTEEN

Black as spilt ink, the night sky is coated with stardust that shimmers dimly in the sea's reflection. I stare at it from the rigging, weary and sluggish from my broken sleep and the alcohol still filtering through my body.

As usual, the faces of the dead were there to greet me the moment I shut my eyes. Father was among them, face shrouded in smoke and his bloodied hand reaching toward me in desperation as the mass of Visidia's fallen grab on to him, weighing him down.

I do everything I can to put the memory out of my mind, humming a quiet shanty as I dip my head back against the ropes.

My first time up here, my palms had sweat so much I'd barely been able to maintain my grip. Last summer, scaling the rigging with Bastian was the first moment I remember feeling truly alive. I remember the heat of his breath on my skin as he steadied me, keeping me from falling. The way his eyes glimmered with delight as a seagull squawked at us in greeting, and he squawked right back. The way the sea salt air tore through my hair and brushed against my face, telling me that this is where I belonged.

It was my first taste of true freedom, before I knew the truth about Father and the Montara family.

Before I lost my magic and Father slid a sword deep into his stomach to protect me.

I hadn't been a queen, then. I'd been Princess Amora Montara—a girl who was naive enough to believe she could protect a kingdom she hardly knew, with a magic that was nothing more than a lie.

It feels like a lifetime ago; when Father's body was sent out to sea, that girl sunk into the depths beside him. Now a queen I hardly recognize has taken her place.

Silver moonlight peeks from behind a curtain of clouds and I shut my eyes against it, stilling hot tears before they come. No matter how hard I try to think otherwise—no matter how hard I try to pull my thoughts from this dark place and focus on what needs to be done—my mind keeps pulling me back to a single thought: as much as my past self yearned to one day sit upon the throne, perhaps I'm not the rightful ruler of this kingdom.

But for now, until Visidia is back on track, I am the ruler they *need*. I'm the only one with the knowledge to atone for my family's past. And until then, I will not cry, but fight to give my people the kingdom they deserve.

Only when the rigging sways beneath me do I open my eyes and steady myself, gripping the ropes tight. I jerk my attention down, expecting Bastian. But my protests stop short when I see it's Ferrick who's inching his way up. His forehead is knitted with nerves, and every few inches he climbs he stops to curse under his breath.

"Stars." I sigh and unravel myself from the ropes, descending a few feet so that he doesn't have to torture himself by climbing any higher. "You should be sleeping."

"I could say the same for you," he tries to say, but his

teeth chatter so fiercely that his words quiver. He winces as a particularly vicious tide slams into the ship and he grips the rigging desperately.

I roll my eyes and press a hand to his back, helping Ferrick regain his balance. The sea doesn't take kindly to visitors during the winter. The dusky water is thrashing and vicious, and every movement feels amplified here on the rigging.

"Casem snores like a drunken sailor," Ferrick mutters, shrinking his neck into his coat like a hermit crab. Some of his breath escapes, pluming the air around him in smoky wisps. "I was going to steal a candle from Bastian's room to melt the wax and stuff my ears. But then I saw you."

I imagine his smile would mirror mine if he weren't so busy burrowing as much of his exposed skin into his coat as physically possible.

At his stubbornness, I can't help but laugh. "Wrap your hands in the ropes." They're the same instructions Bastian gave me on my first climb. "The sea's rough tonight, so it's best to be cautious. We can go lower too, if you're scared—"

"I'm fine." Bracing himself against the cold winds, Ferrick retreats from the warmth of his coat. As instructed, he winds his hands around the rigging for safety and hesitates for only a second before flipping to face the sea. When I lean back against the rigging, he follows suit.

I trace his eyes to the tides, which no longer feel quite so dark. The moonlight shines brighter, igniting what looks like thousands of tiny crystals upon the water. They brighten the sea like a gemstone.

Now more than ever, I wish I could learn time magic. I would freeze myself in this moment, moon-soaked and overlooking the ocean. I would become *Keel Haul's* figurehead, glued to this ship for all of eternity. Traveling forever, rather than sitting on a throne built upon blood and burned by lies.

"It reminds me of the night we fought the Lusca." Ferrick's voice comes gently, as if aware he's coaxing me from my own dark thoughts. "The sea was calmer then—at least until the beast showed up—but it was dark like tonight. Beautiful, too . . . if not for the giant monster trying to kill us."

I'm surprised by how genuine my laugh is. It's not like back on Arida, where I must play pretend.

Ferrick was there the night my life changed. He's been there for all of it. With him, there's no pretending.

"That night, you became the bravest person I've ever met." It's surprising even to me how natural it feels to be around him. How comfortable.

His laugh is soft, nearly swept away by the wind. "I could say the same for you."

I think back to that moment when I threw myself onto the Lusca. How I'd thought about the stories Visidia would tell in my honor, and how proud Father would be when I showed him proof I'd bested the beast. I never did have the chance to show him Rukan.

Silence weighs heavy between us, but it's not tense or awkward. Moving closer to Ferrick, I settle into that silence, letting my eyes shut and my head fall upon his shoulder as he winds an arm around me. I'm not sure how long we stay like that, but it's only when Ferrick stirs that I lift my head to eye him.

"Are we doing the right thing?" His lips are pressed thin, and his green eyes are bothered and distant, as though he's trying to piece together a puzzle.

"By 'we,' are you asking me if I think *I'm* doing the right thing?"

Foot bouncing against the rigging, he nods. "I don't feel good lying to everyone. Vataea deserves to know about Blarthe, and even Casem's trying his best to make this easier for you. He's in communication with your mother and the other islands every day, trying to make this as smooth as possible. The Montaras lied for ages; you don't have to be the same as them."

Staring at the cloudless sky, I wonder if any gods can hear my sigh.

"I stopped knowing what the right thing to do was a long time ago, Ferrick. All I can do is what I think is right. And for now, that's making Visidia the priority. I won't be the same as my family; I'll tell everyone the truth when the time is right. But for now, I stand by my decision." I kick at the rigging, letting the ropes tangle in my boots.

Ferrick's scoff is so soft I nearly miss it. "You're too used to doing things on your own. Give the rest of us some credit, would you? We *want* to help."

I hide my scowl, tired of hearing that. I spent eighteen years relying on someone else, and look where that got me. The best way to get something done is to do it myself. If they can't keep up, that's not my problem.

"I appreciate you looking out for me." There's a sharpness in my tone I don't bother masking. A warning that it's time for this conversation to end. "But I'm doing what I believe is best for my kingdom."

"Well, tell me how I can help you, then," he argues. "I'm trying to do everything I can to be there for you. To be a good friend, a better adviser, a stronger fighter with more magic. What can I do better?"

As my heart drops to my stomach, I clench my fists around the rope. "You're perfect, Ferrick. I promise, this isn't about you."

His chest falls as he sinks deeper into the rigging, and for a long moment he lets the silence expand, the only sound between us that of thrashing waves and sharp winds. When he eventually turns back to me, his eyes are as sharp and as clever as a fox's. So quietly that I'm uncertain whether I've made the words up in my own head, he says, "If that's how you want it to be, fine. But your stubbornness will be the knife in all of our chests one day, Amora. Gods help us."

SIXTEEN

Even my bones are tired as I claw my way up to the deck the next morning.

I spent hours on the rigging well after Ferrick left, until my fingers had numbed from the cold, my grip had grown slack, and I could no longer keep my eyes open. Only then did I sneak back into my hammock, stealing a few hours before thoughts of Father and visions of the dead woke me again.

Bastian's the first one I see when I step onto the deck. He's seated alone on the starboard side, while Vataea and Shanty sit portside. They have an unrolled burlap sack filled with dehydrated fruits, hard cheeses, and dried meats spread out between them. While they play a strange card game that requires flipping cards and being the first to slap their hands on the deck upon seeing certain ones, Bastian busies himself with a familiar item. I'm breathless the moment I see it—my satchel.

He's emptied it of its contents, scattering bones and teeth over the canvas. Though he doesn't yet use the magic—I'd feel it if he did—I can sense him considering it as he holds a bone between two long fingers, using his other hand to gently scratch the bone with the edge of a small push blade. His will pulses within me, and I know at once that he's trying to call soul magic to him.

It doesn't come.

"You never told me you were having trouble with it." I take a hesitant seat in front of him, running my fingers along the familiar ridges of the bones. While part of me hates the longing that springs to life within me, there's no denying its existence.

I hate what I was forced to do with my magic. I hate that I spent eighteen years learning to kill for the sake of a beast within me that never even existed. I hate that my magic was nothing more than a lie.

But I don't hate my magic; I could never hate the most intimate part of me. And one day, I'll get it back in its true form. Gentle. Peaceful. Protective. The way soul magic was created to be.

Bastian squeezes the bone between his fingers, tighter this time. He scrutinizes it as though it's some kind of puzzle, and my heart practically trembles as I remember the last time I saw that expression on his face, back when I'd been creating Rukan. It was the first night we truly kissed.

My skin itches with the discomfort that urges me to get out of here and distance myself from Bastian, but the pulse of my magic within him keeps me seated.

"That's because only now, when you're stranded on a ship in the middle of the sea and have limited places to hide from me, do I get to talk to you." His voice is cheery enough that I roll my eyes.

"Well, I'm here now. Tell me what's going on."

He makes a faint tsking sound under his breath. "You seem far more fascinated in what I have to say, than I care for the answers you might have. But I do have an idea—something to satisfy both of our needs." He looks up, stars dancing in those dazzling hazel eyes. "Have you ever considered asking nicely?"

What I wouldn't give to throw this blasted pirate overboard.

I bite my tongue and twist my lips into the iciest smile. "Would you *please* tell me why you can't use soul magic? You arrogant, oafish, bast—"

"You really ought to learn how to stop when you're ahead." He sighs but scoots closer. "Don't worry, we'll work on that. Now, for your question, it's simple. I just don't know what to do with this thing."

He holds up a bone, squinting to peer at it in the sunlight. I lean in, trying to see if he's looking at something different than I am. But all I see is a normal finger bone.

"What do you mean you don't know what to do with it?"

"I mean I know how to summon the magic. I can feel it. But whenever I've tried to practice with it—whenever I've tried to see what it *feels* like—I don't know what to do. You have your fire, your aunt has that whole stomach acid thing when she swallows a bone, your father used water . . . But I don't know what to *do*. How did you know you were supposed to use fire?"

I lean back on my hands, trying to remember if there was ever any sign. "It was something I just knew," I eventually admit. "It was instinctual."

His sigh is far more dramatic than necessary as he waves the bone at me. "All I want to do is break this awful thing." Plucking up the bones and teeth, he stuffs them back into the satchel. "Curse magic is so much easier."

"That's because you grew up learning it." My skin chills without the touch of the bones, and I smother the feeling. "All new magics are hard to learn at first. Look at Ferrick."

I nod toward the bow, where Casem tries to teach Ferrick

mind speak. All Ferrick's done since he's been home is dive back into his training, and my heart tugs at the sight of him. I should have known that if I gave him the role as my adviser—as my most trusted partner—that he'd take it more seriously than anyone else. Watching him, I know I've made the right call. I've no idea how long they've been at it, but the skin around Ferrick's mouth is tinted red, and within seconds of watching him he's already nursing a fresh nosebleed.

Across from me, Bastian winces. "Fair point. Still though, it doesn't feel great knowing I've got the strongest magic in the kingdom and no idea how to use it."

"You shouldn't use it anyway," I say. "That magic was never meant to be practiced by anyone other than a Montara. When Kaven tried to have others learn it, the majority of them died."

"They did," he agrees with a small nod. "But it wasn't the same. They didn't have the real thing."

"It's not worth the risk." The anger within me flares. "We don't know what will happen if you use it, and I want you alive. We've got a curse to break, so leave it alone. If you ever have to use it, gods forbid, you'll know how."

"You say that, but how—"

"You just will, all right? I promise."

To my surprise, the rest of his argument dies on his tongue, and the tension in his body eases.

"Are you two going to work all morning, or are you going to join us for breakfast?" Shanty calls, hands cupped around her mouth for effect. Today her hair's a fresh mint green that matches her eyes, which are winged out with beautiful fluorescent-pink liner. Though I know it's nothing more than a glamour, she's dressed sharper than anyone traveling on a ship has a right to be, donning a shimmering pink cape that puffs lightly around her like a beautiful cloud. Her loose collared shirt hangs with two of the top buttons undone, so faint a pink it almost looks white, and is tucked into beautiful lavender pants that billow out at the hems. Today, she's distinctly Ikaean, with taste as expensive as mine and Bastian's.

"What happens when you Ikaeans run out of unique themes for your outfits?" I nod teasingly at her clothes as Bastian and I move to join them, followed closely by Ferrick and Casem.

Shanty flicks a grape into her mouth. "Impossible; the world's too interesting. There will always be too many ideas, and not enough time for them all. Now, breakfast?"

Only when I pop a cube of cheese into my own mouth does she resume shuffling her cards, pleased. As she shuffles, her nails turn from a pretty plum color to a deep, vicious red.

"You trying to earn back everything you lost on Kerost last night?" Bastian teases, and I notice he's toying with a small amethyst box.

Unbothered, Shanty bats her hair over her shoulder. "You wish. I don't know how to *lose* money, pirate. All I do is win." She clears her throat to draw our attention to the inside of her coat as she peeks it open, flashing a fat rose gold coin purse tucked into one side. She does the same with the other side, and this time there are two coin purses.

It's all the rest of us can do not to gawk at her.

"That's all from last night?" Bastian asks, not bothering to hide the jealousy in his voice.

"The house always wins, right?" Shanty muses. "For part of the night, I played as the dealer and pocketed some chips to use when I turned back into a player. Coupled with Ferrick's winnings, we could have bought that whole den. You know, they ought to figure out some counters against enchantment magic. Everyone might as well have been handing me their money."

Vataea's bark of laughter is so sharp and genuine that it's impossible not to join in.

"Stars, Shanty." Bastian shakes his head. "You're a monster."

"I appreciate that." At some point, without me noticing, she's drawn out a thin knife. She stabs it into the grapes, piling them up onto the blade. As quickly as she maneuvers it, she never once misses. Several times though, she presses her blade down too hard and digs the steel's tip into *Keel Haul*. Every time it happens, Bastian's frown grows more severe.

"What's the update on Curmana?" Ferrick asks Casem, trying to distract from Shanty's clear attempts at irking the pirate. Sweeping some seagull jerky and cheese into my palms, I shift focus to my guard.

"I was able to get in contact with their adviser as we left Kerost," Casem says between mouthfuls of jerky. "They're expecting us in two days' time, and are 'thrilled to finally have the chance to have the queen on their soil.' Apparently, it's been ages since they've had a visit from the royal family, and they'd love to throw out all the stops. Baroness Ilia Freebourne will be there to greet you, and they'll have all bachelors ready and waiting to sweep you off your feet."

He pauses for some cheese, not bothering to force any enthusiasm. For him, this is nothing more than a trip away from Mira and all the wedding planning he's dying to do. I've no doubt that half of his time on this ship has been spent using mind speak to communicate with his fiancée like the sappy romantic he's become. "There will be food and wine,

and plenty to restock on when we're done with our celebration. All you have to worry about, Amora, is making them
fall in love with you. That's a note that comes directly from
your mother, by the way. She's not thrilled about the change
of itinerary, but she's glad you're taking precaution."

Gods, I can't wait to find Ornell and end this ridiculous
charade. When my people learn the truth of what I've done,
they'll either love me for it, or they'll hate me. But either way,
my job will be done.

"I can't wait." I manage to keep at least some of the
bitterness from my voice as I tear off a bite of jerky. "Now
what about the island itself? Have any of you been there?"

Ferrick and Vataea both shake their heads, while Shanty
bites a grape from her knife and says, "I've been there on
business. I'm happy to share the details if you're all interested?"
It's clear she's talking about more than the island's geography.

While part of me hates to admit it, I *am* interested. Ferrick,
however, looks queasy.

"I've been there plenty," Bastian says, sparing us from
having to hear the details. As he speaks he pushes the small
amethyst box toward me, as if needing a distraction to do it.
"It's impeccably clean, but there's not much to do. They grow
hundreds of different herbs in the jungle that wraps around
the northern edge of the island, and use them to develop
powders, potions, and the majority of the medicine that gets
shipped directly to Suntosan healers. Their spas are popular
because of those herbs; they'll throw them into the water you
bathe in, or make them into tonics and oils they use as they
massage your skin to relax you. They say that in Curmana
there's an herb for everything. You remember that powder I

used on the guards back in Arida's prison last summer? That's where it came from."

"Sleeping powder?" Shanty guesses aloud, smiling when Bastian doesn't correct her. "Oh, I love a good sleeping powder."

"It's a beautiful island," Bastian continues. "But it's quiet. Consider Curmana simple elegance. For those looking for an adventure, I wouldn't recommend it. Everything closes early, and it's all a bit stuffy."

A place that's quiet and relaxing sounds better than anything right now. Besides, if it's truly that calm and quiet, that should make my job of finding Ornell even easier. "It sounds lovely," I say, and though Bastian shrugs, his lips curl into the tiniest of smiles. I take the box he slid toward me and open it. "If you could arrange it, Casem, I'd love for us to be able to visit those spas—"

Inside the box is ginnada, and my heart leaps to my throat.

"Where did you get this?" It's a silly thing, but just the smell of the sugary almond paste is enough to make my heart heavy. They remind me of Arida, back before Kaven. Of my parents and me stuffing ourselves full of the dessert every time the cooks made them for a celebration.

Father loved them even more than I do.

I breathe in the smell of them and shut my eyes. Since losing my magic, I'm not as hungry as I used to be. Back then, I had an appetite that was practically insatiable, as I constantly needed to replenish my energy for my magic. But even without my old appetite, I would put down an entire ship full of ginnada if given the chance.

"I know you love those things." Bastian doesn't look at me when he says it. Though there's no trembling or shyness in his words, the anxiety within him buzzes in the pit of my half-missing soul. He scratches the back of his neck, boyish and anxious. "I picked them up back in Kerost, it's no big deal."

But he's wrong. Because all I see as I stare at the ginnada is the warm brown of Father's eyes. All I hear is his bellowing laugh.

I wish Bastian would stop being kind. That he'd stop caring, at least until I remember how to care that same way. At least until I'm no longer so empty inside.

"I can't accept this." I press the box back into his chest, unable to steady my trembling hands. I don't watch to see the look in his eyes, but that doesn't stop me from feeling his pain.

"It's just ginnada. You don't have to—"

"Eat it if you want." I can't keep the chill out of my voice. Each breath is too tight in my chest, constricting me until I'm on the verge of bursting. "Or throw it overboard, I don't care. But get that out of my sight."

All I hear is Father's laughter. All I see is his blood on my hands. The sword in his stomach.

Gods, why won't he stop laughing?

"Amora—"

Shanty takes hold of Bastian's shoulder, slowly shaking her head.

I hate the pity in her eyes.

I hate the pain in Bastian's, and how it mirrors my own.

I hate the way they all look at me, like I'm some hurt animal to be consoled.

And I hate more than anything how alone I feel when they're all right in front of me.

Shanty said they might understand, but looking into their

147

eyes, I know now she was wrong. They'll never understand.

"I'll be in my cabin." I force myself not to stumble as I stand. "Someone fetch me when we arrive."

One foot in front of the other, I force myself away from their eyes. Down the stairs, to the cabins. I barely make it to a basin before I throw up.

SEVENTEEN

Curmana is every bit as beautiful as I imagined, and nearly identical to how Bastian described it. And I'd tell the others as much as we file off the ship, if only I'd talked to them at all in the past two days.

We arrive to sand so pure and white that, despite the five Curmanans standing before me as our crew descends *Keel Haul*, it's difficult to believe anyone even lives on this island.

"Welcome, Your Majesty." A beautiful woman with silky ice-blond hair dips into a bow so low that the fabric of her cotton pants—cut short at the ankles—sweeps against the white sand. Her porcelain skin is so smooth and poreless that she looks more spirit than human. A tall, lithe, birdlike spirit, with a sharp nose and pale, round eyes.

The woman wears a black silk top with straps made from delicate silver chains. While it's significantly warmer here than it was in Kerost, there's still enough of a bite to the air that she wears an onyx cape inlaid with a silver emblem I recognize as a zolo leaf—Curmana's most popular medicinal herb, used in almost every remedy across every island. At once I know this is no spirit, but the Baroness of Curmana, Lady Ilia.

I glance to her belly, still swollen from her recent pregnancy, and notice the deep shadows beneath her eyes that come from having a newborn. Though I'd seen Ilia in passing during Father's reign, we've hardly shared words with each other. Her brother had stood in Ilia's place during our recent advisory meeting on Arida because she'd only just given birth.

Ilia straightens, a smile plastered tight to her lips. Unfortunately, that smile doesn't quite reach her eyes. "I hope the sea offered you a kind journey?" she asks by way of friendly conversation. I'm quick to oblige, fully used to this polite charade.

"It did, thank you. I'm glad to finally be here, Lady Ilia. Though I hope you know you didn't have to come see me yourself. I would have understood if you were busy with your newborn."

Her pale pink lips pucker. "Just Ilia is fine, thank you. And it's no bother, Your Majesty. I may be a mother now, but I am still this island's adviser; there are duties to uphold. My wife, Nelly, is watching our child, so don't worry yourself. It's such a pleasure to have you here on Curmana, and to finally have the opportunity to show you our island." Even her voice is a frigid breeze. Her sharp face remains expressionless, not entirely matching her words.

The rest of the crew is quiet behind me, but from the corner of my eye I catch the uncertainty in Ferrick's expression and know I'm not the only one Ilia is making anxious. Her beauty is ethereal, but that only makes her more terrifying. She leads me across the flat white sand, so dense that my boots hardly sink into it. "I'll show you to your room, where you can clean up for the party tonight. You'll be meeting—"

"There's a party tonight?" I hate the spark of joy that flares within me, wanting to stomp it out. I'm here on a *mission*, not to slip into a dress and dance the night away. And yet I can't stop the buzz of excitement that prickles my skin, wanting desperately for the distraction.

Not to mention that a party means there will be crowds. And in that crowd, perhaps Ornell will be waiting.

"Some might call it the best party Visidia has ever seen!" It's a new voice that speaks, one far less shrewd and much more boisterous. Another woman is barreling excitedly down the shore, beautiful honey-blond ringlets billowing behind her. Her eyes are a bright and familiar green—a shade I've seen before but can't for the life of me place—and her smile is warm enough to melt the iceberg that's Ilia.

"*Nelly*," Ilia begins, though her voice is warmer. "You're supposed to be watching the baby."

"Oh relax, Elias is watching him for a few minutes. I wanted to meet the queen!" Nelly leans over to press a quick kiss to Ilia's cheek, and though the adviser's brows furrow, she ultimately relents to sighing.

"I'm the one who planned the party." Nelly doesn't wait for me to extend my hand before she takes it and gives two firm, quick shakes. "We had to make a few changes given the short notice, but I promise you're going to love it. We've got the best catering Curmana has to offer; imagine cakes and wine imported from Ikae, more desserts than you've ever seen in your *life*, fresh fish with mango slices . . ."

The more she lists, the more intrigued Casem becomes, taking a long step forward to listen more intently.

"Your Majesty," Ilia gently interrupts only when I can't imagine what food will possibly be left in Visidia after this party, "let me introduce you to my wife, Nelly. She came here from Suntosu, and works as a resident healer for the island."

Nelly's peachy-pink cheeks flush. "Apologies, Your Majesty. I've just been so excited for your visit. We know how important it is for you to find Visidia's next king; I want to make sure our part in that goes as smoothly as possible for you. If you're going to find love tonight, the atmosphere has to be absolutely perfect!"

Behind us, Bastian scoffs.

While Nelly's look is one of determination, Ilia's is bemusedly apologetic. The look she casts me is one that says at least she knows this has nothing to do with love or romance, but is for Visidia. I'm sure her brother, Elias, filled her in after the council meeting.

"My wife is very much a romantic," she offers, to which Nelly grins.

"And there's nothing wrong with that! Besides, nothing *ever* happens on Curmana. Having you here will be a nice change of pace for the locals."

"But first, we should show Her Majesty where she and her guests will be staying." Ilia keeps her shoulders squared and her body tall as she walks, as though she's balancing something as heavy as the eel crown. Though the two couldn't be any more different, there's a familiarity in the way they stand side by side. A naturalness to the way Nelly's hand slips into Ilia's and their fingers lace.

Jealousy blossoms within me, so bitter and encompassing that I turn away, attempting to smother the emotion before Bastian notices.

What must it be like to be able to feel your emotions so freely and naturally? To trust the way you feel about someone else, without the complication of a curse in your way?

I hardly remember anymore.

"You'll be staying at one of our spas, if that's all right," Ilia says, drawing my attention back from its bitter depths. "I thought it'd be the most fitting place for a queen and her attendants."

"Attendants?" Vataea starts to protest, but Shanty nudges her swiftly.

"After you see the perks you're about to get, V, you're not going to care what they call you," she whispers.

Half distracted by the chattering around me, I turn back to Ilia and nod, trying not to look as eager as I feel at the idea of not only having a few nights away from sharing a small cabin, but also being at one of the spas my cousin Yuriel and Aunt Kalea always raved about. "Will the festivities be held there, as well?"

Nelly's lips quirk, telling me I must have asked something funny.

"Curmana prides itself on being as tranquil and relaxing as possible," Ilia says curtly. "If you've been to Ikae, then you've seen their fast-paced lifestyle. They're frivolous; every-thing is a party to them." My tongue sharpens, ready to argue, but Ilia continues before I have the chance. "People who visit Ikae are looking specifically for a taste of that life. But people come *here* to relax. To feel as though every day is the length of three, and that there's never any rush. Tourists come for a taste of our calm lifestyle—a chance to *breathe*. Our spas are our most sacred areas for this; we wouldn't want to disturb that environment with a party. Our festivities will take place closer to the water, along the shoreline. Will these plans work for you, Your Majesty?" Her bright amber eyes flicker to me.

More than anything, I wish I could drink myself silly and

dance in the arms of a dozen handsome men, laughing and feeling more like myself than I have in ages. But it's as they said—we've only three days on Curmana. I need to maximize my time to find Ornell.

"The plan is perfect." I smile despite the tiredness that weighs my bones. "Tonight will be wonderful. I'll just need a few hours to prepare. I'd rather not smell like fish while meeting these people for the first time."

"Funny." Bastian's teasing tone takes me by surprise. Though I figured he'd still be mad about the ginnada, he's smiling. "I must smell like fish all the time, then. But you've never had an issue with it before."

"I *am* a fish," Vataea cuts in. At first her expression is flat, and we all still, wondering if we've offended her. But then her lips curl into a smirk. "I think people actually like it."

It's jarring to find myself relaxing into everyone's laughter, and doubly so when Bastian's sends a white-hot fluttering through my body, making my breath hitch in my chest.

Bastian catches my eye, and my heart stutters. Gods, the things this boy does to me.

"It's okay, Amora. I'm not mad." His eyes warm beneath dark lashes, but I tear my attention away. It's hardly fair that he can sense what I'm feeling so easily. I have to center myself as Ilia and Nelly escort us into the spa where we'll be staying, pushing all thoughts of him away.

The inside of the building is even more gorgeous than I could have imagined, built of natural gray stone and slate flooring interlaced with large pebbles. One wall is taken up entirely by the largest stone hearth I've ever seen, while the one across from it's made from thick yellow moss, rich green leaves, and dark ivy that snakes into intricate patterns. Three small, gently flowing waterfalls trickle from beneath the leaves, and the soothing sound is amplified by the large space.

"Is this the spa?" Ferrick asks skeptically, to which Nelly laughs.

"This is just where to check in! The spas are farther back in the building."

My skin warms. Mission or not, I'll be paying the spa a visit before I leave.

The moment we reach our rooms, I realize we're the only ones staying here. We have the entire floor to ourselves, and Ilia and Nelly are quick to leave us to explore our rooms, insisting there's more to do before tonight's party.

"You *have* to try the baths," Nelly says excitedly before the attendants take over for her, helping load our luggage into our suites. "There should already be one drawn up for you."

And sure enough, as I make my way across slabs of unfinished stone flooring, I find a perfectly heated bath waiting for me inside with a collection of herbs floating atop steaming water. Hints of lemongrass and sage lure me toward the deep stone tub, where tendrils of heat spiral and lick my skin as I lean forward to breathe the scents.

Behind the bath is an iron wall of spice jars. Upon closer inspection, I find each of them has a tiny label written in elegant script, describing contents such as sandalwood or lavender. Rosemary and sea salt. There's everything I could ever imagine and more—scented oils for your skin and hair. A bowl of warm, shimmering liquid that promises my curls will be glossier after using it. There are potions and tonics to scrub my skin clean and then replenish it again, and a wall lined with beauty products that sends my heart fluttering.

There are jars of rouge in every shade I can imagine. Dozens of lip stains, and kohl for the eyes. There are brushes and hair accessories, and absolutely anything I could ever want. And if I were to somehow want for something that's not here—as impossible as that feels—there's a rope in the corner where I can tape a note with what I need—whether it be food, a drink, fresh water for the bath, fresh clothing, a stylist, anything—and pulling it will alert the staff.

Stars, it's no wonder my aunt and cousin frequented this place. I'd live like this forever if I could.

Goose bumps roll up my bare skin as I step into the water, and there's a brief moment where all thoughts of my curse and mission melt away. I am not a queen; I'm just Amora.

And this, I could get used to.

I can't fathom what silent creature must have delivered them while I was bathing, but as I return to my room there's a collection of Curmanan outfits and jewelry laid out on the four-poster bed.

They're nothing like the extravagant gowns I've worn to parties in the past; rather than thicker material like crepe or chiffon, the garments are comfortable linen or feather-soft silk. There are none of the tightly structured tops I'm used to. Everything is fluid and elegant.

While not outright lavish, the details built into the pieces are exquisite, from the intricate shoulder embellishments to the plunging neck and back lines. One satin dress has almost no fabric in the back at all, but golden gossamer threads that hold it together, shimmering like a dampened spiderweb.

Apart from the dresses, I've also been provided pantsuits as an option, and am immediately drawn to one made from silk. The top is a deep inky black with delicate shoulder straps made entirely of small onyx gemstones, cropped above the navel. There's a lightweight cape resting beside it, shimmering and so sheer that I wonder whether it's meant to provide any warmth at all.

I pull on the matching pants, cropped to my ankles. They billow out widely, so comfortable that I'm annoyed with Arida for not yet having adopted this style of fashion. As much as I love our tight, structured gowns, being able to eat without feeling as though I might suffocate will be a welcome reprieve.

I've just slipped on jeweled sandals and have fastened my curls back into something I hope looks passably elegant, when there's a sound at the door.

"Five more minutes," I say, figuring it must be Casem on the other side. "I still need to put on my jewelry."

But the sound comes again moments later, so quiet I barely hear it this time, and I realize it wasn't a knock at all.

Someone's fiddling with the handle.

Immediately my thoughts jerk to the two men who'd attacked me in Kerost. I sweep Rukan from its sheath on my bed and clutch the poisoned dagger tight at my side, hating how fast my heart races. I creep toward the door, every hair on my body raised and alert.

I am Amora Montara, Queen of Visidia. Even without my magic, I can still fight. And with Rukan, all it takes is a cut deep enough for the blade's poison to seep into the bloodstream to end someone's life.

The thought gives me the courage to throw the door open with my dagger held at the ready. But as I raise it into the air and prepare to strike, Bastian stumbles back, throwing himself against the wall.

"Stars!" He chokes on the word, voice three octaves higher. "I thought we'd gotten past the stabbing phase of our relationship!"

Rukan turns to lead in my hands, and I sheathe the blade. "What are you *doing*? Why didn't you say anything?"

"Considering our situation, I thought you would have *felt* me." Righting himself, he smooths the wrinkles from his shirt with a grimace. "I know you're not thrilled about our curse, but could you find a better solution than murdering me?"

I ignore him, anger hot in my throat. "Were you spying on me?"

"Of course not." His eyes skim away, hands flexing at his sides. "I was just . . . Stars, I was putting a curse on your door, okay? After what happened in Kerost, I figured a little extra protection couldn't hurt."

I nearly lose my breath at those words, skin warming. "Why wouldn't you just tell me? I'm fully capable of—"

"Of protecting yourself?" He levels his face to mine. "Knowing you'd say that is exactly why I didn't tell you."

At first I throw my shoulders back, defensive. But then I see there's blood on his finger, and a bead of it has been smeared onto the door's handle. Though I want to be mad at him, there's nothing to be angry at. In fact, more than anything, it's embarrassment that makes my voice quiet and my cheeks hot.

"Thank you," I mutter, folding my arms around myself.

"And . . . I'm sorry about the other day. I didn't mean to lose my temper."

He stills, nerves prickling the air. "You don't need to be sorry. I should have known better."

"There was nothing to know, all right? Just . . . come in and get washed up."

Only then do I allow myself to fully *look* at him, and heat stretches up my neck. I've never seen him so polished. His shoulders are broad and his chest proud in a coat of rich onyx with shimmering gold buttons and trim. His hair has been smoothed back, and his warm golden-brown skin glows from the oils and creams. As he steps into the room, all I can think is that he looks like an entirely different man, handsome and self-assured.

He looks like a noble.

"Is that cedar?" I lean in and breathe the air around him, searching for the brine of the sea that belongs on his skin.

"It's vetiver, actually." He holds his chin high, as if proud I've noticed. "It smells good, right?"

I curl my nose. "It doesn't smell like you."

As soon as the words are out, I want to shove them back into my throat and swallow hard. The surprise that flickers in Bastian's eyes heats my skin so fiercely I fear I might burn to ashes right here and now.

"Ah." Bastian clucks his tongue, brow arching. "So you *like* the smell of fish."

Gods, even his smile looks different. Brighter. Sharper. More cunning. It beams at me, glinting with mischief that has my heart stuttering. I've always thought Bastian was handsome, but seeing him so cleaned up, dressed head to toe in a rich, velvety onyx, is doing things to my body I'd prefer it didn't.

This isn't the Bastian I'm used to—the pirate with a crooked grin and mischief in his eyes.

This is Bastian Altair, the eligible Visidian bachelor who is here to make his presence known.

Unfortunately for me, it's worked. My fingers ache with the desire to comb through that polished hair of his and make it wild again. To undo a button or two of his onyx shirt and see just how much of him glistens with oil.

I'm glad for a moment to gather myself as he disappears into the wash room to wash his hands, though I lose myself again the moment he's back.

"Let me escort you tonight." His declaration is cool water against my skin. I feel the anxious pulse of his soul, but he doesn't show it. He holds out his arm, and I have to pull myself back when I instinctively reach for it, desperately wanting to touch him.

"Jewels," I choke, needing to distract myself. This isn't the time to be having *these* feelings.

"Jewels?" Bastian's brows furrow, then steady when I point to my bed and the collection of jewelry laid upon it. "Ah. Right. I can wait out in the hall if you need some more time?"

He starts to back away, and—though for the life of me I can't understand why—I shake my head before he can get to the door. Bottom lip sucked tight between my teeth, my voice betrays me. "Stay. You can tell me what looks best on me."

"Everything looks best on you." His smile burns bright with charm. When I say nothing, however, Bastian's quick to wipe it away and take a seat at the edge of the bed, waiting.

I run my fingers over the jewels, pretending to contemplate

them for the distraction of it. But gods, all I can think about is how being so close to him warms the ice in my veins. I can't stop thinking about how frustratingly handsome he looks in these clothes, but I'm also imagining what he looks like outside them. Not to mention, he's on my *bed*.

Maybe my feelings for Bastian *are* real. It's as though, from the moment I first met him, his spirit has called directly to mine.

I hope you give it your best shot with those boys, he'd challenged. *Because you're going to be sorely disappointed when you discover that not one of them is me.*

There isn't a single part of me that doesn't want to take off on *Keel Haul* and explore Visidia with Bastian at my side. I remember moments when I thought that Bastian could be it for me; that he understood my soul in a way no one else would ever be able to. But our curse has muddled those feelings.

I very well might be in love with Bastian Altair. But until our curse is broken, I cannot trust myself to make that decision.

It's all I can do to force the thoughts away. To scoop the closest necklace and hold it up as if I'd been eyeing it all along.

"This one?" I ask, only now seeing it's an elegant silver chain with teardrop of black pearls and matching earrings.

He takes the time to look them over, then nods as I fasten on the earrings—simple pearls that dangle from an onyx chain, understated and elegant. When I go to put the necklace on, however, Bastian watches me struggle with the clasp. Taking pity on my attempts, he stands.

"Give it here." He takes the delicate jewels in his broad, calloused hands. I shiver as they graze the back of my neck, and my lungs tighten until my breathing comes in quiet, short rasps.

Bastian doesn't appear to notice my struggling. He manages to clasp the necklace quickly and adjusts it so it sits straight.

"There." The huskiness in his voice does strange things to my stomach. "Beautiful." But he's not looking at the necklace, and his hands don't move from my shoulders.

Every part of me is simultaneously chilled with goose bumps and drowning in fire, my body igniting under his touch. Under his voice.

I can't take it for another second.

I turn, and Bastian knows exactly what I want, because he wants it, too. His firm hands grip my shoulders and he pulls me into his body with every ounce of desire that roils through my own. I wrap my arms around his neck, hating myself for kissing him, and hating myself for ever considering otherwise. I back into the bed and drag him over me. I don't have it in me to break our kiss and wince at a pair of earrings that dig into my back, but Bastian tries to sweep everything aside all the same.

For fear of breaking this moment, neither of us says a word. One wrong word, one wrong breath, one wrong look, and it will all be over.

His lips find the crook of my neck and I exhale a contented sigh as my body threatens to melt beneath the comforting weight of him. His lips trace delicate patterns against my skin at first, but the longer it lasts the greedier and more desperate we become. Kissing each other. Touching each other. Holding each other.

But then he says, "Are you sure about this?" and we unravel. My skin burns while my lungs stretch and fill, breathing far easier than they do when he and I are apart. If I could curl into this bed with his skin against mine for an eternity, I would.

I run my tongue over dry lips, trying to find the right words, though I'm not sure *what* I want. My willpower around Bastian is abysmal.

"I get it." He spares me from having to answer by being the first to speak. Gently his fingers glide through strands of hair that have fallen free from their coiffed style. He twirls a finger around one of my curls. "I may not have been cursed to a person, but I was cursed to *Keel Haul*, remember? As much as I love that ship, my curse made me resent it. I don't want that for us.

"I know what you're feeling is terrifying," he continues, shifting so that he's more to my side than on top of me. "But we need to work together if we're going to get through this, Amora." The way my name sounds from his lips stokes a ravenous fire deep within me. "Whether you like it or not, I'm in this mess with you. You don't have to put the weight of the world on your own shoulders. Let me carry some of it, too."

"That's easier said than done." I pull away from him, but he takes hold of my shoulder, pleading for my gaze. I don't give it to him; if I do, I fear it might shatter me completely.

"Maybe it's easier for you," he says. "But stars, I need help, too. Only unlike you, I'm not afraid to admit it. After everything that's happened, sometimes it feels like the world's going to crash down on me at any moment. But being with you steadies me. I know you've wanted space, and I tried my hardest to give that to you. But I can't do it, because being apart doesn't only hurt you. I've tried so hard to be there for you, and to give you time, but . . . I need someone to be there for me."

I can't imagine the strength it must take to admit those words. But still, I can't look at him. I clench my hands into the fabric of my pants.

"You don't have to love me." His voice is gentler this time, so soft it's little more than a whisper. "You don't have to do anything. But we need each other right now, and we went through too much for our relationship to waver because of a curse that we're going to fix, together."

The plea in his voice is enough to knock the wind out of me. No longer is the weight of his body a comfort; it's suffocating. I push myself free from Bastian and clutch my tightening chest.

The sides of the room sweep inward, until all I can see is a tunnel ahead. My breaths come fast and hard, and my body is too heavy and too cold for me to be able to focus enough to do anything about it.

I can no longer see Bastian at the end of that tunnel, though somewhere in the back of my mind I know he must still be sitting in front of me. Instead I see Father, dead on the ground. I see Kaven smiling over him, a blade dripping with Father's blood raised to his lips. When I do see Bastian, it's him convulsing on the ground, eyes rolled backward into his skull as a crowd of the dead swarm around him, watching with hunger in their smiles.

Then, all I see is the blood, weaving itself over my vision.

Red.

Red.

Red.

Red.

There are sounds now, coming from the tunnel. I can't decipher them at first, but they grow louder and louder until they're beating against my skull like the painful hammering of a struggling Kerost.

I try to drown them out, humming a familiar sea shanty under my breath, trying to steady the rhythm. I try to focus on it amid the pounding of the hammers, but I keep losing it. I keep losing—

The sudden weight on my body is enough to give me pause. To make the tunnel expand just a little as the hammers cease their pounding. The shouting I'd heard becomes clearer, and I recognize now that I'm not the only one humming.

The tunnel snaps.

Bastian holds me tightly from behind, arms wrapped firmly around my chest. "It's okay," he says with a soothing firmness. "It's okay, I'm right here."

I wrap my hands around his arms and sink into his chest as the shaking steadies and the tightness in my lungs ebbs away. He picks up humming the shanty when I can no longer continue, not needing to be asked. My body is lead against his, so heavy and tired I can barely move. But at least I can see, again. At least I'm back in reality.

"Are you with me?" he asks, to which I manage a quiet grunt in response. The tension in his shoulders relaxes some, and he loosens his grip. I tighten mine in response, anchoring myself back in reality and away from the memories I've desperately been trying to keep shelved in the farthest crevice of my mind.

"Take your time," Bastian whispers. "Just breathe. We can stay like this all night if we need to."

And though I know he means it, I also know he's wrong. Because I'm not a tourist here for a spa trip; I'm the Queen of Visidia, and there's an entire island expecting me tonight.

There's nothing I want more than to remain exactly like this for the rest of the evening. Unmoving, protected and whole, listening to the soothing sound of this boy humming spectacularly off-key. I don't know if I physically *can* move. Even breathing is painful, and my vision is still so bleary that I worry it'll never normalize. But I don't have the luxury of sitting in my feelings, no matter how much I might need to.

"I have to get up," I tell Bastian, though neither of us takes any step toward moving. Instead, we sit there for another long, quiet moment before he eventually stirs.

"Is this what happened a few days ago? When you saw the ginnada?"

I swallow the slowly shrinking lump in my throat. "It's happened a few times." I worry he may ask for more details, like the things I see when this happens, but he doesn't. Instead, he presses a kiss to my temple, still cradling me.

"I'm sorry you're going through this, Amora. But we're all here for you."

I'm not sure how long we sit there, but Bastian holds me until my muscles relax, the tension ebbing away. My body aches as I force myself to roll off his chest and rise shakily to my feet. He's standing within the second, waiting to see if I need him as I fix my ruffled hair and smooth my pants. Looking in the mirror, I see my lips are swollen and my eyes red-rimmed and puffy. But in the darkness of the night, I'm hopeful no one will be able to tell.

Once I'm ready, I take hold of Bastian's offered arm and let him lead me through the hall, grateful for his presence. My body feels as though I've overused my magic, thoroughly exhausting myself. I focus my energy into every step, hoping that with some food and distraction from my own thoughts, I'll be able to ease up enough to believably participate in tonight's festivities.

"You've got this," he says, and I try to sink into those words. To wrap them around myself as armor. "I'll be right there if you need me."

"Thank you." I squeeze his arm, just once, and feel his body go lax. "And I can try to be there, too."

His expression softens and he looks ahead, knowing just as I do that there's no turning back, now. Not from him, and not from the hundreds of bachelors hungry for the title of king as we throw ourselves into the fray.

EIGHTEEN

Parties on Curmana are far from the loud, bustling events I'm used to.

There are no merchants perched behind stands of sugary-sweet ginnada. No cooks with sweat on their brows as they dole out skewers of freshly roasted meats or glazed Ikaean desserts, and no uninhibited laughter from dancing partygoers who flock around barrels of wine and ale that line the streets.

Instead, there are Curmanans dressed in sleek onyx robes who use levitation magic to float tiny portions of food and moderately filled flutes of sparkling red wine around the crowd. Swapped for the loud drums and horns I'm familiar with is a harpist who's positioned off to the corner, playing music that's so soft and beautiful one could easily fall asleep to it. Hardly anyone speaks, and when they do their voices are smooth and quiet, offered with only the politest of smiles.

Back in Arida, we wouldn't call this a "party."

My skin crawls from the silence. "Why is no one talking?"

"They are." Bastian takes one cursory look around the bay, looking from bachelor to hungry bachelor. The tension in his shoulders swells. "Just not out loud. Mind speak, remember?"

Gods, I can only imagine the things they're saying about me. I've enjoyed mind magic when Mira's used it; she always has the greatest gossip to share about the kingdom. But on this side of it, it's possibly my least favorite magic of all.

I spy Ferrick making conversation with a grinning Nelly, who sneaks looks behind her every so often at Vataea, who Ferrick is clearly talking about. His entire face is scarlet as Nelly leans in and whispers something to him conspiratorially. Ferrick nods, listening intently to whatever romantic advice she must be offering.

Ilia stands beside them, listening with only a quirk of amusement upon her lips. While Nelly's dressed in a gorgeous gossamer gown of black with brilliant emerald touches, Ilia wears a velvety onyx suit and rich matching cape. Her hair's been fastened into a long plait that drapes over one shoulder, while Nelly's has been elegantly curled and piled atop her head in a fashion that shouldn't work but miraculously does.

While Ferrick wears clothes similar to Bastian's, the harsh color makes his pale skin almost ghostly. A few yards opposite him stands the focus of his interest—Vataea's beside Shanty, who has taken an entire tray of food from one of the workers and holds it between them while sipping on sparkling wine. A crowd of admirers linger around them, casting hopeful glances toward the girls, some working up the nerve to ask them to dance. Vataea looks positively ferocious in the silk gown that sits on her body like a second layer of skin. Used to cooler temperatures, she's neglected any form of coat or cape, showing off the full extent of a plunging neckline and thin diamond straps. Shanty's chosen to ignore Curmana's signature color and style in favor of enchanting her own slinky dress to be as startling a lilac as her hair and eyes. The short dress hugs her curves fiercely, and she revels in the attention she's receiving.

Behind them, I see Nelly give Ferrick a small shove, and he makes his way to the two girls, nearly dragging his feet with every step. He looks like a fish out of water, fiddling with the neck of his shirt as though it's too tight. Eventually though, he makes it to Vataea, speaking words I can't hear with cheeks that are red as wine. But they make her smile, and the moment he reaches his hand out, she snatches it. Vataea practically drags him to the dance floor.

It's the small boost of morale I need to drop my arm from Bastian's as we approach the party. Immediately my skin cools with the chill of his absence, and it takes everything in me not to reach out, again.

"Save me a dance." There's a tightness in his smile that crinkles the corners of his eyes. "I'll be around."

He disappears into the crowd as Nelly hustles over to me. Casem follows behind her, looking like a proper guard with the royal emblem shimmering bright on his shoulder. Or as proper as he could look, I suppose, given that he's holding a plate of five meat skewers.

"Isn't it beautiful?" There's excitement brimming in Nelly's voice as she tilts her head to admire the hundreds of white, twinkling lanterns that hover in the sky around us. They're like tiny stars, held up by mind magic and swaying pleasantly in the breeze. "Talk about mood lighting. The scene is set, the men are here, and now the lady of the hour has finally arrived. Are you ready for your big night?"

Behind her, Casem's lips twitch into an amused, knowing smirk as he bites off a chunk from the skewer. I ignore him.

"I'm bursting at the seams." I wave down one of the working Curmanans, who responds by using their magic to float over a ridiculously small puff pastry with sweet cream. While delicious, everything is conversation food, too small and dainty. I'm going to need about fifty workers levitating trays my way if I'm ever going to get enough for a meal.

Another pastry floats toward me, and I jolt when this one bursts on my tongue not with cream, but delicious stewed meat. The worker laughs at my reaction, and suddenly I'm surrounded by pastries that dance around me, just waiting to be plucked from the sky.

Talk about service. The moment I reach for more, however, Nelly frowns and takes hold of my hand.

"There will be time for food later." She pulls me alongside her with a surprisingly firm grip, steering us toward the party with determination glinting in her eyes. Excitement buzzes off her skin as she pulls me straight through the crowd and to the edge of a roiling sea of people. Casem's hustling to keep up as Nelly drops my hand to loudly clap her own.

"Esteemed people of Curmana," she begins with a toothy grin. "Tonight, I have the pleasure of announcing this evening's most honored guest, the Queen of Visidia, Her Majesty Amora Montara."

All eyes turn to me. Verbal conversations ebb as backs straighten. Chins lift and chests puff as appraising eyes roam over me. I do my best not to glare at anyone whose stare lingers too long or seems too hungry. Here in public, before the eyes of everyone, I will be polite. Face-to-face, however, I'm not responsible for whether my dagger accidentally grazes those who eye me like I'm a prize to win, or for how many times I step on their toes.

When the crowd lowers themselves into a bow, I politely

wave their gesture away. In the past, I would have reveled in their display, letting their respect wash over me and fill me with pride. Now when I look upon them, all I see are the faces of the dead staring back.

How many of these people lost loved ones during Kaven's attack? During the storms on Kerost?

I am a liar who should not be standing here; the Montaras are nothing more than a facade, no more powerful than the next person. The beast my great ancestor Cato once warned us about was nothing more than a ploy for him to gain power.

And yet these people bow to me, because not a single one of them knows the truth.

I do everything I can to ground myself in the earth, fighting the urge to turn and flee from the eyes watching me. But Ornell could be here in this crowd, and I'll maintain this charade until I find him, no matter what it takes.

Cato Montara was a coward. Aunt Kalea was a coward. *Father* was a coward.

I will not be.

"Please," I say with what I hope sounds like a gentle laugh. "There's no need for that tonight. Do you see a crown on my head?" I wait, smiling. "Call me Amora. And as the night goes on, I hope I have the pleasure to meet every one of you. Not as your queen, but . . ." I stall, drawing in a breath to make myself look a little nervous. I press my lips together, then look up at them from beneath my lashes, playing the role of the friendly queen, demure and hoping to find her king. "Just as myself."

Casem steps up to be my escort down the shore, his lips quirking in amusement, which I take to mean I'm doing my job right. He sets a hand upon my shoulder and faces the crowd to address them himself, having somehow made his plate of food disappear.

"As you all know, Her Majesty's looking for a suitor. Someone who will be *king*." He wags his brows, and I try not to gag because there's no way any random bachelor I meet could ever become Visidia's king as though it were some contest. Not when I've trained so long and so hard for it, and still don't have the faintest clue what I'm doing half the time. And yet I keep that smile plastered to my lips for dear life as Nelly joins in.

"The night is young," she says, "and everyone will have their turn. So, please be patient, and let the festivities begin!"

Gently, Casem squeezes my hand and leads me down the remaining steps. "Make sure you get some wine," he says by way of encouragement. "You're going to need it."

Casem wasn't lying.

Though I expected more courting and less politics, three hours and two glasses of sparkling wine in, I've danced my way from one man to the next, having listened to at least a dozen tell me all the ways in which they're fit to be king, and all the thousand things I'm doing wrong with Visidia.

So far, no one named Ornell is anywhere to be found.

As expected, the majority of these bachelors are foolish enough to believe they can win me over with a smart tongue, but I don't give them the time to hear themselves speak. There are too many people here tonight, but only one I need to find. I have to keep moving.

"I think Visidia's forces need stronger regimented training," one of the men tells me. Nelly introduced him as

Lord Gregori. And because he's connected to nobility, no matter how distantly, it's apparently given him the belief that he has the right to act like a pompous oaf. He's somewhere in his early twenties, with snow-white skin and flaxen waves he must have spent far too long combing to perfection. "After everything that's happened this past year, I think it's time we better prepared ourselves. We should start with mandatory drafts, and look into creating more effective long-range weapons. I have a diagram of one I think you'd like, operated with blasting powder. Imagine a handheld cannon . . ."

"Fascinating." I cut off his thoughts with a wave of the hand. "Tell me, are you familiar with anyone by the name of Ornell? Ornell Rosenblathe?"

Nose scrunching with annoyance, he shakes his head. When he starts speaking again, I finish off my wine and flag someone down for what will be my third flute and more puff pastries, drowning out the boy's haughty words. He doesn't appear to notice, rambling on about the weapons he hopes to create and about how there needs to be a better budget for their development. I pop one of the floating pastries in my mouth, and jolt in surprise at the new flavor.

"This one's mint!" I tell him aloud, glad to finally have a reasonable distraction.

His eyes narrow in offense. "Excuse me?"

I point to the remaining puff pastry and take a bite of it before I show him the green jelly that oozes out from inside, then take another swig of wine. "It's mint jelly. Would you like to try some?" I hold out the remaining half of the puff pastry, and his eyes flick from it, to my flute of wine, and back up. His lips curl.

"Nice to see our queen is taking her courtship seriously."

The words are so ridiculous that I can't help myself from laughing. Yes, I may be a little wine-hazed, but I've still got my wits about me. I'm on a mission, after all.

"And it's nice to see that there's no shortage of men who think they're more qualified for my job than I am," I say casually. "Tell me, were you born with your delusions of grandeur, or did you grow into them?"

Gregori's mouth falls open, but in his surprise, no words manage to tumble out. Even the quiet *pop pop pop* of my bubbly is louder than he is as I take another sip and tell him, "I've spent every day for eighteen years training to wear my crown. I am the one who defeated Kaven and ended the threat to Visidia. So *please*, continue to belittle me. Tell me all about your silly weapons, and how they'll solve our political strife." I shove my empty wine flute into his hands. "Actually, come to think of it, I'd rather you not. Excuse me."

I leave him without once looking back, annoyance burning my skin. Half a year ago, I would have strung that boy up by his fingers for making such a mockery of the crown. It's unfortunate I no longer have that option.

It's not that I was looking *forward* to this, but stars, I assumed there would at least be a little more dancing and flirting. It would have been nice to have even a small reprieve from being forced to consider and discuss the changes happening within the kingdom.

"Smile, Amora," I grumble to myself. "Laugh, Amora. Make them love you, because the standards are different for us, Amora."

In the midst of the crowd, I catch sight of a short, squat man dressed head to toe in a soft pastel blue. I've no idea

175

what theme he's going for with his wardrobe, but the oddity of his widely puffed collar and shoulders are enough to know he's from Ikae. His yellow eyes catch mine briefly before swirling behind me, to where an enraged Gregori still stands with my flute glass clenched in his hand.

When the Ikaean jots something down on a piece of parchment, I clench my teeth tight so that I can keep my scowl inward, knowing at once he's one of the reporters Shanty warned us about. And I'm giving him a great story.

Heart squeezing, I try to flag down a worker when I bump hard into someone's chest. I stumble back, but the man catches my hand before I can fall, steadying me.

"Careful," he says, voice deep and husky. "I wouldn't want to get into trouble for accidentally injuring the queen."

I peer up to a face that's surprisingly familiar—Lord Elias, the younger brother of Lady Ilia and the man she'd sent to stand in for her during Arida's advisory meeting.

He's got a hard, square jaw and wide shoulders. Focused on the meeting, I didn't pay him as much attention the last time I saw him. This close though, his face is handsome enough to make my mouth dry. I press my lips together, trying to collect myself as I stare into deep, sea foam eyes that are beautiful against his suntanned skin. He towers over me, flashing a smirk that makes me notice day-old stubble I'm surprised to find myself wanting to touch.

"You'd be thrown into the prisons for that," I find myself saying, forcing the words out. My stomach flips when he laughs, low and deep. I want to ignore it, but I can't help feeling the familiarity that strikes me hard. He reminds me of a blond Bastian, strong and broad, with a deep laugh and a husky voice.

"Surely you'd come and bail me out?" he teases. "I know my queen is far too benevolent to allow me to rot away underground."

I pretend to consider this, squinting at him. "It sounds like you don't know your queen at all. But, I'll tell you what. I can help you with that problem, should you help me find another glass of—"

"Bubbly?" Nelly stands behind Elias, beaming as brightly as the moon as she presses flutes of bubbling pink wine into our hands. "I'm so glad to see the two of you chatting. That dance floor sure is looking a bit empty, though . . ."

Elias's chuckle is low and tinged with awkwardness. "Apologies about my sister-in-law." He flashes her a look, eyebrows knitting. "She's been trying to pawn me off all year."

"I'm just trying to help," she says innocently between sips of wine. "You need a good girl in your life, Elias."

"And I am quite capable of finding one on my own, I assure you." He sighs, thoroughly charming me with the way his cheeks flush a light pink. He's swift to extend his flute toward me. "Regardless, Your Majesty, I hope this settles our grievance?"

"It's a start." I tap my flute against his, my own skin warming as Nelly slowly backs away.

"I'll leave you two alone, then." She starts to retreat into the crowd, where Ilia is quick to grab her hand. There's a stern, serious expression on the adviser's face as her focus shifts to me for little more than a few seconds.

Nelly's lips press together. She gently peels her arm away, muttering something under her breath that I can't make out. It's clear they're arguing, though they do it in low voices so as to not draw attention to themselves as they disappear into the crowd.

Though my curiosity spikes, there's nothing I can do about it as I catch sight of the Ikaean reporter lingering in the edge of my vision. I consider Elias. He's everything Mother and Visidia's people would eat up—charismatic, handsome, and of noble blood. And with the reporter watching, I know my chance to find out what the two were arguing about has already passed. There's no room for politics tonight, and with Ornell nowhere to be found, I may as well give Visidia a show.

"I must admit, I didn't expect you would be here tonight, Lord Elias." I make my voice softer. My eyes gentler. "You never struck me as someone interested in the crown."

"I'd never given it any thought," he says with an easy shrug, taking the bait and settling into a comfortable place beside me. "But after meeting you back on Arida, I decided I was interested in who *wore* the crown. I figured why not give tonight a shot and see if there was a connection?"

"Funny," I say. "You didn't seem very interested before."

"Would you believe I'm painfully shy?" Show or no show, his smirk nearly strangles me. No matter how many men I've talked to tonight, I haven't once been able to get Bastian out of my head. I've compared every new face to his. Every voice to the way his words make my stomach flip. Every pair of eyes to the way I enjoy looking at his. So far, no one has been even comparable.

But Elias is at least similar. So much so that if I don't look at him too closely or listen too intently, he could make for a wonderful distraction.

"Did you know that the name Amora means beautiful sun?" Without having taken a sip, he's switched out his bubbly for blood-red wine. "That's even what you look like,

178

too. Radiant and beautiful, like a giant ball of sunlight."

I meant to take only a nursing sip of wine so as to keep my head straight, but I choke as I tilt the glass back, accidentally swallowing a giant mouthful that nearly comes out of my nose. "Blood of the gods, where did you hear *that*?"

A coy smile plays upon Elias's lips. "I didn't. But that's what it *should* mean."

And gods do I laugh, even if it's mostly from the alcohol and the ridiculousness of my burning nose.

"Just how many times have you tried to woo a girl with that ridiculous line?" I give him a teasing elbow to his gut, and he rubs at it with a deep laugh.

"I promise that one was crafted specifically for you."

Music swells in the air around us, no longer excruciatingly soft and slow. It kicks up enough that others find their way onto a makeshift dance floor set up upon the sand, looking so bemused that I'd believe they've never before danced. When I peek at Elias, about to ask him to join me, his hand is already stretched toward me.

"Ladies I've danced with in the past have told me I have two left feet," he says with a crooked grin, "but I've never been certain if I should believe them. Do you feel qualified to make that assessment?"

Smooth talker, this one.

I don't stop to consider the offer because if I do, I might think better of it. I should be moving on to the next person, hunting down Ornell. But maybe it's because I know I need to put on a show, or perhaps because he just made me laugh so hard that I nearly choked. Or, maybe it's because he reminds me of Bastian, or how during the night back on

Arida when I'd faked my magic for the advisers, he was the one who hadn't turned away in horror. Whatever the reason, I take his hand.

All eyes are on us as he leads me to the dance floor, including, I'm sure, Bastian's. But I don't let myself think about him.

I stiffen when Elias sets his hands on my hips, goose bumps fleshing their way up my skin. I set one hand on the arm that holds my waist, and the other on his broad shoulder, stepping closer into him. The music, while faster than it's been previously, is still slow and elegant enough to keep us in each other's arms.

Elias's grip is strong and comfortable, familiar even when he's not. I find myself relaxing into it as we dance, the world slowly morphing into a blur of lights and jewels. Elias certainly does not have two left feet; he's an excellent dancing partner, and an even better conversationalist. At first I'm able to keep up with his wit, but the longer we dance, the more sluggish and jellylike my limbs become. My feet slow and the blur of lights and jewels is no longer beautiful, but painful enough to make me squint. Even when I stop moving, the world around me continues to spin.

Stars, I must have had more alcohol than I thought.

The moment the song is finished, I pull away from Elias, breathless and clammy. This isn't my first time drinking; I know what it feels like when I'm getting too close to my limit. I made sure to eat and pace myself, but it must not have been well enough.

"I have to stop," I manage to grit out. "I'm so sorry."

Though his eyes widen a bit, I'm glad to see Elias doesn't look offended. "Don't worry about it. You're looking ill, though. Is there something I can—"

I shake my head, not wanting him to see me like this. "You're a lovely dance partner, but I owe it to the others to continue on with introductions." Now that we've stopped dancing, the world has steadied some. My vision still blurs at the corners, and if I move too quickly my balance sways, but it's better. "Why don't you find me tomorrow? I could use someone to show me around the island." Even light-headed, I don't miss the way his chest swells, and I laugh quietly at his eagerness.

"I'd be honored." He doesn't miss a beat. "I'll wait here for you around midmorning?"

I don't have the chance to answer. The burn of bile rises in my throat, and I shut my eyes to steady it, not about to make a fool out of myself before the entire island.

"Your Majesty? Are you sure there's nothing I can—"

"You can get out of the way and give her some air."

From the immediate wave of warmth and relief that floods me, I know the voice belongs to Bastian. Opening my eyes again, I see he's there before me, pressing a glass of water into my hands. When Elias hesitates, Bastian's eyes flare darkly, voice lowering into a growl.

"Turn around and walk away. You're going to draw attention if you keep staring."

But it's too late for that. The Ikaean reporter in the corner is working his magic on the parchment in his hands, and I'm sure there are a dozen others I can't see who are doing the same.

"I'll see you tomorrow, Elias," I say urgently, trying to smile but failing miserably as a new wave of nausea rolls over me. Fortunately, he takes the hint and bows his head before backing away.

"Tomorrow, then. Feel better, Your Majesty."

The moment he's gone, I sway but don't fall. Bastian's hands are on my shoulders, steadying me. By the look on his face, it's clear he's been watching all night. Not that I expected he wouldn't be.

"Well, you certainly have a type." Though some of the bitterness in his voice left with Elias, it's still far from thrilled. "What happened?"

I keep hold of his arm to steady myself. "I think the wine must have hit me at once. I thought I'd been pacing myself, but . . ." My voice trails off as he nods and sets a firm hand on my waist. The feeling of it there sparks a heat in my belly as I remember all the places those hands trailed my skin earlier, back in my room.

"How do you feel right now?"

"Light-headed. But there are still so many people I need to meet. I have to—have to go meet them." I spent too much time dancing with Elias; I should have spent that time making sure I'd met everyone. I'm about to pry myself from Bastian and hunt through the crowd when his fingers splay across my hip. Tense, I eye them. "What are you doing?"

He straightens, avoiding my eye by looking upward. "You're slurring your words, Amora. The last thing we want is for people to talk about how their queen got too drunk on her first visit to Curmana, or to share those blasted moving pictures. I'm not letting you go back out there on your own." He turns to the crowd, raising his voice for them before I can argue. "This will be the last dance of the evening for Her Majesty! She has an early morning tomorrow, and plenty more time to meet everyone. If she'd like more time with you, you'll be summoned tomorrow."

He says the last several words with audible annoyance, gritting them through his teeth with much effort.

"Another dance?" I grumble, head pounding and feet aching.

"We can't rush out of here without looking suspicious," Bastian says gently, at least having the decency to look as though he regrets making me do this. "Humor me with one more dance, and then we'll make a clean escape. We'll get you some food and water, so you can sleep off that wine and spend tomorrow with my look-alike. But for now, one more dance."

Though he keeps his voice light and teasing, there's fear in his words. Through our curse, those feelings of his seep into me so fiercely it's as though they're my own.

This time I give in to them and lean into Bastian's chest. Over his shoulder I spot Ferrick, watching and ready to sweep in should I need him. But right now Bastian's touch is exactly what I need to help with this sickness. The feeling of his skin against mine calms my swaying vision, but it's not enough to dull it entirely.

I've been drunk before, but it's never felt anything like this. Our "dance" is nothing more than him holding me on my feet as the world once again blurs around me.

"Have you eaten?" His smile is wide and proud, fake for all those watching.

"I heard Ilia and Nelly arguing," I answer instead, not remembering what he asked me.

"Do you know what it was about?"

"Maybe she was mad because this is all fake?" I laugh into his shoulder, no longer able to see him. My skin is so hot. So sticky. Everything is white. "She must have spent so much money on this party, and it's all *fake*."

I laugh again as the music stops, feeling Bastian tense beneath my hold. "Hang on a second longer. I'm going to get you out of here."

"Apologies," someone says. Ferrick, maybe? By the gods, I love Ferrick. "But we're under strict order to get Her Majesty to her room by a reasonable hour, to prepare her for the rest of her time on Curmana. But please feel free to continue enjoying this wonderful party. Eat, drink, dance!" He says something else that makes the crowd laugh, but I don't hear it.

Bastian turns my back to the crowd when I can no longer pretend. It's all I can do to hold his arm and allow him to lead me.

"What's wrong with her?" Distantly, I recognize the voice as Vataea's and wonder when she arrived.

"She said it was too much wine," Bastian says, keeping his voice low. "Just act natural. Laugh or something. Stars, Vataea, you draw too much attention."

She laughs quietly, as Bastian suggested. But as we get farther away she whispers, "Are you sure it's the wine?"

"I'm fine," I try to argue, but I'm not sure if the words ever make it past my lips, or if everyone is ignoring me.

"Food poisoning, maybe?" Casem asks. We must be far enough from the crowd, because my feet slip away from beneath me and my body floods with warmth as Bastian pauses to scoop me into his arms, cradling me against his chest.

"We need to get her to the room without anyone seeing," Bastian says. "Shanty, a little help here?"

Those words and the press of two warm hands against my cheeks are the last thing I remember.

NINETEEN

When I wake the next morning, the first thing I do is vomit into the metal basin at my bedside.

Though I don't remember this happening already, something in the way I reached out for the basin, expecting it, assures me this isn't the first time.

Only after a wave of dry heaves do I notice Bastian's on the chaise beside me. I startle when I see him, my stomach clenching even fiercer, and his jaw screws tight.

"Looks like you're awake this time." He stands to gather my fallen curls in his hands and fasten them back into a clip that hadn't been there the night before. "Here, drink some water." Wordlessly, he picks up the basin and disappears with it. Two minutes later and he's back, placing a clean one next to me. "How are you feeling?"

"Better, I think." Stomach empty, the nausea has subsided some. No longer is my skin slick with cold sweat, but sticky with the memory of it. "What happened last night? I remember I was dancing, and then we were leaving, and everything after that is . . . fuzzy."

There's a clatter from the bathing room, and both Vataea and Shanty poke their heads out.

"I told you she was awake," Vataea huffs, slipping out of

the room to join us. There's worry etched into the hard lines of her face, and as Shanty trails in behind her, even she looks concerned enough that my skin crawls.

"You're scaring me with those faces," I attempt to tease, but the joke falls flat at the worry in their eyes. "Relax. I had too much wine, but I'm fine, now."

Ferrick appears then, opening the door of my room carefully as he balances a heavy tray of food. Though I expect one of the elegant gourmet meals that Aunt Kalea and Yuriel have always raved about, I'm surprised to find that everything he's brought comes from *Keel Haul*'s stash. Dried meats, cheese, fish, and nuts. Casem follows behind him with a small barrel full of water we had stocked on the ship.

I pinch my brows at it, surprisingly hungry for having thrown up. "They didn't offer us breakfast?"

"They did. But this is what we're giving you." Ferrick sets the tray down and, only a little grudgingly, I take a bite of jerky. Hungry as I am, I don't let the food distract me. The crew looks at me with such pitying faces that it reminds me of when I'd been nearly killed by the Lusca or injured by Kaven. Their bodies are tense and jittery, as though they believe I might fall over at any moment. I'm about to reassure them that I'm fine, that they can all go get ready for our day, but the look they share stops me.

They're not just being overly protective. Something's wrong.

"Amora, we need to tell you something. But we need for you not to freak out, and to trust us."

Chills flood my body as I recognize the tremor in Ferrick's voice as genuine fear. He reaches his hand out and I take it without delay. Vataea sets a hand upon my thigh, and though

186

she's not the touchy-feely type, even Shanty's lips are pressed firmly together, looking more angry than upset.

"We knew that tension was high within the kingdom," Ferrick says. "We knew going into this that some were going to be resistant. But Amora, we don't think your sickness last night had anything to do with alcohol. We think you were poisoned."

I yank my hand from him as a sharp breath seizes hold of my lungs and stalls there. "Why?" I demand more tersely than I mean to. "Why would you think that?"

Bastian leans forward so that his elbows are on his knees and looks at me with the most severe expression I've ever seen. "You were throwing up blood. Ferrick was here all night, trying to keep you alive. I imagine you'd be dead without him; you didn't stop until the sun was out."

"You saw it, too?" I ask Ferrick, whose neck retracts in surprise. He starts to answer when Bastian's voice turns to gravel.

"You think I'm lying?"

He has no reason to, but I don't want to believe it. I hadn't felt threatened last night. I felt like I'd been putting on the show Mother told me our people wanted, minus the occasional slipup, like with Lord Gregori.

Most of my people had seemed receptive to me. Had one of those faces truly been lying?

"No," I offer quietly. "But could you have mistaken it for something else? I had a lot of stew in those puff pastries."

His scrunches his nose and leans back in his seat. "It wasn't stew. Curmana specializes in herbs, remember? Most of the ones you'll find around here are for healing. In small doses, they're relatively harmless, like the zolo leaf on Curmana's emblem. But . . . not all herbs are safe, and let's just say I used to know my way around Curmana's marketplace. If you know where to look, poison isn't hard to find." His eyes flicker up to Shanty, whose lips clamp even tighter.

"He's right," she admits. "I've bought my fair share of it, using many different faces. There are many different forms of poison, but this one was lethal. You're lucky Ferrick was here, and that whatever it was you consumed, it must have been only a small portion."

The cold sweat is back, licking its way up my spine as realization sets in—I could have died last night. If Ferrick hadn't been here, I *would* have died.

Vataea draws the blanket over my shoulder, and there's a fierce protectiveness in her eyes that, if I didn't know was for me, would be terrifying. "I will kill whoever did this." Her words are flat and casual, like she's telling us she'll have toast for breakfast. Ferrick sets a gentle hand on her shoulder.

"If you don't, then I will." Bastian's fists clench. "But first, we'll need to find them."

Ferrick nods and takes a seat on the edge of the bed. "Oh, we'll find them," he says without an ounce of hesitation. He dips his chin, making each of his words firmer. "*We* will find him, Amora. This isn't something you get to do on your own. If we're going to find whoever did this quickly, you have to let us help you."

Much to my surprise and his, I can't find the words to protest. For so long I've felt alone, even with my crew beside me. But now, seeing the anger in their eyes—feeling their fear—I want their support. I want to find the person behind this, and this isn't an obstacle I *want* to face on my own.

Father died because of the throne, and the decisions he

made while upon it. I knew the moment I set the crown upon my head that death would try for me, next. There's a certain strength you get by being in power, but there's also a unique danger. And without my magic—without *any* magic—it's not a danger I want to brave alone.

I want to let the others in, more than anything. I don't *want* to find everything on my own. It's just . . . hard. But maybe in small doses. Maybe this can be the first step.

The tension in Ferrick's body eases as he lets out a breath heavy with relief. If I weren't so sick to my stomach, I might have even laughed at how over the top it was.

"Good." He drops his voice low enough that the rest of us have to lean in, careful for any eavesdropping attendants who might be passing by. "We'll meet up in the afternoon for a trip to the marketplace, to figure out where the poison was bought and who it was sold to." Then he turns to Shanty, whose body straightens with understanding as he says, "We're going to need your help."

"Just say the word." Shanty's smile is as lethal as a serrated blade, though it flashes for only a moment before she's looking at me, again. "But before that, there's something you might want to see, Amora."

Ferrick's head swivels toward her, face pinched and stern. "I thought we were going to wait on that."

"She needs to know—"

As each of their faces sour, I sigh. "Whatever it is, show me. It's not like this day's going to get any worse."

As she plucks a piece of parchment from her pockets and goes to unfold it, however, I know instantly upon looking at the moving parchment how wrong I am.

HER MAJESTY, QUEEN AMORA:
AN ACCOMPLISHED NEW RULER,
OR A CHILD IN A CROWN?

Last night, Queen Amora's royal officials were seen escorting Her Majesty from her own party several hours before it was set to end. With reports from Curmanan staff claiming that Queen Amora was throwing up well into the morning, we have to wonder: Could the queen be pregnant?

With the Montara lineage dwindling, it's no secret the queen will need to quickly produce an heir to the throne. Sources claim the child could belong to a dark-haired male seen entering Her Majesty's room, alone, prior to the party.

But perhaps there's another answer. According to Lord Gregori, grandchild to the Suntosan representative, Lord Garrison, Her Majesty was heavily intoxicated throughout the night's festivities.

"I tried to get her to slow down," he told us in an exclusive interview. "We spent most of the night together, strategizing about Visidia and discussing the expansion of weaponry. At first Amora seemed fine. She was smiling and laughing, and we were having a wonderful time. But perhaps the night was too much for her, because as the party went on, I started to notice she was drinking more heavily. By the time I thought to stop her, she was already nearly six glasses of wine in, and was growing increasingly irate with me. When I noticed something was wrong, I quickly found her staff and sent them to collect her. I'm not sure how she's doing, but I'm going to be sure to check

in on her today. We have a date set this afternoon."

If Lord Gregori's right, then we have to wonder—in the hands of a freshly minted eighteen-year-old queen, just how safe is Visidia? Is it too much—

I crumple the parchment in my hands without finishing it, hating the moving image of me shoving my empty wine flute into Lord Gregori's chest.

"Your mother's not happy," Casem says timidly. "She's been yelling at me all morning." His eyes are milky white, hazy with the look of someone using mind magic. As the color returns to them, he sighs and tiredly rubs his temples.

"Tell her it was food poisoning." My voice shakes with an anger I don't try to rein in, letting it fuel me. "If she learns it was anything else, or if she thinks I'm out here making a fool of myself, she'll try to bring me back to Arida."

"Would that be a bad thing?" It's Ferrick who asks, a hand on his scabbard. "You've had two assassination attempts already. Maybe we should return home and try to plan something else."

"I will not cower before my kingdom." Ferrick, more than anyone, should understand why this is so important. When he opens his mouth to protest, I fix both him and Bastian—who looks ready to take Ferrick's side at any given moment—with a sharp look. "I am Visidia's queen. I'm here for a purpose, and I'm not leaving until I've accomplished everything I set out to do." My body is weak as I try to stand. "We'll carry out our morning as planned and then meet in the afternoon to find whoever did this. And Casem, do me a favor in the meantime. Find the reporter who wrote this parchment, would you? I'd like to have a word with him."

TWENTY

No matter how bone-tired and weary I feel, I must present myself with smiles and continue with the unsuspecting charade that everything is fine.

After kicking out everyone but Vataea—who lounges in a chaise in my room, glaring at the door as though it's about to come to life and attack at any given moment—I journey to the attached bathing room to try to breathe some life back into my skin.

I lather the tub with powders and tonics all meant to energize me, scrubbing my skin with scented creams and my hair with shimmery oils. Stepping out, I slick my curls back and coil them into a bun, using rose water and rouge to liven my cheeks. By the time I'm done, I look far less tired than I feel, and am passable to journey out into Curmana. Primarily, for my date with Lord Freebourne.

Though I thought to cancel it, Ferrick insisted we didn't want to draw suspicion. However, I'm not to consume anything, be it water or food, unless it comes from my crew directly.

"You look nice." Vataea stands to stretch out her long limbs as I emerge from the bathing room, fully dressed and my face made up. "You look as though you might actually be trying to impress this man."

The questioning lilt of her voice itches at my skin. *Was* I trying to impress Elias? He's handsome and sharp, I'll give him that. But my thoughts don't linger on him. He was a fun distraction for the night, but little more than that.

"It's all of Curmana I'm trying to impress," I tell her instead, though the words make my tongue bitter. How hard should I be trying when someone here attempted to poison me? I hate that I can't be bold in my actions and alert the kingdom so that we might find who did it. I hate that I have to pretend.

Vataea hooks a satchel to her hips, skimming her fingers over her poniard to ensure it's in place. Back on Arida, Casem and I had helped her design the long, serrated blade. It's thin and light enough that it wouldn't weigh her down if she were to take it in the ocean. But there's danger in the deadly jagged edges. Though Vataea's true weapon will always be her voice and the water surrounding her, she needed something for protection here on land. To my surprise, she's grown rather attached to it.

"Well then, let's go impress them." Shoving her feet into a pair of black boots, she tosses me a coat and we head out. Shanty waits cross-legged on the floor outside, picking at her nails. She looks relieved to stand, and I'm relieved to have her. Both of these girls are by far the fiercest and most capable of my crew in a fight; should anyone try something, I'll be glad to have them on my side.

But unfortunately, Shanty's not alone. Bastian's beside her, broad arms folded across his chest.

"We need to talk," he says, brow arching when Shanty slyly scoots an inch closer to eavesdrop. "Alone."

"There's somewhere I need to be," I start, but he ignores me, quick to take me by the wrist and walk me right back into the room, shutting the door behind us. Outside it, Vataea growls a few choice words.

"Freebourne can wait." He drops my wrist, eyes starless and steely. "I know I said I didn't care if you kept your secrets, but I lied. We're playing with fire, and it's time to tell me the truth. Why are we really here?"

My chest numbs. It's everything I can do to keep my attention level with his and not give myself away. "Visidia needs an heir—"

"Don't give me that." There's venom in his growl, raw and fresh. "We both know this is nothing more than a charade, Amora. And let's not forget I can feel your *soul*. You were searching for someone last night, but it wasn't a suitor. Every time someone introduced themselves to you, you were *disappointed*. You were looking for someone, and I want to know who. No more games."

My tongue grows heavy, useless as the weight of the truth settles between us.

"Why have you been lying to me?" he presses, and to that at least, I have an answer.

"Because I needed my space from you, Bastian." My words come in a rush of breath that nearly knocks me back. "I needed to feel like I'm my own person, again. Like you're not right there with me for every decision I make!"

"And you think I don't want that, too? For both of us?" He clenches his fists at his sides, trying to ease their angry shaking. "You're acting as though I've somehow wronged you, like this was *my* choice. I didn't put this curse on us, Amora; I don't want this any more than you do. But gods forbid you be honest with me, so that we can work together instead of you trying to do everything on your own. Gods forbid I don't have to be miserable every day, thinking that the woman I love isn't off pretending that she's searching for a *husband*! That I don't have to watch her parading around while the kingdom tries to murder her, and she won't even let me *try* to protect her."

The moment the words pass Bastian's lips he freezes, eyes going round as an owl's as he realizes what he's said. Even the room seems to sucks in a breath, still and waiting for someone to crack the silence.

My skin goes clammy, and I've no idea whether it's right to keep looking him in the eye, or turn away. But before I can decide, Bastian turns and groans into his palms, smoothing his hands over his hair in frustration.

"You know what, I'm not doing this right now. I hope you have a wonderful time with that pretty poster boy. He seems like a real charmer."

I think to stop him. The words might have even left my mouth, I'm not sure. But Bastian throws open the door regardless, storming down the hall and leaving two confused girls blinking back at me from behind the door.

"So," Shanty muses as she turns back at Bastian's retreating figure, then to me with a purse of her lips. "I take it that means you're ready for your date?"

Seething, I grab my cloak from the bed and jerk it over me, wishing I had Valukan magic so that I could light something on fire. "Let's get this over with."

Elias waits upon the powder-white sand, his lips pressed together as he paces small circles. He straightens when he catches sight of us, appearing almost surprised. "Amora! I read the papers this morning; how are you feeling? I tried to stop by your room to check on you myself, but that guard of yours gave me a rough time. I don't think he's keen on me." He looks surprisingly boyish, and my skin cools at the sight of him, remembering what Bastian had called him—pretty poster boy.

He wasn't exactly wrong. Yet while part of me wants to gloat in what is clearly his jealousy, the other part wants to track Bastian down and . . .

I'm not sure what. Set his coat on fire? Push him into the sea? Kiss that annoying face of his?

Gods, I hate the uncertainty.

Peering over my shoulder, Elias nods his head in greeting toward the two girls, though his attention lingers on Vataea a beat too long. Even if her clothing makes it impossible to see scars on her neck and thighs from her gills and fin, it's clear there's something different about her.

"Your chambermaids?" he asks.

Vataea's eyes narrow into dangerous slits. "If chambermaids are the ones who will tear your heart out with their teeth or put a dagger through your eye if you so much as look at the queen wrong, then yes. We're her chambermaids."

The knot in Elias's throat bobs as he swallows. "Not chambermaids, then. Duly noted."

I think to tell him not to worry, or that Vataea and Shanty are more bark than they are bite, but it'd be a lie too easily found out. So instead I loop my hand through his offered arm, though my heart is far from in it.

"I must admit that I was disappointed when I didn't see you again last night," he says as we start down the beach. "You

196

snuck away so quickly. But it'll be nice to have a day just for the two of us to tour the island."

There's a genuine excitement in his voice that I wish I could match. Last night, drunk off wine and apparently poison, touring the island with Elias had seemed like a wonderful idea. Now though, I'm too distracted with thoughts of Bastian.

That bastard said he *loved* me. But there's no way that's right. His emotions must be as muddled as mine, so how dare he say something like that? And then to just *leave*!

It takes all my power to tear my thoughts away from Bastian; to compartmentalize him away someplace else, so that I might focus on my time with Elias, who knows Curmana better than most, given his position. I came here to find Ornell Rosenblathe, and today I need to make some progress.

"Have you lived here all your life?" Vataea and Shanty are keeping an appropriate distance away, but I quiet my words regardless, letting this time between us feel more intimate. The more relaxed he is, the more information I can pry.

"All twenty-two years." His smile is far too charming. "I've traveled to most of the other islands, but Curmana is my home. Should anything happen to my sister, I'm on the lineup of potential advisers to take her place. So I try to stay on Curmana for the most part, to keep abreast with what's happening on the island."

Curiosity prickles my skin, but I don't let myself show it. Instead, I keep politely interested. "Anything interesting happen, lately?"

Something related to poison, perhaps?

It's possible he doesn't know about the seedy underbelly of his island, just as I was unaware of how bad things in the kingdom were getting while I was stuck on Arida. I watch his face for a sign, any break or hesitation that might show he's aware of something stirring in Curmana that has yet to be reported to royal officials. But his expression remains confident and unwavering, betraying nothing.

"Nothing too exciting, no. We have milder weather this far north, so we don't get the same storms that plague the southern islands. Revenue has continued to increase throughout the years as we expand our spas and inflate the prices of our more luxurious services. We're incredibly stable and self-sufficient, as we also produce the majority of the herbs and oils we sell right here on the island."

"What about the crime?"

And there it is. Brief and so fleeting I nearly miss it—a quick tic of his jaw.

"Pardon, Your Majesty?"

"The crime rate," I repeat. "What's it like?"

"I dare say Curmana is the safest places you'll ever visit. I recently visited Ikae, and it's astounding how much petty theft tourists get away with there. The tranquility here makes residents and tourists alike happy; because of it, our crime rates are low."

Curmanan residents eye Elias and me as we walk along the sleek white shore, the sand so powdery that I wonder if this is what the snow upon Zudoh might feel like. Most bow their heads, but there are a handful of children who gawk up at me, much to the horror of parents who hurriedly try to get them to dip their heads.

Shanty's watching them too, eyes narrowed as she scouts their faces, looking for others with enchantment magic who are only here to look for a story for tonight's gossip parchments. Briefly, I wonder what today's might say.

QUEEN AMORA AND LORD ELIAS
FREEBOURNE—WE HEAR THERE'S
SOMETHING IN CURMANA'S WATER.
COULD IT BE LOVE?

Or, perhaps:

A LORD OR A PIRATE—COULD ONE
OF THESE CHARMING BACHELORS BE
OUR NEW KING?

Before my face can give away my anger, I peel myself from those thoughts, refocusing on the mission at hand.

"We had a family friend from here who would always rave about how wonderful Curmana is." I make my voice light, as if recalling fond memories. "Are you familiar with the Rosenblathe family, by chance? Ornell Rosenblathe? He always told me about the food and spas, and that Curmana could make lying in a tub full of warm mud feel like the most luxurious thing ever. I'd love to see him while I'm here."

Everything in my body seizes when Elias squints his eyes, forehead creasing as he scans his thoughts. Hope balloons, threatening to burst within me. I clench my fists tight and dip my nails into my palms to contain it.

But it deflates when Elias puckers his lips and sighs. "Sorry. I know it's familiar, but I can't place where I've heard it."

I try not to let my disappointment show, left with no choice but to settle into our walk.

Curmana truly is another world. A wondrous, relaxing, beautiful world.

A group of tourists stretch themselves upon the sand, catching up on the latest parchments or tomes. Many wear giant hats and glasses to shade their eyes, while they cover their skin with loose pants and billowing tops. Curmanan workers in black linen use mind magic to float an assortment of goods around them, offering tourists food and drinks.

More tourists sit nestled comfortably beside a fire pit, while others in the distance relax upon flat cots, their bodies glistening as attendants massage oils into their skin and rest steaming stones upon their backs.

As relaxing as it may be, it's difficult not to notice how quiet all of Curmana is. In a way it reminds me of when I first met Zale in her camp back on Zudoh. Only this silence isn't made from fear. Because so many Curmanans use mind speak to communicate, the tourists have naturally followed their lead by keeping quiet. Even when they do speak aloud, their chatter is little more than a whisper.

"We could go in if you'd like," Elias offers as he catches me admiring a beautiful stone hut with steam billowing from within. "It's a building meant for meditation. It's supposed to help detox your mind and soul. Some claim to even use it to try to communicate with the gods."

I snort. "Like the gods would ever bother themselves with a human."

He laughs. "We'll pass on the steam room, then. No worries, there's more to see." Elias paves the way deeper into

Curmana, steering us away from the docks.

My morning is spent being toted around while I'm forced to pretend my head isn't pounding from the poison.

It's not that my time with Elia is *bad*, but the more touristy destinations we visit, the more my thoughts wander to what a date here with Bastian might be like. If I let him show me around his home island, Zudoh, he'd never show me places meant for tourists. He'd show me the cavern he used to explore as a child, or the best vantage point on the island. And even if it took us two hours to reach, it would be worth it. He'd never show me the places anyone could find; he'd show me the places that held small pieces of his soul.

Even here on Curmana, I'm certain he'd have far more fascinating things to show me than a quaint lunch establishment I couldn't eat at, or a journey through the various spas.

With Elias, I can't help but wonder—where's the fun on this island? Where's the underbelly? The gossip and the secrets of the island that you have to dig through the surface to find?

Being with Bastian has spoiled me; anything less than that doesn't even feel worth my time.

"That head of yours sure is up in those clouds," Shanty whispers as she cranes her neck at the sky, squinting against the sun. "If we look hard enough, do you think we might be able to find it?"

Focus pulled back to the world around me, I roll my eyes despite her grin. "Ha ha, funny."

A thicket of banana trees lies ahead in the distance, wildly overgrown with their large leaves hanging haphazardly. Beyond them, farther north, is a landscape so dense with flora that I can't see even so much as a gap within it.

"Up there's the marketplace," Elias offers, following my gaze. "Most of the locals live out this way. We try our best to ensure the area by the water stays quiet to maintain the peace for the tourists. Many of the locals like to live farther out; they can be noisier, and the rules are less strict. It's also closer to the marketplace, and any of the jobs that involve work in the jungle, like collecting herbs for Suntosan medicines."

"And for poisons," I grumble under my breath to Vataea, who straightens her shoulders and peers warily around us in response.

As the sand gives way to snaking roots and dead leaves that crunch beneath my boots, humble buildings take shape, marking what I know must be the edge of the market. At the base of it sits a small stone building decorated with moss and the leaves from hundreds of thick trees that loom over it. There's a tiny painting of a teacup and billowing steam on a hanging wooden sign over the door.

"This is one of my favorite places on the island," Elias says as he draws the creaking door open. "It's private, too. I figured it might feel more . . ."

"Intimate" is the word he's looking for, but my skin crawls at the idea of it.

All I hear are Bastian's words banging around in my skull.

The woman I love.

The woman I love.

I love.

I take a deep breath and try to clear my mind.

No matter how mouthwatering the scent of baking honey bread wafting from the tea shop, I'm about to suggest to Elias that we find another plan when Ilia's willowy, ice-spirit figure emerges from the store's depths. Elias stiffens immediately, clearly as surprised as I am.

"Lee?" He squints at his sister. "What are you doing here?"

"Looking for you." Even her voice is sharp as an icicle, impaling me. "As we discussed, you've duties to uphold today. You should be in the woods now, helping the rest of the gatherers. There's no time for . . . this." She waves her bony hand between us, the sharpness of her cheekbones deepening her scowl.

Elias looks mutinous. "Amora's only here for a few days—"

"I'm sure she'll understand." Ilia's eyes blaze so fiercely that I nearly draw a step back. There's something lethal in her eyes that wasn't there yesterday. Immediately I find myself wondering if she's angry I'm still here, today. If she's angry that I survived.

It's as though she's disgusted by the idea of her brother anywhere near me. Even Vataea and Shanty are rigid at my side, ready to intervene.

"I understand perfectly," I growl, suspicion itching at my skin. I could easily tell her to turn away and leave Elias and me, but even with the girls at my side it's not worth the risk. I won't put them into that situation when it's avoidable.

"Perhaps we could reschedule for dinner?" Regret fills Elias's voice. His shoulders slump, face apologetic.

"Perhaps," I say, though I'm not looking at him. I stare back at Ilia's pale, icy eyes as she holds her chin high and defiant, waiting for me to challenge her.

"I read the parchments this morning," she says coolly. "I'm glad you're feeling better, Your Majesty. Feel free to explore our humble island to your heart's content, but for now I must take Elias. I'm sure your chambermaids will be wonderful company."

Though Vataea scowls, Ilia doesn't see it. She turns instead to her brother, taking him by the arm and pulling him from me as though I'm diseased. She has him out the door within seconds, leaving the three of us in the middle of this small, empty tea shop. Only then do I notice the woman behind the counter, thin and elderly. Her eyes have rounded with surprise as we've caught her staring directly at me, looking as though she's about to faint.

In a croaking, nervous voice, she asks, "Tea, Your Majesty?"

TWENTY-ONE

"This might take a lot less time than I anticipated," Ferrick says, assessing the marketplace that lines the road.

Late that afternoon, after several hours of entertaining the shop owner by pretending to drink her tea—all but Shanty, anyway, who claimed to be immune to most poisons and was able to happily sample everything—the marketplace has grown busier.

It's built at the edge of the dense jungle, upon the meeting place of sand and root. While some merchants sell their wares from wooden huts, others lean against thick, gnarled trees. They use the canopy of leaves for shade, with their goods spread onto a blanket before them. But unlike Ikae's marketplace, here there are no shouting merchants touting overpriced snapper or yelling about their daily goods. No one is selling fine gowns, or sampling ale from a street full of competing vendors.

Curmana's marketplace, like the rest of the island, is so unsettlingly calm that I can't shake the nerves that skitter down my spine. It's not that people aren't talking; there's some chatter and laughter. Barter, even. But so many conversations are happening without words. I catch a couple locking eyes now and then, nodding along to something the other must silently be saying. A child runs, trying to play among the vendors. But before she can stray too far, her father uses levitation magic to lift the girl into the air and bring her back to his side. The girl does little more than blink, unsurprised, before darting away again.

If they're having a conversation, they too have it in silence. And while I admire the privacy of the magic, there's something odd about humans being so . . . . still.

"This place is horrifying." Bastian's voice is a low rasp, trying his best not to be heard amid the eerie silence. The loudest sounds come from the insects in the trees behind us. "Are you sure we're not trapped in a curse?"

This many silent bodies are more frightening than a curse could ever be, but I don't tell him that. Since what he said to me back in my room, we haven't so much as looked at each other.

From the corner of my eye I can barely glimpse the thick blond curls and the baby-blue eyes Shanty enchanted him with. He no longer has manicured stubble along his cheeks and jawline, but a full beard I can't help but stare at. I've never kissed someone with a full beard before, and I'm annoyingly curious to know what it feels like.

Bastian isn't the only one of us whose appearance has been altered with Shanty's enchantments. She's given herself flat brown hair and a meek appearance as to not make herself stand out. While she's tried to conceal some of Vataea's mermaid qualities, it hasn't fully worked. Her scars are concealed, but anyone who looks at Vataea—with her now long auburn hair, rounded eyes, and full pink cheeks—would surely still wonder how one person could be so beautiful.

Ferrick and Casem appear to be twins, both sporting heavy onyx robes that match the inky blackness of their hair.

206

Casem wears his short, while Ferrick's is long enough to tie into a knot at the back of his neck. His long face has been broadened, and his shoulders made leaner. Though I haven't seen myself in the mirror since Shanty altered our clothing and appearance outside the tea shop, there are loose red waves at my shoulders, and I know my face and body must be as cleverly disguised as everyone else's.

"We draw too much attention as a group," Bastian says. "It's time to split up. It'll be easier to find information that way. And if anything happens, Amora and I will be able to find each other."

At least our curse has one good use, I suppose. No matter where Bastian is, I can sense him like a lighthouse in a moonless night.

"Just don't go too far." My hands wrap around my stomach at the memory of the white-hot pain that comes when one of us strays too far from the other.

"Everyone plan to meet back here by sunset." Ferrick sets a hand over what I know must be the pommel of his sword, though it's hidden by the thick fabric of his robe. His enchanted blue eyes catch mine, waiting for me to nod before he relaxes.

Bastian clasps Ferrick on one shoulder and Casem on the other. "Let's get going. You three"—his eyes find mine for only the briefest second before he brushes hair from his face and turns away—"stay safe."

Vataea sets a hand on her hip. "As if I'd let anything happen."

And with that our group separates, diving farther into opposite ends of the marketplace. We pass several wooden huts that have been built into the trees along the jungle's entrance, painted white to stand out against the canopy of leaves and monstrous curving tree trunks. Mostly they're selling casual things, like spices for everyday cooking, medicines, or health elixirs. Shanty points to a bottle of wild carrot seed—a popular method to prevent pregnancy—and wags her brows at me teasingly.

"Focus," I growl back, ignoring the heat that rises to my neck and chest.

Aside from the lack of voices, nothing about this place feels strange or dangerous, and yet Bastian's words from last summer ring in my ears. *Every town has an underbelly. You just need to know where to look.*

"What are we meant to be looking for?" Vataea asks, batting gnats from her face.

I'm glad she asks, because while Shanty plods ahead, confident and determined, I've been trying to figure out the same thing.

"We're looking for something obvious," Shanty says, "but that's not quite right."

How helpful.

The longer we search, politely declining gentle offers of spices and elixirs, the clearer it becomes that I'm not the one in charge of this group. Far from meek girl she's glamoured herself to look like, Shanty hunts through the stalls like a predator starved for prey. Vataea and I exchange a look as we watch her, neither one of us having any option but to follow her lead.

Shanty pretends to examine a cart full of produce; as she's admiring a small melon with one hand, she slips a peach into her pocket with the other. Only when we're out of sight does she retrieve it and take a bite, wiping at the juice that runs down her lips and chin.

"You do that just like Bastian." I recall the deftness of his fingers. The clever way he can slip a coin from one hand to the other before there's time to blink.

Shanty's laugh is hearty and genuine before she takes another bite and says through it, "Who do you think taught him?"

Surprise has me nearly tripping over my own feet. It's no secret that Bastian and Shanty knew each other in the past. When we first met, she'd told Bastian that he owed her money, which led me to believe it'd been a fleeting thing. I thought perhaps he'd spent a few days on Ikae and happened to run into her, or that he'd hired her for a job. But there's more to it than that.

Shanty tosses the peach pit onto the sand. "It's when we were kids, back before the barracudas even had a name. I'd left my home the season prior, and he'd been on that ship of his for about the same time.

"We met in the market," she continues, rubbing her peach-dampened hands on her pants. "He was vying for some bread, and I was eyeing a pair of pink diamond earrings. I was hungry too, don't get me wrong, but I thought Bastian used to think too small. Why go for the bread when you can go for something that could buy you a whole bakery? I didn't have full control over my magic yet, but I'd learned from a young age how to alter my face enough to prevent anyone from recognizing me. After enchanting myself, I'd go into the stores and pretend to shop. Sometimes, when I had spare money, I actually *would* buy something, so they'd grow to trust one of my faces and not pay close attention when I got too close to the jewels.

"I'd spent a week trying to figure this shop out. I went there every day with a different face to see who was working, and figure out which shopkeeper would make the easiest mark. Every day Bastian was there too, roaming the streets, stealing small things like pastries and fruit. I didn't think he'd ever noticed me; I was used to being the one who did the watching, since no one was ever able to recognize me. Except, one day, Bastian did." Shanty shakes her head when she says it, a smile playing on her lips.

"The second I finally got those earrings, I booked it back to where I was staying—I think it was some shack that'd been out of business and was having a difficult time being sold. I didn't think I'd been followed, and yet there was Bastian. He showed up at my place to tell me he'd seen me use magic to enchant my face back on that first night, and that he'd known it was me ever since. While I'd been watching him, thinking him so silly for going after such trivial objects, he was the one who'd been in it for the long con. He knew I had the earrings, and had seen what I could do. If he wanted to, he could have told the authorities and been rewarded for it. Those earrings weren't the first pair of jewels I'd stolen; shops were complaining about theft, and soldiers were cracking down to try to catch me. He knew this, I'm sure, but when I asked if he was going to turn me in, he laughed and said not if we partnered up. Clever bastard. I didn't have any choice. I tried to give him the slip a few times at first, but he always managed to find me again. He was far more precocious than he let on."

It takes me a moment to realize I'm smiling, and I try to smother it before either of the girls can see it. The Bastian from her stories sounds exactly like the pirate I first fell for.

"What happened?" It's Vataea who asks, keeping her melodic voice low in public. "Why did the two of you separate?" I'm curious too, and Shanty notices.

"It was never anything romantic, if that was your impression. Men aren't my thing. Bastian and I had a business partnership for a while, but he never settled on Ikae the same way I did. He left every night to sleep on his ship, and returned early the next morning ready to work. He kept a lot of secrets, but it worked because I did, too. Neither of us ever pressed each other for answers; having a partner was too beneficial, and I imagine we didn't want to ruin it. Stealing by myself worked, but there's so much more to be done with two people. One of us could be the distraction, the other a thief. We started stealing not just small jewels, but also weapons. Expensive clothing. Everything.

"As Bastian got older though," she continues, "we realized that smile of his could win him more than petty distraction; it could win him hearts. He started wooing girls from affluent families, and I think both of us started to realize that he no longer needed someone to help him alter his face. He knew how to use his own too well. He took whatever he could from Ikae, and left when there was nothing else for him. He stopped needing me, which sounds bad, but I wasn't too upset." She shrugs. "We never had what I'd call a true friendship; I don't think Bastian knew how to have one of those. But working with him made me realize how much *I* enjoyed working with others, and that there could be success in numbers. So when he left, I found others who were living on the streets like we'd been, and I started the barracudas."

"What about the money you said he owed you?" I press. "Back when we first met?"

"He used to stop by the lounge occasionally. One of those

days, he stole my damned earring." I'm surprised when she says it with a laugh. "Those pink diamond ones, from the night we first met. I never ended up selling them; I loved them too much. I still have one, but Bastian managed to steal the other that night."

I recall seeing an earring like that last summer, back when I'd been working on creating Rukan at his desk. At the time I thought little of it, suspecting it was nothing more than a lost memento from a past relationship, or perhaps expensive jewels he was preparing to sell whenever he next had a chance.

Bastian wouldn't have been against making friends. I know more than anyone how much he wanted to settle, but also how he didn't believe he could. If he spent that long with Shanty, it wasn't because he needed her or felt forced. It was because he wanted to make it work.

He cared for Shanty, which is likely not only why he took that earring, but also why he still has it. As a reminder, in case he never had the chance to see her again.

As much of that pirate charade as he puts on, Bastian's a good man.

"Amora?" Vataea says again, her honey-rich voice warming my skin. "You all right?"

I start to wave her off, but as I go to lift my hand, something stops me. I trust Vataea to give me the truth more than I trust anyone. Mermaids, from what I've been able to tell, rarely lie. They've little sense to conceal the truth simply to spare someone's feelings.

"Do you think that, without the curse, I'd be with Bastian right now?" The only way for me to get the words out is to force them quickly, not lingering to think about what I'm saying. "Do you think I love him?"

She stares me dead in the eyes, and without so much as blinking, says, "I think you already know the answer." She continues past me without looking back, not realizing that I've lost my breath.

How can she be so sure?

"There's no time for personal revelations." Shanty knocks her hip against mine to get my attention and nods her head forward. "See that up there? On that merchant's sleeve? She's our mark."

It takes me longer than I care to admit before I see what she's referring to—a golden zolo leaf on the sleeve of the merchant's long onyx robe.

"*That's* the symbol we're looking for?" Vataea asks, voicing my same skepticism. "Those leaves are on everything, here."

"That's the beauty of it." Shanty's voice is practically admiring. "Zolo leaves are known for having two veins down their center. You'll notice that this symbol, however, only has one. The smartest way to hide something is by concealing it in plain sight."

I blink, realizing she's right. But without her there, I never would have noticed it.

The woman bearing the symbol smiles the same polite smile as the others, though hers doesn't quite reach her eyes. "Rosemary bread?" She doesn't have a proper merchant booth. Instead, she sits against the trunk of a gnarled tree, a wooden basket of bread in front of her.

Shanty takes a loaf and lifts it to her nose. "Must be a hard business right now, given the competition. I think we've passed at least four bread stands so far." From the corner of my eye, I notice Vataea slowly drawing back, positioning herself several

213

paces to Shanty's left. She nods to me, and I follow her lead by positioning myself opposite her, to Shanty's right. Together we form a triangle to block the woman in against the tree.

"When you sell the best, visitors still come," the merchant says.

"That's a beautiful robe you have on. I love the embroidery." Shanty takes a tentative bite, considering it for only a moment before she spits it onto the ground. "Yup, this is the one. What is that? Moonseed? Must be a mild dose, you can barely taste it over the rosemary. Is it supposed to be a light sedative?"

The merchant's face drops, and with a heavy sigh she says, "You're that girl everyone warned me about, aren't you? The face-shifter? We're not supposed to sell to you anymore."

Shanty grins wide, as if pleased to have done something that warranted someone needing to be warned about her. "Good luck with that. Take us to your shop and make this easy, otherwise I'll have to convince you. And you'll find I can be incredibly persuasive."

"You're a *thief*. If you think we're going to entertain you after you stole the entire—"

Shanty tuts her tongue. "Ah ah ah. Let's not discuss the past when we're in the present." Her eyes flicker to me, then to the dagger at my hip, and she bounces a brow. I roll my eyes and draw Rukan, only because it's the flashier of the two. I grip it tight in my palms, and the merchant's throat bobs.

Shanty reaches for the weapon, and I begrudgingly hand it over. Immediately I feel naked, now without not only my magic, but also my next best source of protection. I try to steady my breaths as they sharpen, anxiety taking hold.

My vision begins to tunnel, but before I can spiral, I

catch sight of Vataea. Her eyes bore into mine, and I try again to steady myself.

I try to think of her laugh, of her song that shifts the sea and steers our ship. Of the one I hear her singing on the bow as she sits above the figurehead late in the evening, when she thinks no one's listening.

I don't speak the language or understand their words, but I play the melody to myself in my head until my chest is no longer so tight, inflating with the full breaths I'm finally able to take. I lift my chin higher and stand taller, giving Vataea a small nod.

I'm okay.

She nods back, and though it's clear from the tension in her shoulders that she doesn't believe me, she leaves it alone.

"You're familiar with poison," Shanty casually tells the merchant as she brandishes Rukan, admiring the strange flecks of iridescent blue and the jagged, hooked navy tip. "Tell me, have you heard the legends of the Lusca? Did you know each of its tentacles has barbed hooks full of lethal poison unlike any other kind? It's unlikely they'll ever figure out an antidote; the only way to keep from dying is to cut off your infected limb, or drain your blood before the poison can spread too quickly. This blade *is* the barbed hook of the Lusca, because this woman here, our *queen*, bested it on the sea." When Shanty tips her head toward me, having far too much fun with this, the merchant blanches. Her fingertips dig into the earth and she readies her feet, clearly preparing to flee.

"Just one slice of the pretty neck of yours, just one *jab*, and you're as good as—"

The merchant jolts upright, but I'm ready for her. I lunge,

knocking her feet out from under her in one swift kick. She hits the sandy grass face-first, and before she can push herself back up, I'm straddling her back with one hand wrapped around the hilt of my steel dagger. The other is fisted in her hair, pulling her face from the sand.

"Next time keep your speech shorter," I grumble at Shanty, who makes a huffing noise under her breath.

"It takes a lot of work to come up with creative threats," she sighs. "They ought to be appreciated."

Heat prickles my neck, keeping me focused. My blood pounds, veins bursting with tiny jolts of eager energy. For the first time in gods know how long, I feel *alive*. Though in the back of my mind I know it's wrong—though I know I *shouldn't* love the fight—I do.

I crave this feeling more than any other.

The merchant curses and tries to take a swipe at me with her long nails. One of them is tipped with thin, elegant metal that extends from her finger like a long, embellished fingernail. She scratches it against my trousers, and though she doesn't break through the fabric, it begins to sizzle. Whatever poison is in the tip of that metallic finger *burns*, and I curse as it eats its way through my pants quickly, knowing that can only mean it'll go through my skin, next.

I drop my hand from her hair and slide the dagger across my pants, tearing off the fabric before it can melt into my leg. The merchant tries to use my distraction to throw me off balance and escape, but Vataea has her foot pressed against the merchant's neck before she can flee. Her golden eyes are nothing short of lethal.

"I'm starting to get hungry." Vataea's voice is pure frost.

"Try that again, and I'll skin you alive and filet you like a fish."

"Ooh, good one, V," Shanty chimes in. "Make sure to remember that one. We'll have to use it again."

Skin pale, the merchant stills. "You're not human."

"How kind of you to notice," Vataea says. Her words are as barbed and lethal as those golden eyes. "Now if you value your heart, you'll make this easy. My friends and I have some questions for you." She removes her foot from the merchant's neck, and I ease off the woman's back enough for her to gather her breath and straighten.

"I'll take you there," the merchant rasps, rubbing her throat. "And I'll tell you whatever you want to know. Just hurry, please, before someone else sees us."

∾
TWENTY-TWO∙

Humidity clings to my skin as we journey into the jungle, venturing far past the marketplace and deep into the thicket of overgrown trees and lush flora. Buzzing insects swarm us, drawn by the sweetness of our sweat, and I bat them away with a steady stream of curses as they try to get a taste of my skin.

The deeper into the jungle we journey—and the wider my distance from Bastian grows—the heavier my limbs become as my curse settles into my bones.

"How much farther?" I demand as the merchant hesitates by a misshapen trunk, inspecting its bark. Squinting my eyes, I notice a tiny zolo leaf has been crudely carved onto it. The tension in my shoulders eases. The merchant isn't misguiding us; she's searching. In a jungle this massive, it's impossible to tell anything apart. Wherever we're going, it must be well hidden.

"We're nearly there."

To Shanty I ask, "How'd you find this place last time?"

"I've never been to the base before." A mosquito takes a swipe at her neck and she smacks it dead, grimacing at the guts on her palm. "I glamoured myself to look like one of the merchants and stole their wares." She grins when my brow arches. "A girl's got to work, Amora. No one got hurt who didn't deserve it."

There's a pang in my chest from my missing soul magic; what I wouldn't give to take a peek into Shanty's soul and see what it's like in there.

As we travel deeper into the jungle, the canopy over us thickens, clotting the sky. No sunlight sneaks through the branches, making it impossible to decipher how long we've been out here or how close it may be to sunset. My heart gives an anxious squeeze and I turn to the merchant. "For your sake, you'd better hurry."

While her footsteps hasten, the woman scowls. I drag myself after her, boots struggling to keep pace through the thick damp moss and overgrown weeds that reach out to ensnare us. Vataea, after perhaps her fourth time tripping over something, snarls and stabs her blade into the weeds.

"You know they're inanimate, right?" Shanty asks casually. "That they're not actually *trying* to hurt you?"

Regardless, Vataea spits at the ground. "The land is too cluttered. At least with the sea there's empty space. You can see where you're going."

I shudder as I recall the time she brought me into the sea with her, so that we could get past Kaven's barrier and onto Zudoh. The sea had felt vast, but it certainly hadn't felt empty. Its depths held too many unknowns, things I couldn't see but knew were watching.

Fortunately for Vataea, there's not much longer to travel. The merchant raps her knuckles on the bark of another tree, and this time the three of us still when hollowness echoes back. The merchant digs her fingers into the gray bark and peels it back as if to open the tree.

"Stairs?" Vataea squints her eyes, keeping her blade drawn at her side as she approaches the merchant. Rukan held tightly in my own hand once more, I follow and peek down into the base of the tree. Sure enough, there are stairs built from the trunk, lowering into the roots of the tree and descending into the darkness of what appears to be a hollowed-out room.

It's ingenious. A person could search forever and never find this place.

"I'll go first," I offer. "If she's a mind speaker, there's a chance we'll have company down there." Though I make a move to climb down the stairs, Vataea presses a hand to my chest to hold me back.

"You're the queen," she says simply, flat and factual. "You need to survive."

Not about to take no for an answer, she steps before me and descends the stairs. I'm quick to follow her, with Shanty and the merchant tailing us.

"Try anything funny," Shanty warns the woman in a deceptively pleasant voice, a thin knife pressed against her back as they walk, "and you'll be dead before your next breath."

The stairs are creaky makeshift boards of rotting wood atop earth, hardly stable. We take them slowly, weapons held at the ready despite the silence that waits for us.

The tunnel is a stifling blackness, so stagnant my lungs tighten and so dark that I test each of my footsteps before making them. Only when the stairs end and the floor levels out do my eyes adjust enough to make out the shape of a small wooden table and the oil lamp beside it. With practiced ease, the merchant lights the lamp, bathing the tight quarters in a dim amber glow.

No faces wait to attack us. No weapons are drawn, aside from our own, and no fights are imminent.

"They're over there." The merchant nods to a small room carved out in the corner, and I exchange a look with Vataea. Her knowing stare confirms my own suspicions—something here isn't right. This is too easy.

"Don't linger," I tell her. "We need to hurry and get out."

Vials of liquid poisons and cotton pouches stuffed with powders fill the walls, each of them labeled not with what's in them, but what they do. My skin crawls as I realize there's a tiny skull symbol on the label of more than half of them, and already I'm coming up with a hundred different ways in which I'd like to burn this place to the ground. To think that such a place could exist right under my nose.

Had Father known about any of this? After everything, I wouldn't be surprised if he did. Just how long has the Montara family allowed this kingdom to destroy itself? With each passing day, it feels like my duty to repair it is getting that much harder.

"Someone tried to kill our queen." Shanty skims the shelves, not bothering to be sly when she slips three different vials and two pouches of powders into her pockets, much to the merchant's protest. I bite the inside of my cheek, hating that I wonder what she intends to use them for. Shanty's proven nothing but helpful so far, and I pay her too well for her to be a threat to me.

Unless someone were to offer her more . . .

I hate that I think it, and yet Vataea watches the face-shifter as intently as I do. Her eyes are pinched, trying to decipher what, exactly, Shanty's taking. The air around Shanty grows fuzzy as she paces, and I ignore the dull throbbing of my temples as the poison from last night acts up.

"We think someone snuck something into her food," Shanty says. "It would need to have been something easily masked."

The merchant snorts. "You think someone would be able to do that at a party? To sneak something into *her* food, specifically? There'd be too many people. Too many risks. More people would be sick."

Rukan's weight is suddenly heavy in my hands. "If not in the food or wine, then what?"

"What were your symptoms?" The merchant examines the shelves, squinting at their labels in the dim light. Vataea keeps close to her, inspecting the vials with sour lips.

"I was throwing up blood, and everything felt like it was spinning. I woke up feeling like I hadn't drunk water in a year, and last night, no matter what I ate, it wasn't enough. By the end of the night, I couldn't keep sense of what was happening. I passed out."

"That rules out a bloodstream poison. The timing is too long for that, and you're back on your feet too quickly." She heads to a different shelf instead, still squinting. "It could have been an ingested poison, but . . . no. Too risky. It would've had to enter the body in another way. Perhaps—"

"Through the skin." As soon as the words leave Shanty's lips, my stomach drops with understanding.

My bath. Something was in the oils and the tonics I put in the water. The ones I breathed in through the bath's steam, and soaked my body in.

The one Lady Ilia had prepared for me when I arrived on Curmana.

I hadn't thought anything of it when I showed up to my

room with the bath already drawn for me. I'm the queen, after all. That's normal enough.

But it hadn't been someone trying to make a strong first impression; someone was trying to kill me.

I grab hold of a shelf to steady myself, knocking into it so fiercely that one of the vials rolls off and topples onto the floor, shattering shards of glass dripping with fluorescent-yellow liquid.

The merchant shuffles through several more shelves until she makes a clucking noise with her tongue and draws a vial, having found what she was looking for.

"Did it smell like this?" She offers me the bag, but Shanty takes it first and draws a deep breath before passing it to me.

It smells like lemongrass and sage.

Bile rises to my throat. "Who was the last person you sold that to?"

The merchant's face remains impassive. "It must have been a while ago. I can't remember—"

I slam a fist against the shelf, letting more vials shatter to the floor.

"I'm not playing games." I grab the merchant by the hand and yank her forward, ignoring her sharp breath and plea of protest as I draw Rukan along the back of her index finger, pressing the hooked blade deep enough for her blood to bubble up. Lines of blue crisscross immediately over her skin as the poison enters her bloodstream. She screams, and I stuff my hand into her mouth to smother the sound. When she bites down, I press Rukan deeper into her finger, until her biting breaks into sobs as the blade nearly cuts clean through.

"You have one minute to give me a name." I wrench my hand from her mouth, and the moment she starts to scream, my knee finds her stomach and knocks the wind from her lungs.

One life is not more important than the kingdom. If I die, so does the people's chance at freedom. Unlike the fight on Kerost, here I can and will attack freely after what she's done, out of sight from any wandering eyes.

Slowly, ensuring the merchant feels every inch of this blade, I drag it across a second finger.

"The more poison that's in your blood, the quicker it works. You try that again, and you won't get another chance to speak. I'll cut your throat."

She tries to glare at me through watering eyes, but the fear is too potent as I steady Rukan against her neck. She trembles, her resolve splintering.

"Someone ordered them a few days ago, that's all I know! They never came to the shop, but they knew who I was. We used mind speak to communicate, and they hid their face with a cape. We exchanged goods, that's it."

I don't remove my weapon, but instead press it deeper against her skin. "For your sake, I hope you think of something else to give us."

"Amora—" Vataea starts, but I don't turn back.

Panic quickens the merchant's breath and makes her skin clammy against my hands. "B-blond! I saw blond hair, and they were tall. And . . . gods, I don't know anything else! I think their voice had been enchanted somehow; it was different every time I spoke to them. But I never saw a face, I swear."

I draw back to look at the other two. "It would have been someone who knew we were coming. They'd have known which room I'd be in."

"*Amora*." Vataea's voice is tense now, her eyes on the

stairs. "She said they communicated through mind speak."

The implication in those words stills me. Dread sinks its way from my fingers to my toes, and my grip on Rukan falls lax.

"We need to get out of here." The merchant hadn't been lost through the jungle after all. She'd been stalling. "V, Shanty, go!" These tight quarters are the last place we can afford getting sucked into a fight.

The girls don't hesitate. They sheathe their weapons and dart for the stairs, and I jerk Rukan back from the merchant, whose head falls back with a cold, pained laugh.

"I'd always heard our queen was vicious," she snarls. "I should have given that customer a stronger poison."

I leave her on the floor and take hold of the oil lamp.

"We're not going without you," Vataea warns from the base of the stairs, beside a fidgeting Shanty who very much appears to be having a mental struggle over that promise. "What are you doing?"

I look to the wall of powders and poisons. I might not be able to stop these poisons from being made, but I can certainly stall their sales.

"If you make it out of here alive, good luck cutting off your own hand," I tell the merchant. "That'll be the only way to stop the poison."

The woman stumbles to her feet, rivulets of fresh blood trailing like wine from her fingertips. She makes a choking sound as I kick the shelves, letting the vials fall and shatter.

I don't turn to look at her horror. Instead, I send a prayer to the gods, toss the lamp onto the leaking poisons, and turn to run as fast as my legs will carry me, pushing Shanty and Vataea ahead. Thankfully it takes longer than I expect for the poisons and oil to catch fire, but the explosion nearly knocks the ground out from under my feet when I'm halfway up the steps. One of us screams in the darkness, and the next thing I know the blackness is awash in snarling red flames.

The merchant stumbles after us as Vataea kicks open the makeshift door, pushing open the trunk. She reaches for Shanty and me, dragging us out. I barely have time to pull the merchant through before Vataea slams the door back shut as if in hope to snuff out the fire.

Rukan's poison is tearing its way through the woman; navy lines make a feast of her skin, devouring her fingers and spreading through her arms. If she's to save her life, she'll need to work fast. But beyond pulling her out before the flames could make a meal of her, I'm through helping. She dug this grave herself.

At some point in our distraction, Shanty's enchantment wore off. I don't notice until she stumbles to me and lets the warmth of her magic settle into my skin like melting candle wax, coughing. In my periphery I see she's made my hair appear to be a warm copper red, and has tightened it back into curls. From where she touches, I know she's altering the shape of my jaw and my nose before masking my clothing.

Her work with Vataea is swift, making the mermaid's face smaller and rounder, and her hair a warm brown. She works on herself last, aging her skin, tiring it with heavy bags under her eyes, and lightening her hair to a short crop of gray.

"You horrify me," I tell her as I get my bearings. My eyes sting from smoke and poison, whether from last night or from breathing in fumes, I can't be sure. "The boys' disguises will have worn off as well. We need to hurry, and—"

A blow to my face strikes hard, making me stumble. Gasping, my hand flies to my aching jaw on instinct, anticipating blood. But there's nothing there, and no threat stands before me.

"Did anyone see—"

Another blow. This time it knocks the wind from my lungs, and I clutch my arms tight around myself, hunting for the source through watering eyes.

Realization strikes a beat too late. My breaths hitch into sharp, tiny breaths. It's not me who's being hit—it's Bastian.

"The boys are in trouble."

∾

TWENTY-THREE

Though my body protests, aching with pain that's not my own, I force my burning legs into a sprint. Neither of the girls asks questions, keeping close as I break through the jungle. Unlike on our way in, I'm not lost. My soul knows where to go; it's my body that's struggling to keep up.

I feel us fast approaching the others when all breath is stripped from my lungs. I drop to my knees, clutching my throat. Darkness plagues my hazy vision, reminding me of the time I was in the water with the Lusca, drowning as the ocean held me in its clutches.

And then it's just gone. I clutch desperately at the roots beneath me as I gasp in my breaths.

Bastian's suffocating.

"Keep going," I rasp, shaky as I drag myself from the tree and force one foot in front of the other until I can regain the ability to run. "They're close. Keep sharp—"

Another wave of breathlessness hits, and I start to sink when the other two hook their arms beneath mine and haul me up between them until I can steady my trembling knees once more.

Damn this blasted curse.

My chest seizes, skin warming in a sign I know means Bastian's near. But the jungle is dense and dark beneath the

228

canopy of thick leathery leaves, and I can't see him.

Why can't I see him?

"Look out!" It's Ferrick's voice, but the warning comes too late. Oversize roots rip from the ground beneath me, forcing us back. They lift into the air, and I realize what they're doing just in time to push Shanty and Vataea back. The roots triple in size before they smack onto the ground at full force, striking me hard in the chest. I wheeze, but there's little time to gather myself before more roots are torn up, stretching and elongating as they reach to ensnare us.

"That's enchantment magic," Shanty whispers, awestruck. She shrinks back, narrowly avoiding the roots that wrap around my legs, slicing her knife through them to free me. Quickly, she reaches into a pocket and draws out one of the poached vials of poison with a skull on the label. She dunks several needles into it, then pins them against the underside of her fish bone bracelet. Two of the needles, however, she keeps tucked between her fingers.

"And levitation magic, by the looks of it." I drag myself closer to them, throat raw.

"Which one of you is the queen?" The low, familiar voice twists my chest, creating knots that threaten to steal my breath. "Show yourself and I'll let everyone else go."

Before I can say anything, Vataea's nails are digging into my wrists. "Not one word."

When none of us step forward, there's a break in the canopy overhead and a shift of movement. I clutch Rukan's hilt tight when I see them—the boys hover in midair, suffocated by the vines that threaten to drop them at any given moment.

If they were dropped, Ferrick might stand a chance with

his restoration magic, and Casem could use his affinity to air to cushion the blow, but it would undoubtedly kill Bastian.

"Stay back! It's—" Bastian's words are cut off as a vine snaps from around him and whips to his mouth, lodging itself in his throat. He chokes on it, gagging. I *feel* Bastian's pain in my bones, like it's my own. It takes everything in me not to show that pain. Not to choke on the ghost of the vines squirming in my throat.

I won't reveal my curse before my enemy. Besides, I don't need Bastian to tell me who I'm fighting. With a pit in my stomach, I realize I already know. While several people knew I was coming and which room I'd be staying in, only one person was in Ikae recently, and would have had the chance to study enchantment magic.

"Stop being a coward and show yourself, Elias." I wrench my hand from Vataea's and step forward. Shanty's enchantment magic may be all over my skin, but Elias takes the gamble that it's truly me. Perched upon a too-thick branch, he uses levitation magic to float his body to the ground, hazy white eyes locked to mine.

"I was hoping you'd be dead before morning." His voice thins. "You're smarter than I gave you credit for."

"That's what all the boys tell me." I clutch Rukan close, trying to figure out how to get near enough to strike. "I thought you practiced mind speak."

"Have you never considered there are a few of us who practice both?" His pride is sickening.

I hate that I scream when the ground falls out beneath me, my body yanked forward by his levitation magic. When he catches sight of Rukan, however, he gives pause to whatever idea he'd been brewing and drops me back to my feet. Behind us, there's a sharp whooshing in the air followed by both a scream and a series of vibrant curses as the boys tumble to the ground. They fall so swiftly that my entire body seizes; Casem barely has the chance to cup his hands around his lips and blow, creating a gust of air that knocks Ferrick and Bastian to the side seconds before they hit.

But there's little time to protect himself. He's barely able to cushion the blow, hitting hard enough for his scream to tell me he's broken something, but not so hard that the impact kills him.

Elias's frown deepens at their safe landing, and his frustration is enough to give me pause—Elias is no fool. I've been in enough fights to know not to take risks when you don't know your opponent's magic. He knew nothing of these three, and yet he risked allowing them to fall back onto the battlefield and out of his clutches.

At once I think back to Ferrick trying to learn mind speak on *Keel Haul*, remembering the blood that poured from his nose and the headaches Casem nurses when he uses the magic too frequently.

New magic takes growing into; it's taxing on the body. And Elias is no exception to this rule; he's revealed the flaw of his magic too easily—it has limits. Weight, time, or distance; one or all of those factors prevented Elias from being able to fight me without releasing the boys.

This fight won't be easy, but Elias isn't invincible.

"Why are you doing this?" I have to dig to find my voice. "I'm trying to *help* Visidia."

His response doesn't come with anger, but with deep,

unsettling resentment. "Do you really think *you're* what's best for Visidia? For centuries my island has been at peace, in spite of your family's rule. We've taken every precaution to protect ourselves and maintain that. But from the moment you took the throne, you've been a threat to Curmana. You're encroaching on our independence. Our power. You're the last thing this kingdom needs."

"Your *power*?" I find the steel in my voice and bite into it. "What about the power of the other islands? Should your stability mean their ruin? Why should they have to struggle, just so you can be comfortable? Look at Kerost—having multiple magics is *helping* them."

He snaps his hand to the side, irate. "You said yourself that Curmana has always been self-sufficient. Why can't the other islands be the same? Why must we share our resources, our strength, because we are forced to live under your rule? Why can't we govern ourselves?"

My throat's dry, aching from the smoke and the vines that had suffocated Bastian. I try to speak, but find I have no answer. Only a question. "You want Curmana to secede?"

"I want *every* island to secede." He spits the words, tensed and seething. "I'm tired of seeing my island responsible for the lives of others. We work hard; why shouldn't we reap our own benefits? Why should we have to share them?"

"I don't understand how you can be so callous that you're willing to watch others suffer when you have the ability to help them."

"And I don't understand how your family has managed to convince an entire kingdom into following the Montaras for centuries when you've done nothing for us! We don't need you."

Try as I might, my mind struggles to keep up with his words, still lingering on the idea behind them. I've never considered it seriously, but Elias's words strike hard—why *does* the kingdom need one ruler?

To keep them safe with the royal soldiers? To ensure safety in the prisons? To be the deciding factor of passing laws?

What do we do for the islands that they can't do individually? Am I doing any good for my people at all?

Heavy footsteps distract me, and I turn in time to see Bastian's broadsword raised in preparation of an attack. But his movements are too slow, and it's with a sinking realization that I can *feel* the poison coursing through his body, slowing him. Though I know it's not within me, it bites all the same, making me sluggish. If it comes down to physical combat between Elias and me, there's no way I'll win. Lack of magic aside, this curse has hazed my mind and made my body weak from the poison inking through Bastian's veins. If I'm going to end this, I'll need to be quick.

"If you died, it would be enough to stir the kingdom," Elias says, using his magic to pull the vines protectively around him. They swell until they're thick as trunks, hovering over us. "We could start a revolution of freedom for each of our islands. We'd be responsible for our island, and no one else."

His conviction gives me pause; the confidence in his words and the way he squares his shoulders reminds me of Kaven. Of someone who perhaps once truly did have a sound idea, but who has lost themselves in their ideologies.

"You don't want freedom." I take a step forward as he appraises me with caution. "You want power." Even without my magic, I will not stall. As I lift Rukan, I see in my mind's eye all the blood this blade has spilt. I may be weak, but I am not helpless. I will defeat him.

The next step I take, wind rushes from my lungs and I'm jerked off my feet, reeling toward the wall from his levitation magic. Casem reaches up, trying to stop it from happening, but his body buckles, unable to summon the air in time. My back slams into a tree and I cry out as blinding pain tears through me. My shoulder shatters, cracking in a dozen places.

Vataea and Shanty are there to catch me, while Ferrick still hasn't moved from the vines constricting him. His eyes are shut, and my heart seizes, thinking the worst. But then I notice the creases of concentration between his brows, and it dawns that he's not hurt—he's healing himself from the same poison Bastian's fighting against. It's something Casem is undoubtedly struggling with, too.

I look at Elias as Bastian moves behind him, though I've no idea how he's still standing. It must be adrenaline alone that has him taking another swing at Elias, though the strike never lands. There are vines at Elias's back within seconds, smacking Bastian in the jaw and winding tightly around him. He hits the ground with a pain so fierce that I grab my chest, gasping against it and my throbbing jaw.

As he struggles to get back onto his feet, body shaking, I realize three things:

First, there are enough of us to outnumber Elias. But because he practices mind speak, we need to keep him sufficiently distracted so he can't call for backup.

Second, Bastian needs healing for the poison that's clawing its way up his throat, threatening to overtake both of us at any moment.

Third, I know how to win this fight.

As Shanty tries to help me back to my feet, I grip her hand and squeeze it tight, slipping the bracelet from her wrist as slyly as I can manage. Her eyes flash with a warning to be careful, but she doesn't ask questions or let on as I slip the needles tucked within it between my knuckles.

"You bastard." Bastian, stubborn as he is, has his sword raised against Elias once more. He looks as he did with Kaven, rage in his eyes and his body poised to kill. His movements sway, and though there's no way he'll win, he refuses to back down, buying us time. "You'll burn for what you tried to do to her."

"After today, there will be no more *trying*." Without lifting a finger, Elias knocks Bastian to the ground once more. Steel flashes as he draws a thin blade from his belt.

Fear crashes through me cold as ice as he ducks over Bastian, brandishing the blade. I rush to my feet, breathless, but I'll never make it in time.

And yet it isn't fear I sense swelling from Bastian. It's pride.

Slick as an eel, he kicks Elias in the chest and draws a push blade from somewhere in his coat, ramming it into Elias's hand.

Elias stumbles back, clutching his bloody hand to his chest. "You'll die for that!"

Bastian casts me a fleeting, almost apologetic look and reaches to his side—to a satchel at his hip.

Understanding dawns the moment before I feel the pulse of my magic as it flares to life within him, white-hot and all-consuming. It's fire in my veins, scorching through me until I'm on my knees, suffocating beneath it.

I try to take control of it; to open myself up to its familiar

235

pressure. But the magic refuses to obey. Because it's not *me* the magic rests within. It's Bastian, and he has no idea how to wield it.

He clutches a shard of bone in his fists, coating it with Elias's blood from the push blade, and I buckle. His muscles tense with determination, yet his confusion rolls over me like a wave as he stares at the bone.

You'll know, I'd told him. *If you ever have to use it, gods forbid, you'll know how.*

And with a sickening understanding, he does.

Bastian puts the end of the bloodied bone in his mouth, clenches his teeth down on it, and snaps it roughly in half, splintering the bone and nearly taking one of his own teeth with it.

Elias's scream is followed by a series of snaps as his arm contorts so grotesquely that the bones protrude from his skin. He roars, dropping to his knees as Bastian spits the bone out, gagging on the blood that coats his lips and tongue.

The breaths Elias takes are through gritted teeth, seething and desperate. Lost to the heat and power of the magic, Bastian shakily draws another bone from his satchel, but buckles before he can use it, the soul magic raging against his body.

Elias's hazy eyes turn white as milk as he jerks his uninjured hand out, and once again I'm being pulled against my will. He drags me across the jungle floor until his hand is around my neck, squeezing as he pins me down and stabs his blade into the meat of my thigh.

"Make another move," he seethes between angry breaths, spitting with each word, "and I'll kill her."

I can't conceal my anguish as Elias grinds the blade

deeper into my thigh for emphasis, then yanks it back out. From either Bastian's pain or my own, my vision blinks white. I feel every inch of the cold steel in my body.

Hands trembling, I clutch for Elias as though I'm falling. And gods do I want to fall. To give in. But I didn't put myself through this pain to have him not fall with me.

He stabs through my thigh again and roughly jerks the blade back out. But this time as he bends to do it, I grab a fistful of his hair with one hand, summon every inch of will left in me, and hoist myself up enough to punch the poison-soaked needles between my fingers deep into his throat.

Elias jerks back, bulging eyes going bloodshot as the cloudy haze fades from them. Pressing shaking fingers to his neck, he gags as they brush against the needle. A tiny, terrified sound slips through his lips. "What did you do to me?" The shakiness of his hands turns to a full tremble, though he tries hard to steady his hold on his blade. "What did you do?"

I laugh, half delirious as my fingers warm in the small puddle of blood forming around my open wound. It won't take long for me to bleed out like this; I can only hope the poison is fast acting. "Poison's a bitch, isn't it?"

Fat beads of blood bubble at his neck and roll down the length of it. Squinting through the haze threatening to eat my vision, I smile when the blood isn't red, but inky black.

Elias screams and clenches both hands around his dagger, and I know exactly what he plans to do with it. But before he can stab me again, a knife spears through his stomach. Bastian drops his hand from the pommel, panting. His eyes are beginning to roll up to his skull from aftershocks of the soul magic his body was not made to use. The poison eats through him as well, and the cloud over my vision blossoms. My own breath sharpens as my eyes mirror his, rolling back into my skull.

When he seizes, so do I.

TWENTY-FOUR

I wake to the scent of sandalwood and the chatter of concerned whispers.

For a moment I contemplate keeping my eyes shut tight so that I might return to the heavy siren call of sleep. But when I recognize one of the low voices as Bastian's, my attention can't help but stir; his voice is more ragged than usual. The longer I listen to it, the more the puzzle pieces in my head snap together until I remember the poison. The sword. My thigh. And another person dead by my hand.

"Amora?" Nelly's airy voice beckons. "Your Majesty, can you hear me? I think she's waking up." There's a clatter of footsteps against the wood, and the air around me constricts. Slowly, although I wish I didn't have to, I open my eyes and take in the circle of anxious faces staring back at me—Vataea, Shanty, Ferrick, Casem, Ilia, and Nelly. My brows furrow when I notice a face is missing, until warm fingers graze mine and I turn.

Bastian's lying on the cot beside me, his hair a mess. "We should really try to work on our fainting. Perhaps we can make it a once-an-adventure type thing?"

"How about a *never* thing?" Ferrick chimes in, ignoring Bastian's wrinkling nose. "I didn't sign on to be a personal healer."

"I'm not sure we'd even be able to call it an adventure if there was *never* fainting, mate."

I curl my fingers around his outstretched hand, letting the warmth of our connection settle between us. My forced laughter sounds like a croaking frog, hoarse and painful. "How long have we been out?"

"You?" Bastian's teasing tone takes a serious edge. "Two days. I was awake after the first, but they put me on bed rest because of my . . . symptoms."

"You both were having *seizures*," Nelly clarifies sternly, her eyes narrowing when Bastian tries to edge around her words. My chest falls when he steers his attention from my face, refusing to look at me. But I don't need Nelly's words to know that something's wrong with him. I feel as though my body's been struck by a cannon, each movement sluggish, the pain dull but distant.

This pain belongs to Bastian, and I know at once it's because he used soul magic.

Though Bastian has access to the magic because of Kaven's curse, he's not a Montara; his body isn't equipped to handle it. Every one of Kaven's followers who chased after soul magic either wound up dead or deteriorated. It even got to Kaven in the end, skewing his perception and driving his bloodlust until it consumed him entirely.

I try to catch his attention, but once more his focus turns flighty, purposely avoiding me.

"You were too reckless." Ferrick's the one who breaks the silence, white-knuckling the sheets of the cot I lie upon. "You're the *queen* now, Amora. You need to stop throwing yourself into danger."

"I always seem to make it out okay." The words are out before I can stop them, tense and bitter. "It's everyone else around me who gets hurt."

Bastian's lips screw tight enough to tell me it was the wrong thing to say. But it's also the truth. No matter how many times I dive into a fight, there's always someone left worse off. Father. Aunt Kalea. Mira. Bastian.

Nelly clears her throat as if to ease the tension away. She's seated by my leg, cleaning it with a cloth that drips with a thick yellow liquid. Ferrick's seated across from her, watching intently.

"I can close your wounds as many times as you need me to," he grumbles, as if able to sense my stare, "but I can't manifest more blood. I appreciate what you did for us, but it's our job to protect *you*. Our kingdom needs you right now."

His edge of warning gives me pause, and I fight back a cringe I don't want him to see.

"I'm sorry." I grit the words out, not favoring the taste of them. Rage pulses Ferrick's jaw.

"Your wounds are sealed." He stands but doesn't move, having nowhere to go. "Between you, Bastian, and Elias, I only had the energy to keep you from death's door. You're going to have a scar, but we have ointments to help with that, and once we're done here I can try to heal it, but it might be a slow—"

I sit up too quickly, blood rushing to my head and a dull throbbing in my thigh making me bite back a curse. "Elias is alive?"

Ferrick's spine straightens, guilt eating into the edges of his frown. "I didn't know what else to do. He was watching me as I was taking care of you and Bastian. He kept *staring*, and . . . Yeah. He's alive."

I steal a look at Bastian, whose cool eyes cut to mine. Elias saw Bastian use soul magic. If word about that got out before we were ready to tell the kingdom the truth, it could ruin everything.

"There's something you should know." Though Ferrick speaks gently, something in his tone draws my attention. "The poison . . . It's affected his mind. He doesn't seem to remember who he is."

If it's true, then it's a relief. But I can't afford to take any risks; already my mind is spinning on how to keep this a secret.

"What you did to Elias . . . did you plan that?" Until now, Ilia has remained silent. Shadows fill the hard lines of her face, aging her.

"I did what I had to do to stay alive," I tell her, recalling the anger in her eyes back at the tea shop, and the way she practically ripped Elias away from me. I'd thought she hated me, but perhaps it wasn't me she was worried about at all. "Did you know he was the one who poisoned me?"

Her chair practically swallows her, and the streaks of dried tears on her face tell me she'd be thankful if it did. "I had my suspicions." She sits up only to set a hand upon Ferrick's shoulder, a tremor rattling her voice. "I will never be able to thank you enough for saving him. I never expected . . . I knew he wanted things for Curmana and for the kingdom that I didn't agree with. But I never thought he'd take it this far."

Nelly takes Ilia's hand, cradling it in her lap as if to let her wife know she's there with her. "It's my fault, Your Majesty. Ilia warned me of what she feared he was becoming, but I didn't want to believe it. I've known him since he was a child; he's truly like my own brother. I thought maybe if he met you, or maybe if he heard you out, he'd understand there are other solutions out there than just his own. I wanted him to learn."

The guilt from Nelly is so palpable it hits me in dense waves that roll off her as I ask, "So you both knew about the poisons on your island? And about the changes Elias wanted for Visidia?"

While Nelly's head drops and tears spring to her eyes, Ilia screws her jaw tight and lifts her chin higher.

"We were trying to put a stop to the poisons ourselves, before the royal soldiers needed to intervene," Ilia says. "I didn't want to believe that my brother was capable of this. But I promise you, I will do everything in my power to make it up to not only you, but to this entire island. I thought it was the right time to give him a chance to prove himself and step up to the position of a ruler. I wanted him to see how challenging the role truly was . . . But I underestimated his arrogance, it seems. He's so young, and the power must have gone straight to his head."

"I'm younger than he is, and I am the queen of this entire kingdom." They're words that give Ilia pause, crumpling her shoulders as I turn to Casem. "Men don't always need lessons; sometimes they need punishment. His age is no excuse for attempting regicide. Casem, I need you to take him to Arida immediately, where he'll wait in the prisons until my return. I'll oversee his trial myself."

Ilia flinches as though I've struck her; we both know it's not a trial he'll win. Her mouth opens, closes, and ultimately she says nothing as Nelly's bottom lip trembles.

For their sake, I wish I could make an exception. But Elias made no small grievance, and even if he doesn't yet realize it, he knows too much. Even if I put him in the prisons, he has mind speak. He could share the information he has far too easily.

"I should stay with you," Casem argues quietly, though there's no conviction in his voice. His face is a stark white, knowing as well as I do that we'll have to find a way to silence Elias permanently. If he's already poisoned, it wouldn't be a stretch to believe he died on the ship during his journey to Arida.

"Ferrick will take over your position as mind speaker," I say. "This takes priority."

Ilia makes a strange choking noise in the back of her throat, and Ferrick reaches to squeeze her shoulder. For a moment, I hate him for being able to do that. For being able to apologize to her, and for not being responsible for this decision. While I'm the one lying here on the cot, nearly having bled to death for stopping someone who wanted to commit regicide, someone else gets to be the good guy.

Nelly holds Ilia's other hand tight, and as if to break the tension of the situation, Ferrick nods to her and says, "Nelly's on the staff of Curmana's healing ward, and has studied the development of Curmanan herbs and medicines firsthand. She made the ointment on your leg."

I blink, peering down to see that my leg's been thoroughly numbed by a thick green paste that smells of mint and basil.

"If Amora ever decides she'd like a new adviser, I'm coming here to study." Ferrick's awe as he eyes the ointment is undeniable. "There's so much here. So many herbs and plants for tonics, and medicine, and—"

"Poison." I lift my brows while Ferrick's furrow.

"Yes . . . And poison. But there's good on this island too, Amora. Those herbs have done a lot of amazing things."

"I should have alerted you the first time I heard about it." Ilia's voice is fraying at the edges, her sorrow and guilt easily the most palpable emotion I've yet to see from her. "For every incredible medicine we create, there's someone out there who finds a way to make it into something foul. I had soldiers scouting, some of them even undercover, and we've made arrests of our own. I thought we could handle it internally; we didn't want to scare anyone." She pauses. "But I see now that it wasn't enough. As good as we've gotten at hunting them, they've gotten even better at hiding. I never thought my brother would involve himself in something like that."

"You're right," I say. "You should have alerted us the moment you discovered this was an issue. But now all we can do is find ways to control these substances. We can shut down access to the jungle. Put soldiers on patrol, and ban access to anyone who isn't certified to use the herbs for the development of medicine. Even then, no one should be able to journey into the jungle alone; they'll go in teams."

"Amora." I only notice how heavy the bags are beneath Bastian's eyes when he rolls them. "You nearly bled to death. Policy can wait until you're feeling better." Carefully, he lifts himself with a wince and reaches his hands out to me again. "I think we should heal up and get moving. The less people who know about this incident, the better. The only ones who ever need to know are here in this room."

Get moving.

I tense.

Four days on Curmana. Four wasted days, no closer to finding Ornell Rosenblathe. It's not an outcome I can accept.

"Where do my people think I am?" My words are hesitant, almost afraid to ask.

"We told them you had a horrible case of food poisoning," Nelly says softly, "and that we were busy trying to nurse you back to health and keep you inside, because all you wanted to do was see them."

"All the parchments are talking about it," Shanty chimes in. "It's a good thing. People are angry at Curmana, not at you. It's created sympathy among Visidians."

Grateful as I am, that doesn't stop the aching in my chest. In every regard, I'm failing miserably. Whether I'm to meet my people and put on a show for them, or find Ornell and the artifact, nothing I've attempted has gone right.

On Kerost, I was challenged for engaging with my people.

On Curmana, I was poisoned by someone who wished to end my reign.

I don't even want to imagine what might happen at our next destination.

I'm half tempted to give up now. To accept my curse and my lost magic, and sit on the throne until someone comes for me. I can leave it up to the next poor bastard to fix this kingdom's mess.

And yet I can't convince myself to take that step. I can't convince myself not to care.

Because to my core, I am still Visidia's queen. My people deserve everything and more for what my family has done to them, and unfortunately, I'm the only one with the power to give that to them. Until my last breath, I must keep trying.

"Elias told me you were good with names," I say to Ilia. It feels like I'm swimming in muddied water trying to find my words, but I get there. "Have you ever heard of someone with the surname Rosenblathe? There's an adventurer by the name of Ornell Rosenblathe, and I have reason to believe he's here on Curmana. Before I leave, I need to meet him."

The moment Ilia's eyes widen, relief bursts within me so fiercely I could cry. Silently, I thank the gods for taking pity on me just this once.

Ilia recognizes it. I don't need her to answer to see that. But, curiously, her eyes dip to Nelly, whose tearful eyes have gone owlish.

"How," Nelly asks, "do you know my birth name?"

TWENTY-FIVE

I was a fool for assuming Ornell was a man. All this time I'd been expecting a bachelor, and here she was, right under my nose.

"If you want my help," Bastian says to me tersely, "then it's time to tell me what's going on."

Only the two of us are left in the room. By my command, Nelly waits outside while the others have vacated entirely. Looking at Bastian now, my skin flushes hot and my stomach twists. I can't help but think of when we were last together, and the words he'd admitted.

The woman I love.

The woman I love.

Something between us changed here in Curmana. From the moment I caught him placing protective curses on my door, to him distracting Elias enough to save me despite the poison in his body and the toll of soul magic, my frustration with him has waned. Curse or no curse, I trust Bastian with my life, no matter how hard I've tried not to.

"I found a way to break the Montara curse." It's time I tell him everything—about Blarthe and the clue he gave me, and how I can't sleep. About the faces I see every time I shut my eyes. I tell him of the power said to be left behind by the gods, and how, with it, I can repent for the damage my family has done. All the while he keeps his eyes to the floor, wordless, contemplating. I talk enough for the both of us, because once the truth starts, I can't stop it. There's freedom in releasing it.

"Does Vataea know you're working with Blarthe?" is the first thing Bastian asks. "You need to tell her."

My shoulders cave in. I know I should; Vataea deserves to know we've captured the man who caused her years of pain and trauma. But I'm closer than ever to my goal, and I can't risk losing this opportunity. Besides, what might she think now that I've kept it a secret this long?

"When the time is right," I tell Bastian, "I'll tell her everything."

I tense when he stands and runs a hand along the dark beard that's beginning to take shape over his jaw, waiting for his reaction. Waiting for him to yell, or to tell me how naive I'm being by risking it all on Blarthe's word.

"I want this, too," he finally says. "I want my freedom, and to travel freely. But if we're going to do this, you and I need to be on the same page. I'll help you, but only if you promise that we'll work together from this moment on. No more secrets."

I flinch, remembering saying those same words to him last summer. I never expected how guilty I'd feel being on the opposite side.

"You'd forgive me?" I ask hesitantly. "Just like that?"

He huffs a small, quiet laugh. "You've forgiven me for worse, Amora. Do we have a deal or not?"

I nod, skin hot. "We have a deal."

"Then it's time to find out what Ornell has to tell us." Bastian crosses the room to fetch Nelly, who waits anxiously behind the door. "Did you bring it?" he asks, to which she nods and hands him a large, smooth stone. He's quick to set it upon the small table he drags between them, and takes a seat close to Nelly.

"All you have to do is think about what you want us to see," he instructs. "Let your memories flow freely. Can you do that?" As he speaks, he tries to still his trembling hands on the stone as another aftershock of soul magic seizes his body. It makes my own feel like it's boiling before it passes. Shakily I exhale a breath while Bastian only grips the stone tighter, as if to pretend he hasn't felt a thing.

While Nelly could simply tell us her story, memories fill the gaps where words cannot. Using Bastian's curse magic, she can show me everything she knows about the artifact, though it'll be up to me to decipher what it means.

"Nelly, since we're accessing your memory, all you have to do is add your blood to the stone," Bastian says. "You're the one doing the work. I'm just here to guide you through it and attach the memories to the stone. Don't pull away until you've shown us everything."

Nelly nods and peeks at me as I lounge against the cot, leg propped up, trying not to let my pain show.

"Are you sure this will work?" I ask. "She doesn't have curse magic."

Bastian cuts me a look. Drawing his push blade, he takes hold of Nelly's hand and gently presses its tip into her index finger, enough to draw blood. Lifting the stone, he dabs her blood onto its surface. "It'll work because I'm here guiding her. It won't be any different from when you saw Sira's memories about Cato last summer."

It's odd, seeing how versatile curse magic is. For years

I believed the magic only had one purpose—an eerie and frightening ability to trap people into a state where they see whatever strange images the magic wielder wants them to. But seeing it used like this—to transfer thoughts, images, or memories from one person to another—is a showcase of how diverse magic can be. It's always shifting and evolving, never staying stagnant. It's how I want my kingdom to be, too.

Nelly wraps her fingers around the stone and shuts her eyes when Bastian presses a finger to it as well, his own eyes closing tight.

"Amora, touch the stone," he says, and I obey.

Forehead knitting into lines of deep concentration, I settle back as the distant pulse of magic swells within me. Bastian's magic feels cool and placid. It's nothing like the starved, scorching beast of soul magic, and it's strange to be reminded that this is how magic is *meant* to feel. That what I practiced all my life was not truly magic, but a curse. While this magic may drain Bastian after a while, his tiredness can be cured by sleep. It's not the bone-tired, life-threatening exhaustion my magic brings.

Once more the magic swells to a peak, and as Nelly feeds it her memories, I'm swept away within them.

His name is Rogan Rosenblathe, and there's nothing I want more than for him to look at me.

I'm pulled into the memory in the same fashion I was pulled into Sira's memories last summer. Only this time I am not a woman, but a young girl of perhaps eight, and the one whose attention I want so fiercely it feels as though the emotions are my own, is my father's.

I watch Papa through the crack of his office door, left ajar just enough for me to peek inside. As usual, he's seated at his desk, poring over a mess of parchment—notes, maps, charts, guides of the constellations, and even leather-bound tomes of old seafaring legends.

I'm told Papa used to be a sailor once, years before I was born. But he doesn't speak of those times.

Empty decanters filled with ale and stale wine are strewn across the desk and floor, and Papa's hair is mussed from running his fingers through it so many times, tugging at the ends and cursing words Mama told me I should never say.

"It should be here," he's muttering to himself, voice so low and frantic my skin crawls. "It should be here. Blasted godwoken, why isn't it *here*?" Jerking from his seat, he slams a fist against the already splintering wooden desk. An unlit oil lamp tumbles to the ground, oil splattering onto the thatched floor. The hungry wood soaks it up, but Papa doesn't notice. It's not until he hears my sharp, surprised breath that his attention lifts to the door.

"Mariah?" The razor-sharp edge of his voice has me teetering away from the door, wondering if I should run. But there's no time. His boots fall with heavy, drunken steps that grow closer by the second. "I thought I told you never to—"

Papa throws the rickety door open, confusion awash on his face. It isn't until he looks down that he notices me, trembling and pressed back against the wall, trying to make myself as small as I feel.

"Y-you didn't come down to dinner," I stammer. "I wanted . . . to check in . . ."

He sighs, and here in the light of the hallway I notice his

eyes are dewy and bloodshot. Kicking the door open behind him, Papa says, "Come in," though there's no fondness in his tone. There's none of the warmth I keep hoping I might someday find.

But I don't care; Papa has never let me into his office, and I can't so much as remember the last time I spoke to him. I cling to what I can get.

"I like maps too, you know." From the corner of my eye, I watch to see if he's impressed. "And I know all the major constellations, and how to navigate with them. My friend and I are going to be sailors one day, just like you! She'll be the captain, and I'll be the navigator. Unless . . . you ever decided you wanted to sail again. I could be your navigator instead, maybe? If you wanted me to."

"I will be sailing again." He says it so plainly that my heart soars. "Just as soon as I figure out where I'm going. But you won't be coming with me."

My heart crashes back down, straight into my throat. Though I never truly let myself *believe* otherwise, I'd hoped Papa would at least consider me. I've been studying every night, just like him. I know I could be so helpful, if he'd let me try.

My sadness swells, but I won't let him see it. Papa never shows his emotions, after all. Maybe sailors aren't supposed to. Maybe this is a test, and I'm not meant to show mine, either?

"Are you looking for something?" I take a seat on the edge of the small bed behind him. Then I lift my chin high, trying to sound serious and worthy of his notice.

To my surprise, it works. Papa doesn't tell me to leave, or cast me a withering stare. He simply sits in his chair and runs both hands through his blond hair, tugging at the ends with a sigh.

"Yes" is all he says at first, and I hesitate, unsure whether to press or keep quiet. In the end, I decide to go for something in between.

So quietly I almost hope he doesn't hear, I ask, "What is it?"

The chair beneath him squeaks as he tips it back and draws a long sip from his decanter. Even from here I can smell the sweetness of rum on his breath. "Do you truly want to know, Ornell?"

Something in my gut stirs, telling me I should leave; I've never seen Papa like this before, and something about it doesn't feel right. But before I can move, he's talking again, and I can't bring myself to disturb him. He's never talked to me so much at one time; I should *want* this.

Slowly, I nod.

"I'm looking for the one who has my heart." His voice is smooth and factual, each word like a punch. "I'm searching for the way to bring the woman I love back from the dead."

Everything in my body numbs. "But ... Mama's not dead." I know they're naive words even before I say them, but they tumble out. Never has Papa spoken like this; never has he put emotions like love into his words. It must be the rum bringing it out of him, for his eyes grow more glazed and bloodshot and the words tumble out faster with each sip.

"No, but Corina is," he grits out. "And no matter how many times I've tried to save her, I've always failed. Tell me, have you read this?" Kicking his feet onto the table, he toes at the edge of the leather-bound seafaring book that sits open to a sketched picture of a bird flying into a town that sits upon the clouds. I've never read it, but I've skimmed enough to know it's about the legends of Visidia—things like kelpies, hydras, and the

254

Lusca—legends Mama told me were forged by drunken sailors who needed to find ways to get through long, lonely nights.

"There's a legend in here about the godwoken—four deities who were the first of the gods' creations, each tasked with a duty—the protection of land, sea, sky, or humankind. They protect our world with bodies that hold the power of the gods. One scale from their skin or a feather from their wings, and someone would be the most powerful human ever known." His eyes are alight with a hunger that has my hands trembling. Desperately, I steady them into my lap. "But their magic comes with a price—to have what you most want, you must give up what you most love.

"When I was eighteen," he continues, "I was engaged to a woman I would have moved the stars for—Corina. We were set to marry the next summer, when one day she joined her father for a fishing trip and never returned. Little did she or I know, it wasn't truly a fishing trip at all, but a poaching trip to capture mermaids and steal the scales from their bodies. In the end, those mermaids used their voices to win the fight, and they took the lives of every one of the sailors aboard that ship. I was never meant to see Corina again, but that was a fate I couldn't live with. I knew from the moment I heard of her death that I needed to find a way to get her back, no matter the price I had to pay.

"It took me five years before I discovered the secret of the godwoken—if I could get their power, I could use time magic to amplify it. To turn back the clock and win back her life. And I did it." His voice is a low whisper, as though he's no longer telling a story, but speaking for only himself. "I did it. I hunted the water deity—a beast made from coral and the weeds of the sea—and stole a scale from its back. That day, I changed my fate forever."

His long, pale fingers clench tight around the decanter. "But gods are tricky bastards. I never stopped loving Corina— she was the reason I lived. The reason behind every breath I took. I didn't know what I was getting myself into with that magic; I thought I could offer something else, and that so long as I got Corina back I could make anything work. But what I wanted most was her, and what I loved most was also her.

"I turned back the clock, and I brought her back. But she didn't remember who I was. And try as I might to win her over, she was repulsed by me. No matter what I did, I couldn't win her heart. And in the end, none of it mattered. She got back on her father's ship that same fated day, and the mermaids stole her from me again.

"So I tried a second time. The guardian deity of the sky was said to have wings as soft and as white as clouds. I sailed to an island far beyond this kingdom, to a place with mountains so tall they touch the skies. It was the last place anyone had ever seen it, and I searched there for two years before I found what I'd been looking for—a fallen feather, imbued with its magic and power. Again I turned back time, and again Corina slipped out of my reach and back onto that blasted ship. I don't know what I lost that time, but I gained something even more important: the knowledge that I needed to love something else, something new, before I tried again." He takes a long swig from his decanter. "I thought to start a family. If I had that, I could give those blasted guardians something new, in exchange for Corina."

The glow of the oil lamp feels dimmer, and the draft in the room cooler as it gnaws into my bones. The room tightens with shadows that crawl from the darkest crevices, stretching toward and across the floor. They take me by the throat, making my voice hoarse.

"You wanted to trade me and Mama? But . . . we would die." My voice doesn't sound like my own; it's too squeaky. Did I misunderstand? Surely, that's not what he could have meant?

Papa would never trade me . . .

His profile is shadowed by the dim amber light, turning him into nothing but sharp and shadowed angles—a monster in the night. He doesn't turn to me; doesn't try to ease the fear boiling hot in my gut, making me too numb to move.

"I just have to find a guardian." He turns back to the parchment at his desk, and I see now that one of them is a map scrawled with notes. Several of the islands are circled or crossed out, with notes scrawled along the map. They're words like *"leviathan?"* and *"fire serpent?"* accompanied by page numbers for source material and scribbled-out notes and drawings of the beasts. The air deity is so beautiful even in the artwork, with feathers so thick and white it almost looks like fur, and a curved obsidian beak. Though it's got four massive claws, it doesn't look like a vicious beast. It looks peaceful, and as though it should be a crime for anyone to even imagine hunting it.

I wait, deathly still, to see if Papa starts laughing or offers anything more. His back remains bent as he huddles over the parchment, shuffling them with a stream of whispers too quiet and quick for me to decipher. It doesn't take long to realize I've been forgotten.

Praying to the gods to keep it that way and to make my feet and breaths as noiseless as possible, I slip off the bed and out of the room, my heart beating so fiercely I worry he may hear it even as I'm halfway down the hall, sprinting for Mama's room.

Mama's always said Papa had his own way of loving people. But as I climb into her bed, tears falling faster than I can process them as I tell her what happened, I realize we both know the truth, now: Papa doesn't love us, and he never will.

That's what the gods took from him that second time he tried to steal their magic—his heart.

Rogan Rosenblathe truly was a heartless man.

It feels as though hours pass before Nelly breaks away with a gasp that Bastian and I echo, ending the curse at once. Even back in reality though, my mind lingers to the final parts of Nelly's memories.

She and her mother snuck away that same week, leaving Rogan far behind. They went to live with her mother's family in Suntosu, where Ornell changed her name and took up restoration magic at the age of twelve before later moving to Curmana for work. She never saw her papa again, and I'm glad for it.

And yet it's not Nelly who's at the forefront of my mind as the memories drag to an end, nor is it the fact that using this godwoken magic has a steep price I'd never known until now—*to have what you most want, you must give up what you most love.*

Right now, that doesn't matter. All that matters is that Rogan Rosenblathe had successfully used the godwoken's magic to reunite with the dead.

And if he could do it, what's stopping me from doing the same?

❧

TWENTY-SIX

Nelly's cheeks are soaked with tears, and there's surprise in her wide emerald eyes.

"Sorry." She's quick to dab her cheek with the hem of her shirt. "I'm so sorry, I don't know what came over me. It's just . . . He's not someone I like to think about."

"There's no reason to apologize." Bastian's expression is one of deep sympathy. "Some memories are easier left forgotten." I don't miss the shadows that sink into his skin, hollowing his eyes. I feel the emotion brewing within him, and though I can't read his thoughts, his yearning is enough to tell me he's thinking of a time long before this. A time when he was still on Zudoh with his family.

A time before his brother stole that life from him, and took my father from me.

"It was actually cathartic, in a way." Nelly's smile is thin as a reed, and her airy voice too sharp. "He was an awful man, and yet I spent years obsessing over him and his damn maps. I guess . . . I think I saw some of my father in Elias. I hadn't been able to help my father, but I thought that maybe I could help Elias, you know? It's hard to admit sometimes that others aren't your responsibility. There was nothing I could have done to help either of them."

Bastian's eyes are all over me. Unlike Ferrick, who'd be sending me silent messages to be more sensitive, Bastian looks as intrigued as I am when I ask, "Nelly, were you ever able to find anything out from those maps?"

Nelly's eyes darken, lips screwing tight. "Whatever my father was after, Your Majesty, you don't want to touch. The magic he used is something that shouldn't be part of this world. It's something no human should ever know."

I straighten as well as I can to look her in the eye, putting every ounce of power I have into my voice. "If you figured out where to find the godwoken, I need for you to tell me. Don't give me a reason to make it an order."

Though it lasts only a moment, her resolve cracks. Fresh tears spring to her eyes. "Valuka" is all she whispers for a long moment, as if struggling with the moral battle of dragging the words out of herself. "As I said, I was obsessed with him. Even when my mother and I fled, I read everything I could about the godwoken. I wasted too many years tracking them, as if finding one could make my father love me, or realize I was worth something." She scoffs, lowering her head. "There were many rumored sightings of the godwoken, especially around Kerost. People believed that since storms are so frequent there, it must have something to do with angry godwoken living in the waters near it. But I never liked that legend. It seemed too easy.

"There was another one that stood out to me, though. About a mythical serpent that lives in the depths of Valuka's volcanos," Nelly continues. "The volcanos are active, so it's challenging to confirm if such a creature really exists. But I traveled there one day, just to see. I couldn't get anywhere near the volcano; the smoke is too thick. It's unnatural. But . . . there's this *presence*. I can't explain it, but it's like there's something within the smoke, something powerful. I'd bet my life that's where it's hiding. But for your sake, Amora, I hope you never find it." With that she stands and makes her way to the door. "Remember to use ointment twice a day to help with the scarring. And keep doing your stretches. Take it easy, Your Majesty, and good luck."

When the door shuts, Bastian's eyes bore into me, searching. "Did you know what the artifact could do?"

The longing within him intensifies, as does my own. With the power of the gods in our hands, we could change everything.

"I didn't know everything."

We could raise the dead . . . I could bring back *Father*.

The hunger in Bastian's eyes tells me his thoughts aren't far from my own, and for the first time since having this curse, I wish I could pry myself deeper into his mind to see what he's thinking.

"You really miss them, don't you?" I ask.

Bastian rolls back his shoulders, straightening himself before he answers, "Every day."

"And it never gets any easier?"

There's a long moment where he says nothing, screwing his lips tight in thought. Then, slowly, he crosses the floor to the cot I'm on and settles himself upon the edge. As he takes hold of my hand, my skin cools.

"Loss can drive people to do shameful things." His thumb brushes slowly across my knuckles, though his eyes are distant, lost somewhere within Bastian's thoughts. "For me, it made me flee my home for years, leaving my people to suffer. For Rogan, he gave up his ability to love, and was willing to sacrifice his wife and child.

"I don't know if it ever gets easier," he continues. "If it does, then I'm still waiting. Because no matter what Kaven did—no matter the pain he's caused and everything he took—I still miss the days before he found Cato's damn knife and decided his purpose was to change Visidia. I still wonder if I could have changed things. If there was something I did wrong, or an opportunity I missed that could have saved my family."

Bastian doesn't look at me; I can feel his soul is tearing at the seams. It's the same as my own. Even without this curse between us, Bastian and I are the same.

"Loss will rip you apart, Amora." There's a sense of urgency in his hazel eyes. "It will take whatever you give it, and it will never be satisfied. So don't you dare give it yourself."

His grip on my hand tightens, and I know exactly what he means without needing to ask. Bastian doesn't need to read my thoughts to understand my soul. If he could have brought back his parents, I'm sure he would have done it.

Father wasn't always a perfect man, and he was far from the perfect king. But gods did I love him.

I could live with my curses forever if it meant I could use the godwoken's magic to see him again.

To seek his advice. Sail with him. Go on an adventure, and chase down the fiercest beasts of the sea.

Gods, what I wouldn't give to hear his laugh one more time.

But no matter what I use the godwoken's magic for, I must pay a toll far heavier than I ever imagined.

To have what you most want, you must give up what you most love.

There are many things I love; but what is it that I love *most*? What, exactly, will I be forced to pay if I'm to use this magic?

"Promise me you won't use that artifact." Bastian's voice is as soft as I've ever heard it. "When we find it, we'll figure out a way to use it that doesn't require such a steep payment. I don't want you touching it, Amora. Not before we figure out a better way."

Fear rolls from him in waves, but I'm not offended. He's right to doubt my intentions.

If I had the power to bring Father back, he and I could heal Visidia together. We could find a different way to restore soul magic to the kingdom. He could atone for what he did.

"I promise." The lie passes my lips before I think to stop it. "Once we find the artifact, we'll find another way to use it."

I peel from my bed beneath Bastian's scrutiny, effectively ending this conversation as I peek out through heavy satin curtains to confirm it's nightfall.

Ilia was wise enough not to take us to the healing ward for recovery, but to her personal home. Though I've only seen the guest suite, its beautiful white stone flooring and lattice ceiling is enough to tell me this place is grand.

While my leg has mostly healed, there's still an aching in the muscles of my left thigh that screams with every small step. I grit through the stiffness of the muscles, and take Bastian by the forearm as we climb down a spiral stone staircase.

"The others should already be waiting," he says, going as slow as my needs dictate. Which, unfortunately, is little more than a slow crawl.

I'm expecting a silent night upon the shore when Bastian tosses the door open, but what I receive is far beyond that.

The shore is lined with Curmanan citizens dressed in their finest, their heads bowed and hands lifted with offerings—silks, fruits, sweets, stretching the entirety of the way down to *Keel Haul*.

I stumble at the sight of them, surprise snatching my breath. Bastian presses a steadying hand to my back, grinning at the display before us.

"I know I wasn't supposed to tell them," Ilia's voice comes quiet and timid from the porch, "but your people didn't get long to see you, and they wanted to say goodbye."

Carefully I unlace my arm from Bastian's, straightening to hide my injury as I make my way onto the shore.

The first person waiting there is a man I recognize from the night of the party, someone who made polite conversation. He lowers to a knee, and offers a gorgeous silk shawl. "To keep you warm on your journey," he says as I take the silks slowly, brushing my fingers along the luxurious fabric.

Beside him, a woman with a loose chignon drops to a knee and offers a bottle of sparkling red wine. "To keep you free on your journey."

I laugh and thank her, handling the bottle to Bastian, who lingers protectively behind me. Even the Ikaean reporter waits upon the shore, hands trembling as he offers apologies in the form of sweets. To him, I turn up my nose and walk away. While I never had the chance to say anything to him, it looks as though Casem's given him quite the lecture.

I wish I could sample the food my people offer, or the lotions and oils they place into my palms. I want to trust them, but the aching of my thigh reminds me I'm safer if I don't. I'll smile and accept their offerings, but it will only be to later dispose of anything that could be laced with poison. As painful as it is, it'll be safer that way.

Even the Curmanan soldiers help carry the offered goods

up to *Keel Haul,* and for one of the first times since summer, my chest swells with pride.

Perhaps Elias truly was an anomaly. Perhaps not everyone thinks I'm doing such a horrible job after all.

Casem waits for us on the base of *Keel Haul*'s ramp. "I'll pray that your time on the other islands will be safer and grander than what you've experienced so far." He stretches out his arms, scooping me into a tight hug. I laugh weakly against his chest, returning it.

"Give Mira my regards," I say as I ease away, letting Casem linger back toward the edge of the ramp. "And tell my mother we're headed to Valuka, next."

Casem keeps his face stern as he smooths pale fingers through his honey-blond waves. "I'll let them know to start preparing. If you need anything, have Ferrick contact me. He's a horrible mind speaker—always sounds like he's yelling through a conch shell—but he should be able to reach me."

"I will. And I'm sorry to ask this of you, Casem, but . . . you know what to do with Elias."

He nods swiftly, not needing me to elaborate. "I'll deal with it. You focus on taking care of yourself, all right? We're going to get through this."

Nodding, I release him and start up the ramp to where Shanty and Vataea wait for me, wearing proud smiles.

As we draw up the anchors, drifting away from the docks, Bastian casts me a look over his shoulder. "To Valuka?"

"To Valuka."

Bastian lifts a compass to the air and twists the helm, setting our course westbound. "Hang on tight, Ferrick, and try to keep that stomach of yours. We're in for a bumpy night."

TWENTY-SEVEN

Not even the gentle pull of the waves is enough to lull me to sleep. At this point, I'm convinced I'll never again have a full night's rest unless I'm poisoned or ill. I should have stolen some sleeping powder from Curmana while I had the chance.

It's the aching in my thigh that keeps me awake and alert, tense from every creaking floorboard and every slam of the wind against the ship. I know it's irrational—nothing can get me in the middle of the sea, unless the Lusca decides to test its luck, again. But even so, memories of Kerost and Curmana rattle against my skull, tricking my eyes into seeing strange stirrings in the shadows of beasts that aren't truly there.

Some of the Kers had turned their noses up at my rule, believing it to be too little too late.

Elias had tried to poison me to shake the throne and upturn the monarchy. He wanted Curmana to rule itself, and was willing to kill me to do it.

And no matter how I spin it—no matter how power hungry Elias may be—perhaps he had a point.

After all this time and everything we've done, why should the Montaras still rule Visidia?

But there's another thought warring against memories of Elias, as well.

I'd thought I had my plan ready—find the artifact, break my curses, and restore Visidia to what it always should have been. But now the inkling of hesitation sinks into me, burrowing itself deep.

If I find this artifact, I'll have the power to bring Father back. And despite Bastian's warning, despite every awful feeling within me that says breaking the curse is the right move for Visidia and that Father was an awful king, I want to be selfish. I want to hear his laugh one more time. I want to see his real eyes, and not the two holes filled with smoke and shadows that wait for me in my dreams.

But if I give myself that gift, what would happen to Visidia? Without the truth—without magic restored to them once and for all—how am I better than any other Montara?

Not to mention there will be a price to pay, no matter what I choose to do.

To have what you most want, you must give up what you most love.

But what exactly is that?

"Are you going to tell me what the problem is, or are you going to keep sighing all night?" Vataea's voice cuts the silence of our dark room. Even heavy with sleep, her words still sound like a lullaby.

"What will happen if I choose the sighing?" She'll either roll her eyes or eat me alive for the joke, but either way, I'll know if this is a conversation she's awake enough to have.

To my surprise, Vataea snorts. "Then I'll melt a candle and stuff my ears with its wax, and you may go on sighing for as long as you wish." It's too dark in the windowless cabin to see her, though I can tell she shifts from the rustling of her hammock. When she speaks again, her voice is louder and more focused. "What's wrong?"

My injured thigh pulses as I turn to face her. Even if we can't see each other, it feels better this way. "Why are you still here, V?"

Given the long silence that follows, I know this isn't the question she'd been expecting. She hesitates for a moment, and only when it appears she'll never answer does she ask, in a voice unusually quiet for her, "Would you rather I be somewhere else?"

"That's not it at all. But you could be anywhere right now, doing anything. So why are you here with us? Why would you risk your life for us, when there's so much more you could be doing?"

Her sigh comes after a brief pause, long and dramatic. "If I knew we were sharing our feelings tonight, I would have stayed asleep."

I roll my eyes, thinking to chuck my pillow at her face. Remembering those teeth of hers, however, I think better of it.

"Humor me," I tell her. "Just this once."

She flips onto her side, and though I can't be sure, I swear those yellow eyes of hers can see me in the darkness.

"If you really want to know, I'll tell you. But I'll say it only once, and will never repeat myself." The words sound like a warning at first, but quickly turn timid, dipping to little more than a whisper. "I didn't ever think I wanted friends until I met you, Amora. My kind is different; we have bonds, but not the kind of kinship you humans have. And I suppose . . . I like it. For some reason, I find myself annoyingly fond of you guppies. Besides, I always wanted to see this kingdom, and sometimes it's preferable to do that upon a ship rather than with my own fins."

Her words cleave through me, splitting me straight in two. I know at once I have to tell Vataea the truth. I have to tell her everything.

"V, there's something—"

"No more of this conversation," she says in a brisk voice I recognize as embarrassment. "Tell me what's wrong with you. What are you sighing about?"

"I don't—"

"Tell me, or I'm sleeping outside."

Guilt crawls at my skin, but the moment to tell her has passed. Instead I do what she wants and ask, "Do you think Elias was right?"

Her response comes slowly, thoughtfully. "I think Elias wanted power."

"But do you think he was *right*? That maybe Visidia's problem is that we have one sole ruler?"

This time, she pauses for so long I fear she's fallen asleep. "Where is this coming from?"

I tense and turn toward the shadows on the ceiling now, thoughts whirling. "I think his methods were misguided, but he made a good point. The Montaras have ruled for centuries, and yet I can count the good things they've done for this kingdom on one hand. My family has too much power, and Visidia's grown stagnant under our rule. Look how much Kerost has flourished since they've been able to learn multiple magics, since they've been able to help themselves. Can you imagine a world where they were given that right all along? I can't stop thinking about how different that world would be, if . . . if my family hadn't been in charge of everything."

Vataea considers this, then asks, "But would it truly be a better one?"

And that's just it. That's what I keep coming back to. No matter how much thought I give it, it's impossible to know the answer.

"What would you do?" I try to catch her eyes in the darkness, faintly able to make out their dim glow. "If you were me, would you step up, or would you step back?"

"If I were you, I would stop blaming myself for the grievances of the dead, even if we did once share the same blood." They're callous words, but they're why I can talk to Vataea so easily. There's no pretending with her. "Sometimes stepping down means the same thing as stepping up. This is your situation to figure out and be at peace with, Amora. But you need to get out of the past if you're ever going to see a better future. You love your kingdom more than you love anything—you'll do what's right for it."

It's as though all of *Keel Haul* stills with those words.

You love your kingdom more than you love anything.

It's with a paralyzing sickness that I realize she's right—I love Visidia more than I love anything else.

Should I use the magic of the godwoken, losing my kingdom is the price I'd have to pay.

But what would that mean? Would I be unable to rule Visidia? Would I be forced to live somewhere else, far away in an unknown kingdom? Or would I stay and simply lose my love for my kingdom? And if that's the case, could I handle that?

"Amora?" Sleep honeys her words, and I know she's drifting.

"Get some rest, V." I tuck my arms behind my head, wishing I could do the same. "I'll be fine."

And one way or another, I will be.

Just as I do every time the siren's call of sleep finally comes, I dream of Father.

I dream of the smoke that builds around him as he plunges a sword deep through his stomach. Of the way the fire chars his skin inch by inch.

He reaches out to me, his face shrouded by smoke and his body covered like a coat by the faces of Visidia's fallen.

I run, desperate to save him. Desperate for the smoke to clear so that I may see his face once more. I pray to the gods for it—to give me one last moment with him.

But every step sends me farther away, until his body is nothing more than smoke, ash, and the memory of a hand that reached for me to save him.

Again, I watch Father burn, knowing I was too slow to save him.

And again, I wake up.

TWENTY-EIGHT

Valuka's bay is awash with turquoise flames when we arrive
in the early morning, three days after leaving Curmana.
The flames move like a dance, wisps of fire shooting from the
sea and blazing through the sky, raining down in a thousand
dazzling pink embers. My breath catches as they shower over
Keel Haul, fizzling out just before they touch the ship.

Valukans fill the docks in their finest ruby garb, looking
like a sea of blood in the distance. They shift the tides around
us, swirling them into shimmering tide pools that suck us
into vortexes of air that whip my hair back so fiercely I clutch
Keel Haul's railing, laughing.

The wind is music on the water, pushing and pressing
against it, howling and whispering. A group of Valukans on
the bay stretch their arms high above their heads, letting the
sea flow through their fingertips and heed the call of their
magic. The waves expand and contort until they form a body.
Then a face. A mouth. A saltwater dragon takes shape before
me, wind hissing from its mighty jaws. With each movement
the Valukans make, the dragon follows, snaking around the
ship. It dips into the water only to emerge again before me,
its angry, gaping mouth and watery whiskers inches from my
face. My heart pumps fast, threatening to burst.

Wind moans around the dragon, and fire blossoms in its chest before it tips its head back and breathes embers into the sky. Steam sizzles around the magical beast, and I stumble back in awe.

"Is all of this for us?"

"No." Bastian steadies me, his hands settling gently on my waist as we watch the dragon sprout massive watery wings. "It's all for you."

I don't push him away.

With a final fiery breath, the dragon soars into the sky before its body shatters, showering the sea with thousands of water droplets that dazzle like fallen dragon scales as they rain onto the deck.

Suddenly, even with so many people, the sea feels too quiet as the dragon disappears. The tides shift to draw us to the docks now, where a dozen Valukans are quick to help secure *Keel Haul*. It's impossible not to notice—especially as I ease away from Bastian's rigid body—that nearly all of them are young men.

Vataea steps to the portside railing beside me and looks over, whistling low. "Bring on the bachelors."

Ferrick steps beside her, surveying the crowd. "They certainly don't waste any time."

"And they certainly don't hold back," Bastian huffs. "Stars, it's not even that hot out. Put your shirt back on, there are ladies aboard!" he calls to a bashful Valukan who grins up at him.

Vataea smirks. "Are you jealous, Bastian?"

His shoulders straighten as he takes on a dismissive air. "Of course not. Have you seen the way Amora tries to undress me with her eyes? I've got nothing to worry about."

As *Keel Haul*'s ramp is lowered, I take my time looking over the railing to spite him. One of the young Valukan men catches me looking and flashes a sly grin. His skin is dark brown and his curly hair is shorn close to his scalp. He has a smile the gods made for charming. When he waves at me, I wave back.

"Really?" Bastian asks.

"I've got to keep up appearances, don't I?" I whisper back.

Vataea captures my hand, and with a laugh she ushers me down the ramp and onto the shore, where I'm immediately greeted by no less than fifty Valukans. At the head of them, both Lord Bargas and Azami stand proud. They're dazzling in rich scarlet coats embroidered with golden stitching similar to the one Bastian had been wearing when we first met, with the emblem of two eels winding around a smoking volcano on the trim of the cuffs.

"Welcome, Your Majesty," Azami says with the most genuine enthusiasm I've felt this entire journey. Forgoing formalities, she pulls me into a swift but firm hug as Lord Bargas watches with a grin.

I notice now what I didn't back in Arida—his shoulders are beginning to curl forward into a hunch, and the skin beneath his eyes weighs heavy from age and exhaustion. There are small tremors in the hands he presses against his sides.

"To think that the little girl I watched growing up is now here, as the Queen of Visidia. Your father would be so proud." He sets a hand upon Azami's shoulder. "You'll have to forgive me, Your Majesty, but my old bones aren't what they used to be. I've tasked Azami with the duty of watching over you during your time here. It'll be a good chance for the two of you to get to know each other; she'll be Valuka's newest adviser soon enough."

Azami practically glows with excitement. "Welcome, Your Majesty. I hope our performance was to your liking?"

I laugh, not missing the spark of light in her eyes. "It was incredible. You didn't have to do all of this just for us."

Docked at the center of earth and water territory, Valuka stretches endless miles ahead of us in all directions. The island's divided into separate quadrants devoted to each element, and far to the right I can make out a thicket of trees that leads to the swampy water territory. To the left, spires of rocky mountains sweep into the sky, disappearing into clouds that mark the border of earth territory, and the air territory I cannot see.

Far to the north, three massive volcanos loom in the distant fire territory. While the two smaller volcanos appear dormant, one towers over all Valuka with plumes of thick gray smoke that twist from its neck like a serpent.

"That can't be a good sign," Vataea says skeptically.

Both Lord Bargas's and Azami's attention flickers briefly to the volcano, confused, and then they laugh.

"There's no need to worry," Azami says. "It looks scarier than it is."

"Doesn't all that smoke bother you?" Vataea presses.

Azami's voice is easy as she leads us to the swampy eastern edge of the island, toward the water territory. "Not at all. Legends say there's a beast that lives deep within that volcano, who protects Valuka from danger. We take the smoke as its way of letting us know it's still there."

This close to the artifact—this close to having the power of the gods in my hands—my bones ache to turn and run straight for the volcano until I find the fire serpent. Not only a legendary protector, but allegedly a deity made by

275

the gods—one of the godwoken.

As a child, I'd listen as Father read me legends of the fire serpent, always prattling on about how he'd one day find the beast and steal a scale off its back, just to prove he could do it. He'd said he'd bring me with him; it would be an adventure just for the two of us.

We had no idea the beast was a godwoken, but the serpent was right up there with the Lusca in terms of seafaring legends: something so powerful and otherworldly it couldn't possibly exist. But I always believed, and ever since the first time Father told me about it, I've wanted to one day face this beast. But I wanted Father there by my side when I did it.

"Have you ever seen it?" I ask, trying to keep my thoughts from wandering. If I'd come to Valuka for the first time with Father, under different circumstances, it would have meant the world to see his face when we saw the serpent. I'd give anything to have that moment with him.

"We like to give it space." Azami's voice is soft, as if she can sense something mournful in my tone. "It's widely believed that the serpent protects the island, but we Valukans have a different belief. If that volcano erupted, this entire island would be destroyed. We don't think that the serpent is protecting the volcanos from *us*; we believe it's protecting us from the volcanos. And so we give it its space to work. Besides, we couldn't get close to those fumes even if we tried."

This change to the myth takes me by surprise. I grew up with stories that told me the serpent had fangs longer than a person's body. That poison hot as fire ran through its veins, and how one touch of a scale could melt away skin. The stories said it was never seen because people were too afraid to track it down, not because it was too busy protecting an entire island from peril.

"Never mind the volcano, Your Majesty. We have something even grander to show you!" Azami's voice is rich with genuine excitement. "This season has been one of the greatest our island has seen in some time. I know there's been some hesitation around the changing laws, but they've been wonderful for Valuka. Please allow us to show you."

"Please," I say. "Call me Amora."

Azami smiles and politely bows her head.

"I admit that when she first presented her idea, I was hesitant," Lord Bargas adds in his gruff baritone. "Things have worked the same in this kingdom even longer than I've had my title; but that's part of why I'm stepping down. Azami is young; she's able to adapt to the changing times in ways I struggle to see."

"Last summer, we were on the verge of a crisis when many of our hot springs started to run dry. But, now . . ." Azami's words trail off with a grin that has my blood warming. "Now, you'll have to let us show you. Follow me right this way! We'll have your belongings waiting for you in your rooms."

Every bone in my body is aching, and the absolute last thing I can imagine doing is making small talk with strangers. Especially when I need to hurry and get to the fire serpent. Though I'm still not certain how I'm going to use it, I can't do anything until that artifact is mine.

But I'm still here on a false mission, after all. And it's practically guaranteed not all in the crowd are Valukans. Though everyone wears the same brilliant shade of ruby, I've no doubt some of those faces are truly Ikaean reporters trying to blend in. With them watching, I'll need to bide my time for the right moment.

Not to mention that Azami's excitement is infectious. Despite everything, I find myself drawn to her, wanting to follow.

And so I say, "It'd be my pleasure," because what does one more night matter? Just one more night, before I'm forced to choose my fate.

"Come on then." Azami grabs hold of my hand. "Valuka's waiting for you."

Winters on Valuka are too hot for a cloak. Even my thin linen shirt sticks to my clammy skin in the clotting heat.

Gods, I can't imagine living here during the summer.

We're deep in the water territory, surrounded by swamps with water so thick and green it's impossible to see even an inch down into it. Overgrown vines and gnarled roots snake from the ground, forming crooked, uneven pathways between the water. Most of the trees have been cleared away, creating a stretch of swamplands and marshes with wet earth that mucks onto our boots.

"Our island is the largest in the kingdom," Lord Bargas says, hands folded behind his back as he assesses the terrain around him, wrinkling his nose at the mud on his boots and trousers. "Because of that, we've adopted some alternative methods of transportation. This is where I'll be leaving you today, I'm afraid. But not without a gift."

He sweeps both hands into the air, and all around him the marshes come to life, muddy water spiraling out of them. But the water doesn't fall; instead, it takes shape as it did back on the bay, turning into a smaller, watery green dragon that hovers in the air. Beside it, more water springs from nearby marshes and takes shape into four horses that stamp their misty hooves against the ground and shake the strands of algae and vines that form their manes.

"They'll get you where you need to go," Lord Bargas offers. "Azami, I'm putting our queen and her companions in your care."

Azami grins, making a fist that she punches down at the earth. A chunk of it splits beneath her feet, lifting from the ground so that she's hovering upon it.

"She'll be in good hands, Uncle. Are you ready, Amora?"

The dragon winds around me, dipping between my legs and hoisting me onto its back in one quick motion. I gasp, expecting to be soaked, but every part of the dragon that I've touched has turned to solid ice.

"Are you sure there isn't a more . . . sanitary way for us to get there?" Ferrick grimaces at the cloudy water while Shanty gleefully climbs atop her steed. Vataea's more curious than she is cautious, running her fingers through the water. I can practically see her mind working to decipher whether she could produce something like this on her own.

"I'd no idea Valukan magic could be so versatile," Bastian says as he eyes his horse.

"Oh?" Lord Bargas asks with mock surprise. "I would have thought that someone impersonating a Valukan would have known more about it." He doesn't give Bastian the chance to bite back. Instead, he gives his wrist a small flick, and the water horse throws its head into Bastian's stomach, tossing him onto its back.

"Don't you dare, you old man—" Bastian's voice cuts off with a sharp yelp as the water horse takes off and Bastian's forced to hold on. All the while Lord Bargas laughs with such gusto his belly shakes.

The rest of our mounts take off as Lord Bargas, still laughing, waves his goodbye, and I clench my thighs tightly around the makeshift beast beneath me and hang on.

Wind whips against my cheeks, and my fingers numb against the dragon's icy body as it races across the terrain, hovering above the others.

Shanty hoots with laughter, using the horse's makeshift mane as reins. "Faster!" she yells, and the horse gives a hiss of misty breath as it obeys, stomping over the swamp water as though it were flat ground.

Not ones to be beaten, Vataea and I share a quick look before we're charging after her, laughing. I spread my arms wide as the dragon soars past them, feeling as though I'm flying as the wind beats against me. We weave between crooked and half-fallen trees covered with moss that twists around their branches.

Below, the earth pushes Azami forward, moving her swiftly across the terrain as she tails us, having to work harder to form her path around the obstacles.

Squinting against the rushing wind, I keep my head tucked and my mouth shut from the mosquitoes that swarm the stagnant swamps. We cover several miles in minutes, finally catching sight of the Valukans who wait for us in a soggy marshland. They're huddled together in a large expanse of land where all the trees have been uprooted and cleared away. Grins spread wide across their faces when they spot us.

My dragon trembles as it lowers to the ground, dissipating into steam as it drops me onto my feet before them. I sway as I land, body dizzy from the motion, but my adrenaline is surging.

Stars, I'd pay to do that again.

"So how are you enjoying our humble island so far?" Azami asks with a knowing lilt.

My responding laugh is brisk and breathless. "I'm already planning my next visit."

Her grin couldn't possibly beam any brighter. "Then you're going to love what's next." She drops the earth from beneath her and it settles back into the ground as if undisturbed. "I'd like to welcome you to the greatest show in Visidia!"

The moment she says those words, all the waiting Valukans snap into action. Those with an affinity to earth stomp their left foot against the marshland and swipe sharply through the air. The ground trembles beneath us before it breaks through the surface to form half of a curved ring, with long benches made from mud. Other Valukans harden it with white-hot flames that surge from their mouths or their palms before Azami motions for us to sit upon them. Only then do I notice that, unlike the rest of us, Bastian's soaked to the bone, his hair lying flat on his head.

"Not one word," he grumbles, settling into his seat with folded arms while more Valukans take their place, still as statues as Azami steps between them, back to us. The five of us hold our breath, and there's a split second where I wonder if this is all a trap. With this many Valukans, we'd be overpowered in an instant.

But then Azami turns around, and we're no longer in the swamplands of Valuka, but transported into the grandest performance I've ever seen. It's like the water show they performed while greeting us, but larger, and more elaborate than anything I could ever have imagined.

Perfectly in sync, the water-affinitied Valukans lift from their crouch, dragging bodies of dusky swamp water with them. In their palms, that water merges into perfect spheres they toss back and forth. Every time they do, the water splits and morphs into a new shape, until each Valukan is holding a tiny, watery dolphin, every one of them a different color.

Several Valukans lean forward and breathe onto the water, their breaths steaming with frost that freezes the dolphins over. They fall from the hands of the performers, but instead of cracking, it's as though the ground swallows the dolphins. It spits them back out again so that the dolphins look as though they're swimming on land, with ground that twists and rises around them like waves.

"Stars." Shanty draws a sharp breath as she leans in, eyes blazing with a hunger I've started to recognize in her, a hunger that happens when she's presented with something valuable that she wants for herself.

Valukans with a fire affinity are next, breathing hot spheres of flames they toss toward those with an affinity to air. The air stokes the flames, creating an inferno beneath them. Each one of us gasps as the four Valukans let themselves fall back into the inferno, diving as gracefully as swans. I release my anxious breath when I see the flames don't burn them; instead, the Valukans manipulate the air around them so that they're torpedoed back into the sky. They split off as the vortex spits them out, gracefully weaving the air beneath their feet so it looks as though they're riding upon clouds.

Some of the Valukans also practice enchantment magic; they shape and mold the air beneath them, enchanting it into shapes like dark navy clouds filled with stars, or a fierce and seething sea beast so it looks as though they're riding into battle.

When they do fall, they do it delicately, landing noiselessly upon their feet with soft bows and satisfied smiles.

We're on our feet clapping within seconds, and Azami beams, hands clasped excitedly to her chest. "You liked it? Truly?"

"Of course we did, it was incred—"

"I have so many ideas!" Shanty interrupts, the words practically exploding from her. "I've never seen elemental and enchantment magic mixed like that, it's brilliant! I think you should perform it at night. Make the colors brighter. And you can add music that syncs with what everyone is doing!" Though Azami's face twists with surprise at first, she laughs as Shanty throws an arm over her shoulders excitedly. "You're going to grow this, right? Monetize?"

"That's the plan. We'll need to get better with enchantment magic, but it's a start. We want to adapt with the changing times and show off that change doesn't have to be scary."

No longer is my guard up as she turns to seek me out, so excited and relieved that I've no idea how I ever could have suspected she'd be capable of hurting me. "I want Valuka to feel like a place brimming with magic," she says cautiously, as if hedging her bets against my input. "I want it to be a place where you can ride water horses or take off on the wind. I want there to be performances, and for it to be so beautiful that people want to come back again and again."

"It's ingenious." Shanty's grin is so hungry and crooked I almost think to pull Azami away from her. But the up-and-coming adviser is too excited, grin so wide it threatens to break her face as she clutches onto Shanty's arm happily.

"This was all your idea?" I ask.

Azami no longer appears shy when she answers. She squares her shoulders and bats away black strands of hair so she can look me straight in the eyes.

"Visidia has been stagnant for ages," she says confidently. "And many of its people are the same, afraid to embrace change and truly see what Visidia could be if we allowed the kingdom to prosper. You're changing the foundation of this kingdom, and I believe in your mission. I believe in what you're doing, and I want to be part of it."

The smile that comes with her words strikes me hard in the chest, filling an emptiness I hadn't realized I'd been sitting with.

"I want to help you mold a new Visidia," she says, voice as smooth and as confident as rain. "Together, I believe we can reshape our kingdom for the better."

And to my surprise, I believe her.

"Azami Bargas," I tell her, "I believe you're going to be one of the greatest advisers Visidia has ever seen."

$\backsim$

TWENTY-NINE

O ur first day on Valuka has only just begun.

Men buzz excitedly around us, checking their hair and breath when they think I'm not looking. Unlike on Curmana, they do not wear their finest attire, but loose tunics and cotton pants—clothing that allows their movements to be as free and flexible as their magic calls for.

"*We* wanted to be the ones who put on a performance for *you*," Azami tells me. "Not the other way around. I know you're here with a purpose, Amora, but I didn't want you to have to feel like you were on display. I wanted everything to feel as natural as it could."

"Which I'm guessing is why you didn't give me time to clean up?"

Azami offers an apologetic smile. "You're only going to sweat, anyway. I figured it'd be fun if you spent the day testing out magic with us. We can figure out your affinity!"

It's as though all the heat is zapped from the island at once, leaving me cold and tense. "I . . . thought people got to choose which element they practice?"

She tucks sleek black hair behind her ears. "You can, of course. But usually people feel drawn toward one more than the others. You'll know it when you feel it. Once you find yours, it

285

consumes you. Like you were always meant to have it, and it was always part of you." Azami grabs my hand; there's no time to stop her as she leads me from the marshes and to more solid ground.

"My affinity is to earth," she announces as a handful of Valukan men approach, offering bows and their names as they settle in beside us.

Normally Azami would be right; this would certainly be my preferred way to meet the people of each island—relaxed, and in their daily lives. But with half my soul missing, I can't practice magic, no matter how much I may want to. The High Animancer is meant to be the strongest in the kingdom— what will my people think when they discover I cannot learn Valukan magic?

She was right to say I'd be sweating—more than she could ever have imagined. My body's numb, freezing, and yet beads of sweat slick my hairline, making me nauseous.

"Start by grounding yourself to the earth," offers a young man with rich suntanned skin and freckles dusted beneath green eyes. "Let it steady you. Feel its strength from your toes." He draws a deep, exaggerated breath and waits for me to mimic it. "Do you feel it?"

I curl my toes into the earth, waiting, but all I feel is the need to scrub my feet clean.

I peer over at the others. Vataea has taken to sitting, dramatically declaring it's too hot here and that we should toss her back into the sea before she shrivels away.

Shanty, Ferrick, and Bastian all concentrate as well, trying their best despite the sweat glistening their skin. Within the hour, we discover that not even one of us has an affinity to earth. The Valukans pat our discouraged shoulders, and though Azami looks mildly disappointed, she remains upbeat.

"It's no matter," she declares with the same determination I imagine helps her choreograph such spectacular shows. "We've got all day to find your affinity!"

But we don't find it at the swamps either, where a charming man guides us through the magic he tells us is like a dance— soft and flowing, or angry and precise. I recognize the lesson as the same one I'd seen the Valukan girl giving back on Kerost.

Vataea picks it up quickly, impressing a group of starry-eyed Valukan men who clap for her. Only when they're not looking do I see her lips moving in a quiet chant to the water, and I know it's nothing more than her siren magic she's tricking them with.

Even though I'd love to be able to create my own water dragon to ride upon, it's not until we get to a roaring bonfire that desire truly stirs within me. When I had my magic, I needed fire to use it. If I had the power to create that fire myself, gods, I would have been invincible.

While we all stretch our hands toward the fire pit, trying to follow the instructions to calm our minds and reach within ourselves for the heat that's meant to somehow be in our core, it's Ferrick's hands that ignite into flames. I jolt at his surprised gasp, and jealousy flares within me as tiny embers flicker up his arm.

"Keep calm," says one of the Valukans guiding us, taking Ferrick by the shoulders. "Breathe deeply. One must have a clear mind to control this magic. Concentrate on how it feels in your palms. Breathe, and let it go."

I breathe deeper, trying to do the same, hoping and praying for the magic to come. Hating that it's not me who gets it, but heavy with guilt for my jealousy when the embers spark excitement in Ferrick's eyes, opening a new world of possibilities for him.

A tiny bead of blood starts to trail from his nose, but he wipes it away; even the difficulty of practicing a new magic doesn't sway his excitement.

My frustration and guilt only grow worse by the time we're practicing the final affinity—air. Azami watches me with curious eyes, waiting expectantly, but it's Bastian and Shanty who weave tendrils of it through their fingers, lifting leaves into their palms and laughing as they blow gusts of air into each other's hair.

Bastian's grin brims with excitement, and from the emotions I feel swelling from within his soul, I understand why—by mastering wind magic, he'll be able to help guide *Keel Haul's* sails, possibly never needing a full crew. It's brilliant, but I can't help but feel as though he's leaving me behind.

They're *all* leaving me behind.

And why shouldn't they? Ferrick and Bastian each practice three magics now, and I don't have so much as one. My blood is directly responsible for the ruination of Visidia. My own people are trying to kill me.

I'd leave me behind, too.

"Didn't you feel a spark with any of them?" Azami presses. "Maybe we missed it. If you need more time, I'm sure the others wouldn't mind staying longer to help you learn."

Azami is genuine; I know this. Like the others, she believes I'm here to find Visidia a king, and she was at least kind enough to try to make meeting Valukan suitors as natural as possible for me by working with them. Nothing she's doing is *wrong*. And yet the pressure in my chest is mounting, tearing its way through my body and leaving behind a poison that makes my chest so heavy I can barely breathe.

There's disappointment in the eyes of the Valukans. A lingering expectation that's replaced their desire to win me over. Visidia's High Animancer is meant to be the most powerful person in the kingdom, and they've just watched me fail.

Seeing them look at me like that brings me back to the night of my birthday celebration, where my magic took me over in front of a crowd. The memory is an anchor upon my chest, sinking lower and lower until it shatters whatever armor I've built around myself. I clutch my stomach, my throat, trying to force air into my lungs as my ears ring with the memories of that night.

She'll destroy everything!

She's the one who should be executed! She'll kill us all!

Bastian's head snaps up so that his eyes find mine quick as a lightning strike as my vision begins to tunnel in. He doesn't need for me to tell him I need help before he's at my side, hands squeezing my shoulders to let me know he's there.

Why am I doing this?

So what if everyone thinks me weak for not being able to learn their magic? Why is that my fault?

Why am I doing any of this?

Why does it matter what Visidia thinks of me when I'm this close to holding the key to their fate? I could free soul magic for them. I could restore Visidia to what it was always meant to be, and finally tell them the truth. I could lead our kingdom into the future it was always meant to have.

Or I could be selfish. I could have Father back, and with his revival, the pressures of the crown would no longer lie solely upon me. Mother would smile, again. I could hear his laugh, and show him Rukan. He and I could restore Visidia together, and I wouldn't feel so alone.

It doesn't matter what anyone else thinks. Visidia's fate is in my hands, and I'll do with it what I will. A queen doesn't need to smile. She doesn't need to play games.

A queen needs to rule.

"I won't do this anymore." The words don't feel like my own. They're a bitter whisper, quiet enough that Azami leans in.

"Amora?"

My knees buckle.

"The party's over." Bastian's voice is distant. "Everyone return to your homes, the queen will see you all tomorrow—"

"No." The moment the word leaves my mouth, I can breathe easier. The freedom of it brings a laugh bubbling to my throat. "No, I don't think I will see them tomorrow. I think . . . I think I'm done."

Azami's face goes ashen. Behind her, others stare dumbfounded. "Is something wrong, Your Majesty? I'm sure I can fix—"

"You've been brilliant." With each word, the pressure on my chest eases. With every breath, I feel a little more like myself. "I appreciate everything you've shown me, and everything you're doing for Valuka. I'm sure every one of these men are wonderful, but I've worked too hard for this throne; I've sacrificed too much of myself for my people. No one, no matter how kind or wonderful they may be, will ever understand or be prepared to take on the burden of this crown, and I'm tired pretending that I would let them. Tell Lord Bargas to let the kingdom know I'm done with this charade."

On every island we've visited so far, I've lost too much

time keeping up appearances. Twice, I've nearly died trying to persuade others to like me. I'm tired of pretending to be something I'm not, just to be accepted.

I am Amora Montara, and I will no longer be a pawn. I will be a queen.

"It's about time you stopped this charade," Vataea tells me as we settle into our room that evening. "I was surprised it lasted this long."

Drawing a pillow over my head, I inhale the freshly laundered lavender scent deeply, doing everything in my power to disappear into it. While I'm glad for the freedom of no longer having to parade around with suitors, there will be a storm in the parchments tomorrow.

But it doesn't matter. I can't *let* it matter. Come tomorrow, it's time to find the godwoken and change the fate of Visidia one way or another.

Only when added weight creaks the bed do I stir, peeling myself from the pillow long enough to see Vataea's golden eyes boring into me.

"Are you pitying yourself?" she asks so plainly that, for a moment, I'm reminded of how inhuman she truly is. "Or is this because you're missing your father, again?"

"I always miss him." When I sit up, she follows my lead.

"There are many whom I miss, too." While she says it casually, something heavy burdens her shoulders, caving them in. Light flickers and dims within her eyes. For centuries mermaids have been poached, harvested for their scales and for the most abominable reasons. For someone who has lived as long as she has, I'm sure she bears the loss of many.

"I know his reign was built on lies. And that he did everything he could to uphold them," I say eventually, struggling to make my voice audible. "I *know* that. But . . . I'd give anything to see him again. Even if only for a moment." I can't say what causes it, but something within me splinters beneath her glowing stare. The emotions flood through me like a dam has been broken, pouring freely and all at once. "No matter what he's done, he's my father. I can't help but feel that if he were here, he could help me fix this mess."

"You can't undo centuries' worth of lies in two seasons." Vataea takes a firm hold on my shoulders. "You are doing your best, Amora. That's enough. There are many I have lost, but I do not allow myself to become lost with them. They wouldn't want us to pause our lives because their time is up. Grieve, but do not lose yourself to your mourning."

Her words are far easier said than done. As many people as she's lost, she was never responsible for the pain—for the deaths—of so many.

"The gods are cruel to have taken him from me." My words feel pathetic, but I mean them with everything in me. So much so that I send each one at the gods like a punch, hoping they can feel every ounce of my rage with them. "I just wish they'd give him back." Together, we could restore magic. Defeat Kaven. Spare so many lives.

If I didn't know any better, I'd think the look on Vataea's face was pitying.

"Even I know it's unwise to curse your gods, Amora." Vataea slips from my bed to crawl into her own, putting out the candle on her way. "You never know when they might be listening."

292

⚝
THIRTY

S omeone's watching me.

I bolt upright in my bed, breathless.

The only light in the room is from the moonlight that bleeds onto the floor from gaps in the drapes. I squint through its silver haze, yet all I see is Vataea sleeping soundly in the bed beside mine, her breathing heavy and undisturbed.

Cautiously, I settle back into bed, confident it's my nerves catching up with me as I try to find my breath. But I'm back on my feet the moment a shadow crosses my window, clutching Rukan and poised to wake Vataea when I hear the shadow laugh.

It's a booming, proud sound that rattles my lungs and nearly brings me to my knees. I'd recognize that laugh anywhere. But . . . it couldn't be.

"Father?" My voice comes hoarse and quiet, yet his laughter echoes again in response. It's all I can do not to weep at the closeness of it.

When Vataea still doesn't stir, I pinch my wrist hard, knowing this must be nothing more than the cruelest dream. My breath catches when the pinch stings, and I don't wait another second before I throw a cape over my nightgown, steady Rukan's sheath around me, and run. I escape through the house in a blur, the cool marble biting my bare feet.

"Father!" I call again, louder once I'm away from sleeping ears. He laughs again, and this time I see what I know must be him—a blur of shadows and light sprinting across the terrain ahead.

I don't think. I just follow, moving farther and farther away from the house until the earth turns to little more than mountain and stone, pain creeping into my soles. I know with everything in me that this can't be real. It's a curse. A mirage. *Something*.

But Father's right there in front of me. He moves so quickly that, if I want to catch him, I can't hesitate.

"Wait for me," I whisper after him, fists clenching as a stone digs into my heel. "Wait a second!"

No sooner have the words passed my lips before a glowing figure emerges before me. A beast made from shimmering blue flames stands tall and proud. It's taken the shape of a wolf, overly large and burning so fiercely I struggle not to shut my eyes against it.

Its smoking paws stomp impatiently at the ground, a constant stream of fresh embers falling from its glowing fur. Orbs of white fire have taken over its eyes, and I find myself reaching for my dagger as they fix upon me.

Spotting my movement, the beast snorts as smoke flares from its nostrils, as if trying to tell me not to bother. It's not here to fight.

"Will you take me to him?" I close the space between us and offer a tentative hand to its neck, sucking in a breath of surprise when the flames don't so much as singe my skin. Forcefully, I work up the nerve to lift myself fully upon the beast, not wanting to stray too far behind Father.

The moment I'm mounted, the wolf takes off in a sprint that rivals the wind, scattering blue embers in its wake. Only there, upon the back of this fiery beast, does my mind catch up to my body, warning me that I'm a fool for following it so easily. This wolf didn't create itself, and it clearly knows where it's going. But still, Father's laugh was too real. Too close.

I can't turn back, now. Not when he's within my reach.

Father's back is to me when we find him, his body made from the red flames he shares with his own steed, a giant elk with silver antlers. Together they charge through the mountains, weaving around geysers that burst into a sky thick with shooting stars, their mist spraying down upon my skin and making the beast beneath me sizzle and steam.

"Look at me," I whisper, urging Father to turn and face me. Urging him—begging him—to show me his face and prove it's him, but fearful I'll wake up the moment he does.

But as I urge this to happen, Father turns and the fire around his body fades. For the first time since I watched him burn, I see his face.

There's his suntanned skin, wrinkled from years at sea. Warm brown eyes that glow with pride as they look me over. And a smile. Wide and wondrous and beautiful.

"It's you. It's really you."

Father doesn't respond. Instead, he lifts a hand to the sky, using magic I've never seen to draw a string of swirling constellations into his palms. They wrap around his hands and dance their way up his arms and shoulders, swirling between shades of pinks and blues and green. Again he laughs, stretching his hand to me. This time, the constellations swirl between his fingers and through my hair. I laugh as they sweep around me before exploding back into the sky, swallowing me in a sea of magic and stars.

I barely notice my cheeks are tear-soaked as I tilt my head back at them, and I don't care.

Though I'll have to wake from this dream, I pray to any god listening that reality will not come for me soon. I want to stay in this moment for as long as possible. Listening to his laugh. Seeing his smile.

All my life I've wanted this adventure with Father. Now that it's here, I pray it will last forever, until the galaxy swallows us whole and our world is no more.

But even the gods have their limits, and they've been too kind to me already.

Father's body begins to smoke at the edges, and with one swift kick to his steed, he's charging forward again. Only this time he's lifting higher and higher, as if racing into the sky. I lean into the wolf beneath me, clutching its fur tight in my fists as it charges forward, following.

Every second, more and more smoke fizzles from Father's body. It turns the air around us hazy, constricting my lungs and searing my throat. But still I follow, because there's no way he's slipping through my fingers a second time.

"Don't stop," I whisper into the wolf's ear, flattening myself against it as the smoke begins to shroud us. "Get to him."

The beast burns brightly against the haze of smoke, warming my fingers as it charges forward, stopping only when it stands before Father's halted form.

He sits tall before me, a gleaming light among smoke and shadows. He's stolen the moon and wears it as his smile.

"You certainly did get my sense of adventure." His words

swell with a pride that pierces through my chest with a might more fearsome than any blade.

"Gods," I whisper around a mouth thick with cotton as I dismount. My throat scorches with every word. "I miss you."

There's so much I want to tell him. So much I want to say. But Father's fading into smoke that's dissipating into the air too quickly. I reach out for him, desperate to find a way to keep him here with me, but he doesn't reach back.

"I miss you more than you could ever know. But I need you to be brave, Amora." His body is fading like smoke into the stars. "Be brave, my girl, and do what I could not."

I try to call out. Try to grab for him again. But my hand falls through empty air, and every ounce of my breath falls with it.

As quickly as he came, Father is gone. And yet wisps of smoke still linger in his place, taking shape into something that waits behind where he'd stood only a moment earlier—something he promised me the two of us would one day find together.

Something with large, blood-red eyes.

So the child has finally made her appearance. Welcome, Little One. I've been wondering when you would arrive.

I stumble back as the shadows stir, taking shape into a massive creature that slinks closer. Only then do I realize where I'm standing, and that Father's body wasn't purely responsible for the smoke surrounding us.

He's led me to the base of the volcano, where the deity I've been searching for waits.

He's led me to the godwoken.

But how? It should have taken hours to get to the volcanos from where we were staying. And yet my moments with Father felt like seconds.

The serpent's sleek body towers over me as it straightens itself. It's as though it's built by the night sky, growing and stretching and shrinking as the shadows ebb and flow from the glowing lava light of the volcano. Scales of onyx glisten as I stare at the slithering form, up and up until two piercing red eyes blink down at me, more curious than threatening. The serpent slithers forward, power radiating from it in waves so extraordinary I struggle to gather myself. Every limb in my body is numb; it takes excruciating effort to move even my hands.

My trembling fingers grip Rukan, and the serpent's eyes flicker to it before it hisses, forked tongue grazing my cheek.

I see you've been doing some hunting.

I force myself to look back into its eyes. The snake's mouth never moves, and yet I swear I hear those words clear as day.

Keep that weapon sheathed, or I'll make a meal out of you, Little One, destiny be damned.

I sheathe the weapon at once, quicker than I ever have despite the trembling. "You can use mind speak?"

Lowering itself, the beast coils tight, head poking out to set upon its body as it observes me. *I am a creation of the gods, Little One. I know all magics that were, are, and ever will be. You dare question me?*

I swallow, an apology hot on my tongue until I realize that the serpent is *smiling*. Its tongue forks out in what can only be described as amusement, and I grit my teeth.

"How am I here?" I ask, unable to stop my voice from trembling no matter how hard I try. "Was that . . . Was he real? Was that really him?"

He was as real as he could be, the serpent answers, voice a slow, lazy drawl. *You wanted to see him again, didn't you?*

I clench my fists, trying to will some sense back into my limbs. "Then why did you take him from me, again? There was more I wanted to say! There was more I needed to tell him—"

I have seen your burdens, Little One. Alone as you think you are, we have watched, and we have known. Tonight was the gods' gift to you; a kindness, for all the burdens you have been born to face. You were given what those who grieve often seek—one final moment. Why waste that moment with words?

"So you conjured a vision of him to lure me here?"

It was no vision. Your father's spirit lives within you, Little One. All I did was give it shape, if only for a short time.

I want to cry. I want to brandish my dagger once more and drive it into the beast again and again until the godwoken gives Father back to me. But it's right. I wouldn't have changed a single second of seeing Father tonight; it just wasn't long enough. It could never be long enough.

But it was something.

It was a chance to see that Father is not surrounded by the dead. That he's not reaching out, begging me to save him.

Father is still having his adventures; only now they're among the stars.

"Which godwoken are you?" I ask, finding my trembling voice.

The serpent appears to consider this for a moment. *Well, I'm not the one guarding the sanctity of the heavens, nor am I the one who guards the wrath of the tides. Perhaps I guard the wrath of the flames? Or perhaps it's the innocence of humans I protect? I am one of those.*

My eyes sink to Rukan, thinking of the Lusca, and the snake hisses again with distaste.

That beast you killed was no guardian. If it had been, you would not be standing here before me today. Now tell me, Little One, why have you come here? I have seen you in my head for years, but I do not know what it is that you seek in this moment. This is no place for your kind.

The serpent's right. Already my chest is getting tighter and my breaths shallower. As a thin haze forms over my vision, I suspect the only thing keeping me standing amid these fumes and smoke is the beast's magic. If it wanted, it could let me die on the smoke at any moment. But this close, there's no way I'm giving up without trying. "I'm here to borrow the magic of the gods."

The serpent slithers closer so that the glossy scales of its body brush against mine. I try to reach out to them, or to grab for my blade so that I may cut one off, but the overwhelming power of its body keeps me knocked back.

What do you wish to do with such power? There is a fork in your path; which road is it that you plan to take?

"As queen of this kingdom, I'll do whatever I'd like with it. My answer shouldn't matter to you."

I am favored by the gods. What use have I for the construct of queens? Though it doesn't physically laugh, its voice rings in my head with dark amusement.

Construct? I bristle, though the serpent couldn't care any less. It presses against me, body coiling around mine.

I have watched you little ones since the dawn of time, and every queen and king I have ever known has cared more for themselves than any other. You were given a gift tonight, and still you are greedy, wanting more. But ah, I see you know that already, don't you? I see you imagine how thriving the world and its magic might be if not for your greed. You imagine what a different world this place could be. There are many possibilities; I find myself curious what the world will look like, as well. Perhaps one day I will know.

"Not everything the Montaras have done has been bad." I don't know why I'm arguing. It's like the serpent is echoing my own inner thoughts, and it feels futile to debate a deity. But I push myself from its coiled grasp and spin to face it all the same. "There's been at least some good."

But which outweighs the other, I wonder? The wrongs, or the rights? Because all I see when I think of that answer is the possibilities. I see the "what could have beens" for this world, but never the "what will be." The new magics that could have been discovered by now, but not the ones that will be. I see the changes your kingdom could make, but know not which changes you will choose. I can only imagine the world you dream of, Little One. And I hope for it just the same as you do.

The serpent's voice grows thick and melodic. I fall into it, lulled by its words. I drown out the heat. The smoke. The sting. And I envision what the serpent wants me to: a world not built by the division of magic, but by growing with it and adapting. Expanding. I imagine a world bursting with magic—a kingdom that was allowed to spend centuries building and exploring their magic, rather than a kingdom restrained by greed.

And it's beautiful.

I see magic in the form of flowers growing from the tips of fingers. In a young man who sings songs to the birds, and who understands every word they sing back. It's a world full of color and magic I've never seen, and the beauty of it stings my eyes, making fresh tears burn within them.

I see it so clearly that my heart aches. This "could have been" world really might have been, if not for my family.

"I'm trying to make up for it." My voice is faint, grating against my raw throat. "I *will* make up for it."

What the world becomes is in your hands, you are right about that much. But one does not change the future by altering their past.

The serpent's voice is a coolness that spreads through my veins, freezing me in place. "If you didn't want me to bring Father back, then why show him to me? Why tell me it's possible?"

We are not so cruel as you believe, Little One. You did not ask to bear these burdens you were chosen to carry. For them, you were given a gift. Is it not enough to see him? To know that he is still here, still watching?

Even though I've seen him at peace, it still doesn't feel like enough. Unless Father's standing here next to me, it will *never* be enough.

Once again, my hand finds its way to Rukan. This time though, I undo its sheath, summoning every ounce of courage I have to keep my body from shaking.

"Since you seem to know everything, then you know I'm not leaving without that scale."

What I know, Little One, is but a few certain things. The first being that you and I were fated to meet; there is no timeline in which you do not seek me out. And the second being that you have a choice ahead of you—one that, no matter what you pick, will alter the fate of this world as we know it. One that will bring it into chaos, and another that will be its salvation. Choose wisely.

I know the choice it must mean—it would mean putting

the power to bring Father back and change Visidia's history there in my hands but telling me not to use it. To choose to move forward, rather than try to change the past.

"So you want me to say goodbye to him again." It's not a question. "That's a cruel punishment, even for the gods."

I do not want you to do anything, Little One. There is no right or wrong answer, there are only possibilities. The serpent blinks its beady red eyes as if to study me. *That naivete is the thing I admire most about you little ones. For even if I told you the choice you should make, you would do whatever you wanted in the end. It would matter not what I say. Besides, I am no god. I do not fully know whether destruction is what this world needs, or salvation. But I will tell you this—the gods do not take kindly to those who try to steal back their dead. It's only wise to move forward, never back.*

"Tell me," I demand, trying to still my trembling hands. "Did I do something to deserve this?"

You did nothing but what you were created to do. That is your fate, and it is why you were given that gift, tonight. Your journey is one I do not envy. It is one that will leave many scars. But those scars will heal, and in them you will find yourself. You will find what you are supposed to do. The serpent's body turns another full coil around me. *Remember that all beings have their time, even myself. You are the queen of Visidia, and with that title, you bear a responsibility no one else will ever know. As you said, it is a cruel fate, but it is yours. And what you do with it will determine Visidia's future forevermore. This goes beyond you. Remember that.*

Remember that. *Remember* that?

I don't need a reminder when all I *do* is remember. I

remember the way magic used to fill me; how it was a mighty flame in my soul, inextinguishable. I remember a time when most of Visidia wasn't living in fear. When I wouldn't need to *distract* them in order to pass a new law. When I wouldn't have had to travel to each of the islands with my guard up, fearing someone might try to kill me.

I remember a time when I could kiss whomever I wanted without doubting my feelings.

When Father's laugh would boom across the bay as we stood at the helm of *The Duchess*. The way so many trusted him, before Kaven ever became a threat.

I remember the ghost of his kiss on my forehead. The memory of blood draining from his body as life dimmed from his eyes. The sword speared through his flesh, buried deep in his belly. The nightmares of his hand reaching for me, and a face shrouded by smoke.

I remember *everything*.

I squeeze my fists tight and lift my chin to the serpent. "I won't leave here without a scale."

It dips its head, tongue forking out. *I am not the guardian who will try to stop you from getting it. I am only tasked with protecting the earth.*

My balance sways as the ground trembles beneath me, but I will not go down so easily. Clutching Rukan, I bring my blade down upon the serpent, slicing through its skin and ripping off a piece of it, scale attached. The beast hisses but doesn't jerk away, almost as though it wants me to take it. The scale comes off easily in my hand.

I curse and nearly drop it when it sears my skin. But the longer I touch it, the more power sinks through my skin and deep into my bones. For the first time since losing my magic, I find myself trembling beneath the weight of power, having to steady myself before I'm brought to the ground. Just one scale and some skin from this beast contains more magic than I've ever felt in my life.

I'm quick to tuck the scale close, backing away from the serpent that coils back, lifting its head to watch me.

As I said, I am not the one tasked to protect it, Little One. They are. The serpent's eyes flicker to the volcano behind me as lightning strikes the sky above it. Clouds black as tar billow from its mouth as the volcano erupts, white-hot magma pouring from it and bursting into the sky.

In the middle of that magma, a strange form takes shape as it stretches into the night, growing bigger and bigger until breath flees my lungs, and I understand.

There is not one guardian deity here; there are two.

This is the fire serpent.

THIRTY-ONE

Unlike the earth deity that slinks back and coils tightly into itself to watch what unfolds, the fire deity does not speak before it bares its fangs, hissing steam against my cheeks. Its entire body is made of fire; lava burns hot around it, melting everything in its path. Magma drips from its fangs, and its eyes are the heart of a fire, white hot. The heat radiating from its body is stifling, nearly suffocating me.

You are a fool to allow this girl to hold so much power. Have you not learned from the past? This guardian's voice is booming as it condemns the other, whose blink is slow and calm.

The little ones will do what they want, says the earth deity. *Her being here was fated.*

The fire deity's tongue lashes out in distaste before it slinks closer. I choke on its presence, smoke gripping my throat as I stumble back in search of the fiery wolf that brought me here. Miraculously, it still waits for me, curling its claws into the ground and flaring a bright white. As I reach for it, it heeds my call and helps me onto its back, taking off down the mountainside as I clutch the snake scale to my chest.

Stop helping her! hisses the fire serpent as it slams its body into the ground, chasing after me. The earth deity doesn't pay the other any mind as it coils into a corner, body fading into the shadows.

With every inch closer that the godwoken slithers, fire and lava flare. They devour the ground beneath the beast, as if attempting to crack the island itself wide open.

I don't know how the black, poisonous fumes of the volcano haven't gotten to me, yet. It must be the same magic that has me on the back of this fiery beast, racing down the mountain as fast as the wind.

Drop that scale and leave, human. I won't ask you, again.

I ignore the serpent and clench the rich onyx scale to my chest, pouring all my focus into it, using it as a beacon to focus my thoughts and keep myself standing.

I will not give in. I will not let go when I've come this far.

The godwoken rears its head back, bares fangs as long as my body, and strikes.

I cling tightly to the wolf beneath me as it banks a sharp left, digging the fingers of my free hand into its ember fur for balance. The heat of the godwoken's body is all consuming, making the earth swim and my skin slicken with sweat.

The ground trembles and roars beneath us with every movement, steam trailing from the ground. I'm about to twist away from the threatening geysers beneath us when I see a flash of black hair in the corner of my eye.

"What are you doing?" I yell. "Get out of here!"

Vataea stands barefoot at the edge of the mountainside, nightgown clinging against her clammy skin. She grounds her feet into the earth, assessing the steam of the geysers beneath us.

"Keep running" is the only warning she gives before a song consumes her. It's honey and wine, intoxicatingly sweet but soured with a bitter edge that makes my head spin. As she sings, the trembling amplifies, so fierce that even the godwoken jerks back.

But it's too late. Vataea's song commands the water, and as she lifts her hands to the sky, the earth cracks and water erupts, striking the serpent firm in the chest. It roars, twisting to her, but I'm quicker. Tugging on the embers of my wolf, I steer it sharply for Vataea, grabbing her palm and jerking her behind me, onto the wolf's back.

"You could have already been down this mountain," she growls, breathless. Her grip on my waist is weak, floundering like a fish out of water in the midst of this heat. "What were you *thinking*, Amora?"

Behind us, the serpent cries out. The sizzling of its body is so loud my ears ache, and the steam burns my eyes. I can barely squint through it all, disoriented as we race ahead. The scale in my palm burns, ready to tear a hole through my flesh. From the shaking ground and the steam that follows me, I know the serpent's still behind us, slowed but not stopped.

"There was no time for thinking." My lungs squeeze, starting to feel the effects of the volcano. "Can you call the water again?"

"I can try." Vataea's voice trembles with a song as she calls another geyser. This time though, the water not only gets the deity, but also the wolf. It sizzles beneath us, buckling with the effort until we stumble off its back.

Vataea hits the ground on her knees, snarling from the pain. Her breaths are too tight. Too loud in the overwhelming heat. She wouldn't be able to summon more of her magic even if she tried.

Pushing her behind me, I clutch Rukan tight and spin to

face the serpent that looms above us, raining steam and embers.

Its fangs are lava that drip from its mouth and onto its molten body. They're startlingly bright, and white as Curmana's shore. And they're about to devour me.

Until, suddenly, they're not.

The serpent throws its head back with a roar, and I jerk back in surprise, trying to find the source of its pain.

Bastian's behind it on his own steed, his palms pouring blood that's been coated on a group of rocks he floats beside him, using Valukan air magic. He throws the cursed stones at the beast, eyes raging.

But this beast isn't like the Lusca. A curse doesn't hold it for more than a few seconds.

I turn in time to see Ferrick's here too, hauling Vataea onto a blazing orange horse. "The next time you ask me on a blasted adventure, I swear to the gods, it had better be a vacation!" he yells.

"If we get out of here, I'll take you wherever you want. Now hurry and get Vataea somewhere cooler." I choke on burning breaths, doing everything I can to keep my focus on Bastian.

"My duty is to protect you—"

"I'll buy the queen some time." The voice belongs to Shanty, who follows at a respectable distance behind, clearly wanting to be the first to get herself out of here if things go awry. "Get Vataea out of here, Ferrick."

Vataea hisses at the words, but the knot in Ferrick's throat bobs only once as he swallows, then nods.

"Just get out of here alive, all right?" he says to me.

I nod. "All right."

Wrapping his arms around Vataea to keep her stable, he

kicks the horse's side and it takes off, leaving nothing but embers in its wake.

"You need to get out of here, too," I tell Shanty, who rolls her eyes.

"Trust me, I'm on it. But not without a little parting gift." Dropping to the ground, she slams a palm against the earth. Like the strange door from when I first discovered the Barracuda Lounge, the world around us twists into an illusion of enchantment.

Extra trees spring from the earth. Mist rolls in, concealing us. Visions of fiery wolves take shape, pacing back and forth in the darkness and tricking the eye.

By the time she's done, Shanty sways and grabs on to her fiery steed. "Use that to your advantage."

"We will. Now hurry and get to *Keel Haul*."

I don't wait to see her off. Instead I spin to see Bastian's still fighting the godwoken with curses that have almost no effect on it. Though it stills for a moment each time Bastian hits it with a stone, it snaps out of the curse no more than a few seconds later, spitting fire. It's enough time for Bastian to get back to my side, letting the godwoken struggle to find us in the mist.

Enough! Magma swells, brightening the night at once. And it's clear that, no matter how magnificent Shanty's power or how fast these steeds may be, there's no way we're going to outrun the godwoken.

"Do you have it?" His voice is harsh from the smoke.

I wrap my fingers around the scale and the handful of bloodied snake skin it's attached to and nod. "We're going to have to fight."

"We can't even *touch* it," he argues. "How are we supposed

to beat something that'll melt our weapons?"

He's right; not even Rukan is any match for this beast. To have even a chance of it, we'd need the power of the gods. Fortunately, we have that.

The fire serpent's above us now, its heat and power all consuming, a true beast of legends.

But I've bested one legendary beast before, and I can do it again.

"We have to use soul magic. It's the only way." With the scale in one hand, I take Bastian's hand in the other, as though my body knows exactly what to do before my mind can catch up. The moment our skin touches, it's as though the fire all around us is now within me.

With the power of the gods in my palms, I can feel my magic pulsing within Bastian. It burns in my blood and takes root in my veins, spreading like wildfire.

Bastian rips his hand from mine, fizzling the fire away at once. Even in the sweltering heat, it makes me cold as frost.

"You saw what happened last time." He scowls. "I can't control it. Not to mention I had to put Elias's blood in my *mouth*. I can't exactly do that with lava, Amora."

"Then we won't use yours." We won't make it much longer in this smoke. Every one of my breaths comes in a rasp now, thin and painful. "We'll use mine. My soul magic isn't a gods-created magic; we can use it against the godwoken."

Panic contorts his face. "But you can't use your magic."

"I can't use it *alone*. I need you to trust me, Bastian."

And though I know he's scared—though I know he wants nothing more than to run—Bastian grips me by the shoulder. "I trust you."

That's all I need.

I slip the crinkling snake skin from my wrist and hold it like a cup, praying that this will work. The other godwoken hadn't been worried about the fire; it wasn't worried about being burned.

Its skin is immune to the flames. Why else would it live so close to the volcano?

When I work up the courage to lunge, it's not for the guardian, but for the lava that drips from its body like a second skin. To my relief, it sits in the makeshift snake skin cup, not burning me.

The fire serpent sinks backs, angry and cautious, with seething white eyes. *What are you doing?* Its tension tells me it already knows—I have a fire and now its skin. I have everything I need for soul magic.

The fire is building, and now there's only one way to know if my plan works. I take Bastian's hand and let the magic between our souls swell once more as I hold on tight. "We have to try."

"It's my soul, Amora. If I let you in . . . there won't be any going back. There's no more running away from me."

"I know." I squeeze his hand. "It's my soul too, remember? Bring me to it."

There's no time to worry about whether there will be consequences, or what this will mean for him and me. Bastian pulls soul magic around him like a shield, and despite the danger, I shut my eyes and follow his lead as it consumes us.

I *feel* him everywhere. In my skin, in my soul, in my mind. I feel his spirit. Taste the salt on his skin as he opens his soul to me. As he lets me into the most intimate parts of him.

Bastian's soul is one of pain. Of longing. Yet it shines with adventure, brighter than any I've ever seen.

He's beautiful.

I hesitate as I feel the familiar sensation of magic prying at me, trying to delve into my soul the same way I'd seen it done with Father the night he died.

At first, I don't let it. My body tenses on its own, rejecting the attempt. For nearly a full season I've hidden from Bastian. I've hidden in my own thoughts, avoiding my own feelings. But not anymore.

Now, I let him in. And the moment I do, magic consumes us as he extends it out to me.

I press the snake skin and molten fire into his hands, and Bastian drops the piece of the fire serpent into writhing flames, keeping the earth deity's skin in hand.

We are two people, but we are one soul.

Soul magic flows through Bastian and into me, and I relish its coolness in my veins. In the way it fills me, making me whole.

I shut my eyes to focus on the magic flaring to life within us, helping guide it through Bastian and into me. This time, with the two of us, the magic obeys our command.

We feed the serpent's skin to the flames, and its fire fizzles out at once. The deity rears its head back as the lava peels away from its charring body. Without its fiery armor, it's no longer as big as it looked, or nearly so threatening.

When the magic between Bastian and me snaps, I nearly fall to my knees before he catches me. There's something different when our skin touches this time, a spark of whatever just happened between us. I feel him stronger than ever. The tension in his muscles. The awe as he watches the deity slink back.

Together, no repercussions come from his soul magic. Together, we were strong enough to take it down.

Heed my warning, human, the godwoken warns, voice a vicious hiss. *If you choose the wrong path, there will be no coming back.*

But we don't listen. We only run.

∾
THIRTY-TWO⊙

We make it to *Keel Haul* breathless and battered, stumbling onto the deck as though it's our salvation.
The others have prepared the ship for departure. The moment we're aboard Vataea begins chanting at the water, wasting no time. She's already significantly improved, her dripping-wet hair enough to tell me she must have cooled off by taking a dive. Though I wish there was a chance to say goodbye to Azami and thank her for everything she's done, there's no time.

I fall to my knees, lungs gasping for the clean sea air, raw from smoke and breathlessness. My head spins, vision blurry as I fight the urge to pass out, as my body likely should have done ages ago. But I refuse to focus on the spinning, and I won't give in to my blurring vision.

"I see none of this crew cares about beauty sleep," Shanty grumbles as she wraps her arms tightly around herself. "Must we get into trouble at *all* hours of the night?"

Ignoring her, I clutch the snake scale close to my chest and let its magic pulse against my skin. It's lightweight, with a warmth that sinks into my core. Its latent magic is powerful enough to clatter my bones and make my skin feel as though it wants nothing more than to crawl into itself.

This is magic. I thought before that I was strong, but I held nothing on this power. This feels impossible. Gods-like.

I want this magic, forever. This power. This ability of the gods. It's mine.

It's mine.

It's mine—

"Amora?" My body goes rigid as Ferrick crouches beside me. Sweat and ash lick his brows and dust his face, though it's the worry in his eyes that I focus on. "What is that?"

The snake scale's no longer warm—it's scorching. I gasp and set it before me on the deck when it burns my palm, wincing at the pain. Ferrick's presence steadies me, and I realize with dawning horror that those thoughts were not entirely my own.

This magic is powerful, dangerous.

"It's a scale from the godwoken." Drawn to touch it again, I clasp my hands together and press them tightly against my lap, resisting. "This is what's going to fix everything."

When Bastian reaches out to touch it, I slap his hand away on instinct, going still as I do. Even Shanty and Vataea are watching now, and everyone recoils with surprise. Again I clasp my hands together, fingers twitching. "I . . . I'm sorry. Just, please, don't touch it."

Bastian's brows knit with worry, but he withdraws his hands. "What were you thinking, going after that alone? You could have been killed."

Dragging my trembling limbs to a stand, I wordlessly scoop the scale and cradle it close again. There are no words for the things I saw, tonight. For the things I experienced.

In my hands, I hold the chance to bring Father back. I have a chance to bring back everyone who died that night on

Arida last summer. All I have to do is take it.

Even if it means Visidia must wait longer to be fully restored, and I'm forced to find another way to break my curse.

Even if it means losing my entire crew.

My body trembles from the weight of the power I cradle in my arms, and the anticipation of what's to come. "Set our course to Arida."

"That's *it*?" Vataea's honeyed voice is too bitter on the tongue. I level my stare, though it's impossible to match the ferocity in her eyes. "Bastian's right. You snuck out in the middle of the night after *multiple* assassination attempts, didn't tell a single one of us, and nearly got yourself eaten by a giant snake. Are we your friends, or are we your subjects? Because I almost died for you, Amora. And I can't understand why you'd put yourself in that position without saying anything to the people who *care* about you."

I clutch the snake scale closer, leaning into its power. It calls to me even stronger than a siren's song, and I want nothing more than to obey it. I just don't know which path to choose—what could have been, or what could be.

"You are both," I tell Vataea gently, unable to speak any louder. "I'm sorry, but wherever I drag you along, there's always danger waiting. As a friend, I'd like to protect you, and would hope that you trust me to do that. But as your queen, I'm asking you to obey."

Vataea turns her head away, fists clenched, while Bastian steadies a hand on my shoulder. There's tension in his jaw. "Just tell us if you're all right."

I try to focus on the magic pulsing against my fingertips. On the possibilities of the future I could give Visidia if I turned back time. If I had more help. If I had Father back at my side, my people would have more trust in their ruler. The fire serpent had meant to give me a moment of peace with Father, but all that's done is make me yearn for a true reunion even more.

If I brought him back, I could sleep again, no longer plagued by the faces of the dead watching over me.

But the cost of this reality is growing more profound with each passing day. And to answer Bastian's question, no, I don't know that I'm all right. Perhaps I'm not. But I can't waste this time dwelling when, one way or another, everything's about to change.

I think of the all-consuming emotion of standing hand in hand with Bastian as we performed soul magic. Even now, I feel as though our insides have been cracked open and exposed to each other, raw and bleeding. And yet I can't look away.

I don't *want* to look away.

Because in opening myself to him, I know the truth now. Bastian Altair feels like home, and I never want to leave.

I take hold of his hand, squeezing it briefly, just once. Before I can let nerves get the better of me, I say, "Get this ship on course, and then meet me in your cabin. There's something I need to talk to you about."

THIRTY-THREE

Stepping into the captain's quarters feels like walking into a memory. I cross the floor, heart heavy as I eye the luxurious four-poster bed and the warm flicker of the oil lamp, which reminds me both of my and Bastian's first real kiss, and of the days I spent down here after I first lost my magic.

My fingers trail along Bastian's desk, admiring the atlases and maps strewn neatly across it, organized in a way I know only him to be. His closet is color coded with fashions from each of the islands, with shoes carefully lined beneath them according to height and style. Seeing them like that, not an inch out of place, I smile. As abrasive as Bastian can be, it's charming how meticulous he is with his belongings.

Every passing minute feels like an hour as I make my way to his bed, sitting cross-legged upon the navy sheets. I've tucked the snake scale away in my room so that I'm no longer tempted to touch it, so there's nothing here to distract me from the nerves roiling within me, making me pick at the skin around my fingernails, peeling until they bleed.

When the door to the captain's quarters cracks open, those nerves leap to my throat, thickening it so fiercely I fear I may never speak again. Bastian shuts the door behind him, the fall of his boots slow as he makes his way down the creaking wooden stairs. His throat bobs when he sees me, and he hesitates.

"I know you're going through a lot, and I'm sorry for it." He takes a seat at the edge of the bed, careful to give me space. "But . . . you know you can talk to us, right? Any one of us. We're all here for you."

Bastian must sense my nerves, because he reaches out a cautious hand. Pressing my lips together, I take it, lacing my fingers through his. The moment our skin touches, a weight lifts from my chest and shoulders. I can breathe easier against him.

And though I've hated this fact, now I lean into it, wanting to sear the feeling of his touch into my memory.

"I've hated this past season, you know," I say softly. "I hated making myself stay away from you."

Something in his demeanor cracks. His breaths are too sharp, and his grip softens in mine. "Amora . . ."

I shake my head before he can say anything more, and push onto my knees. Eyes never straying from his, I close the space between us, waiting for him to stiffen. To hesitate. To tell me that after everything I've put him through, I'm not welcome.

But Bastian does none of these things. Rather than push me away, his hands find my hips and help pull me onto his lap. As my legs kick over his hips to straddle him, his hazel eyes glint with hunger and his grip on my hips tightens.

"You're going to have to tell me what we're doing here." His words are husky and low. "I don't want to misread you."

I press my hips firmly against his, stroking my fingers through his hair as his head rolls back with a low groan. "There's nothing to misread. I'm terrified of the things I feel for you, Bastian Altair. But to say that I felt none of these things before my soul was cursed to you is a lie. I wanted you

320

then, and by the gods, I want you now. But only if you still want me, too. I won't blame you if you don't."

But please, please do.

He looks me over, as if taking in what he's being presented with and trying to determine whether it's real. Eventually, his confident eyes meet mine. "I want you, Amora. All of you. Now and forever, that's all I've ever wanted."

There's a sweetness in those words I wasn't expecting, and it's jarring. This isn't how any of my previous nights with men have gone. They'd all been a series of tangled limbs and wanting bodies, pressed together to satiate a temporary hunger. None of them had ever satisfied *this* desperate hunger I have now. This bone-deep want.

No one else has ever looked at me the way he does.

"All of you," Bastian repeats firmly, not daring to look away. "That's what I want, if you'll have me."

"I will." I lean back on his lap and unclasp my cloak, letting it fall to the ground. My shirt is next; I don't look away as I strip it over my head and toss the garment to the floor, for once not caring whether it gets ruined or dirty.

The moment my clothes hit the floor, Bastian takes me by the hips and flips me onto the bed. He's swift to remove his shirt before he's the one straddling me, kissing me from the ear down, taking his time to reach my lips. My neck. Taking the skin of my collarbone gently between his teeth. I wrap my arms around him as he drifts lower, dragging my fingers over the pronounced muscles of his back, or taking fistfuls of his chestnut hair when he gets too low for me to reach. His lips trail from my navel to my hips, where he hesitates. There's a question in the eyes that glint up at me, and my entire body heats with desire that flares from that single look. I understand exactly what he's offering, and I want it.

When I nod, his fingers fumble with the buttons of my pants, and he eases them off, kicking them to the floor before his lips are against my skin once again. This time though, they travel even lower, and as he finds the most sensitive area of me, I unravel. I dig fingers into his hair. Into the sheets around us. Into anything I can get my hands on until my body shudders around him. I'm breathless, reveling in what he's given me. But I'm not done with him, yet.

I pull Bastian up so that his body's over mine, and I kiss him firmly. "More," I say against his lips, igniting at his low laugh.

"Are you sure?"

"Yes." I've never been so sure of anything in my life. "And I have wild carrot seed to take after, so we'll be safe." I start at Bastian's pants, but as he stands to finish undressing, my only job is to lean back on the bed and admire him.

The warmth of his brown skin glows like the sun in the flicker of candlelight. His chest and shoulders are broader than I remember. When he takes too long, I lift to my knees to drag Bastian down to the bed.

His eyes widen when I don't pull him over me again, but instead drag myself onto his lap.

"Why do you look so surprised?" I laugh, smoothing my fingers through his hair and peppering kisses along his neck to quell his nerves. "Have you been with someone before?"

"I have." His hands settle onto their familiar place upon my hips, and I shudder as his thumbs trace patterns over my bare skin. "Just not . . . like *this*."

He nods to my body, and I understand at once that

Bastian's used to being the one in control.

Perhaps it's selfish, but tonight I want him in all the ways *I* want him. Because no matter what comes after this—no matter what choice I make—it's me who's going to lose something when the time comes to use that scale. So for tonight, I will be selfish.

I take his face in my hands and plant the softest kiss on his mouth. "That's okay. If there's anything one of us doesn't like, we'll stop."

He brushes his fingers through my curls, tucking a strand back behind my ear as his thumb strokes my cheek. He smiles as he does it, soft and content, and kisses me back.

It's a slow kiss, soft and tender, melting my body against his. But it grows into something fierce and desperate, until it feels as though there isn't a single thing in the world that can satiate me except for him.

When we connect, there's nothing I want more than for this moment between us to last. Curse or not, being with Bastian in this way is unlike anything I've ever experienced. It's like our bodies are made for each other. Where he touches, my skin turns to fire. When I kiss him, his body bends to mine.

I've no way to know how long we've been tangled together before we relax on the sheets, both of us breathless and veiled in sweat. Yet neither of us makes any motion to pull away.

Bastian holds me close against his bare chest, burrowing his face against the crook of my neck. I want to live in this moment long enough to capture it. To remember the feeling of his soft, contented breaths. The way his body feels against my skin. How he combs his fingers through my curls, wrapping them around calloused fingers.

He's more vulnerable than I've ever known him to be, and I can't help but wonder what would happen next between us. If the snake scale weren't waiting, where would Bastian and I go from here?

"You have something planned." He speaks the words against my neck, sending chills down my spine and goose bumps along my arms. "I trust you, Amora. We all do. But we're also worried about you. Is this . . . Is it about what we saw in Nelly's memories? About the choice her father made?"

I still, and for a moment Bastian tenses as if he's worried I might pull away. But I don't, even while guilt weighs my stomach like lead.

"Kaven changed the landscape of this kingdom forever." I keep my voice flat. "Our people no longer trust me to lead them, even if I'm one of the few who knows the truth behind our history. I'm trying to help fix the damage my family has done. But if Visidia knew the truth about the Montaras . . . there's no way they'd listen to anything I say. With the artifact, I could have a chance to change things. I have a chance to fix Visidia."

"Amora." Instinct makes my body relax at the way my name sounds coming from his lips. I shut my eyes, focusing on how his fingers toy with my curls as he talks. "Sometimes, beautiful things come from our most painful experiences. Before your reign, Zudoh was nearly wiped out. The Kers were killing themselves by trading time off their lives to Blarthe, just for the possibility of one day having their homes back. Magic was being kept from our people.

"Your family made mistakes that changed the history of this kingdom, you're right," he continues. "But if you don't tell them the truth, what makes you any better than the rest of them? No Montara ever gave Visidia a choice until you took the throne. I know it's hard, and I know . . . I know you have the power to do some things that look pretty appealing right now. But the Amora I know? She'd do whatever it took to give her people their freedom. To give them the future they deserve. And *that's* the Amora I'm in love with."

A knot coils tight in the center of my chest, making the words even more difficult to grit out. "I miss him, Bastian. I feel like, if he were here, he'd know what to do about all of this. I feel like he could fix everything."

Bastian presses his forehead to the back of my neck and kisses the skin there with a gentle sigh. "You don't need his help; you already know what needs to be done. The king may have been a loving father, but he was not a great ruler. He fixed *nothing*. He would have done whatever was best for him and his family alone. You're not like that; you can't be. Visidia may be changing, but it's only getting stronger. It may still be finding itself, but one day it will stabilize again, I promise you."

The king may have been a loving father, but he was not a great ruler. The words strike something within me, fierce and gutting. My entire body tenses, thinking back to the serpent scale once more. All I need is someone who can use time magic, and Father's as good as alive. In two days, my entire world could change, and I could have him back.

All my life I believed I was made to sit on Visidia's throne, but being on it now, I know with certainty I'm as wrong for the throne as Bastian believes Father was.

I suppose the real question then is which one of us is worse.

"Do you think he *could* have been a good king?" At first, I'm not sure my words even come out, they're so quiet. "If I'd gone straight to him about Kaven, do you think he would have listened? That there's a reality where he would have taken our side?"

Bastian's hesitation is enough of an answer, though it's not the only one he gives. "I think your father's love for you was so great that he didn't even know what to do with it. He knew you idolized him. I think the last thing he would ever have wanted was for you to grow to despise him. Because of that, I think he would've tried to keep his truths hidden from you forever. So no, I don't think he'd have taken our side. And that's the difference between you two. I think everything happened in the only way it could happen. But I also think that there's no good that can come out of this conversation." With a gentle stroke to my cheeks, he bends to plant a kiss against my skin.

"Sometimes it's hard as a man to be open and share what you're feeling," Bastian continues. "The kingdom expected him to be stern and strong, and so that's who he showed them he was. But he broke that facade every time he saw you. The two of you loved each other in a way I wish I'd been able to know with my own father. I hardly knew King Audric, but I saw it when you two were together the night of your birthday.

"No one can tell you how to grieve." He curls his fingers into mine. "You need to mourn in whatever way is right for you. But he wouldn't have wanted to see you thinking like this. He believed in you; he died so that you could live and help the kingdom in a way he was not able to. The last thing he'd want is you giving up the sacrifice he made."

Never once have I spoken about what happened that night. Mother wanted to know details, but no matter how hard I tried, I couldn't give them. Every time I tried to think about them, I'd think of the blood. I'd think of the life draining from his body and eyes, and I'd lose myself to the pain of that night all over again.

But tonight is different. This time when I think about Father's death, it's not the blood or the sword I see. It's the moment when he took me to the deep, secret place within his own soul, and I'd spoken my last words to him: *I can't forgive you for this.*

For so long I've tried to avoid thinking of that moment, of the words I've wanted for so long to take back.

My last moment with Father was spent telling him how wrong he was and blaming him for the many mistakes he'd made. And tonight, even if it wasn't truly him, I still hadn't managed to tell him I was sorry.

I don't realize I'm crying until Bastian winds his arms around me tight and bundles us into the sheets. He's saying something between soothing sounds, but I can't focus enough to make out the words. I bury my face in his chest, unable to stop every feeling that floods through me at once. Pain, mourning, and an absolute, unending numbness.

"I told him I couldn't forgive him." I nearly choke the words into Bastian's skin, and his shoulders slump with understanding. "Those were my last words. Not goodbye. Not how much I love him. I told him I could never forgive him."

"You didn't need to tell him how much you loved him." Bastian holds me tight no matter how hard I cry on his bare skin, making a mess of his chest. "He knew. I promise you, if there's one thing King Audric knew, it's that you loved him."

And gods, I want him to be right. I want nothing more than to believe that as my truth. But there's no way for me to truly know.

Father is dead. And if I choose to break my curse, I will never have the chance to tell him how much I love him.

❡

THIRTY-FOUR

I wake before dawn, peeling from the warmth of Bastian's bed and quietly pulling on my coat and boots. Avoiding the creakiest of the steps, I sneak out of the captain's quarters and back to my own cabin well before anyone should be awake.

To my surprise, it's not a sleeping Vataea who waits for me.

Both she and Ferrick stand in the room, him a disheveled mess and her feral. She speaks in a low and angry hiss while Ferrick tries to placate her, hands held up in defense.

My hand slips from the door as Vataea's golden eyes cut to me, far more lethal than I've ever seen. Even while pulling men into the sea, she never looked half as frightening as she does now.

She jerks from the floor and has me against the wall with no warning, her forearm pressed against my throat. "To think I ever called you a *friend*." Her words are a snarl worse than the Lusca's and more fearsome than even the godwoken. Her other hand is beside my head, claws out and grating into the wood. "You've been using me like everyone else, haven't you? You're no better than any of them!"

"Let her talk, Vataea!" Ferrick grabs hold of her shoulder, but she whirls so quickly I don't understand what's happened until Ferrick reels back, stumbling and clutching a bleeding arm to his chest. Only then does the light snap back on in Vataea's eyes. Horror-struck, she clutches her hand tight against her chest and draws a step back.

"Everyone told me not to trust humans." The sea lashes around us, the tides swelling with a ferocity that matches her words. "I thought you were different, but all you humans do is lie. You take what you want, and you *lie*."

I clutch my throat, choking on the words I force out of them. "What are you—"

"Blarthe!" she yells, nails digging into her palms as she clutches them into fists. "You have Blarthe, and you didn't tell me!"

My fingers are numb on my throat. Ferrick drops his red-rimmed eyes to the floor. The stone with Nelly's memories sits between them, and I know at once that she's realized everything.

"She knew you were hiding something, so she went looking for clues." Thoroughly miserable as he slumps against the wall, Ferrick doesn't bother to even heal his own arm. "We should have told her the truth sooner."

"V," I say softly, "I'm sorry. I wanted to tell you, I swear. I just . . . I was afraid to."

"My name is Vataea." Each syllable is sharp as ice, ready to impale. She kicks the cursed stone with her boot, and I flinch as it scuffs the wood. "I am not fragile. You asked me why I stayed, why I risk my life for you, and I told you the truth. You had plenty of chances to be honest with me, but you are a coward." She kicks the stone again, her anger swelling. It's like she's barely able to contain it, drawing sharpened breaths and raking her bloodied fingernails through her hair.

"I have to break this curse." My voice trembles more than

I'd like it to. "I needed Blarthe alive until I found what I was looking for."

"And *will* you break your curse?" I've never heard a voice so cold as hers. "Ferrick and I saw what that man in the memories did. He altered time to raise the dead, Amora. Tell me you don't intend to do the same. Tell me that you're not planning to waste every moment of our lives these past two seasons. I didn't come this far to go back to where I was, and neither did this kingdom."

My hesitation lasts for a beat too long. Her scowl sinks deep into her face, as though vying to become a permanent fixture.

"I—no. I'm not sure, yet." My words aren't coming out like I want them to.

"You are a disappointment, *Your Majesty*," Vataea spits with pure venom. "I would have helped you regardless. I would have helped more than you will ever know, had you been honest."

I follow after her when she turns to take the stairs two at a time, climbing up to the deck and wasting no time peeling out of her cloak, then her pants, tossing them to the floor as she grabs hold of the rigging and hauls herself onto the railing.

"My people were right to never concern themselves with you humans." She casts me a glance from over her shoulder. "I will not be anyone's *subject*. I hope you find yourself again, but right now you're lost, and I've been used enough for one lifetime."

In that moment, Vataea is more human than I've ever seen her. There's sorrow in the way her brows knit together before she slowly turns to the sea. And then she jumps.

The moment her body hits the water, my knees threaten to give out from beneath me. I buckle, breath caught in my throat, choking me.

In the distance, I watch as a rose gold fin lifts from the sea and smacks down upon it with a final goodbye before disappearing.

Just like that, Vataea's gone.

I try not to look at Ferrick, but my body betrays me. His shoulders sag, body wilting into itself, and I force myself to turn away as grief crumples him.

"I'm sorry." His words are barely a whisper for the wind. "She found the stone, and I had to tell her. I couldn't lie to her anymore."

"Why were you even in my cabin to begin with?" I rip my eyes toward him, and though his cheeks flush red and flustered, he doesn't answer. "You should have let me be the one to tell her." I can't stop the way his words swim in my head.

I couldn't lie to her. I couldn't lie . . .

I hear the judgment in his tone. The disappointment. The warning of the godwoken, telling me that all must die.

The gray skies tunnel around me, their shadows reaching and consuming. I fall deeper and deeper into that tunnel, to where Father waits for me as I shut my eyes, not on his steed with his smile burning bright, but with his face trying to emerge from behind a swath of shadows. His hand is outstretched, waiting for me again.

Be brave, he'd told me. But what did that *mean*? No matter which choice I make, I would be losing someone I love. No matter what I do, I will lose Visidia by using the power of the godwoken.

"We're not letting you disappear on us, again." I barely hear Bastian's voice through the fog of my brain and my muddled thoughts. It isn't until he presses a hand to my shoulder and I feel him there, presence warming my body, that the fog dissipates and I'm able to focus on his words. "Come back to us, Amora."

One of them drapes a coat over my shoulders, easing me down to the deck where we lean against the mast. Being here with nothing but the sea stretched endlessly before me and the briny air on my tongue is steadying. It grounds me enough that my fingers stop searching for the satchel they won't find, and I lean back. I tip my head to the sky, and for a while the three of us sit like that. It isn't until Ferrick brushes my boot with his that I stir to attention.

"I admit that I prefer the land," he says, surprising me with the softness of his tone, "but there's something about being out on the sea that can't be replicated. It feels like we're alone in the world; like it's all ours. The sea, the stars, all of it. It feels like it's ours to grab. I've always understood why you love this life so much."

"You love it, too," Bastian mumbles, keeping his eyes to the sky. "Don't pretend."

"I've gotten *used* to it. But it's not the same for me. You two love the adventure of it. The being able to go wherever you want, and seeing whatever you'd like. I prefer the land. The stability—always knowing where everything is, and the routine of it all. But what I've loved is the time I've spent with you all. I didn't have a crew like this back on Arida; I barely had friends, other than Casem. Spending these past two seasons with you all has . . . Well, it's taught me a lot about myself. I feel like a different person from who I was before, and I can't imagine never having been able to have that."

They're words that tear into me, melting my heart and

ripping it apart with guilt. In our time on *Keel Haul*, Ferrick truly has grown into himself.

"I'm sorry for what I asked of you," I whisper. "I'm sorry that she's gone."

"So am I." He tips his head back to the sky, emptying his lungs. "But I have a feeling it's not for good. Vataea processes emotions differently than we do, I think. She has every right to be mad, but I hope she'll give us another chance."

Carefully, I ease closer to Ferrick and rest my head on his shoulder. He bends too, so that his cheek sets against the top of my head.

"You know I will always love you." He kisses the top of my hair, and my heart softens. "I will always be here for you, because you're my best friend. But this decision you're about to make affects so much more than just you. Talk to us."

"The kingdom is crumbling." My voice wavers. "It's changing too quickly for everyone to keep up, and there's nothing I can do to help it. People want me *dead*. How am I supposed to lead a kingdom that tries to poison me? Who wants me dead and gone? If I had my father here . . . he could help. The kingdom would feel safer."

"Just because things are difficult right now, that doesn't mean you're doing anything wrong. You're trying to make up for centuries of mistreatment. It's okay if it feels hard; it should feel hard. But you can do this, and we can help you." Ferrick shows none of the anger I expect as I pull away to look at him, nor is there sympathy in his expression. Rather, there's pity in those green eyes. He sets a gentle hand on my shoulder, willing me not to look away.

I brush it off me. "Don't treat me like I'm a child," I snap, though the moment the words are out, I wish I could bite them back. "I'm fine."

"If you're fine, tell me what you were thinking of doing with that scale," he challenges. "Tell me you weren't considering twisting time so far back that we'd have to do this all over again."

I look away, saying nothing. Ferrick knows me far too well.

"You made me your adviser." His voice is commanding. Powerful. "And some advising is exactly what you need. So suck it up and listen, because we're stuck on a ship in the middle of the sea, and there's nowhere else for you to go." There's an almost wild look in his eyes that tells me he's determined to say his piece, and as the wind pushes against me, whipping my hair back and forcing my body to stay seated, it's as though the gods themselves are demanding I listen. "The last thing you are is *fine*. Think of the ramifications if you do this. All your life you've wanted to rule this kingdom, Amora. So rule it. If you give up now, you'll be no better than your ancestors."

"I *have* thought of the ramifications! I've thought of everything."

"Have you really? Then tell me what good can come from this decision. How will you be saving Visidia, by putting it back to how it was?"

I know this is a conversation I need. They're thoughts that've been swirling in my head for so long, and I know I need to get them out. And yet I can't help my defensiveness. Being confronted like this makes my skin prickle and my voice bitter. As much as I might *think* I want this conversation, the actuality of it is grating.

"If we can stop Kaven before he attacks Arida," I offer, "we'll be saving lives."

"And you'll also be destroying them." He doesn't miss a beat. "There's no doubting that Visidia's in a period of hardships, but before something can heal, it scabs. It gets ugly and painful, and you just want to skip ahead to the easy part where everything's fine. But if you go back, you'll be putting Vataea back in captivity. Kerost and Zudoh will go back to the struggle they were in before. And what if we take too long to get them stable again? How many lives might we lose, then? Do you remember every single soldier who was on Kaven's side? Because if you don't, and information slips, he can attack at a different time. Or he could reinforce the barrier around Zudoh and make it even harder to penetrate. It's too risky. You'd be starting from square one, trying to convince your father that they're worth our time to help.

"I loved King Audric, too." Ferrick's voice falls when he says it. "But he wasn't that kind of man, and we need to stop pretending that he could have been. We can't count on him to change his mind, and if he doesn't, then how else will you ever help Visidia? You will single-handedly put this kingdom in more jeopardy than it's in now."

I try to resist them, but the words resonate. Even though I loved Father to my deepest core, he knew the truth. He could have stopped all the lies in in Visidia, but he didn't. Back on the night of my birthday, Bastian gave him the chance to step up, but Father ignored it. I'd pressed for information, and he'd lied to my face.

Ferrick's right—if I brought Father back, there's no saying that I could make things go any differently. Even if I hadn't failed my performance—even if I'd claimed my title as heir that night—Father had lied to me for too long. That's the way he knew how to rule.

Visidia deserves better than him. It deserves better than either of us.

It is a cruel fate, but it is yours. And what you do with it will determine Visidia's future forevermore. Remember that.

"The kingdom may be off-kilter, but you're doing right by our people to let it run this course," he says. "Look at Kerost, at how they're thriving. The only reason they've been able to is because you sent Valukans to help them rebuild, so that they can learn to protect themselves and their homes. They're better off than they've been in years because *you* made magic available for all."

"Think of Zudoh," Bastian interrupts, each word pressed firm with belief. "My people are finally part of the kingdom again. You've freed them from Kaven and sent soldiers to help them rebuild. Valuka was already in danger; giving them the use of multiple magics is going to do wonders for them."

"What about what happened in Curmana?" I demand, because they're only seeing half the picture. For everything good I've done, there are a million worse mistakes I've made. "People want me dead."

Though I want my words to sway him, Ferrick is quick to shake his head. "It was one person, and Elias was power hungry," he says. "He recognized a shifting climate and wanted to take advantage of it. He used you as an *excuse*, not a reason. I find it hard to believe that a man who wanted power as much as he did would never have tried something else, if the opportunity to go against you had never arisen. You can't blame yourself for that. If anything, you *helped*

Curmana's people by discovering what was happening and bringing their struggles to light. The new laws you'll create are only going to help protect them from harm."

As much as he challenges me, I recognize this is why I asked him to be my adviser; even in times like this, he has the ability to be the most rational person I know. No matter how annoying it may be.

I clamp my teeth on the inner skin of my cheek, biting down as a rush of adrenaline courses through me. I can't determine what, exactly, is causing it, because I feel everything. Pain. Confusion. Frustration. Guilt.

Somewhere within me, I *know* what Ferrick is saying is the truth. I know I *should* be listening. But with every word out of his mouth, I feel myself being pulled farther away from Father.

I flinch as Ferrick's hand encompasses mine, warm and firm.

"I've lost a parent, too." His words are tender, but they're another knife twisting into my heart. "All of us have. I know it hurts. Losing my mother hurt more than any physical pain I've ever felt. I wish I could heal that feeling for you, Amora. I wish I could take away that pain, because I would do it for you in a heartbeat. But no one can give you that relief, and I'm sorry for it. I'm so, so sorry. But Bastian and I have been there. And we're here for you. We're not going anywhere."

That's all I can take. Everything swelling within me bubbles to the surface, and it can no longer be contained.

The tears come hot and fast as my chest rattles with breaths I can hardly take. I sink to the wood, and Ferrick is quick to follow, drawing me into his arms. I don't know the words he says, but I feel him whisper them against my hair as he holds me close.

"I'm not ready," I whisper into his shoulder, again and again like a prayer. "I'm not ready to say goodbye."

At first, I've no idea if Ferrick responds, because all I can hear are my own sobs. All I see is Father's body, bleeding and on fire, fading from me. The ghost of him reaches out, and my hand aches to reach back.

"He would want you to." Ferrick's voice cuts through the haze of smoke clouding my vision, and I falter. The hand I reach toward Father turns to lead, too heavy to keep up. Slowly, it begins to fall to my side. "He would want you to live the life you deserve."

I stare at Father. At the hand he reaches out to me. I take a step toward him, and this time I don't fall back. Bastian and Ferrick's presence steadies me, and the smoke around him begins to take the form of his fiery steed.

Father's eyes lift to mine, clear and warm and wonderful, and my chest burns as my hand falls back to my side. His lips curve, and he smiles.

I love you. I try to shout the words to him. To tell him everything I didn't have the chance to say before. But all that comes out is, *I don't know how to do this without you.*

Slowly, eyes never leaving mine, he lowers his hand. It's as though all the daggers that have been stabbed through me these past several seasons twist at once, gutting me as I realize he's not asking me to save him. He's not reaching out to me. He's been trying to say goodbye.

"You might not know now, but you'll learn." I don't know where the voice comes from, but I hear it loud and clear. "Make this life everything it should be."

The smoke is back, filling my lungs. It shrouds Father's

body once more, and he disappears entirely.

Whether this was another gift from the godwoken or entirely my own imagination, I can't be sure. But what I do know is that Father is truly, finally, gone.

As the sea crashes back into view, and my eyes open, I find my sobs no longer come in gasps. My cheeks are still soaked with fresh tears, but I can breathe again.

Father's smile lingers in my mind, his words echoing. *Make this life everything it should be.*

Finally, I know what that is. I know what I must do.

I sit on the bow late that night, legs dangling over the serpentine figurehead as I feed tiny slips of parchment into the water.

I'm sorry.

Please come back.

I am the worst human in the world, and you can tell me so as much as you want if you come back.

I drop slip after torn slip into the water, my heart as dark as the tides that pull them under. Vataea will probably never see these. She's likely long gone by now. But still, I have to try something.

And so I scrawl my notes and toss in one after another, until there's no parchment to be found and I've given all the apologies left in me.

Except for one.

Lifting my head to the sky, I shut my eyes and summon whatever remaining pieces of courage I can find.

Ferrick was right when he said that, here upon *Keel Haul*, it feels as though we're alone in the world. Like the entire sea is ours for the taking. I imagine years of myself at the helm, my hands worn with calluses and skin warmed by the sun, sharing the telltale signs of a sailor that I'd spent years admiring on Father.

"I'm sorry for what I have to do." I speak the words solely to the heavens. "I don't know if it's what you would have wanted, or what you would have done. But I hope that when you look upon me, it's with pride. I know this is our path forward; this is how we're going to make up for what we've done to our kingdom."

No Suntosan is powerful enough to heal my pain. It's in every inch of my body, shredding it apart and rebuilding, only to begin shredding anew. That shredding may never stop entirely, but one day, I hope it might slow.

"I love you." I send my words to the gods so that they might deliver them to him. "But this is truly our goodbye."

And as the sea breeze picks up around me, brushing across my skin and filling my lungs with the sea salt air, I know Father's listening, and that this is his goodbye, too.

A WEDDING? OR A ROYAL RUSE?

It appears that the search for Visidia's future king has been called off nearly as suddenly as it began.

It's been reported that on her first day visiting Valuka, Her Majesty Amora Montara suffered from what witnesses can only describe as a "complete and utter mental breakdown," where she refused to participate in any of the island's prearranged activities after being unable to find her Valukan affinity. Witnesses say that Her Majesty disappeared shortly after her outburst, and that they've not seen her since. Allegedly, both she and the ship she's traveling on disappeared from the island in the middle of the night.

Despite our reaching out with our concern for the queen, Lord Bargas and up-and-coming adviser Azami Bargas both refused to provide any comments on the matter. Though the queen was to have remained in Valuka for several more days, little is known about Her Majesty's current whereabouts.

Given the reports of the witnesses, we're left with no choice but to form our own theories, of which we have a few:

Could Her Majesty's outburst have anything to do with the tragic, early death of Curmana's very own Elias Freebourne, who Amora was reportedly cozying up to several days prior?

Is it possible that Visidia's future king has already been found?

Perhaps our queen has been scorned by rejection?

Or are we giving Her Majesty too much credit? Perhaps there is no obvious answer for her outburst other than teenage indecisiveness and lack of experience.

Whatever the reason, it looks like all we can do now is wait for Her Majesty to show up somewhere, and to explain herself once and for all.

✑
THIRTY-FIVE

This time as we approach Arida, it's not to the cannon fire and smoke of an attack. It's not the screams of my people as they fight for their lives.

This time, it's with nothing but a set jaw and determination. This time, it's with hope.

"Brace yourselves."

The winter sea is fierce and jarring. I grip the helm tight, wrapping my fingers firmly around the wood and refusing to let myself be bullied by the tides.

Sand red as blood waits for us on the shores of Arida, marking our destination. I focus on it as the sea drags us in, and so does Bastian. Ferrick and Shanty brace themselves, grabbing on to the rigging to keep stabilized. Bastian's truly taken to Valukan air magic; he whirls briny air through his fingertips, using it to billow and twist the sails while I take the helm to direct *Keel Haul* to the docks.

We make a good team, he and I.

Shanty's the first one off as we dock, not bothering with the ramp, and Ferrick is fast behind her. He happily crouches upon the sand, dragging his fingers across it and looking like he's half ready to roll himself in it. I wish I could share in his enthusiasm, but worry claws my throat, knowing how much there is to do now that we've arrived, and not knowing how anyone will respond to the changes I'm about to make.

The worry dwindles when a calloused hand wraps around mine, flooding me with warmth.

Our arrival has alerted the royal soldiers, some of whom gawk at our appearance, not having anticipated us back on Arida so soon. They flock to our side and to our ship to help unload the cargo, but I'm quick to stop them.

"Spread word that there's something I'd like to discuss with my people in one week's time," I tell them. "Make sure every island is alerted. Everyone who can is encouraged to attend. And make sure that, this time, Kerost is here."

The lead soldier, Isaac, hesitates. "It'd be best if you let me escort you to the palace, Your Majesty. We need to let Visidia know you're safe. There's been a lot of talk in the press . . ."

Ferrick had seen the parchment through mind speak and informed me of its contents. But I can no longer concern myself with appearances or gossips. I've already made up my mind, and I'm not about to give anyone or anything else the opportunity to convince me otherwise.

Besides, I've kept Blarthe from justice long enough.

"You should do as I say, Isaac." My voice is unwavering. "Right now, I need you to fetch a prisoner for me. His name is Blarthe, and he's dangerous. Be careful."

It doesn't take long for the soldiers to find him. Feet and hands chained, Blarthe looks more haggard than ever as the soldiers drag him down the shore. He squints at the unfamiliar sunlight, deep shadows beneath his eyes. Time magic has taken its toll on his body; each footstep looks painful and deliberate, and he babies his left knee. His skin looks as though it's tightened into leather, riddled with sun spots. Upon seeing him, Bastian grimaces.

Blarthe doesn't look concerned to see me, nor is he too eager. Hungry eyes scan my hands, then my coat, looking for any sign of the artifact.

"Did you find it?" are the first words out of his mouth, and the soldier scowls, yanking Blarthe's chains.

"Bow before your queen," Isaac warns him.

"I don't need his bow," I tell him. Then, to Blarthe, I nod. "Just how many times do you plan to go against the gods, Rogan?"

At first, I'm only guessing, but the way the hunger in his eyes dims and his hands twitch at his sides tells me I was right to gamble.

"I met your daughter, but she wasn't in Kerost like you thought she'd be. She's happy and thriving somewhere far away from you, where she'll never have to see your sorry face again."

"I don't care if you found *her*. The artifact. Where is the artifact?" He reaches chained hands out for the scale, and for a moment I pity the way those hands tremble. But I let that thought pass; this is a man who has been given far more years than any one life deserves. Who has turned back time not once, but twice.

Back on Kerost, he'd been using time magic to make himself look as he did when he knew Corina. All this time, he's been trying to chase that period of his life.

I won't make his mistakes.

"It's not for you." I fold my arms behind my back, keeping my chin high.

His neck retracts, a fire in his eyes that reminds me of

the night we fought in Kerost. My first instinct is to pull my magic around me for protection, but I settle a hand on the hilt of Rukan, instead.

"Careful, Amora," Shanty whispers, sensing the same threat in him that I do.

"I know," I tell her. "Stay back."

"I'll tell everyone your secret." Blarthe's voice is brittle. "See what they think of you then, little queen. See how they tear the crown from your head."

I unsheathe my steel dagger in one swift motion and press it deep against Blarthe's throat. "Go right ahead." And I mean it. This is why I'm back on Arida; I don't care what my people think of me, anymore. It's time they know the truth.

But what I don't anticipate is that my getting close to Blarthe is exactly what he wants. Because like the rest of Visidia, he's been practicing a new magic, too. And it's one he's been hiding.

Startling blue flames blaze across his body, burning so fiercely that the Valukan magic shatters his chains and sends the guards reeling back. I don't have the time to pull away before those flames catch the steel of my dagger and sear the skin of my palm. I jerk back, dropping my blade on instinct, and my gut sinks when Blarthe dives for it.

He turns on the soldiers first, quicker than lightning with his time magic, and has the dagger through their bellies before I can blink. My heart seizes as Isaac falls. Blarthe's movements aren't anything like they were during our fight in Kerost. There's no time to track him. No time to prepare. No longer using the time he stole from others to maintain his youthful appearance, he wields the full force of his time magic.

Blarthe is on top of me with the dagger at my throat.

"Where is it?" He rips open my jacket to search the pockets, kicking off my boots to see if I've hidden it there. I struggle for breath beneath the weight of him, hand searching blindly for Rukan, but I can't reach around Blarthe to get it. Again I try to summon my magic, but it's useless. When Blarthe doesn't find what he's looking for, the dagger's cool metal presses against my skin, and I realize this is what it feels like to be truly powerless. No magic. No weapons. Just a man twice my size, holding me down with fury in his eyes.

It's all I can do to grab hold of his arm and fight the blade off, but it's not enough.

It's not enough.

"Hey!" Blarthe rears back at Ferrick's yell, and I fill my lungs with the air they've been desperately needing. "Is this what you're looking for?"

And gods bless this idiot; Ferrick has the scale I thought was still tucked safely aboard my cabin on *Keel Haul*. It catches the sunlight, glistening like water, and suddenly Blarthe is no longer on me.

Only my crew would be foolish enough to fight a time wielder. *Those who practice time magic make some of the finest soldiers*, Father once told me. *They'll have their sword deep in the enemy's gut before anyone can blink.*

Seeing it in action, I know Father was right.

Blarthe's in front of Ferrick within the second, but the boys anticipated him. Bastian sends a surge of wind that knocks Blarthe off his feet, giving Ferrick enough time to slip the scale away somewhere I don't see. His eyes find mine and I nod, telling him I'm fine. He doesn't have time to be distracted.

Stumbling to my feet, I finally grab Rukan tight. I'm done playing nice.

When Blarthe gathers himself, it's not Ferrick he dives for this time, but Shanty. He's got my dagger to her back, eyes gleaming wicked.

"Give me the artifact or she'll die," he grits through his teeth, breathing heavy. But Shanty is easy to underestimate. She tosses her head back so it smacks hard against his nose, cracking it. As he snarls through the pain, she slips from his grip and tosses a cloud of bright yellow powder in front of her. With one long puff she blows it into Blarthe's face and ducks away, drawing two long knives from her belt.

She may not like to get her hands messy, but from the deftness of her fingers on those blades, it's clear that doesn't mean she won't.

The powder slows Blarthe's movements, making him sway, but it doesn't stop him.

"Those beasts told me I would see Corina again," he spits. "Give me the scale! I *will* see her again!"

In another time, I might have pitied him.

His eyes flash from Ferrick to Shanty, and so quickly I nearly miss it, Blarthe is on her again. Though Shanty's blades are held at the ready, she's no match for the speed of a Ker. Blarthe knocks her back, but Ferrick must have seen through his plan. He tackles Blarthe to the ground a second before the dagger can strike Shanty; instead, it cleaves straight through Ferrick's side.

My heart seizes. Ferrick buckles and wheezes, but already his restoration magic is working to close the wound from the inside out. But Ferrick's magic can only focus on one injury at a time, and Blarthe's raising his dagger again.

Both Bastian and I lunge, but neither of us reach him before the ocean roars to life behind us. The tides wrap around Shanty, pushing her across the shore before swallowing Ferrick and Blarthe whole. Bastian grabs hold of me as the waves crash down, slamming us against the sand. I hit shoulder first, and something in my arm snaps. I choke, swallowing seawater, but the tides are gone a moment later, and I blink through salt-stung eyes to see Blarthe on all fours, panting on the blood-red sand.

Behind him, the tides ripple and raise around Vataea. Relief floods my veins so fiercely that the throbbing in my arm disappears.

"You don't get to touch him." Vataea's voice is a thousand songs, making my head spin and my ears threaten to bleed. "Stand up, Blarthe. Did you think you'd seen the last of me?"

His chest hitches with fear, and he refuses.

"I said STAND." She is the eye of her own storm. Behind her, even the sky darkens as the gods shield their eyes in fear of her. Water snaps beneath Blarthe, taking him by the throat and tossing him onto his feet.

To his credit, he doesn't beg as Vataea steps from the sea, shedding her fin as she crosses the sand. The tides wait behind her, seething and shifting, as starved as she is.

"I have thought about what I would do to you for years." She doesn't flinch when he lashes out with the dagger. The sea is her shield, swallowing the blade before it can strike and spitting it out at my boots. I swipe it into my wet palms. "I *dreamed* of pressing a dagger deep into your throat and bleeding you dry. Of taking my time, cutting you piece by piece over years, slowly enough that you would remain alive, begging to die. In other dreams, I would call you to the sea. I would rip your heart out and devour your body limb by limb. But it seems your gods favor me today, because not one of those dreams could ever beat the opportunity they've given me."

The sea splits behind her, and I realize now that Vataea is not alone. Another mermaid waits, skin pale as sleet and full lips blue as a corpse's. A crown of blond waves spreads around her in the tides, and she stares at us with piercing lavender eyes, slit like a cat's.

The instant Blarthe sees her, his shoulders fall and a sob rattles his chest. "Corina." The name is a prayer upon his lips, and my stomach lurches at the sound of it.

Corina. The love he'd lost to the mermaids. He'd never truly lost her at all.

Corina parts her lips, and I yell for Shanty and the boys to cover their ears. Her song isn't silks and honey like Vataea's; it's gravel and steel, something not quite right about the tone. But Blarthe's enamored all the same. He stumbles across the sand, trying to halt every few steps to look at Corina. He screams her name, willing her to stop, but she won't.

"You traded away her love for you," Vataea says with a laugh so vicious I draw a step back, sinking against the sand. All this time I've been grateful to have her on my side. Now though, I'm not so sure that she is. "Now, you'll spend an eternity within the sea as our pet, and she will never remember you. No matter how hard you try, no matter how much you might beg, she will not care for you or your pleas. You will spend your days in the ocean, mourning the one who is right in front of you. And when you wish to die, I will make sure that you live. You are *my* trophy, now. And it's time I show you off."

Corina wraps her fingers around Blarthe's throat as she

presses her lips to his. But rather than wake him from a trance, she turns Blarthe's skin blue as ice, and amid the first of his screams, Corina drags him into the water.

They never resurface.

Vataea stands before me, and I scramble from my knees up to her. "I'm sorry," I say. "And not because you're terrifying, but because I mean it."

At that, the smallest smile cracks her lips, but I don't stop.

"Vataea, I never wanted to hurt you, I swear it. I was going to tell you the truth when we got to Arida, and Blarthe was always going to be held responsible for his crimes. But . . . gods, I'm sorry. He hurt you worse than anyone, and I'm so sorry."

She sets a hand on my shoulders, and I try not to flinch at the long claws, sharp as knives.

"I understand that you were trying to do what you thought was best." The magic in her voice has yet to wear off. The sweetness of it makes my head ache. "But you've opened wounds within me, Amora, and I cannot tell you when they might begin to heal."

"But we can try?" I set my hand over hers, determined. "Can we try to heal them?"

Ever so slowly, she nods. But there's no time to sink into the relief that comes; down the shore, Shanty screams.

"We need help!"

There's coughing. Wet, ragged coughing, and my body goes cold at the sight of a sea-soaked Ferrick wheezing on the sand. Shanty's got her hands pressed hard against his chest, but blood seeps through her fingers with no sign of slowing.

Blarthe's attack was deeper than I thought. As much as he's trying to heal, Ferrick can't seem to slow the bleeding.

I rush to his side, helping Shanty put force on the wound. Isaac is just managing to stand. He's shaky on his feet, clutching a hand to his bleeding side. But the blood is minimal; thankfully it's not a fatal wound.

"Go get the healers!" I yell to him. "Now!"

Ferrick's blood is hot and fresh, flowing too quickly from his body. I push harder, but Ferrick sets a trembling hand atop mine. Tears blur my eyes when he smiles.

"Thank you for letting me be part of your adventure." His fingers wind around mine, squeezing weakly. "I couldn't have asked for a better crew."

Bastian's beside me now, and Vataea, too. She stares at his blood, chanting as though fighting to control it. Unlike the sea, it doesn't obey. But she doesn't stop, forehead creasing into deep lines of concentration as she tries and tries again.

"Shut up, Ferrick." I pull my hand from his, forcing pressure on the wound. "You and I have plenty more adventures. You just have to hang on a little longer; the healers are coming." His blood's hot against my hands as I press into the wound with everything I have, thinking of Father and the night I let him die right there beside me. "Please, you have to hold on. I can't lose someone else. I can't lose *you*."

He tries not to show the pain, but I see it in the stalling of his words and the way he grinds his teeth, fighting it back. The scale shimmers in his left hand, held tight in his white-knuckled grip. All I have to do is pry it from him and I can fix everything. We'll redo the fight. I'll keep my dagger from Blarthe. I'll—

"Amora." He draws my hand again, pulling it gently from his wound. "Stop scheming and let me say goodbye."

I don't want to. With everything in me, I want to refuse.

But I'm not the only one crying. Bastian's holding Ferrick's shoulders firm, chest trembling as he lowers his forehead to Ferrick's. I don't hear what he says, just that he says it through sobs he's trying to stave off long enough to choke out the words.

"You might be the biggest asshole I've ever met," Ferrick tells him, though his tone is light. "But you became my brother, and I'm glad for every minute we had together. Except for the one where you cut off my arm." And then he turns to Vataea, his smile fraying at the seams. "I'm sorry, for everything. I never should have lied to you."

"That day on Kerost, you were the one to come to me." Her voice is the softest whisper. "You were the one to save me. I've never thanked you for that." She bends, pressing her lips firmly to Ferrick's. His arm wraps gently around her head, threading weak fingers through her hair.

When they separate, he presses his cheek against Vataea's and says something, the words too soft for me to catch.

There are tears in Vataea's eyes when he leans back, though she doesn't cry; she looks more like she doesn't understand what's happening. Like something here isn't right.

And it's not. Humans are too fragile. None of this is right.

I can't imagine the strength it must take, but he lifts his head enough to press a kiss to my temple next, hard and firm.

"Listen to me. I don't want you to mourn me, Amora. I want you to live for this kingdom and for yourself. I love you, and . . . I'm sorry for what I have to do."

"I love you, too," I say, because if there's one thing that needs to be said, this is it. I will not let him leave me as Father did, with too much sorrow between us. But only after I say it do I catch the rest of his words, and chills send me spiraling.

I look once more at his hand, clutched tight around the scale. "Ferrick—"

"This was my final adventure." Each of his words takes more effort than the last, hands fighting tiny spasms. "But promise me you'll have a thousand more."

The scale shatters before I can stop him. Ferrick slams a hand into both my and Bastian's chests, and my veins flood with fire as Ferrick's restoration magic fills me, reaching into depths that shouldn't be possible. Reaching into my soul and making it whole.

Magic stirs from what was once hollowness within me, and I am myself again—Amora Montara. Fully, solely, me.

I open my eyes to Ferrick, whose tears fall freely now, no longer trying to stay strong. I reach for him, breathless, but my hands go through air.

A moment later I wonder . . . Who was I even reaching for? And whose blood is it that stains my hands?

THIRTY-SIX

S pring is here, and change has come with it.
Placid wind greets me as I stand on my balcony, staring past the winding rows of rainbow eucalyptus and far down at the waiting sea. It glitters like a thousand crystals in the sunlight, the most magnificent blue.

"This is a big decision." Behind me, Bastian sets a steady hand on my shoulder. "I hope you're proud of yourself."

I close my hand over his, enjoying the warmth that diffuses through me at his touch. Because this time, he has no sway over me. Finally, we're free to be our own people.

Today, Bastian wears the same striking ruby coat he wore when we first met. It reminds me of the truest version of him—a roguish pirate with a hunger for adventure. It reminds me of the man I first fell for, and the one I hope to have many more adventures with. If only we can get through today.

Though the sight of him in that coat fills my heart with warmth, it can't distract me from the lingering sadness weighing my bones. A sorrow for something I only wish I could explain.

As glad as I am to have things returned to the way they were with Bastian, I can't ignore the gaping hole in my memory from the day both of my curses were broken. I can't ignore the palace bedroom across from mine that's sat empty for a week, lined with rapiers and herbs, with a closet full of emerald-green clothing. I can't ignore how my eye catches the door every time I walk by, waiting for someone to go in or come out, though I can't for the life of me remember who that should be.

No one can remember who it should be.

Something happened the day Blarthe was dragged into the sea. Someone must have used the serpent scale to break the Montara curse, but none of us can remember who did it or what happened.

All I remember is that there was blood on my hands, and that none of my crew was bleeding.

"Don't you feel like we're missing something?" I smooth my hands over not a sapphire gown, but loose linen pants. Today I wish not to look like Visidia's queen, but as one of the people. "It was too easy."

Bastian wraps strong hands around mine, steadying them. "You call this past year easy? We faced the legendary fire serpent. The Lusca. We took down Kaven. We were poisoned and cut open more times than I can count. And still, we *won*." His fingers press into my palms, warm and reassuring. "Yes, one of us must have used the scale to break the curse, but all that matters is that we're all still here. The crew is alive and well. Our curse is broken, and we have everything we wanted. This year's been hard enough; I'm taking what I can get." Leaning forward, he peppers featherlight kisses onto my cheek. "You should do the same."

I know I should; I *want* to. If I was the one who broke the curse, whatever I lost that day is gone, taken by the gods themselves. I will never get it back, no matter how hard I try to remember. But my magic is back, and the Montara curse is no more.

I've gotten nearly everything I wanted most—but what was the price? My family and crew are safe. My love for Visidia remains whole.

I *couldn't* have been the one to use the scale. So who did?

"Amora?" Mother's voice comes from the doorway. "It's nearly time. Casem will be here, soon."

Freeing me from his hold, Bastian presses one last kiss to my forehead before placing a hand to the small of my back, ushering me into the room. "I'll meet you out there, all right? You're going to be amazing."

I nod, though my body stills when I notice it's not only Mother waiting for me, but Vataea, too.

I wasn't the only one who changed that day on the beach. Her eyes are darker now, her words colder. I love Vataea, and I want to be there for her the way I wasn't before. But I can't undo what I've done. I can only try to move forward and hope it's enough.

The moment Mother spots me, she grabs my hands. Hers are bonier than they used to be, but they're getting stronger day by day.

"Are you sure about this?" The words are out of her so fast I can barely make out each one. "It's not too late to change your mind."

But it is. After everything I've been through—after everything I've seen in this past year—I know clear as a night sky what I must do. Tonight, Visidia will finally be free.

"We're going to be okay." I squeeze her hand, just once, and let the weight of Father's absence settle between us. No longer is it an anchor upon my heart, but a reminder of all we had to sacrifice to bring Visidia the freedom it deserves.

Though she's coiled tight with tension, Mother nods and pulls me into her, pressing her forehead to mine. "You are the queen this kingdom has always deserved, Amora." Her warm lips press against my cheek. "I'm so proud of you."

There's too much emotion in the room. Too much pain. With a final kiss to my hand, Mother excuses herself. In her absence, Vataea seems taller, her shoulders squared and sharp chin held high and proud. She's radiant in a sleek sapphire day gown, but there's a look in her eyes that tells me this might be the last time I see her in Arida's color.

"You're leaving," I say, not as a question. But it stings all the same when she nods.

"You won't see me after your speech. Goodbyes are . . . messy. And they're difficult. But it's time for me to go." Each of her words is a crack in my heart, one after the other. I fist my hands into my shirt, needing something to hold on to.

"Where will you go?"

Tears wet her dark eyelashes, but they don't fall. "I'm not sure," she says. "When I'm ready, I'll find you. But I can't be a sidekick in your adventure. I'll remember our time together, and I'll cherish it. But there's an entire world out there, and I intend to see it."

I can't be selfish, and I cannot cry. Because Vataea deserves this more than anything. She deserves the world, and I need to let her have it.

"One day, I hope you'll tell me all about it." I reach forward, hoping, praying, that she'll take my hand. When she does, it takes everything in me to curl my fingers around hers without letting myself fall apart completely.

"I will." She's slow to draw her hand back, but it's a relief when she does. Because if it were up to me, I'd never let her leave.

"I'll miss you, Vataea. But I hope you have the best adventures of any of us." Every word is a dagger stabbing through me, over and over again until I can't take it any longer. I'm the first to turn away, because this pain hurts almost as bad as when I lost Father. Vataea may not be dead, but she's leaving. Another piece of my heart, gone just like that.

I don't turn back even at the sound of her footsteps. Not even as the door cracks open. Not even as her voice comes from the doorway, quiet but firm. "Amora?" I want to remember that honeyed voice forever. I want to embed it deep into my memory, and never let it disappear. "Call me V."

The door shuts and I grab hold of the bedpost to steady my trembling. This is what she wanted, and as a hesitant knock sounds at my door seconds later, I tell myself to be grateful that she gets the chance to live out her dream. Even if I'm not part of it.

Casem waits outside, hands folded behind his back. His blue eyes watch me from beneath long blond lashes. The royal emblem that marks him as Arida's leading adviser burns as brightly as the sun upon his sapphire blazer, almost matching the gold of his hair. He tries to smile, but his mouth skews with worry when he notices the tears in my eyes.

"Everyone's waiting for you. Are you ready?"

I think of Vataea and the thousands of adventures she's about to live. Taking his arm, I decide it's time for my own adventures, too.

After today, no matter what the outcome of this meeting, everything will change. But as I take one look back out my window to see *Keel Haul* waiting for me in the distance, ebbing upon pleasant spring tides, I know this is the right choice.

The gods created me to lead Visidia—I grew up with that belief. They were some of Father's dying words to me. Now, I believe them more than ever.

Back in Valuka, the godwoken had warned me I'd soon be making a choice that would either lead Visidia into the future or be its demise. Today, I know our future is bright.

We make our way farther up the cliffside, into the garden that rests at the peak of Arida. Hundreds of flowers stretch oversize petals to greet us, beautiful in the sunlight, but waiting until the light of the moon to truly flourish and reveal their bioluminescence—a sight people come from all over the kingdom to see.

Once, I considered these gardens a calming place. Somewhere to seek refuge and beauty that doesn't seem as though it should belong to this world. Now though, I can't fall into their beauty so easily; too much has happened, here. This is where my journey started, and this is where it will end.

Every color of the kingdom stands before me in the crowd, the Kers' amethyst included. Gossip and whispers reverberate through the garden so heavily that even the plants tremble with the anticipation of today's meeting.

Every island's adviser is lined up behind the throne, which sits erected in a clearing surrounded by sprouting pink mushrooms and purple flowers that have fallen from the tree above, where they hang like a crown over the gardens. Mother is there too, and Casem takes his place among them as Bastian watches from the waiting crowd. I draw a breath as I pass and take my place upon the throne. Mother fits the High Animancer's crown atop my head. Her hand brushes gently across my cheek as she does, and our eyes lock.

Make this life everything it should be. I hear Father's voice in her smile before she bows and takes her place at the left of the throne. The giant eel crown sits too heavily, eating me alive as I search the crowd for the faces I need to see.

Vataea and Bastian, standing side by side. Bastian watches with pride burning his eyes, while she offers the smallest nod.

Mira stands nearby with Yuriel and Aunt Kalea, whose presence makes my throat tighten. Her body threatens to wilt beneath my gaze, but the time for that anger is over. I cannot blame her for what happened with Father; now, more than ever, we need to stay together. It's time I accept she's hurting as much as I am.

I don't see her true face in the crowd, but when a blond woman with blood-red eyes winks at me, I know Shanty is watching, as well.

I try not to smile at her and begin to search for one more face. Only I don't realize until a moment later that I've no idea whose face I'm looking for. In my mind's eye, I see eyes green as emeralds and hair red as fire.

But I don't know who they belong to. Whoever it is, they're not here.

"Welcome." I find my voice after a hesitant moment, pulling my focus back to the waiting crowd. "I'm glad for all those who could make it today, especially our friends in Kerost. I know our kingdom hasn't been the kindest to you, so know that your presence here is truly appreciated."

As the many faces of my people peer up at me, the first sting of nerves settles into my bones. Gripping the arms of the throne, I let their curiosity sink into my skin and fuel my words.

I will not waver. Everything I've done—every struggle and every obstacle I've faced—has been for this moment.

"For centuries you've put your faith in the Montaras, trusting us to protect this kingdom to the best of our ability. You were told that a fearsome beast lived within the blood of my family, and that it was put there because my great ancestor, Cato Montara, the first ruler of Visidia, risked his life to save this kingdom. You were told to obey him by practicing only one magic, because otherwise that beast would rear its head and destroy Visidia."

I find Bastian's face in the crowd and draw a breath at his tiny nod of encouragement before continuing. "But I'm here today to tell you the truth, because as much as I love my family, Visidia deserves better. Cato Montara was no hero; he was a thief and a liar—practicing multiple magics was never dangerous, and there was never any beast involved with soul magic."

I push on through the growing whispers, telling them the truth behind Visidia's creation and the lies our kingdom was built upon. I tell them how Cato stole multiple magics through Sira, and of her cursing the Montara bloodline.

I tell them everything, my body lighter with each passing word.

"For everything my family has done, and for every one of my own lies, I am sorry. I can't take back the harm that's been done, but I believe there's a way for us to move through it."

I anticipated anger and yelling. But to my surprise, the eyes of Visidia look on in anxious silence, hanging upon my every word. With shaking hands, I lift the crown from my head and cast one final look at the eel bones. For centuries this crown has been worn by nothing more than deceitful liars—Cato, Father, me.

Never again will it sit upon the head of a Montara.

"Let today be the day that we take back Visidia and restore this kingdom to the land it once was." I stand with the crown in hand. "As of today, everyone can practice soul magic. *All* magic is freely available. As of today, no one else will ever wear this crown, or sit upon this throne! After today, there will be no king or queen. There will be no monarchy!

"We are a kingdom of seven islands." Each word is fervent, coming with a passion I cannot control. "And so seven leaders are what we must have. Collectively, we will work together to rule this kingdom. There will be no more blood ties—no more royals. Every two years, our people will vote for the representative they want to have leading their island, and together we will lead Visidia into the future every one of us deserves."

I turn to the advisers behind me, who stand with their shoulders back and chests held proud. "All those in favor, say aye."

"Aye." Casem's the first to respond, his blue eyes sparkling with pride.

Azami echoes him immediately. "Aye."

Down the line it goes, one adviser after the other. Only Lord Garrison hesitates—but, not one to make himself look bad before others, he nods and answers "aye" in his gruff baritone.

And then it's back to me. I'm breathless, the crown trembling in my hands—at once, I know what I'm to do with it.

With hands that hardly feel like my own, I send it

crashing to the ground. The ivory-plated bones shatter into a thousand pieces, and with it goes everything I've ever known. Every day of my life so far.

But it's also the start of a new life. Not only for Visidia, but for me.

Perhaps Mother will be Arida's adviser. I'll help them get started, but I won't be in charge. My job is done, and my future belongs to the sea.

I don't realize how hard I'm breathing until I pull my gaze from the shattered bones to my people. They're no longer standing. Each and every one of them is on their knees, heads bowed, cracking any remaining resolve I was desperately trying to withhold.

This is more than I deserve, but I don't have it in me to stop them.

"Thank you," I tell them through the tears I finally let fall, coming hot and fast. Our troubles are not yet over. A new Visidia is on the horizon, and with it comes a foreign new future we'll have to figure out. Together.

It won't be easy, but it will be worth it. Visidia's future begins now.

"Thank you for allowing me to be your queen."

EPILOGUE

This day is made for sailing.

Balmy spring air bloats the sails, and I tip my head back to savor its breeze.

Bastian stands behind me at the helm, gathering breaths of the briny air with a grin spread wide across his face. "Where to?" His eyes burn brightly enough to challenge the stars themselves. "To challenge the Lusca to a rematch? Hike the trails of Suntosu? Drink ourselves silly in the taverns of Ikae?"

I brush my fingers against the grainy wood of the deck, trying to memorize everything about this moment, from the mist brushing against my skin to the words Bastian speaks. I lean into them, letting myself imagine the adventures that await us.

Imagine learning to alter my appearance in Mornute. Imagine sailing to Valuka so that Azami can teach me how to create a dragon made from water. Imagine spending time with Ephra in Kerost, learning to change the ways my body interacts with time as we rebuild the island.

The world is open to me now, and so are its magics. And I intend to learn them all.

A whisper of winter's memory rests in the cool air, and I shift to pull my coat around myself and sink into my comfort. But as I adjust, something in my coat crinkles and draws my attention. I reach into my pocket, to a small, folded sheet of parchment that's been tucked away inside.

Bastian's still listing off all the places we should visit—Shanty in Ikae, across the sea to finally see Suntosu, and even to find a way to reach the clouds so that we might chase the legendary kingdom rumored to exist upon them. But his words are drowned out as I peel back the edges of the parchment. It's folded so tightly that I'm careful not to rip it, even despite my trembling hands. Though I try to calm them, they won't stop even as I hold the parchment open before me.

> *Amora,*
>
> *If you're reading this, know first that I'm sorry. I knew from the moment I saw Nelly's memories that this is what had to be done. Visidia needs to be free, and it's up to you to get it there.*
>
> *So I'm sorry for what I had to do. But if I'm right, I'm glad to know you won't remember any of it. And if I'm wrong, well, I suppose I owe you an explanation. They say you must offer what you love most to get what you most want, and I can't think of anything I love more than the time I've spent with all of you. My crew.*
>
> *I'd be lying if I said I don't want you to remember me, but this is for the best. You don't need to mourn anyone else; I don't want you to. All I want is for you and Visidia to finally have the freedom you deserve.*
>
> *So take my gift, and be happy for it. But in return, you must do two things for me:*
>
> *First, do what's best for Visidia. Tell them the truth. Free soul magic for yourself and everyone.*

Second, be happy. Even if it's with that blasted pirate. Go on all the adventures I wasn't able to.

And come to think of it, I'm adding a third clause—I'm not breaking your curses so that you can get yourself killed, all right? I won't be around to heal you anymore, so think before you dive in. And can you at least try to trust others more? I know it's hard, but you've got an incredible crew. I would know.

Now get out there and go see your kingdom. I can only pray that, one day, we'll see each other again.

Until then, happy sailing.

F

Pain grips me tight, cleaving my lungs and gutting through my chest. My tears fall freely, so many I can't see straight, though I can't say why they come.

I rack my memory, but try as I might, I don't recognize who could have written this letter. Even so, there's something familiar about it. Something that causes me to clutch it tight to my chest, careful not to let my tears ruin the ink.

"Amora?"

I startle at Bastian's voice, straightening my spine. Perhaps it's nothing more than this past year catching up with me— why else would I be crying for someone I do not know? It must be a prank—a strange goodbye joke from Casem.

But I don't toss the letter. Carefully, I fold it back and tuck it into my pocket for safekeeping, drawing a breath to steady myself. When I turn to Bastian, it's not with tears, but with a smile.

Whoever this letter is from, if what they said is true then

they gave me a gift. And for them, I'll make the most of it.

"How about to Zudoh?" I ask.

Bastian tenses, and it's a sharp and strange reminder that I can no longer tell what he's feeling. But I don't need to feel his soul; I can see it, now. Blazing and beautiful and bright as the stars. He clears his throat, trying so hard not to let tears come that I stand and take one of his hands in my own. I set my other beside his, fingers wrapping around the sea-slickened helm.

"To Zudoh," he repeats, the stars in his eyes burning with pride.

"And to a thousand more adventures."

The sea draws us into its waiting arms — just a girl and a pirate, ready to take our world by storm.

ACKNOWLEDGMENTS

Everyone warned me that writing Book 2 was going to be hard, but I feel betrayed that no one told me writing the acknowledgments was even harder! Where do I even begin?

First, I'm grateful to God for helping me survive the Book 2 Curse, and for putting amazing people and an incredible team into my life. This business has been so much more challenging than I ever anticipated, but being surrounded by such great people makes it so much better.

Mom and Dad, I've already thanked you for your love and support, so for this book I'll thank you for hand selling copies to strangers everywhere you go and embarrassing me. Please don't read past chapter thirty-two, love you.

Josh, for not thinking I had *total* delusions of grandeur five years ago when I said that I was going to build a franchise like Patrick Rothfuss. Thank you for always listening and trying to make sense of the wild world of publishing with me, even when it very rarely makes any sense.

Tomi, I can't imagine this process without you in it. Thank you for the calls, the late nights, the KBBQ and Thai food, the YouTube videos, all of it. There's no one else I'd rather build empires with. *Insert that unofficial Azula quote here.*

Shea, I'm writing this while in quarantine and I miss you

so much! I am eternally grateful that we all just happened to live in the same city and bonded over Thai food, and that I get to have you as a friend.

Haley Marshall, I will never not be sorry for the amount of times I ask you to read things. Thank you for always being there—for your eyes, your ears, brain, heart, and most importantly, Peter pictures.

Kristin Dwyer, my younger twin, where to even begin. Thank you for being one of the most magnificent people I've ever met, for just being you, and for demanding I let K-Drama into my life. I have been forever changed (and also cry way more, thanks). I wonder if I should thank Lee Min-ho in these . . .

Rachel Griffin, this world is not pure enough for you. Thank you for just being a wonderful human who I'm lucky enough to know. I'm very happy to get to be a Winter Witch.

Shelby RapMonster Mahurin, I wish I was half as chill as you, with maybe a quarter of your rap skills. Thanks for not running away when I kidnapped you. #BunkBuddies4Life

Adrienne Young, for a healthy dose of realness and perspective. I respect and admire the heck out of you and your incredible work ethic.

To my agent, Peter Knapp, you have my eternal thanks for stepping in and supporting me and this book. I'm incredibly grateful to be working with such an incredible advocate!

At Imprint, all the thank-yous to my two editors, Nicole Otto and Erin Stein. Nicole, I'm not sure there's anyone who understands this world and these characters as much as you do. I'm so grateful to have worked with you on Amora's story, and now you will never escape me. Huzzah! :) And Erin, your general badassery and editorial prowess are inspiring. Thank you for putting together such an incredible team at Imprint. I'm fortunate to get to "make my mark" with you all.

Natalie Sousa, design god, imagine me bowing down before you right now. Going into this whole process, I was *terrified* about my cover and whether I'd love it or be able to give any input. Working with you, though, that was all so silly. These books are *stunning*, thank you thank you.

John Morgan, Jessica Chung, and Camille Kellogg, for what I'm sure was an endless amount of work helping to get this book ready for the public eye.

Morgan Rath, I mentally refer to you as my Publicist Wizard every time I get an email from you. But that title isn't quite good enough. Grand Master Publicist, maybe? All-Powerful Wizard Publicist? I'll keep working on it to figure out something fitting that's as wonderful as you are!

Allegra Green and Olivia Oleck, I am so happy to get to work with you both on marketing. You are just so clever, so wonderful, your emails always make me happy, and GAH. I just have such an amazing team!

Linda Minton and Ilana Worrell, thank you for your expert eyes and your help getting this book ready (and for catching all the times I randomly changed someone's eye color halfway through the book).

For my wonderful team at Titan, thank you to my editor Joanna Harwood and publicist Sarah Mather for giving this book a home and getting it into the hands of amazing U.K. readers! And thank you to Julia Lloyd for the incredible cover that I cannot stop staring at! I'm so thankful to have gotten to work with you all on this series.

Roxane Edouard, Ema Barnes, and Abigail Koons, thank you for your amazing work helping to get this book into the hands of readers everywhere. It's a dream to see it reaching readers in different countries.

Gemma O'Brien, Queen of Art, thank you for bringing this world to life right there on the cover. It's everything I hoped for and more, and I am just so in love.

Keel Haul's Sea Crew, thank you all for your early support and enthusiasm for this series. It meant the world, and I'm thrilled to get to share this world with you all. Special thanks to members Madison Nankervis, Nicole Faerber, Bianca Visagie, Brithanie Faith Richards, Jennifer Doehler, Brie Chelton Wood, Holly Hughes, Claire Eva Leyton, Bre Lynn R., Nikole Clow, Deidreanna Isak, Chantel Pereira, Mara Hubl, Jessica Olson, Dana Nuenighoff, and Lily A.!

And to all the readers who have come this far—to anyone who has supported me and these books along the way—thank you. Your letters, messages, art, and enthusiasm have all meant more to me than you will ever know. Thank you all for stepping aboard *Keel Haul* and taking this journey with me. We did it!

ABOUT THE AUTHOR

Adalyn Grace graduated from Arizona State University when she was nineteen years old. She spent four years working in live theater and acted as the managing editor of a nonprofit newspaper before studying storytelling as an intern on Nickelodeon Animation's popular series *The Legend of Korra*.

Adalyn splits time between San Diego and Arizona with her bossy cat and two dorky dogs, and spends her days writing full-time while trying to find the best burrito around.